LION HEART

Interior
In Every Face I Meet
Masai Dreaming
Leading the Cheers
Half in Love
White Lightning
The Promise of Happiness
This Secret Garden
The Song Before It Is Sung
To Heaven by Water
Other People's Money

LION HEART

Justin Cartwright

BLOOMSBURY
LONDON • NEW DELHI • NEW YORK • SYDNEY

First published in Great Britain 2013

Copyright © 2013 by Justin Cartwright

Bloomsbury Publishing Plc
50 Bedford Square
London
WC1B 3DP

www.bloomsbury.com

Bloomsbury Publishing, London, New Delhi, New York and Sydney

A CIP catalogue record for this book is available from the British Library

ISBN 978 1 4088 3979 9 (hardback edition)
ISBN 978 1 4088 3980 5 (trade paperback edition)

10 9 8 7 6 5 4 3 2 1

Typeset by Hewer Text UK Ltd, Edinburgh
Printed and bound in Great Britain by CPI Group (UK) Ltd, Croydon CR0 4YY

For Clementine, Isaac and Buzz,
dear to my heart

Fiction:

1. Literature in the form of prose, especially novels, that describes imaginary events and people;
2. something that is invented or untrue;
3. belief or statement which is false, but is often held to be true because it is expedient to do so.

Oxford English Dictionary

If we view ourselves from a great height it is frightening to realise how little we know about our species, our purpose and our end.

W. G. Sebald

17 October 1191

From Richard, King of England, Duke of Normandy, Duke of Aquitaine, Count of Poitou – to Saladin, Righteousness of the Faith:

I shall not break my word to my brother and my friend. I am to salute you and tell you that the Muslims and the Franks are bleeding to death, the country is utterly ruined and goods and lives have been sacrificed on both sides. The time has come to stop this. The points at issue are Jerusalem, the cross, and the land. Jerusalem is for us an object of worship that we would not give up even if there were only one of us left. The land from here to the other side of the Jordan must be consigned to us. The cross, which for you is simply a piece of wood with no value, is for us of enormous importance. If you will return it to us, we shall be able to make peace and rest from this endless labour.

From Saladin, Righteousness of the Faith, to Malik al-Inkitar, Richard, King of England, Duke of Normandy, Duke of Aquitaine, Count of Poitou:

Jerusalem is as much ours as yours. Indeed it is even more sacred to us than it is to you, for it is the place from which our Prophet made his ascent into heaven and the place where our community will gather on the Day of Judgement. Do not imagine that we can renounce it. The land also was originally ours whereas you are recent arrivals and were able to take it over only as a result of the weakness of the Muslims living there at the time. As for the cross, its possession is a good card in our hand and could not be surrendered except in exchange for something of outstanding benefit to Islam.

1

Last Summer

ONE AFTERNOON, ABOUT six months ago, Emily and I walked down to the Globe Theatre. It was an astonishing day, the sort of day that dispels memories of rain and impenetrable cloud and lip-chapping cold. In winter when the winds blow up from the estuary, it can be bitter here. The view back across the river to St Paul's, serene and unmoved, the cheerful throngs around the theatre, the busy traffic on the dense river (almost at high tide), the sense of a teeming history – all these things filled me with eager anticipation for *Richard III* with Mark Rylance as Richard. It felt that day as if we were in a city right at the epicentre of all that mattered, and that there was nowhere on earth I would rather be.

Emily and I were groundlings. From where we were standing, with our elbows on the stage, on the left, in line with one of the marbled pillars, we could see back stage as the actors, in full pleated skirts, stockings, hats (some of these hats looked like flowerpots) and those ballooning and rather comic trunk hose, were preparing to go on. They had an intensity about them; they were looking silently into the distance. They may have been trying to remember their lines, or they may have been looking to find their cores. This core is important for actors, a sort of mythical state of mind. Their task, I thought, was difficult and maybe impossible – to make us believe that a play written in about 1591 concerning events which took place a hundred years earlier could grasp us and move us. (Plays arouse questions in me about the nature of reality.)

I now see that I was already beginning to be irritated by Emily, although I didn't acknowledge it. Also, I was still constantly surprised by her sexual avidity. She was staring intently at the actors, lending them support, as if she had a special relationship with them, not necessarily shared by me. I thought that she had a tendency to look at the world to see what aspects of it she could appropriate for her collection of useful spiritual truths. I notice that women have this habit – certainly the women I know do. It is often accompanied by a kind of manifesto, sometimes shared earnestly with friends in public. The friends, too, have their own gripes, but they nod sympathetically until their turn comes. These manifestos seem to contain goals and objectives, many of which, I think secretly, are unfeasible. Maybe even meaningless.

In the gallery above the stage I could see only one member of the orchestra, a young woman wearing a plant-pot hat and black-rimmed glasses; she was playing a kind of oboe I would have guessed. But I could also see the slides of three brass instruments – possibly sackbuts – but not their operators. Suddenly, unseen, these sackbuts blared out a fanfare. Their imperious harshness suggested a state occasion. Instead, Mark Rylance shambled onto the stage. He was not grossly disfigured, although one leg trailed. His hair was straggly.

> *Now is the winter of our discontent*
> *Made glorious summer by this sun of York . . .*

I felt a deep and pleasurable tremor run through me: in all of Shakespeare there are no more potent phrases.

> *But I – that am not shap'd for sportive tricks,*
> *Nor made to court an amorous looking-glass;*

I, that am rudely stamp'd, and want love's majesty,
To strut before a wanton ambling nymph;
I, that am curtail'd of this fair proportion,
Cheated of feature by dissembling nature,
Deform'd, unfinish'd, sent before my time . . .

Rylance played this great speech as broad comedy. He involved us, the audience. We laughed uneasily, in the knowledge of what was to come: we knew that this vicious bitter little man, with stringy hair, was a psychopath. Emily was in tears before Richard's innocent brother, Clarence, entered, under guard on his way to the Tower. As he was led away, Richard said:

Simple, plain Clarence! I do love thee so;
That I will shortly send thy soul to heaven . . .

It was funny, but chilling.

The shoes of the players, en route for the Tower, passed inches from my face. These shoes were square-toed, like old-fashioned children's shoes. I was enjoying this ground-up vantage point.

Three blissful hours went by in a flash. The sense that time has flown unnoticed provides an inkling of what eternity might be.

Richard III was the last Plantagenet king, killed in 1485 on Bosworth Field in battle against rebels and he was also the last English king to be killed in battle. His helmet was struck with such force that it was driven right into his skull. Recently his skeleton was found underneath a supermarket car park in Leicester. The skeleton suggested that its owner suffered from curvature of the spine, though nothing so serious that could be described as a hunchback, and the skull had an injury to the head. Now DNA evidence has proved that it is the body of Richard.

Emily and I walked along the turbulent river, hand in hand, heading for a cheap Italian restaurant near Borough Market. We were dying to discuss the play. Our verdicts on plays and books were full of self-importance. I knew that the moment the waiter had taken our order there was going to be a personal skirmish, dressed up as a reasonable conversation.

'Now, what are you going to eat?'

I sounded a little stilted, even to my ears. For a provincial, there's always tension when you are ordering in a restaurant; there's the fear of not pronouncing the Italian or French properly; there's the fear of spending too much money; there's the fear that your friends are going to order a second bottle of wine and – God forbid – mineral water in a blue bottle. Maybe I am especially aware of these things because life with my aunt Phoebe on Deeside was always tense; she was terrified she might give offence. She was also poor: she scanned shops to save a few pennies and kept sheaves of special offers cut from the local newspaper. Her nervousness was understandable: she was scared that she could be turned out of the lodge at any time. And a light down was spreading on her face, as a biblical punishment.

I ordered *penne arrabiata*, and Emily chose *spaghetti luganica*. She had a glass of white and I had a glass of red.

I wanted to make comparisons with Richard I – I wanted to say what a pity it was that Shakespeare didn't write a play about him – and I wanted to talk about what Shakespeare was signalling: the end of the unlovable Plantagenets and a new order, which, by God's will, had ushered in the Tudors. Emily spoke first – her deposition was bound to be a little feminist: she said the male actors playing the women – they were taller than Mark Rylance – were clearly supposed to suggest that the women were being used as a sort of ironic echo of the men, by repeating their words at the end of each sentence.

'Interesting, but do you really think this is the most important thing about the play?'

'No, Rich, it probably isn't. It's just something that struck me. So sorry to have an opinion; I'll try to keep them to myself in future.'

'Em, you know I didn't mean that. I meant that there are some very big issues, Catholicism, the end of the Plantagenets, the Protestant future . . . all the things that Shakespeare thought about. I just think these are more important. Sorry.'

'Shakespeare created the English language,' she said.

'I agree.'

And I do, in a way.

2

East London

I WAS NAMED Richard because my father loved Richard I of England, the Lionheart. But I am usually called Richie. My father's surname – and mine – is Cathar, which he adopted when he was at Oxford in 1963 and often under the influence of drugs. Our family name was previously Carter, way too mundane for my father.

There is a small but distinct group of men that I recognise at a distance, and try to avoid. My father was one of them. They have a kind of frayed-at-the-edges charm and a slightly distracted cheerfulness, as though they are attuned to amusing private frequencies. Their hair is long, even if decimated by hereditary patterns of baldness; their clothes are a little threadbare and ill-matched, so that a Tibetan *shari* can be worn with an old pinstriped suit; or perhaps a thick pair of corduroys, of a type found only in a few streets near the traditional London clubs, will be paired confidently with a Jimi Hendrix T-shirt.

This morning, on the first leg of a relatively pointless journey on the No. 30 bus and the Underground to buy some sausages, I saw a woman – a grandmother, but still a ditsy blonde – enter my carriage pushing a pram. She had that unmotivated optimism of my father's generation. She was wearing a short ostrich cape and a yak-wool scarf. The cape had once been – I guessed – an electrifying green, but now, like the Statue of Liberty, it was verdigris. As the air of the train eddied, disturbed by the rushing anxious progress, it caused the cape to spring into a lively but syncopated dance: scores of antique ostrich feathers fluttered onto the floor and into the pram. I could not see the baby within; perhaps it was being smothered by the errant ostrich feathers or maybe it was soothed by their snow-fall touch. I wanted to speak to this woman who, I could now see as she bent over the baby, was wearing a Navajo silver belt low on her jeans. The silver discs on the belt bore important Native American messages. I got a glimpse of a puckered, tripe-textured stomach when her cheesecloth shirt opened for a moment. I wanted to know where she was going with her grandchild. Also I wanted to ask her if she knew that the cape was moulting: if she were going as far as Dollis Hill or Clapham Junction, it would be bald on arrival. She smiled at me as she saw me looking her way: women with babies imagine you are interested in their charges. Her teeth were not good, worn down to stubs, but her smile was complicit. She was old enough to be my mother, but she recognised something in me. She was, I thought, like my father, one of those not securely moored to reality. It is his birthday today, and he has been dead for ten years.

Now, back from my sausage outing, I am throwing things onto a bonfire. A clear-out is long overdue. The accumulated stuff contains an implicit reproach. I am multi-tasking, getting rid of rubbish and intending to use the fire to barbecue my sausages when it has subsided. At the moment it is alarmingly excitable. The cleansing fire of purgatory, my father wrote, terrified people in the Middle Ages. He said that purgatory was designed to finish off the last, few, lingering sins – the sort of thing chefs do to a soufflé or a crème brûlée with a little blow torch: a light scorching before presentation. In 1999 Pope John Paul II pronounced: *Purgatory does not indicate a place but a condition of existence.* As if anyone were listening. What is it with these religious figures that they make absurd statements about sainthood and gay marriage and purgatory and the covering of women? Do they not realise that religion is purely cultural, an explanation and a comfort dating from a world before antibiotics, hospital births and logical positivism?

I am aware that in my loneliness my mind is unruly. It seems to be flying blindly about like a swallow trapped in a building, crashing into windows, unable to make a plan of any sort.

In the toxic, dark, cat-fouled, medieval strip of dank dead clay – once a lawn, still overhung by a few leggy leftover shrubs – the bonfire is casting interesting light and shadow on the derelict Welsh chapel which forms the end of the garden so that it looks incandescent, as though the Holy Fire from the Church of the Resurrection in Jerusalem has appeared here for a moment. The Orthodox Patriarch, who is the impresario of the Holy Fire's appearances, is on record as saying that he has never had his beard singed – not once – as the Holy Fire whizzed about the church on its annual outing. This is the sort of convincing detail you want if you are going to believe in a miracle. Although, like many miracles, this one seems a little pointless – fire of unknown origin zigzagging about for a few moments from one Romanesque pillar to another without toasting the Patriarch. What does this mean?

The Welsh chapel, which once gave succour to the immigrant Welsh men and women, mostly occupied in the milk trade, is alive again. Its walls are host to wild dancing as the garden furniture catches fire. The few remaining panes of the chapel's leaded windows are winking lubriciously. The Welsh dairies closed well within living memory. Fortunately, it happened before progressive people discovered lactose intolerance, which joined gluten, caffeine and cos lettuce intolerance as conditions to be wary of. People speak of their afflictions as if they convey some distinction on them. Something else these Welsh dairy folk did not have to suffer was the slogan *Breast is best*. The incoming classes in this part of East London have adopted the *Madonna Lactans* as their patron saint. Formula milk stunts intellectual growth.

I am aware that irrationality is on the march – I am, after all, my father's son. I know it when I see it.

I am studying the bonfire. The garden furniture went well at first – it was surprising how quickly the patterned seats and the back-rests were consumed – the effect was almost explosive – but now the frames are glowing ominously, like something radioactive, and there is a sharp, choking chemical aroma in the air. I throw on a roll of damp carpet that has surreptitiously become wet in the former coalhole. It gives off a dense, dark smoke, like a tanker on fire at sea. I have to acknowledge that I am cursed with a kind of incompetence in regard to the straightforward and practical tasks of life. For instance, when I tried recently to change a tyre on the Honda inherited from my father, the jack inexplicably collapsed, bending the drive axle. I had to pay someone to scrap it. My cooking has often gone wrong: small fires have broken out, which included a rogue blaze in the cooker hood that could easily have rushed through the building; a pan has been welded to a cooker, any number of fishes and meats have been incinerated, and I once hooked my own nose when fly-fishing on the Dee. I was using a dry fly, a Tups Indispensable.

Emily was becoming exasperated: my charming disorganisation had begun to annoy her. She was increasingly inclined to ask questions with a rhetorical thrust: 'Why are your underpants on the floor of the sitting room?' The only possible answer was that I had dropped them there in the course of my morning progress from the thin shower, but of course no marks were awarded for honesty. She has a literary bent (2:1 in comparative literature, Reading University) and described me as becoming more and more like Oblomov. When I had read up on Oblomov I said, 'At least you think I am amiable.' (If, like me, you don't really know anything much about Oblomov, I can tell you now that he is the astonishingly lazy but amiable Russian owner of a country mansion in a book by Ivan Goncharov. He fails to leave his bed for the first 150 pages of the novel.)

'Actually, I don't. I think your self-congratulatory idea of yourself as being chilled and charming is passive aggression.'

Now she has gone, like her heroine, Anna Karenina. She said she needed her personal space; she needed time to think. She wanted to express herself, and maybe she would take a creative writing course. But I have heard from one of her friends who has spoken to her at length, and she couldn't wait to give me the news that she has a new partner in Sheffield. I've left messages for Emily, clothed in a cheerful (and bogus) reasonableness, but she hasn't replied. I have not even hinted that I know of the existence of her partner, but actually I would like to go to the steel city, like Dickens, *roaring, rattling through the purple distance*, to stick a Sheffield steel knife into this partner. He teaches creative writing, not of itself a crime.

How our friends enjoy, in the guise of concern, giving us the little, lethal, details.

My plans to grill some sausages are delayed by the chemical nature of the fire. They are Norman sausages, flavoured with Calvados and apple. I bought them from a French deli near the Institut français in South Kensington to honour my father on his birthday and his hero, Richard the Lionheart, who was Duke of Normandy, as well as King of England. His heart is buried in Rouen Cathedral. The rest of his entrails are in Fontevraud Abbey.

My father was the author of an unpublished (and unfinished) biography, *The True Story of Richard the Lionheart*. The research was mostly intuitive. My father claimed to have discovered – his sources were never made public – that Richard had indeed returned secretly from his time as a hostage after the Third Crusade and met up with Robin Hood, not in Nottingham, but in Barnsdale Forest in Rutland where he was hunting. They became bosom companions.

The truth is that after his coronation in 1189, Richard set off for the Holy Land and spent only a few weeks of the next ten years in England. England and much of France were one kingdom then, so Richard would have thought of himself as living in greater England.

My father claimed to have had a piece of luck: rooting in the library of a friend, who was himself an earl living in Leicestershire – Balliol man, pass degree – he found an account of their meeting in a letter written on vellum. The Earl was the manager of a rock band at the time, so he didn't mind in the least my father taking away the original for authentication. I imagine him saying, *That's cool, man.* The letter was written in late Norman French. This letter – my father said – contained the details of a secret meeting between Robin Hood, rightful Earl of Huntingdon, and the King, which was to take place in the deep forest. The King promised to stop his awful brother, John, bringing an act of attainder against Robin. If they did meet, I imagine there would have been a little language difficulty, as Richard mostly spoke the *langue d'oc* and Robin would have spoken the East Midland dialect of emerging English. When Richard was back in charge, my father claimed, he pardoned Robin Hood, restored his lands, and often went hunting with him.

Was this not the plot of *Ivanhoe*? I asked him.

He looked at me with compassion. There were secret sources of knowledge, not available to plodders and literalists. If Richard had spent more time in England – more time than the two days of summer required to undermine Nottingham Castle, hang some of the defenders, and pay a visit to Sherwood Forest – who knows? – they might indeed have grown close. My father had no evidence, but he trusted his intuition. People who take drugs often do. To them much is revealed through close, leisurely self-examination. Serious scholars, of the non-intuitive sort, have hunted through the records of Nottinghamshire, Yorkshire and Leicestershire: the first mentions of a Robin Hood, Hod, or Robert Hoode appear over fifty years later.

My father cited a stone on a grave at Kirklees Priory in Yorkshire. It bore this inscription:

> *Hear undernead dis laitl stean*
> *Lais Robert Earl of*
> *Huntingdun*
> *Near arcir der as hie sa geud*
> *An pipl kauld im Robin Heud*
> *Sic utlaws as he an is men*
> *Vil england nivr si agen.*
> —*Obit 24 Kal Dekembris 1247*

> Here underneath this little stone
> Lies Robert Earl of Huntingdon
> No archer as he was so good
> And people called him Robin Hood
> Such outlaws as he and his men
> Will England never see again.

With his scepticism about rational explanations, my father would inevitably have believed that his pal was a descendant of Robin Hood. But the revived title was only resurrected in the sixteenth century, so his lost parchment was most likely a forgery.

The parcel containing the original sheet of vellum, borrowed from his aristocratic chum's library, was unfortunately lost in Orly Airport when my father went into a cubicle to light a joint and comb his hair, which he modelled on Jim Morrison's. He was in transit to Ibiza. When he realised he had left the parcel in the *lavabos*, it was gone and never found. He raged at the border police for their incompetence. Quite quickly they took him into a small room and roughed him up a little because he had called them pigs and had Jim Morrison's dissident hair. But, he said, he was only trying to explain that a precious document written on vellum – calf skin – had been lost. He had not called the police *cochons*. When he told me this story he seemed quite proud of the incident: 'It was 1968,' he said. 'It was a crazy time,' as if that explained everything. One thing he never explained was why he had left Oxford so abruptly during his second year in Hilary Term, 1963.

I have the sausages on a grill borrowed from the oven, which has become terminally carbonised by fat since Emily left. I'm judging the moment to place them on the fire, which contains small vulcans spitting out lurid flames, like a Roman candle. Gazing at fires makes most people introspective: I am acutely, even painfully, aware that Emily really doesn't want to see me again. I find it difficult to think of anything else; it is impossible for me to let go and grant her this personal space. 'Personal space' is a self-serving phrase, and I need to resolve the semantics with her. I know in the rational part of my mind that there is no point in promising to change (for instance, by putting my underclothes somewhere more sensible).

I imagine the Sheffield pedagogue enjoying the tumultuous sex I had once had with Emily, as though I had passed to him a sexual dowry. It was I who had unleashed this sexual fervour, and it sickens me to know that this passion – these private and personal gymnastics – has broken out to a wider audience. The secret pleasure I derived from knowing that the quiet, studious girl I lived with – verging on the mousey, if I am honest – was a sex fiend has come back to bite me. But the irrational part of my brain – like most people, I am a little vague on the precise structure of the brain and how it works – anyway, the discrete coils that deal with love and emotion and artistic yearnings cannot accept that Emily no longer loves me. I try to remind myself that for the last three months when we were together in this suppurating bunker of a basement flat, bought with a deposit from her father, I was often bored and listless – depressed – and we fell into long periods of oppressive silence. It was as if we had no idea any longer why we were together.

It was Emily who made the first move. She has very neat, precise handwriting, and spends a lot of time in shops that sell paper and pens. She particularly loves Parisian *papeteries*. We once made a pilgrimage to Cassegrain in the Boulevard Haussmann. It was quite early in our relationship, so I feigned interest in these *haut-bourgeois* knick-knacks. In the Marais we tried a variety of teas made from improbable botanical ingredients. I particularly liked one from Dammann Frères which offered *un univers riche en saveurs et en surprises gustatives*. An even bigger surprise was the bill. We were intimidated. The French have a way of blackmailing you with their perfectly matched clothes and ostentatious slimness; we took home an ornamented commemorative box of the stuff, just to demonstrate that we were not up from the burbs.

Dear Rich
I have decided that I have to have my personal space for a while at least. Please don't try (this 'try' really enraged me, as if I were a fan with delusions of a relationship) *to contact me in the foreseeable future, because that would be counter-productive. I am totally serious when I say I need a period of reflection. I feel that I have creative energies that I must explore. I am not saying you are stifling them* (precisely what she is saying) *but I want to study creative writing and I need to gather myself. Although you probably won't admit it, I suspect you will welcome my decision to leave London.*
Emily.

No I don't. I don't welcome it at all. Particularly now that you are fucking some beardy, wannabe D. H. Lawrence who pops his fat northern face into Wikipedia half an hour before a lecture and jots down the names of two or three writers he has never read, with a few crafty quotes to lard his talk, which is about showing-not-telling, the use of voices, the deployment of figurative language, the skill of differentiating characters, making a start – and then he mentions writers like Amis and Rushdie and Tyler and Franzen and some others that nobody in Sheffield has ever heard of like W.G. Sebald, Dacia Maraini and William Maxwell, and after that he will ask you to read aloud your own writing, something that is, of course, a lot easier for the tutor – the bastard with whom you are exploring your creative energies – to pronounce upon than to write anything himself, particularly as his last book – I have found out his Pooterish name – it's Edgar Gaylard – his last book sold 306 discounted copies and reached a high of 1,400,000 on Amazon.

I want to send Emily something from Beckett's play, *Krapp's Last Tape*: *Seventeen copies sold, of which eleven at trade price to free circulating libraries beyond the seas. Getting known.* Gaylard's book was published by his father-in-law, who is the proprietor of a specialist magazine about garden accessories: *Everything you need for the garden, from water features to wild-bird feeders.* Were you aware that Gaylard is married? He has two children, popularly known as the Lardies (I am imagining this) aged twelve and fourteen. They have piano lessons out of town at Hathersage twice a week after school. Could that be when Mrs Gaylard (Jacqui) can be relied upon to be safely occupied for a few hours on Tuesdays and Thursdays driving them in her Ford Focus to musical renown? On the pretext of wanting to forward some nondescript mail, I sent Emily a text, asking for a forwarding address, but she did not reply. Actually, I know exactly where she lives. I have stood outside.

The fire has subsided and the toxic fumes have mostly ebbed. The Welsh chapel is sinking back into its accustomed rock-of-ages sleep, which is disturbed only occasionally when young boys throw bottles and stones and dustbins at the few remaining panes of glass. Police cars howl on Mare Street. They do more than howl: they whoop and sob. They make a noise like the brown hyena. The sodium lights of the Nye Bevan Estate, above and beyond the chapel, look as though a dense swarm of excited orange bees is gathering around them; the air apparently contains moving, whirling, unidentifiable particles.

I assess the fire: still a little chemical, but a good even heat. It is one of my remaining conceits that I know how to make a fire fit for a barbecue. I place six sausages on the grill and lower it onto some bricks which are not entirely level so that one of the sausages rolls through a gap where a spar is missing and falls into the embers of the garden furniture. At this moment a fox, attracted by the Calvados and apple scents, appears at the rim of the firelight. Only its muzzle and appraising eyes are visible. The effect reminds me of those puppets in Prague which perform against a black backdrop. Puppetry is a strange art form. I spear the errant sausage with a fork and throw it to the fox. It grabs the sausage and leaps nimbly onto the crumbling garden wall and vanishes. These foxes have an amazing leap on them. I am ambivalent about foxes; on the one hand you have to admire their adaptability and resilience; on the other they tear open rubbish sacks and spread the bones of KFC chicken – a local favourite – all over the place.

With the help of a headlamp bought for a camping trip to Brittany with Emily – it went badly – I grill the five remaining Norman sausages, wrap each one roughly in white bread slathered with ketchup, and eat them fast, as if I have something pressing to do. If anyone, a logician for example, were looking down from the surrounding high-rises and saw a man with a headlamp eating sausages at high speed in the lea of a Welsh chapel he might make some misleading deductions.

There is a damp and unstable cardboard box of my father's papers, which I was planning to burn, but now I change my mind: the fire is too low to burn damp cardboard, and anyway I should read them one day. The fox appears again and fixes me with its wised-up, *nothing-to-do-with-me-mate*, stare. I throw some bread in its direction. The fox emerges into the light just long enough to assess, and promptly reject, slices of Mighty White with ketchup. In this weakly flickering light the fox's pelt has a ghostly aura for a moment, before it vanishes into the charged night.

Now I have a sense that I am a character in a Pinter play: deluded, losing my grip and prey to forces I don't understand. Pinter went to school not far from here, at Hackney Downs. Maybe really to understand London – what could that mean? – you have to live in a liminal place like Hackney. Michael Caine is another former pupil, I think. Pinter and Caine, of Jewish immigrant stock. The rot set in when the school went comprehensive; boys with attitude were decanted there, academic standards plummeted, staff became unhinged, developed sore backs, took sick leave, school closed. No more four-eyed Jewish professors, playwrights and actors.

I'm thirty-three next birthday. Emily has left me. I miss my father. Both of them gave me pain, but now I am dying of loneliness. For my peace of mind I reassure myself: it's not loneliness in the sense of having no one to talk to – I have friends – it's the loneliness of feeling less and less qualified to live in this world. It's *anomie*, which has redeeming associations with the artistic.

The dense air pressing on the garden, the spavined chapel, the rising symphony from the streets of rap, of police sirens, of violent domestic argument, of football chants – as if anybody gives a fuck about which team the morons support – of breaking glass, of cars trembling with bass – all this adds to the sense of being disconnected because it speaks of some sort of human involvement which doesn't involve me: here I am licking the last of the ketchup off my fingers. I turn the headlamp off.

My grandfather, a Harley Street urologist, sent my father to Winchester. But my father considered Pangbourne College more than adequate for me. Alaric Leofranc Cathar (*née* Carter), the intimate of Richard the Lionheart, saw himself as the only licensed intellectual in the family. His short stay at Oxford confirmed it.

Until 1972 Pangbourne College was the Nautical College, preparing boys for life in the Merchant Navy. When I arrived there many years later the whiff of rum, sodomy and the lash still hung in the air. In my time the older boys practised 'bog-washing', which involved pushing the heads of uppity younger boys down the lavatory and pulling the chain. Another jape was called 'divisional scrubs' and involved younger boys being covered in shoe polish and then showered. Personal space was very low in the college's hierarchy of values. Perhaps it was originally thought necessary to prepare pupils for the close and intimate cohabitation of naval life.

At the end of my first term, my father asked me, with that old roué's pointless smile on his threaded face, his hair flapping winningly over his brow and coursing in two wavelets back over his ears, how school had been. I said, 'Oh, fucking marvellous, I have learned how to wash the inside of a lavatory with my head. Thank you, Pater. I'm sure it will come in handy when I join the Navy.'

He laughed: life is after all really just one cosmic joke.

'That's cool, man.'

I hit him, knocking him off his chair. From the floor he appraised me for a moment. I was only just fourteen but had been doing a lot of rowing on the Thames, the college's one and only area of excellence. He was against violence. He stood up, blood streaming from an eyebrow, and walked towards the door. He stopped.

'I will write to the Commodore and tell him that all shore leave should be cancelled indefinitely. I won't see you again until you write me an apology.'

'I had shit in my mouth and hair. Can you imagine what that was like? And then they rubbed my balls with Cherry Blossom shoe polish.' (It was oxblood brown.) 'You should be writing me an apology.'

I was sobbing, but my father was already on his way upstairs to rummage in his bathroom, whistling – I seem to remember – 'Light my Fire'. He was probably stoned. I refused to go back to school and hitch-hiked to Deeside in Scotland, where I boarded with my father's sister, Phoebe, and worked for the rest of the summer as a ghillie; my aunt, whose face was already being colonised by a light – not unpleasant – down, was well-read and kind, although preoccupied. Her husband had shot himself. Gamekeepers are prone to this as they have the weapons. She never told me what happened to my mother. When it was obvious that I wasn't going home, she enrolled me at the local school, from where I won a bursary to Oxford four years later, qualifying as a Scottish student from a state school, and in this way helping the college in question with its admissions record.

I leave the fire glowing a persistent toxic green as I take the box of reprieved papers inside.

3

Jerusalem, Two Months Later

OUTSIDE MY ROOM there is a small mosque. I can see its minaret – modest with a circlet of ironwork at the top – from my window. The first call to prayer – the *adhan* – is at five in the morning. Four times the *muadhin* calls out: *Allahu Akbar*. I lie in bed entranced by the call. Amplified by loudspeakers, the call to prayer makes my body tremble; it seems to enter my bones and agitate the marrow.

What the *adhan* speaks of in this mad, beautiful, violent, restless city is the human longing for certainty. And why wouldn't you want certainty if you lived here? This is a place where horrors, all of them in the name of a higher authority, have been committed for thousands of years, a place where countless people have died for their religion, where the walls have been built and destroyed and rebuilt constantly, where Armenian, Syrian and Orthodox priests sail blandly about – Quinqueremes of Nineveh – where observant Jews with side-locks wear their painful blank devotion on their pale faces, where creased Bedouin women in embroidered dresses and triangular jewellery sit patiently outside the Jaffa Gate to sell vegetables, where young Arab men, in strangely faded jeans and knock-off trainers, push trolleys of foodstuffs, where in countless cafés men contemplate what might have been, their hair failing, their faces turning to yellowed ochre, as though the tea they drink endlessly is staining them from the inside. Or perhaps it's the water-cooled smoke from their hookahs that is doing it, smoking them from the outside. I think of the salmon smokeries up on the Dee. It was my job to take the clients' salmon for smoking. I graduated to leading the Highland ponies, draped in dead stags, down the hillside. Sometimes I was trusted with driving the little Argocats, which could go anywhere, even fully laden with a stag and a couple of stout German hunters trimmed with forest green.

I find the Old City constantly moving: it is astonishing to me that the Syrian priests use Aramaic, the language of Christ. All around I see the evidence of this urge to fix ourselves in the blind uncaring universe. It seems we are crying out for recognition and validation. From the great golden dome of Al-Aqsa to the Chapel of the Ascension, this longing is evident. Both these places – although 'places' hardly does justice to their immeasurable spiritual charge – commemorate miraculous events, the night journey of Mohammed to Jerusalem from Mecca (it was a round trip on a small white flying horse, not unlike, I imagine, the Highland ponies) and the ascension of Jesus into heaven.

Outside my room the early almond blossom is offering itself promiscuously all over the city. I recognise the scent because Emily favoured Roger & Gallet's Almond Blossom soap – also available in the Marais at fancy prices. As I lie here, waiting to hear the call to assemble, I am seized by an intense awareness of the devotion that is spearing the still-dark dawn, even if in my heart I know it is deluded. Also, I am a little frightened of the Palestinians, because they are seething with ancient resentments and the perception of centuries of accumulated slights.

The dawns of Jerusalem are beautiful – lavender and rose and ground cumin. Damman Frères' teas come to mind.

The *muadhin* follows the round of *Allahu Akbar* with *As-salatu khayrun minan-nawm – Prayer is better than sleep*. I have lain awake before dawn for four days now, waiting longingly for the *iqama*, the call to line up for prayer. When it comes, it is particularly plaintive, fraught with longing and disappointment. I think that this thread of sound links Muslims with a loose but unbreakable cord; I see all the Muslims of the world walking blindly together, like soldiers gassed in the Great War, following this guideline to some unknown destination. One thing is for sure: it will be better there, wherever they are headed.

My room, No. 6, is part of the old building of the hotel; it was once the house of a wealthy pasha who kept a small harem. Room 6 is prized; it was built as the bedroom of the Pasha's beloved fourth wife; it has stone flags, smoothed by the passage of soft Turkish carpet slippers. The Pasha's wives, I guess, were as plump and soft as turtle-doves.

As the *muadhin* calls, I feel the ecstasy of solitude. There can be pleasure in thinking of yourself as alone and in this way closer to your true self. The desert around Qumran and Masada, which I visited yesterday in a bus full of upbeat and fundamentalist Christians from Oklahoma, was where Christ was said to have spent his forty days of solitude and I thought I could see in this parched tumbled landscape what it was the desert fathers valued. I also inhaled the aroma of the Dead Sea below, a strange sulphur smell, which Pliny the Elder noticed two thousand years ago.

There is a difference between solitude and loneliness. I was diminished by loneliness when Emily left me. As her retreat for her own period of self-expression, she chose Sheffield and for spiritual guidance, Edgar Gaylard.

I lie eagerly waiting, as if I am expecting some epiphany. Suddenly the *muadhin* finishes his final call. I have discovered that his inflection changes as the appeal to piety winds down. I take my time – I am assuming the habits of a pasha. All these towels and dressing gowns pander to me and encourage me. I shower and anoint myself in the marbled shower room – separate from the bathroom and its giant bath – and finally dress and go for breakfast in the courtyard, which has a fountain in the shape of a scaly fish standing on its tail in an octagonal pond. Real fish – lazy, overindulged carp and their golden cousins – barely move. Their mouths open idly as if they are expecting a little baklava to be popped into their fleshy lips. A small, obese boy in old-fashioned shorts is pointing out the fish to his mother and father who are eating *labneh*, a soft white cheese, at the table next to mine. They scoop up the cheese with wedges of pita. We smile at each other indulgently, encouraging the fantasy that children are uniquely charming... *Ah... children... the little innocent children.* Around the courtyard are pomegranate trees in deep red flower and palms in huge tubs. The sun is already warming the flagstones, which have the smooth sheen of thousands of years of slippered traffic. I feel a tremendous surge of well-being after my period of *anomie*. Durkheim defined *anomie* as a mismatch between the individual and the norms of society, a sort of detachment. Now I am fully engaged. Society and I are matched.

Things have changed in the last few months. Jacqui Gaylard left her husband, and Edgar Gaylard realised that he didn't really want a life with Emily, but without the Lardies. Emily phoned me, just before I left for Jerusalem, but I was distant. She wanted to talk to me, she said. She was back in London. We met in a pub in Islington – it would be too painful for her to return to Hackney – and she burst into tears; she sobbed and she wanted me to hold her, which I did fastidiously. The pubs of Islington are used to this sort of thing – people around here are very highly strung – and no one took much notice, but I immediately felt better, although of course my chivalric role was to listen sympathetically to her drastically revisionist update of her autobiography, sometimes referred to as her goals.

She had been asked to leave the creative writing course – fees mostly refunded – after Mrs Gaylard went to the Dean of Arts to complain about the relationship with Emily – she had been caught *in flagrante* when the piano teacher was ill. Mrs Gaylard and the Lardies had seen Emily trying to get dressed in a hurry. In an email an ambitious and possibly jealous faculty member had given Mrs Gaylard the low-down about what had been going on. Edgar had been put on a warning about his unprofessional conduct. In fact it was his second – and final – warning, and it was this that was particularly tormenting Emily and at the same time cheering me up no end.

In the pub, increasingly loud with drink-fuelled chortles, shouted confidences, braying laughter and proclamations of happiness, little Emily asked if I would have her back. She had let the flat in Hackney, and I was renting a room from a friend in his flat on the down-slope that leads to King's Cross. From my small bedroom I could see the Mad Ludwig towers of St Pancras Station, a cathedral of steam if ever there was one.

Emily's face, newly pale in an ethereal, sun-deprived, northern way, was older and more troubled. Her eyes seemed defensive. It was hard to recall the assertive young woman who had confidently left me in order to explore her personal space and creative energies. It had all been a huge mistake, she said. Edgar was a total failure as a writer, a charlatan who was teaching mainly to get close to troubled young women. He was a devious and inventive liar. He had a drink problem. He had poor personal hygiene. She had lent him money that she would never see again. For months he had denied he had a wife or children. At least, she said, she had acquired self-knowledge. What she actually said was that she had grown.

Many people believe in self-knowledge, and what they mean by that is a kind of self-justification: while confessing to error, they are suggesting that they have become better people in the process. But – it saddens them to recount – they have realised that they must learn to become less profligate with their kindness – it just doesn't pay.

Actually now that she was sitting in front of me in the Albion, I saw that Emily was quite ordinary; her face had a kind of undue boniness and her eyebrows were straggly, so that she seemed to be merging with Virginia Woolf; over the months I had given her imaginary attributes. There was a juvenile-white-mouse look to her face: her eyelids were pink. She might have been weeping a lot. Still, I managed to get her to come to my little bedroom. She cried most of the time; I could not make up my mind why she was crying. Was she missing the unscrupulous Edgar, or was she regretting that she had left me? Our lovemaking took on the qualities of an autopsy. Neither of us was in the happy state of innocence that was required; we were deep in introspection.

'Richie, please have me back. I am very, very unhappy.'

'You remind me of the girl who murdered her parents and threw herself on the sympathy of the court because she was now an orphan.'

'And you are still a smart-arse.'

After her humiliation, I was feeling far better. This equation is disturbing for what it tells us about human nature. I was concerned that she seemed so diminished, but there was still the matter of the sex she had had with Gaylard. You can't just ignore it; I didn't want to start asking how he was in bed, or whether he made her scream with ecstasy, or whether he liked blow-jobs or preferred to do it from behind *et cetera*. I didn't want to try to calculate how many times he had put his fat prick into her: two days a week, during piano lessons, maybe the odd furtive coupling in the classroom, multiplied by twelve weeks . . . And so on. All the things that are normal in your own relationship are disgusting, perverted and painful when your girlfriend leaves you, taking her sexual reper- toire with her.

Naked, she seemed utterly defenceless. God she was pale, her hip-bones poking unnaturally through her skin, which was not so much skin as a delicate membrane, barely hiding her organs. In there somewhere, but too close to the surface, were all the func- tioning parts. I noticed that she had shaped her pubic hair into a tiny Mohican, and of course I wondered why. I told her that I couldn't come to a decision because I was going to Jerusalem on a grant given by my college.

A few months ago, after I had written to him asking for a research grant, my former tutor, Stephen Feuchtwanger, wrote back to say that there were travel and research grants available for pupils from state schools who had graduated from the college and required a short sabbatical. Now, he wrote, he was living in retirement in Cornwall, although as a fellow emeritus he was in close touch with the college and still had some influence. While I was at Oxford he had been fond of me. He believed I should become a writer. He was revered by many of his students. The grant had not been claimed for years, he said; I simply had to write a short proposal for the travel project, explaining how it would ultimately benefit mankind and attract funding to the college. *Please elaborate in not more than one hundred and fifty words.* I turned to my father's damp and mildewed papers, saved from the fire, for help. I saw that he had been exploring the art of the Kingdom of Jerusalem, and I proposed this as a subject.

Now I told Emily that when I got back from Jerusalem – I was becoming lordly – I would give her a call. She raised the question of the rent of the flat tentatively; she felt it was unfair that her father had paid the deposit and I was now getting half the rental while *swanning* around the world.

'What were you doing in Sheffield?'

It wasn't fair, I said, but I had reluctantly come to acknowledge that the markets, harsh though they can be, contain some undeniable logic.

'And by the way, you said you gave money to Edgar Gaylard.'

'I didn't tell you his name.'

'No you didn't.'

I had found in my father's shambolic and almost-incinerated papers a reference to his employment at the École Biblique in Jerusalem, and to a Father Prosper Dupuis. It seemed like a good use of the college's money to go to Jerusalem. Father Dupuis, a Dominican, was still alive, although semi-retired. I wrote to him requesting an interview for a research project, and he emailed back promptly – I was half expecting parchment and plant-dye ink – saying I was very welcome.

After breakfast I head off in a taxi for my appointment with him. Not only did he know my father, but he has been involved in all sorts of research, from the Dead Sea Scrolls to the fate of the True Cross. How difficult could it be to write a short essay on the art of the Crusaders.

The École Biblique stands on the Nablus Road. It was formerly in Jordan, but in 1967 it found itself in Israel. It was here that the Dead Sea Scrolls were first examined by Father Roland de Vaux, the director of the École Biblique, and his colleagues. My father came here – cheerfully hopeful – and managed, on his sketchy credentials of three and a half terms at Oxford, to find work with the team that was trying to preserve and understand the significance of the Dead Sea Scrolls, recovered from caves around Qumran and written on the skin of the local wild goats. The descendants of these goats still roam the hills. We know this because the DNA of the goats matches that of the vellum used by the scribes of Qumran. At that time there were many theories about what exactly the scrolls were: my father, his papers tell me, opted predictably for the theory that they were the work of a group of surviving followers of Christ himself, who had fled from Jerusalem. When the scrolls were translated and transcribed, they would revolutionise the understanding of Christianity. He was wrong on all counts.

Father Prosper is waiting for me under a cypress tree, in the garden. The Nablus Road is dusty and busy and unmistakably Middle Eastern, but here, although the pale dust has settled on the pepper trees and spiky sisal fronds, there is cool tranquillity. Beyond the garden are colonnades and the façade of a huge nineteenth-century church.

'You are the child of Alaric, I can see it in your face. Bless you, my son.'

His English is heavily accented.

'Thank you. Thank you for taking the time to see me.'

'I have time, *inshallah*. Now I am only employed to keep the archive, although I have my own projects. I am eighty-four years old.'

He is a small, neat man, with closely cropped grey hair; I picture him burrowing like a mole in archives and caves and parchment and rolls of vellum and tombs and shards of pottery. His face is childish – perhaps I mean childlike – although creased and sun-damaged. I know that he reads Latin, Greek, Hebrew, Arabic and Aramaic, Anglo-Norman French, Occitan and the *langue d'oïl*. On the journey here I tried to imagine how he has passed the last forty or fifty years. He is wearing a grey habit rather than the Dominican white; under that I can see huge lace-up black shoes. The shoes seem to me at least as monkish as the habit.

'Would you like to see the library where your father worked?'

We walk through a courtyard enclosed by colonnades, to create a sort of cloister. Forming one side of the courtyard is the library. Actually, it seems to be part library and part store. Scattered amongst the desks and the dark bookshelves are complete Roman and Jewish tombs – looking like the lead planters outside stately homes – sections of columns, Latin, Hebrew and Greek inscriptions on ancient stones, Roman busts, ossuaries – some decorated with rosettes and inscribed with the names of the person whose bones they contained – and many jars made from the ochre and pomegranate clay of the area. One of these, Father Prosper says, contained a scroll from Cave 7 at Qumran. It has a single word on it, possibly in Latin, 'Roma', which has exercised many scholars. He shows me a desk on which a terracotta head stands.

'Your father worked here. When he was not in the field.'

He says this with a small smile, affectionate and perhaps complicit, as though we share some knowledge of my father and his habits.

'What did he do while he was here?'

'Well, he liked to go to the excavations, and also he was always looking for something in the library or in the Rockefeller Museum or in the Crusader castles. And Qumran.'

'In his papers I see he believed Qumran was an early Christian settlement.'

'There were many ideas at the time. Many. Your father was not the only one. William Gyngell, also English, believed it and he was a brilliant scholar. Your father and he went drinking. Later Gyngell had a mental breakdown, alcohol-related, you know. He made anti-Semitic remarks publicly. He hated Israel, because he felt it had stolen two thousand years of history and that it was trying to promote Judaism above Christianity. He believed in a thing he called "Christology" and he believed that the scrolls were about a struggle between the high priests of the temple and the followers of Christ. He influenced your father in this.'

Later I wondered if he meant that my father had also become anti-Semitic.

'Did my father ever talk about King Richard the Lionheart?'

'Yes, he did.'

He treats me to his understanding, innocent smile again. My father was obsessed with the Third Crusade, and tried to find documents of that period or casual inscriptions and works of art; he was forever asking Father Prosper to help him with translations; he says that my father became immersed in reports of lost messages sent between Richard and Saladin after they had fought each other to a standstill in 1192. He looked at hundreds of inscriptions and documents in the Rockefeller Museum, and he tried to find the cache of legal documents lost by the Latin Kingdom after Saladin took Jerusalem. The Latin Kingdom, Father Prosper tells me, was run like any medieval European state, with kings and nobility, knights, courts, bishoprics and councils which produced reams of documentation. He says that my father was sure that Saladin, who both feared and admired Richard, had secretly given him the True Cross as part of a deal which would cede Jerusalem, while allowing free access to the holy places by Christian pilgrims. Saladin had captured it in 1187, after it had been in the hands of the Primates of Jerusalem since AD 328, when legend has it Helena, mother of Constantine, found it at Golgotha. What is certain is that the True Cross has vanished.

In the refectory, we have a lunch of hummus and peppers in oil, with a glass of red wine from a Trappist monastery near Latrun. Father Prosper asks me where I am staying; he says I can move to the guest rooms at the École Biblique free, as I am a legitimate researcher. I explain that I have paid for three weeks at the American Colony Hotel, and after that I will take him up gratefully on his offer. He says I may use the library to write my thesis; he will confirm this with the Prior. I don't reveal that my project is a sinecure, possibly with undertones of unrequited Greek love.

Father Prosper tells me that my father spent five days walking all over the battlefield of Hattin, where, on 4 July 1187, Saladin was said to have captured the True Cross. My father slept on the ground at night. Perhaps he was trying to sense through mystic channels the real truth. But I am also beginning to understand that Israel is a place where every rock and wadi is invested with significance; the difficulty is that they are semaphoring different messages to different people.

Still, I can also see why my father might have camped out on the Horns of Hattin: the terrible loss of the Crusader forces at Hattin, and the capture of Jerusalem a few weeks later, were a call to arms that the red-haired, red-garbed, six-foot-five Richard the Lionheart, King of England, Duke of Normandy, Count of Poitou, the poster-boy of the belligerents, could not resist. That year he took the cross: his mind was inflamed with the dream of taking back Jerusalem from the infidel.

4

The Horns of Hattin

I HAVE SPENT the night in my sleeping bag on the spot where
Guy de Lusignan, the King of Jerusalem, pitched his red tent (red
seems to have been fashionable among the Frankish Crusaders) up
on the Horns of Hattin, overlooking the Lake of Galilee. Down
below, along the water, was Saladin's vast encampment. Like Guy
– like my father – I am facing east. In our world-view, all trouble
comes from the east. Down there, the lake is taking on the battered
sheen of old cutlery.

It is not a profound thought, but I am aware that the lake would
have looked exactly the same eight hundred years ago, and exactly
the same when my father spent his three nights here. Now the
surface of this biblical water is being brushed with a gleaming
molten wash, applied in broad strokes. The sky above the low hills
beyond the lake is touched with silver, shot with pink, but the sun
proper is still some way off. These shards of colour are the heralds
of what is to come. I think of the banners and flags of an approaching army. Or of a sophisticated ice cream.

*King Guy's forces had moved out to Sephoris where there was plenty of
water when news came that Saladin had crossed the Jordan and was
heading for Tiberias. Saladin was incensed because Reynald de
Châtillon, Master of Kerak, had attacked and plundered a caravan
from Mecca, despite the truce the Latin Kingdom and Saladin's*

caliphate had made. Saladin wanted revenge. The Grand Master of the Temple, Gerard de Ridfort, in his ceremonial white, emblazoned with a huge red cross, tried to persuade King Guy to move towards Tiberias. One of those besieged was the wife of Count Raymond of Tripoli and she had sent a messenger asking for help. Despite this, Raymond advised against moving towards Tiberias. The besieged, he said, were in no immediate danger: Saladin was preparing a trap; the Crusader army was twenty miles away from Tiberias; it would not last long in the parched countryside. It was up to Saladin to move.

Both Grand Master Gerard and Reynald de Châtillon accused Raymond of Tripoli of being a coward or in league with Saladin. They cited chivalric duty, pointedly. For all that, Raymond's advice was accepted by the council. But Guy, who always listened to the last opinion he was offered, changed his mind when Grand Master Gerard crept into his tent and asked, 'Sire, are you going to trust a traitor?' Guy decided to advance; the heralds were sent out, trumpets blaring. In appalling heat the vast army of one thousand two hundred knights and fifteen thousand infantry marched all day over the Galilean hills until the Knights Templars, the hard men, themselves said their horses could go no further without water. The well they were relying on proved to be dry and Saladin had ordered all the other wells en route poisoned; now he blocked the route to the water below.

Raymond of Tripoli said, 'Ah, Lord God, the war is over. We are dead men. The kingdom is finished.'

The Christian army made uneasy camp on the Horns of Hattin, horribly exposed. The army was made up of large and small contingents of Genoese, Greeks, Germans, Dalmatians, Serbs, Sicilians, French, English, Pisans, Patzinaks, Poitevins, Russians, Bulgars, Langobardians, Lombardians, Provençals, Venetians, Tuscans, Bretons, Brabançons, Flemings, Gascons, Spaniards, Burgundians and Normans. Down below was an army of Egyptians, Kurds, Arabs, Turks, Armenians and Sudanese numbering thirty thousand.

All night the exhausted and dehydrated Crusaders were harassed and kept awake; before dawn they could hear the calls to prayer from below where the thirty thousand were readying themselves for battle. These were the same calls that I had heard from Room 6 in the American Colony Hotel.

As the sun suddenly stripped the darkness off the hills like used sheets, the Crusaders were offered a terrifying sight, described by Saladin's secretary or *kdtib*, Imad ad-Din al-Isfahani:

A swelling ocean of whinnying chargers, swords and cuirasses, iron-tipped lances like stars, crescent swords, Yemenite blades, yellow banners, standards red as anemones and coats of mail glittering like pools, swords polished bright as streams of water, feathered bows as blue as hummingbirds, helmets gleaming above curveting chargers.

The Crusaders were in the trap.

Now the Saracens set light to the dry scrub, sending choking clouds of smoke up the hill, blinding the Christians as the Saracens took up battle stations, with Saladin at the centre, surrounded by his loyal Mamelukes. The Bishop of Acre, standing in for the Patriarch of Jerusalem, raised the True Cross. The Saracens sent wave after wave of cavalry against the Franks who repulsed them, each time more weakly. King Guy had his tent moved to the summit of the hill. He ordered Raymond of Tripoli to break through to the water: a surcoat over his armour, emblazoned with a red cross on a yellow background, Raymond mounted his horse. Balian of Ibelin, his surcoat decorated with a white cross, immediately followed. They led their knights in a charge down the hill; but Saladin ordered Taki ed-Din to open their ranks, so that Raymond and Balian galloped harmlessly and futilely through. They could not attack from behind the lines, and headed for Tripoli, so escaping the massacre that was to follow. Armenian archers sent showers of arrows – 'clouds of locusts' – at the Frankish army. Although tormented by thirst and aware that they were doomed, the Crusaders kept on attacking. A Muslim chronicler, Baha ad-Din ibn Shaddad, wrote:

They were closely beset as in a noose, while still marching on as though being driven to a death that they could see before them, certain of their doom and destruction and knowing that the following day they would be visiting their graves.

Now I hear the armies. It is cold: I am still in my sleeping bag. I can hear a great roar, the clashing of armour, the shouts of *Dieu lo vult* – God wills it, and *Allahu Akbar* – God is great, and *Caelum denique* – Heaven at last rising with the Templar cry, *Le Beau-séant*, honouring their black over white banner. I can hear the ringing of swords, the thundering of galloping knights, the wasp-music of the arrows, the blacksmith collisions of the knights, the whinnying agony of the wounded, blameless horses, the incoherent appeals to God of the injured – all unanswered. There were said to have been rivers of blood. Did the blood really cascade down the hill, across the Roman road, which to this day follows the shoreline, and into the reedy fingers of the lake? I think it must be a figure of speech. The thin soil would certainly have sucked it up.

Thirty thousand died in a few hours. In his red tent, King Guy surrendered and was taken down the hill towards Saladin's pavilion. Imad ad-Din al-Isfahani, who was present, wrote:

Saladin invited the King [Guy] to sit beside him, and when Arnat [Reynald] entered in his turn, he seated him next to his king and reminded him of his misdeeds. 'How many times have you sworn an oath and violated it? How many times have you signed agreements you have never respected?' Reynald answered through a translator, 'Kings have always acted thus. I did nothing more.' During this time King Guy was gasping with thirst, his head dangling as though drunk, his face betraying great fright. Saladin spoke reassuring words to him, had cold water brought, and offered it to him. The King drank, then handed what remained to Reynald, who slaked his thirst in turn. The Sultan then said to Guy: 'You did not ask permission before giving him water. I am therefore not obliged to grant him mercy.' After pronouncing these words, the Sultan smiled, mounted his horse, and rode off, leaving the captives in terror. He supervised the return of the troops, and then came back to his tent. He ordered Reynald brought there, then advanced before him, sword in hand, and struck him between the neck and the shoulder blade. When Reynald fell, he cut off his head and dragged the body by its feet to the King, who began to tremble. Seeing him thus upset, Saladin said to him in a reassuring tone, 'This man was killed only because of his maleficence and perfidy.'

A small detail, which Imad ad-Din al-Isfahani does not include, is that the water that was to be Reynald's last drink was cooled with snow from the summits of distant mountains.

Saladin himself cut off Reynald's head at Hattin, I think, as a symbolic act. Decapitation has a macabre significance for the executioner. It suggests that mere killing is not the object, but that the deliberate severing of the face and the brain from the rest of the body is the most final death, sending an unmistakable message. When Anne Boleyn was beheaded by Henry VIII, I can only imagine that he intended to snuff out a life in the least equivocal way.

Now Saladin ordered the execution of all the Knights Templars apart from the Grand Master, Gerard de Ridfort.

Imad ad-Din al-Isfahani wrote:

Saladin ordered that they should be beheaded, choosing to have them dead rather than in prison. With him was a band of scholars and sufis and a certain number of devout men and ascetics; each begged to be allowed to kill one of them, and drew his sword and rolled back his sleeve. Saladin, his face joyful, was sitting on his dais; the unbelievers showed black despair.

Many Templars volunteered themselves for execution in solidarity. The bodies were left for the hyenas and jackals. Thousands of ordinary soldiers were sent as slaves to Damascus. The True Cross was attached upside down to a lance and taken with the caravan of captives. There were so many captives for sale in Damascus that their price fell to 3 dinars. One of the inhabitants is said to have bought a prisoner in exchange for a pair of sandals.

Count Raymond of Tripoli's words – 'The kingdom is finished' – were prophetic. Saladin kept Guy in custody for months as an insurance policy while he destroyed as many of the Crusader castles as he could before he took Jerusalem in September and only then did he trade Guy. Guy gave his oath that he would not take up arms. He renounced the oath immediately he was free.

The Holy City was lost, the True Cross was lost. It was a catastrophe which shook the whole of the Christian world profoundly.

Richard the Lionheart took the cross in response. It is reported that when Saladin received word of his intentions, he was afraid: Malik al-Inkitar was coming.

But Richard was delayed, defending his empire in France, and resisting his brother's ambitions. He was unable to set sail until 1190.

The sun is now striking the water itself. The lake is still, although a few trucks and taxis are passing, from this distance apparently very slowly; with the advent of the light the sound of conflict subsides. I must now accept that perhaps I was dreaming. But this place makes persistent assaults on one's imagination so that it is difficult to separate the real and the imagined.

I pack up my things. I am stiff after a restless night. There are scorpions in these hills, and many times in the night I imagined they were sharing my sleeping bag. I have arranged to meet an Arab taxi driver down below at a stall on the old road that skirts the lake. On the way back to Jerusalem, he tells me that Mossad orchestrated a recent bombing of a bus in Tel Aviv, which I had read about in *Haaretz*. I feel the urge to reach across the torn seats of the Mercedes. He sees me as a deluded backpacker, lowlife. I want to tell him that right here, thirty thousand people lost their lives for just this kind of persistent ignorance.

We set off for the American Colony. I need a bath – a wallow – in Room 6, but most of all I need to go down to the bar below the hotel, not particularly to drink, but to be among those who go there to escape the tensions and intensity of Jerusalem. Many of the regulars are journalists in search of information; the bar is famous for its meetings and assignations. Down there in the Cellar Bar an ironic good humour prevails; these people are professionally acquainted with delusion. Also, I have been seeing a young woman I met there one night. Her name is Noor, a Canadian-Arab journalist. I call her, and she says she will meet me. The taxi driver turns in his seat.

'You have sweetheart?'

His gold teeth are winking obscenity.

I don't answer.

'She is Jew?'

The obsession that never goes away.

5

The Levant

I HAVE BEEN here nearly four weeks. Already I feel that I am becoming a Levantine. This world of ambiguity and disillusion and the shadows of past glory and the whispers of endless intrigue are getting to me in ways I hadn't expected. I have walked the Old City ceaselessly. I have, with Father Prosper's help, gained access to the closed chapel in the depths of the Holy Sepulchre. This little chapel is said to have been built on the spot where Helena, the mother of Constantine, found the True Cross.

Levantines, I think, don't make a clear distinction between what is true and what they would like to believe is true. As a way of seeing the world, it has its charms; certainly this crypt is ancient, but it is not clear how Helena would have found the True Cross here in AD 328. It was said that she was led here by a vision. I emailed a professor in Oxford, an expert on the Holy Sepulchre: he thought it likely that what Helena discovered was some of the scaffolding left over after the destruction of the Temple of Venus, built by Hadrian on the site of the crucifixion. She found, or was sold, the *titulus*, the incised inscription bearing the words: *Jesus of Nazareth, King of the Jews*, along with some of the beams of the cross itself and part of the crosses of the thieves crucified with Christ. The inscription was in three languages, Hebrew, Latin and Greek. It was in mirror-writing from right to left in the Hebrew fashion. Helena had it sawn in half, and took one piece to Rome. When, in the fifteenth century, this section of the *titulus* was discovered hidden behind plaster in Santa Croce, in Rome, which retains some of the walls of Helena's palace, Leonardo da Vinci rushed to see it. The Oxford professor told me that he believed the crypt was built in the depths of what had once been a stone quarry, used for building purposes. I didn't ask him what special interest Leonardo may have had, for fear he would imagine I was a mythomane.

I have grown very close to Noor. She has red hair, the deep russet colour of a gun dog's coat, which falls around her face and onto her shoulders. Her skin is almost golden. She speaks like a Canadian. (For instance she says 'aboot' for 'about'.) She has the innocence of a Canadian too, although she has seen – she is unwilling to tell me the details – some terrible things in the Middle East. She is also closely related to one of the substantial Palestinian families of Jerusalem. Her glamour makes me feel both uneasy and blessed. Although I know her body intimately now, with all its little uplands and valleys, there is a hinterland to which I am still a stranger. I couldn't say exactly what it means, but Noor is intensely female. She belongs to an altogether different species of womanhood from Emily. Emily has the gawky vulnerability of a newborn antelope, her limbs rather loosely connected, so that there is something of the marionette in her movements. It's endearing in its way, but also needy.

I have maxed out my credit card. It has an insubstantial look at the best of times, entry-level. It's an old student card, never upgraded. I used the last of my credit to book an extra week at the hotel because I can more easily conduct our liaison there, particularly urgent as she is going on assignment soon.

It's a short walk, sometimes a libidinous scamper, from the bar, our feet clacking goatishly on the slabs. (I am thinking of buying some Ottoman slippers.) She leaves early because she is living with her relatives somewhere not far away and they expect her. She is driven away in a black Mercedes. I don't like to ask her if the car is armour-plated, but it does have a bulky look. The driver also has a bulky look, as if he is wearing a bullet-proof vest. Sometimes I stand at the front door of the hotel as she drives away. She looks intriguingly mysterious. I know nothing about her life beyond the hotel. But in bed she tells me that she loves me, which calms me.

After her adventures in Sheffield, Emily was awkward in bed and then, alarmingly quickly, she became distracted as if she was having sex with a spirit, who was standing in for me. She was expecting a healing, even spiritual, epiphany, and when it happened her body was racked fiercely and she cried, and then whimpered, her pale eyes swimming into focus, as if she was trying to remember who I was. Her painful realisation that it was not the hairy littérateur – and fraud – Edgar Gaylard, ruined our last sexual encounter. Also, I thought Emily looked increasingly like Virginia Woolf. She rearranged her hair into a bun, primly, without speaking to me. I had the impression she was trying to destroy the evidence.

Sex with Noor is gracious and unhurried as if it is a well-understood and ancient ritual. The aureoles on her breasts are dark. Lying next to her, eating pistachio nuts, some shells escaping into the bed, a sheen on our bodies, the fragrance of jasmine and almond coming on the night air through the open window on the same breeze that brings the strains of the flutes and the harsh percussion, I think that Noor believes that her role is to please – not a particularly contemporary attitude. She is what the Bible calls the tender and luxurious woman. Maybe she has a Levantine way of regarding sex, not as a Freudian purging of our demons, but as a sensual, courtly expression of being human. When I asked Noor about her life, she gave me an anodyne history; she told me how much she loved McGill and how she learned French in Montreal and studied international development. Now she kisses me:

'And I love you.'

Her parents are Christian: they left for Canada thirty years ago just before she was born. She has a brother in Toronto, something to do with electronics, and she has an apartment there and works for the *Morning Star* and for the CBC. Because she speaks Arabic, she has become a Middle East correspondent. That's about it.

We have a large jug of blood orange juice beside the bed. She doesn't drink alcohol. Her breasts loll slightly to each side. They contain some weighty element, which responds slowly. I pour a few drops of orange juice on her dark nipples and lick them.

'Taste good?'

'The best.'

'My nipples are tightening up.'

'Is that nice?'

'Oh yes.'

I have a swig of beer. It's brewed in the all-Christian village of Taybeh, on the road to Jericho. Noor tells me she is related to the family that owns the brewery. She says that Muslims in the surrounding villages were hostile when the brewery was first set up.

Taybeh beer is pretty good.

'Do you know,' she says, 'there is a belief here that some of us Palestinian Christians have red hair because of our Crusader blood?'

'It could be true. Richard the Lionheart was a ginger-nut.'

'A ginger-nut?'

'A redhead. Six foot five, a red giant. Your ancestor, definitely.'

'If he was gay, of course, it can't be true.'

'He wasn't gay. He's a gay icon only because he spent no time with his wife and had no children. Not officially. He did have one illegitimate child, a boy, who he recognised.'

'I heard he slept with the King of France.'

'In those days it was a diplomatic move to sleep in the same room as another king to demonstrate your trust. There were lots of servants in the room. And by the way, the first time anyone suggested he was gay was in 1948. In medieval times he had a reputation for being very keen to get his hands on captured women. They were part of the spoils of war.'

44

She moves fluently on top of me. Her skin is lubricated by mysterious oils.

'One for the road, old chap?'

'Why not? Noor, just a tip, lay off the accents and stick to what you are good at.'

'I think I can guess what that would be.'

When she has gone I lie on the bed beneath the open window. Bells in the Old City ring briefly and tunelessly. Somewhere there is a party. I hear music, women's voices, percussive clapping, reed flutes and the hand drums. In the Palestinian territories the fundamentalists are cracking down on music. The association of public pleasure with ungodliness had died out in the West: gratification is big where I come from, a human right, even a human obligation.

Noor has gone to her world, as the perfumed night, flooding in, seems to promise ecstasy. I have an invigorating awareness of being alive and somehow connected, although I don't know exactly to what. Without wishing it, I find myself considering seriously whether the only reality is the self. Up until now I have thought of it as a philosophical idea, with limited use. But there is something in the air – the loaded, tendentious air of Jerusalem – that makes people believe crazy ideas: I am possibly showing the early symptoms. Maybe I am more of my father's son than I ever wished to acknowledge.

A little while ago Noor was lying next to me so comfortably and so naturally that I felt we were sharing internal organs, like Siamese twins. It was absurd, but it struck me that our blood, our breath, our sweat had joined forces and were working together.

Sounds of the party have faded on the breeze. The promise of happiness and limitless possibility is intoxicating. Also, Father Prosper has introduced me to various mysteries and shown me objects from antiquity that have affected me deeply. We went to see the Shrine of the Book and there I saw the Book of Isaiah, all twenty-seven feet of it, beautifully copied, probably a hundred and fifty years before Christ, in the hellish heat of Qumran, and hardly a word of it changed in two thousand five hundred years.

Father Prosper pointed out the lines that read:

And he shall judge among the nations, and shall rebuke many people: and they shall beat their swords into ploughshares, and their spears into pruninghooks: nation shall not lift up sword against nation, neither shall they learn war any more.

He smiled.

'Nothing change.'

He told me that, as well as the major scrolls, there are thousands of fragments of scrolls, many of them still to be translated. What is it that inspired such devotion? What was it that caused Richard the Lionheart to take the cross and sail for Acre? Why was Robert the Bruce so passionate that his heart should be taken to the Holy Sepulchre in Jerusalem after his death? His last testament read:

I will that as soone as I am trespassed out of this worlde that ye take my harte out of my body and embawme it and present my hart to the Holy Sepulchre where Our Lorde laye, seying my body can not come there.

In fact his heart – embalmed – only got as far as Moorish Granada, where Sir James Douglas, the Black Douglas, bearing the heart, was killed. The heart was returned to Scotland.

All religions may be logically absurd, but they speak of something essentially human and this, I see, lying complacently naked in the warm night air, is itself a reality that will never go away. And Noor's motile breasts are a reality of another order.

We are crossing the Allenby Bridge over the Jordan. I am disappointed to see that we are not using the old bridge, so famous from a thousand news reports, but a new bridge alongside. On the Israeli side the border police look at me and Noor with interest as they collect the exit tax. Their heads are close-cropped and topped with sunglasses. They want Noor to know that they aren't fooled by the Canadian passport. They are particularly suspicious of her journalist's visa, reading it a number of times to make sure it means what it says. We explain that we are going to Kerak as tourists. The water below the bridge had already died on its journey to the Dead Sea a few miles away.

Now we come to the Jordanian post. There are fees to pay. We show our visas. One of the three men asks me if I support Arsenal. I say of course, oh yes, I live near the stadium, which is only approximately true. They are impressed by my credentials as a modern and metropolitan man. One of them is a fan of Theo Walcott. These men, after all, are stuck out here in the desert, where no grass grows.

'Football, what you call soccer, is the global currency.'

'I have noticed,' says Noor. 'I wonder why.'

'You can talk football with anyone because football is simple; you kick a ball into a net. Sports also have an outcome. Unlike life. I mean they are still waiting in Jerusalem for the Messiah. What's holding him up?'

'Or holding her up. I dunno.'

'I have never understood why people believe in things that they can't ever prove.'

'Maybe they need to believe.'

'Why not believe in something that exists?'

'Like?'

'Like the Arsenal Football Club of Highbury, London.'

'I was hoping you were going to say "love." '

'And that. I believe in it, for the first time.'

'Do you mean that?'

'I do.'

'Will you marry me?'

I am startled.

'If you promise your relatives won't kill me.'

'They won't.'

I stop the hire car and, watched by some world-weary goats, we kiss. Her lips seek and caress mine. It is all part of the process of colonising each other. This is the best phase of a relationship, but I know that, buried in it, the inevitable prospect of sadness is already incubating. In Jerusalem I have been struck by the profusion of delusions that waste the human essences; perhaps love is one of these. It's crazy, it's delusional, it's dangerous. All these things rush through my mind in a turbulent stream as we drive through the vast Jordanian landscape. It is parched and antique; it screams its pain via the voices of the cicadas, as the earth bakes. I look around at Noor; she is asleep, her hand on my thigh, and my blood bounds.

The map shows that at the end of this road is Aqaba; I visited it on a school trip from rainy Scotland. Twelve pink-and-white Scottish adolescents were snatched from the winter to learn to snorkel and to waterski. I was entranced by the fish, which were wearing colourful pyjamas. There was nothing Calvinist about these fish. My aunt paid for me, drawing the money from her post office account and taking it in cash to the school. I kissed Judy McAllister; her lips were blistered by the desert sunshine, but she ignored the pain. When I last heard of her she was a mother of three bairns, and a part-time hairdresser. At Oxford I never once uttered the word 'bairn'.

A Bedouin camp not far from the road looks like one of those Victorian watercolours by travellers: two camels graze near the tents as the women crouch around a camel-dung fire which is sending wispy spirals of smoke skywards like prayers.

We pass a half-built house of breezeblocks. What happens to these houses? You see them all over the Middle East, the work started and then stalled, probably for ever. I turn towards Noor who seems to sense my gaze and wakes. She throws her hair over her face and then she flings it back again and runs her fingers through it. She smiles at me. There is something endearingly natural about her gestures.

'You looked so lovely asleep.'

'Did I snore?'

'Just a little.'

'Do you still love me anyway?'

'More than I dare tell you.'

'Oh, thank goodness.'

We take great pleasure in speaking this language of love. It is a little sentimental, but it rises naturally from somewhere deep.

After an hour or so of cruising happily south, with occasional glimpses of the Dead Sea to our right, we come on the turn-off to Kerak City. For the last twenty kilometres we have been able to see the castle, rising improbably from the folded countryside. It looks as if it has grown of its own volition from the rocky land-scape. The original name of the castle was Petra Deserti, stone of the desert.

It was from Kerak that Reynald de Châtillon attacked and plundered a Muslim caravan in 1187, which Saladin took as an unpardonable breach of the truce and besieged Tiberias in revenge. Foolish, impulsive, arrogant, and possibly a drunkard, it was Reynald who persuaded the King of Jerusalem, Guy de Lusignan, to attack Saladin's army, recklessly exposing the Christian army on some hills above the Sea of Galilee.

Kerak Castle rests on the spur of a plateau above the ramshackle town. A sign announces improbably that Kerak City is twinned with Birmingham, Alabama in Jefferson County. *I have a dream* . . . As we come closer we see how huge Kerak is; it is impossible to imagine how this could have been built in the twelfth century; no other building in this landscape rises more than a few storeys.

Noor has a North American distaste for squalor and disorder;

there are battered tourist buses and some dusty and neglected oleanders in the main street, once no doubt planted to welcome visitors. There are plenty of those clapped-out Mercedes, all riding rather low. Noor wonders why this place hasn't been tidied up; the Middle East, she says with sudden vehemence, is in terminal decline. As we walk hand in hand towards the vast *glacis*, a stone slope that protected the castle against direct assault and undermining, its walls loom, massive, above us.

She whispers, 'Richie, this place is a necropolis.'

I don't know what to say.

'It reeks of death. For two thousand years the whole damn Middle East has been a shrine to death and victimhood and resentment and murder. Look at this pile. Can you even begin to guess how many people have died here, attackers, defenders, children, raped women, people who have been tortured to death? Can you?'

I hold her close to me.

'No I can't.'

She buries her face against my chest and all I can see is her magnificent autumnal hair. It spreads beneath me like a wrinkled Red Sea.

'Look, don't worry, there are tourists in Gap cargo pants.'

Her body is heaving. After what seems a long time, she looks up from under the hair.

'Let's go in now.'

'Are you sure?'

'Yes, yes. No problem. I had a sort of flashback. I'm sorry.'

Her eyes are moist. I wonder what she was flashing back to. I didn't tell her that Reynald, the Master of Kerak, was a sadistic torturer. He ordered his men to strip the Patriarch of Antioch, a fellow Christian, naked, to cover him in honey and to leave him staked out in the burning sun. When his skin began to roast and the red fire ants closed in, the Patriarch quickly agreed to Reynald's excellent business proposition that he finance an expedition to plunder Cyprus. Nor do I tell Noor that Reynald liked to throw his enemies off the battlements.

The castle can only be approached through one gate. Its base in the desert stone has many arched tunnels where horses and their knights could enter or exit at speed and there are other tunnels and chambers where caravan trains and their camels came in to unload. At any time the Master of Kerak had provision for five years in case of siege. There are remains of Crusader architecture and Norman decoration, though the central church has gone. I knew nothing of the complicated history of the place: Muslims, Christian French, Ottoman Turks, Mamelukes, all fought for this castle. If you were a Frank, why would you leave Poitu or Aquitaine or Gascony or Brittany or Kent to set yourself up here in this desert, two thousand miles away from your verdant home, strung with rivers and thick with orchards?

'It was get rich quick,' Noor says. 'It was about land and empire.'

Deep inside the castle, which is so vast it is impossible to explore fully, there is an ancient chill; the rock slabs of the walls are cold to the touch. We make our way up to the battlements where it is blindingly hot. Noor pulls a peach-coloured shawl over her head. It could just about be mistaken for a hijab, except that she wears it loosely and carelessly and very evidently not in the interests of modesty. Even her smallest actions have a sensuality. I feel guilty when I compare her with Emily and her eyebrows and her white-mouse eyes.

I am learning the language of love and empathy, which I have sorely lacked in the past. I always saw myself as having plenty of preoccupations of my own to keep me busy.

'How are you feeling? Do you want to go on?'

'Yes, I do. I am so sorry. I was suddenly reminded of something I saw in Homs.'

'Will you tell me one day? When you are ready?'

'I'll try. One day.'

'Where do you want to be married?'

'Can we get married in Toronto?'

'Sure. I only have my aunt. And you have a huge family, obviously.'

'Yes, I do; we are part of the out-of-control immigration boom. There will be hundreds of us in tasteless brown satiny dresses and the men will be in shiny bamboo blue tuxedos, with clip-on ties.'

She takes my arm. I can still feel her deep unease. It is like the advance tremor the Underground produces as a train approaches.

6

Late October

SOON AFTER NOOR left, I moved to the École Biblique, where I have a perfectly serviceable room and my father's old desk in the library. In bed, I am watched over by a simple wooden cross of olive wood. Father Prosper was very keen to secure the desk for me. I didn't tell him that my father and I did not speak for the last ten years of his life.

Noor has left Jerusalem on assignment. She is covering the aftermath of the elections in Egypt. We spent our last night in the American Colony Hotel. I was trying in some way to imprint myself on the map of her body, because I had a dull, throbbing foreboding of this trip. The black Mercedes came in the afternoon to take her to Ben Gurion Airport. The driver did not speak to me as I helped him load her bags and cameras. Noor looked not so much a journalist, as my lover masquerading as a journalist. I was too conscious of the driver and the hovering staff to kiss her. I wish I had.

In Kerak City we went to an antiquarian shop to buy a ring. I told Noor I had no money but she took that in her stride. We found a ring from Sinai. Noor liked the turquoise inlaid into the copper band. She talked to the owner in Arabic. He said that turquoise was mined in Sinai for thousands of years. It was lucky.

'I want it for luck,' she said.

It was hard to be sure that anything in this place was genuine.

The owner's name was Hasad al-Sayid – I have his card. He took me to one side in a conspiratorial way, although there was no one else in the place. He had something very special, he said, an ancient codex, which came from a monastery built by the Crusaders. The codex was rolled and tied with a thin leather thong. He opened it reverently. He was offering it at a special price because the authorities in Amman were cracking down on the export of ancient documents and artefacts. I took a photograph of it with my phone when the proprietor went to answer his. He was angry with the caller; we could hear him shouting furiously. Noor laughed: she said he was calling the other person a pig. My teacher in Scotland said the antipathy to pigs was because of the tapeworms they carried in hot climates.

The proprietor came back and said he could let us have the scroll for $2,000. He said that the codex predated the Dead Sea Scrolls and that it had been found in a cave a few years ago by a Bedouin and it was his grandson who had brought it to market. I told him, with Noor's help, that I wanted to see documents of any sort that related to the Second and Third Crusades, and particularly to anything to do with the treasures and records of the Latin Kingdom. I gave him my address at the École Biblique and my phone number. Father Prosper had told me that vast amounts of documents and artefacts were lost with the fall of Jerusalem in 1187, some taken away in a mile-long caravan by the Patriarch of Jerusalem, Heraclius, himself.

I am enjoying my conversations with Father Prosper. When I show him my photograph of the codex, he says it is a fake.

'What I can see of the text, the Aramaic and the Greek are from different periods. And the image of the Madonna is a copy of a well-known picture in the museum in Amman. The original dealer from Jerusalem, who got it in Jordan, tried to sell it to some New York dealers. He was arrested. Only a fool would fail to see that the Bedouin, the cave, the Christian resonances are all supposed to recall the Dead Sea Scrolls. But because these dealers have no training, and no Greek or Latin, they sometimes sell things without knowing what they are or what they may be worth. In this country, it is a little different: everything that is found or excavated, an ossuary or a tomb or a bit of wood, is said to be something to do with Christ, or John the Baptist or Judas Iscariot. It was the same with the Dead Sea Scrolls, which are one hundred per cent Jewish documents. In the early days they said they were Christian or about John the Baptist and that the Vatican wanted to suppress them because they contained explosive passages, which would undermine Christianity. All nonsense. Let us have some tea. In this part of the world, tea is a sedative. I hope I wasn't boring you.'

'No, not at all. It's a real privilege for me.'

'The art of the Crusader period is very little written; it would be an excellent choice for your work.'

I am filled with an unfamiliar zeal.

We drink the tea from small glasses under the weary cypress trees, soothed by the diffident approbation of the turtle-doves. It strikes me, not for the first time, just how arbitrary the choices we make can be. I have become very fond of Father Prosper and I think I could happily have done what he has if things had been different. I tell him that I was estranged from my father before he died and went to live in Scotland with my aunt and worked as a ghillie in the school holidays.

'Oh, that is very sad. There is someone here you should meet. She belongs to one of the grand families of Jerusalem. Your father was very close to her. It was difficult and their friendship was seen as a scandal. They drank together and went dancing. Now she is the *grande dame* of her family. Would you like to speak to her about your father?'

'Will she agree?'

'I will ask her, of course, but I think she will be delighted. Her name is Haneen Husayni. She is a very cultured woman. You will find her interesting, I am sure. She is also an art historian. She may be able to help you more than I can about the Crusader art and manuscripts.'

This is my subject – the lost art of the Latin Kingdom. Where did the Patriarch take the loot after the fall of Jerusalem? And what happened to the True Cross, last seen in 1187 attached to a lance and heading for Damascus?

Haneen Husayni's house stands at the head of a wadi that appears to run all the way down to the Dead Sea. From here you can't actually see the sea, but you can see the hills of Jordan on the far side. The house is built of stone, and has huge arches along the ground floor, with one very old, seasoned front door providing the only access. Up above is a balcony of six arches holding up the roof. I imagine that there are cooling breezes up there. A manservant opens the door to me. Haneen Husayni is waiting just beyond the first hallway, extravagantly dressed in a floor-length robe, and above it she wears a sort of turban in yellow shot silk.

'Hello, my boy. My heart gave a short, how do you say? *galipette*. You look so like your father. So handsome. And you must excuse my headgear; my wretched hairdresser is on holiday. He has gone to Cyprus to do garage music. What is that? Come, we will have lunch.'

She is tall and slender; her eyebrows are arched, and her eye sockets are dusted with something that catches the light, something that looks like spice. Her voice is from a lost epoch, as though it is being played on a wind-up gramophone. Every word she utters carries some elements of complicity, drawing me into her own special alliance.

She asks for my arm, and leans on it heavily as we climb the flight up to the balcony, which is more of an open-air room than a balcony. Here we sit on Ottoman divans amid palms in pots. A servant brings us tea and very cold lemon juice and sugared water, which she calls a nimbu-pani.

'It's Indian,' she says, 'a colonial drink. Now you want to know about your father and me?'

She laughs.

'Well, yes, there is a lot about his life I don't really know. We were estranged when I was very young.'

'Estranged?'

She repeats the word as if she is trying to taste it.

'How sad. When I look at you, I see your father. It's quite disturbing. I loved him as I have never loved anyone else, and I have been married twice and had many lovers. He had a rare quality of enthusiasm; he was eager for love, for strange experiences – sometimes hash had a part in this, but it didn't seem to us to be bad. We believed that the world was changing. We believed in love and sex. My family was horrified, not by your father himself, but by the fact that I was in love with this long-haired, wild boy. My mother secretly adored him too. Seeing you at my door has shaken me.'

She rings a bell.

'Are you ready to eat? Your father was always hungry. It was the munchies.'

She says it as if it was an historical period, *the golden age of the munchies*. The servant appears. He glides in the traditional fashion. He bows, holding one hand to his chest. Haneen glances at him disdainfully for a second. I see that people who have always had servants feel no need to ingratiate themselves; this is the natural order. The servant bows again and retreats, sliding backwards towards the door in his slippers, as elegantly as an ice dancer.

She points to the far hills.

'Have you been down there? To the Dead Sea?'

'Yes, I went to Qumran and Masada. Just on a bus tour.'

'You really are your father's son. He, too, was here, there and everywhere. I haven't been there for years. I have asked for our luncheon to be brought up here. It's cool. I hate air conditioning. It dries the complexion.'

I have never heard the word 'luncheon' spoken before. I am my father's son, of course, but I think this phrase means much more and I am unwilling to accept the implications: I don't want to think that his follies and insensitivity have been lodged in me without my consent.

'We were separated by the Six Day War. We call it *an-Naksah*, the Setback, by the way. Our Arab culture is full of tomorrow and yesterday. Today is more of a problem. Right there, on Mount Scopus, the Israelis had a battery. Your father wanted to come to this house but it was impossible and in the end he was sent away by the Israelis. Deported.'

'Did you see him again?'

'Yes. I saw him three times. We met in Paris first in 1972, but it was difficult to get back to what we had before.'

Her folded, haughty face inclines towards the Dead Sea, perhaps angled deliberately to avoid the view of the new Israeli settlements to the West, rows of apartments and condos attended by cranes. She pauses; she is moved by her own recollections, as people are when they speak of the dead at a funeral.

'It was a shock to me to hear of his death. You must make peace with him now, even now. It's not too late. I want you to do that.'

I wonder why the onus is on me to contact him on the other side. Can there not be two-way reconciliation traffic?

Servants bring up beaten copper trays loaded with small dishes. I have come to see that in these parts a profusion of food – tens of small dishes – indicates hospitality and generosity. I wonder what Haneen would make of my aunt's penitential cooking. Her only firm rule is that the plates should be hot. She hasn't yet come round to garlic, although she watches cooking programmes obsessively on her small television.

Haneen guides me through these dishes and tells me that the family cook has been here for forty years; some of these recipes are family secrets. I am unable to distinguish them one from another very clearly, but the family hummus, the aubergines with rose water and yoghurt, the zatar-flavoured flatbreads and the greenish-yellow olive oil are all wonderful, particularly when I compare them, disloyally, with the meals in the École Biblique's refectory, which has now assumed a retrospective dullness.

I make dutiful remarks about how good Haneen's food is. But my words sound hollow and formal, even to me; I don't have the ease of manner or the language of hospitality or enmity, or the everyday courtesies or the talent for intrigue and the taste for ambiguity required in the Levant. I am treading *the stranger paths of banishment* to which Richard condemns Mowbray in *Richard II*.

'Richard. Richard, there is something I must tell you.'

I find that sentences which contain the words 'I must tell you' often bear unwelcome information.

'Is it about my father?'

'No. I am sure we will talk more of him. The reason I asked Prosper to send you here is because Jerusalem is a small place. I know that you have been seeing Noor. There was no reason for her to tell you, but she is my niece. The daughter of my younger brother. He went to live in Canada after some trouble here. Our family was regarded as being too close to the Israelis. You should know that Noor has been staying here. I feel responsible for her. My driver was always close by.'

'Did she tell you about me?'

'She spoke to me frankly, because you young people think that women of my age are harmless. You can't imagine that we were ever in love, or beautiful or carefree.'

'Did you tell her about my father?'

'Of course not. I didn't know who you were when Noor and I spoke, but then Prosper called to say you would like to meet me and he told me you were Alaric's son. It was easy to put two and two together.'

This is where Noor retreated every night – to her auntie's

home, driven by her auntie's chauffeur and bodyguard. I have walked sleeping into the Levantine world; I wonder what else I don't know. Haneen waits while the servants remove the dishes and platters. She gestures imperiously for them to hurry up. They give the impression that they would be honoured to move faster, if only they could. Still, they scurry quietly, looking to her for approbation.

'Do you love Noor?'

The servants can only be heard faintly now, by way of a light clattering of plates from the steps below. The breezes from the desert are now quite cool. I find it difficult to answer.

'I have never met anyone like her.'

'You are infatuated. *Sous le charme*, as the French say. Do you think she is beautiful?'

'Yes, I think she is beautiful.'

'What I want to say to you is for your ears only.'

She lowers her voice, so that the deepish, Turkish-cigarette-rasped tones become a whisper.

'Noor sees herself as a campaigner for human rights. Around here this is dangerous. "Human rights" ' – she adds a little ironic emphasis as if to indicate that they are an illusion – 'are seen as a kind of tactic by the West. The idea that everyone has human rights is mistrusted. I have rights, my family has rights, my religion has rights, but other people don't automatically have rights. I have tried to explain this to Noor, but she is too much a Canadian. She thinks everyone in the world longs for the benefits of human rights, except the leaders, who are, of course, all evil tyrants. Here anyone could kill her. Muslims because she is a Christian, Jews because she is pro-Arab, the conservatives because she is too modern – actually the list is a long one. She is in Egypt now, reporting, but the truth is it is cover for a human rights organisation she works for. Already I hear rumours. She must go home to Canada.'

'I don't know what to say.'

'When are you going back to London?'

'Soon. I have research to do.'

'If she calls you, try to get her to come back from Egypt immediately. And when you go to London, I want you to call my brother and give him a message. At this moment I cannot call him or even email him or use social media. Everybody is watching us. Richard, I believe Noor is in danger. Will you do it?'

'Of course.'

'I will send my driver to the École Biblique with the message for you to give my brother, with his phone number.'

The term 'social media' is discordant here in the thickening biblical light. We settle down with Turkish coffee. I ask her about the art of the Crusaders.

'Yes, Prosper told me and I have some suggestions for you about where to look. Let me give you an example. Have you heard of the Chinon Parchments?'

'No. I haven't.'

'Well in 2001 an academic, Barbara Frale, a palaeographer working in the Vatican Secret Archives, found parchments which had never been catalogued, or a copy of the originals anyway, which gave new information about Jacques de Molay, the last Grand Master of the Templars, who, as you know, were very prominent in Jerusalem and particularly in Acre. The Templars were actually founded to aid the pilgrims but became knights and fought with the Crusaders. They were very popular in France. De Molay was excommunicated and burnt at the stake on the grounds of heresy and sodomy and many of his people were killed in the power struggle. It led, really, to the end of the Templars in France. There is still a rue du Temple in the Marais in Paris. This parchment, Frale says, proves that in 1308 Pope Clement V pardoned de Molay in Chinon, and refuted all the charges against him brought by the inquisition. The Vatican has an authenticated copy of this document, and I can even give you the document number if you want it.

This is the sort of thing you must look for. You may just find a hint here or a misunderstood letter there, which will lead you to the lost art. I hear that you were in Jordan looking for documents. Forget it. They are all forged. If you are looking for something unusual, the best start is to look at the collections. Some of these are wrongly assigned or catalogued, or not catalogued at all. You have to look in the records for the sort of thing you want.'

'Do you know everything that is going on?'

'I do my best.'

I recognise Haneen as a prototype that I have only read about: the strong-minded, grand, intelligent woman who has outlived, and outdone, the men in her life. Richard the Lionheart's mother, Eleanor of Aquitaine, was one of these too.

'Who are you writing this paper for?'

'I have a postgraduate grant from my college in Oxford.'

As I speak it – Oxford helps my cause – my project sounds sonorous and important when in fact it may be flim-flam, just like my father's endeavours.

The lands dropping away down to the Dead Sea are achingly beautiful now; in the deepening darkness the folds in the hills and the clefts of the wadis have turned this landscape into a chiaroscuro. Above, as on a painter's palette, there are smears of pink, of sherbet and of burnt umber in the sky.

'Your dear father was always looking for revelation. He was convinced that there was secret stuff out there that the powers above didn't want us to see. And here we are plagued by this kind of thing.'

'Yes, I had a conversation with a taxi driver who told me that there was incontrovertible, but secret, evidence that Mossad bombed the Twin Towers.'

'Oh, we all believe that. That's a given. The one I love is the story that Mossad released trained Great White sharks to kill tourists in Sharm el-Sheikh. Absolutely true.'

She laughs, apparently forgetting her earlier caution.

'You should try to find out where the Patriarch Heraclius took the treasures in 1187. There were caravans of them. I would guess Tyre or Antioch. It's even possible that the Templars took charge of them, or that your father's beloved Richard the Lionheart found them.'

Now her mood changes: as the last traces of dusk fade, she becomes anxious.

'You should go now. My driver is waiting.'

She doesn't come down to see me off. At the door a servant is standing with a gift of dates, hummus in a small brown bowl, covered with cling film, pistachios, almonds and beautiful peaches, grown somewhere on the ancestral lands, which are fed from a Roman aqueduct. The driver looks around once before opening the door of the Mercedes. I can't make up my mind whether Haneen is a figure to be admired in her grandeur or to be pitied in her isolation, stranded on a barren hillside of half-built houses and uncleared rubbish, of cats with three legs and gummy eyes and a slinking, wary demeanour. They lurk near some randomly placed drainage pipes. I look up and Haneen is standing on the balcony. I wave, and she turns away.

The driver is silent. He has some beads hanging from the rear-view mirror. The lights of Jerusalem have a particular brightness, a kind of chemical intensity like some fireworks. The walls of the Old City are floodlit; they are glowing warmly below the Ottoman crenellations. I try a date. As dates go, they are luscious and sweet, but at the same time powdery as though the dust of the Negev has infiltrated them.

I think that these gifts have symbolic content: Haneen wants to demonstrate that she is generous, and perhaps also that I am part of the family. Gifts have always been big in this part of the world. When Saladin heard from the Byzantine Emperor, Isaac Angelus, that Richard the Lionheart, the German Emperor Frederick, and the King of France were all making their way to the Holy Land, he wanted to forge an alliance with the Emperor in double quick time; he gave him twenty Latin chargers, boxes of gems and balsam, three hundred strings of jewels, a chest filled with aloes, one hundred musk sacs, twenty thousand bezants, a baby elephant, a musk deer, an ostrich, five leopards (surely cheetahs?), a silver jar of poisoned wine and large amounts of poisoned flour, presumably for Isaac to give to Richard and the German Emperor and their knights when they passed through Constantinople.

Despite all these gifts, Isaac could not halt the Crusaders' progress. Richard travelled by ship via Cyprus, which he conquered, and Frederick never arrived in Constantinople; he died trying to cross a river in Seeucia. He was bored with the slowness of the crossing and decided to swim across, but drowned. Some say he had a heart attack in midstream. His flesh was boiled, stripped off the bones and buried in Tyre right next to the lance which Longinus, the Roman soldier, used to pierce Christ's body on the cross. Sadly, Frederick's remains never made it to Jerusalem. To be buried in Jerusalem was a guarantee of eternal rest.

As we drive down the Nablus Road, I am thinking now of what Haneen said: she was warning me about Noor's naivety but her words were also applied to me. She was saying that this world that we know so little about isn't going to change. What the fundamentalists say now about facing death is more or less what the Crusaders said then: *Dieu lo vult – God wills it. Caelem denique – Heaven at last.* I think of the Hospitallers offering their necks willingly to Saladin's Sufis, guaranteeing themselves eternal rest.

My father, of course, also believed that life had many sacred mysteries to be discovered. He wasn't one of the plodders. Haneen told me that he quoted Shakespeare to her:

Dear Kate, you and I cannot be confined within the weak list of a country's fashion: we are the makers of manners, Kate, and the liberty that follows our places stops the mouth of all find-faults . . .

My father was going to show the way to a better life; he was a follower of Timothy Leary who imagined a paradise, peopled, of course, by nubile young women, their minds released from tyranny – and sexual inhibition – by LSD.

As we approach the École Biblique, I realise with guilt that I have not even sent my aunt a card in the last month or six weeks, and this is the woman who harboured me as a bitter and surly adolescent and taught me to read deeply. The gravel crunches under the tyres as we slow. I thank the driver; he nods briefly and makes a neutral sound that contains no vowels.

I remember, with something like nostalgia, a large jar of powder on my aunt's dressing table, which she applied according to some arcane female etiquette; most days her face would be scrubbed and nun-like, but for mundane excursions – a trip to Mr Reid the butcher – it would be dusted like the surface of her Victoria sponge.

In my narrow room, under the olive-wood cross, I wonder what exactly Noor is doing in Egypt. There are no messages from her. It's a strange silence from a fiancée. Also I wonder if I haven't been unnecessarily cruel to Emily. I have barely thought of her because my jealousy and antipathies have been obliterated by having sex – of a very high order – with Noor. Maybe Emily can fend for herself. Maybe she has the inner strength to get over these setbacks. Creative writing courses are, I am guessing, more about self-worth than literature. Fat-arse beardy, Edgar Gaylard, delivered the first blows to her self-worth and I have added my own, mainly because I was hurt. Now, cocooned in the knowledge that Noor loves me – confirmed by Haneen – I am the pasha of magnanimity.

Father Prosper is waiting for me. In his quiet, ascetic way he wants to know how it went. I think that Haneen's beautiful haughty face with its paprika-sprinkled eyelids, sheltering the dark, sensitive, moist and alert eyes, represents to Father Prosper another world. One which perhaps he wishes he were a part of.

Maybe he wonders what it would have been like to have children and the love of women. I have seen that his duties in relation to the Church are now not very onerous. He was a bright, small-town boy from Perpignan, more or less dragooned into the Church. Scholarship and archaeology are his life, but I have the feeling that in his heart he believes that Haneen represents a more glamorous and exciting world.

I tell him what I can.

'Did you speak of your father?'

'Yes. She said she had loved him.'

'He was a very charming young man, as of course you know.'

I wonder what this charm they speak of entailed.

'Did she talk at all about the Latin Kingdom of Jerusalem? She has a great knowledge.'

'She told me that if there was anything to be found now it would be in libraries.'

'I think she is correct. The Bodleian in your Oxford has some documents that relate to Saladin. That would be a good start. The material is now being properly identified at last.'

I see a slight pinch of reproach around the mouth as he says this. It's the sort of involuntary tic some people have in response to lemon juice or the skin of a peach or ignorance.

Before I go to bed I write my aunt a letter on École Biblique notepaper. I tell her of my adventures, adopting the tone of an enthusiastic tourist in the Holy Land. I try to picture her reading this letter in the listless air of her cottage. I want to cheer her up. I certainly owe it to her. My arrival on her doorstep twenty years ago only added to her accumulation of disillusion. She was fifty-two then, but she seemed older. At first she never spoke of her husband Sandy's death, but it was clear that she took his suicide as a reproach. An oppressive nullity hung over the place. Even the butterflies Sandy collected and placed under glass-fronted frames seemed to reproach her with their stillness. There was no one to reason with, no one to blame; the suicide was a statement to which there could be no riposte. Perhaps the purpose of many suicides is to have the final word. She was living, isolated, in this cottage at the mercy of the landowner, a wealthy German, Gunther Graf von Schwerin. If he turfed her out, she would have to go to the local council for help. She told me that my father 'wasn't to be relied upon'. She appeared to resent him. This rresentment wasn't expressed directly, but in little hints. When I asked about him, she would say, 'Oh, Alaric was always a little fey.' I remembered something I had read: 'He's got that fey look as though he's had breakfast with a leprechaun.' In old Scottish, 'fey' means fated to die soon.

I didn't know anything then: I didn't know she had left her husband in Fulham to move in with this Sandy, apparently a russet, strapping man, with limited conversation which she mistook for profundity of the elemental variety. She had met him accompanying her husband and his financial friends when they were stalking. In this limited world he was a prince. But what he knew was stags – preferably with a twelve point rack – trout, salmon, dogs and guns.

My aunt could not go back to London after his suicide, she said, because she would feel utterly humiliated. Also, her first husband had quickly and smoothly married a younger woman in his office. She had been his personal assistant. He had told everyone who would listen – quite a lot of people, as it turned out – that she was the laughing stock of London SW6. His remarks were cheerfully redirected to my aunt by her former friends. True or not, she chose to live out her penance for her folly in this moist cottage, whose Victorian Gothic was far from comforting. Not far from her back door, the blue-grey Dee ran strongly, unconcerned. Once, she said to me that her heart was not in Deeside. She said it as though it was a profound statement of fact. I was not certain she had a heart; I guessed that disappointment had withered it.

Richard I's heart is in Rouen, probably beneath his effigy. In his day the heart was believed to be the lodging of courage and emotion. Then, this was a medical fact, not a metaphor. I have seen in the Holy Land how easy it is for the figure of speech to be mistaken for the reality.

I visit my aunt occasionally. She takes – rightly – a lot of credit for my acclaimed first class degree. She is very well read in her quiet fashion. She pointed me in the right direction and helped me with my homework. She told me that Oxford was the Holy City, although that precept was delivered partly as a reminder of my father's failings; his sending down was a disgrace.

Much later I discovered the facts of this disgrace: he had supplied the drugs that killed a friend in Balliol. This boy was found dead one morning by his scout – college servant – who looked after his staircase. (Oh, how self-congratulatory are the archaic terms.) This boy was the son of the Foreign Secretary, The Rt. Hon. Sir Alan Gordon-Mowbray, Bart. The story was all over the papers in 1963. My father was told to pack his bags and take the down train. He was questioned by the police, tried, fined and given a ten-month sentence, suspended because he was not selling the drugs. And because the young aristo was shown to have been an avid drug user in his own right. I have seen the cuttings. As his barrister argued, my father had no intention of harming his friend: however misguidedly, he was just sharing his drugs. Although my father was keen to make a statement from the dock, his barrister advised him not to. Perhaps he feared a dissertation on the deep and potentially world-changing importance of the philosophy of *turn on, tune in, drop out*.

Now I think that being sent down from Oxford encouraged my father in the belief that he had a spiritual rather than an intellectual destiny. He went out into the world to join what Timothy Leary called *a new species, a young race of laughing freemen.*

7

Back in London

THE DAY I arrived back in London, I saw a disturbing sight. Across the road is a small grocer and supply store. It is one of those places that stays open late and sells stuff that is often way past its shelf life. There is always a profusion of fast-drying baklava sinking into a small swamp of honey and there are small packets of mouldering nuts. Outside there are rows of plastic tubs in racks, containing fruit and vegetables, some of them almost at pavement level. As I looked across the road I saw a dog peeing on the lowest rack, which housed the cabbages and carrots. It was a big dog with that malevolent squashed face, bred to fight, a walking advertisement for canine eugenics. Its eyes were vacantly looking for trouble: I thought it was considering the merits of an unprovoked attack.

I went across the road, bypassing the dog carefully: 'Never show fear,' my father had said, moments before a dog bit me. 'I warned you,' he said.

I told the proprietor what I had seen. He turned out to be the owner of the dog, so I spoke more calmly than I had intended. He went inside and fetched some water in a plastic bottle and poured it over the carrots and cabbages. The dog watched.

'The kids roun' 'ere steal everyfink. That's why I gotta 'ave the dog, and I am Muslim.' The word 'Muslim' is pronounced 'mooselimb'.

Personally I thought that having a dog that pees on vegetables was worse than a little shoplifting.

I felt a sort of deadening of the spirits. In Jerusalem under the golden clear evening light, I have dined with Haneen, looking down to the Dead Sea. In a pasha's room, flagged and luxurious, I have made love with Noor and I have walked with her through Crusader castles with all their grandeur and folly and longing. I have seen the old city of Acre, already ancient when Richard the Lionheart captured it from Saladin within a few days of landing. I have looked at the remains of the city's Templar church; underneath it was the charnel, where the skulls and the bones of Crusaders and pilgrims were piled. I have seen the chapel where early Christians had arrived in Jerusalem from far away, and I have seen their proud and heart-breaking incision in the rock: *Domine ibimus: Lord, we have come.* I have been in the depths of the Holy Sepulchre, and seen the hundreds of small crosses, some still with faint traces of red paint, incised neatly by the pilgrims on the stone columns beside the stairway leading down to the crypts. I have learned from Father Prosper about the Dead Sea Scrolls, the Essenes, the Maccabees, the use of Aramaic, the True Cross, Jewish settlements on the West Bank, which Father Prosper – who understands *realpolitik*, and finds it thrilling – says will never be given back because of the political balance in the Israeli Knesset. I have heard about the irreconcilable claims to the Temple Mount and I have seen Al-Aqsa; I have visited the tomb of Absalom and the Sons of Hegir in the Kidron Valley, and I have crawled into rock tombs and looked at the inscriptions on ossuaries. I have seen the oldest known synagogue in Israel.

I was looking, in fact, at the doomed struggle to make sense of the human chaos. And I felt encouraged, licensed to think expansive thoughts about life and death and love. And now, back in London, I have seen a mastiff with frightful shark's eyes peeing on vegetables. This same dog, I am sure, reissues onto the pavement, as large, moist piles of shit, the farinaceous dog food that its owner keeps in the back of the shop.

I am very worried about Noor. I have called her number at least ten times. Her phone no longer takes messages. It is dead. In Jerusalem, before I left, I told Haneen that she hadn't called me for four days. I hoped that Haneen had received a call. Now seven more days have gone by. I have delivered her message to Noor's father in Toronto. I gave him his sister's warning as instructed. He was guarded and a little impatient. Perhaps he had reimagined himself as a North American, free of ancient preoccupations and prejudices of the sort I was milling cheerfully. He didn't ask me what my relationship to his daughter was. But I felt the need to explain that I had been speaking to his sister on academic matters – I cited the École Biblique – and that his sister had asked me to pass on the message that Noor could be in danger and should go home to Canada.

'Why did she ask you?'

'I think she was worried about phone tapping. And because I was going home to London. She knew my father.'

'Who is your father?'

'He is dead.'

I feel closer to my father these days. Perhaps I have taken on board Haneen's advice to attempt to make peace with his memory, even if I don't know precisely how you do that. The least I can do is to share some of his experiences.

I am in Oxford to work in the Bodleian Library. The Keeper of Western Manuscripts himself confirmed, as Father Prosper had told me, that the documents relating to the Crusades and Saladin are being examined and will be scanned. It may be here or in another library somewhere, he said, that there will be something unnoticed that points to a letter from Richard to Saladin, or even to Robin Hood. And there may be clues about the lost art of Jerusalem. He directed me to a book by Jaroslav Folda, *The Art of the Crusaders in the Holy Land, 1098–1187*, which he described as definitive.

Libraries have always eased my mind. Because I loved the libraries in Oxford, it was no hardship for me to work. I wanted desperately to do well, possibly to reproach my father. But also when I arrived in Oxford, I had begun to think that the only reality was the one we create of our own thoughts. This theory had a large element of self-justification because I was lonely and I was not fully socialised when I wandered overcome that first October day into my college. It wasn't *Brideshead*, but there were a lot of confident and loudly articulate people everywhere. In libraries I made myself, for better or for worse: *I taught myself freestyle*. I had been exiled for four years from interesting people, apart from those in books. At first I tried to be contemptuous of the Etonians and the other self-assured undergraduates who practised what was said to be an Oxford manner, a playful and caressing suavity. Nobody on Deeside had a playful and caressing manner. Instead they went in for a harsh and taciturn manner, a bullying kindness, which was maintained only if you didn't get too big for your boots. The world in general would always let you down. Burns wrote:

> But pleasures are like poppies spread,
> You seize the flow'r, its bloom is shed.

I was grateful for my aunt's instruction when I discovered that, thanks to her, I had read many more books than most of my contemporaries. They had been surrounded all their lives by an awareness of culture; their parents knew people who were musicians and authors and painters and actors. My information came from books. I wasn't a good conversationalist, and it took me a while to understand the nature of close reading, then required by English tutors.

* * *

Now I am back in the Bodleian reading Folda. It's twelve years on and I am keenly aware that I am not fully part of this: the undergraduates in the streets and in the Upper Reading Room seem to be children. We too must have looked like them. I had read somewhere that in Oxford the scenery stays the same, but the cast moves on, year by year; only the academics remain in place and grow old. The years between twenty and thirty have accelerated out of control, and here I am, almost thirty-three, without ever having had a proper job, sitting down like a student again.

I am staying with my friend Ed who has a small house in Jericho just up the road from Worcester College; after six years in an investment bank, he is working on a doctorate on Adam Smith, which will emphasise the social and moral concerns of his *Theory of Moral Sentiments*, rather than the trickle-down benefits of capitalism of *The Wealth of Nations*. In the bank he was involved with a hedge fund called Lion Fortress, which went disastrously wrong and now he has left banking and gone straight. I see, although I don't say it, that both of us are taking refuge. Life has given him a few whacks. He has also put on weight, so that he looks as if he is trying on his middle-aged self for size. He has quite a lot of money in severance pay and bonuses and is happy to let me live rent-free until I have found somewhere permanent, here or in London. He's lonely; his wife left him when he was fired. At times he is jumpy. In truth we are both a little bruised.

In my small bedroom I have a selection of my father's manuscripts and letters. There is a strangely naive quality to them, a sort of Dalai Lama innocence. He seems to imagine he has access to channels of understanding not granted to many, certainly not to academics. His papers are alarmingly random. I also see that he bought a collection of old silver fish knives at Christie's in 1969: the handwritten receipt fell out of a folder labelled 'Healing crystals'.

I have tried to dull my fears about Noor by spending long hours studying Arabic documents of the twelfth century with the help of a graduate student. I had hoped to find some correspondence or something about the art of the Latin Kingdom. But instead I found myself looking at elaborate illustrated manuscripts about siege engines and the trebuchets – the catapults that hurled enormous boulders – lovingly described and beautifully illustrated by Ali al-Tarsusi for Saladin's better understanding. One of the manuscripts describes Greek fire, which was a naphtha mixture fired in pottery containers over the walls of the enemy castle or town. A Crusader wrote:

In appearance the Greek Fire looked like a large tun of verjuice with a burning tail the length of a longsword. As it comes towards you it makes a thunderous noise like a dragon flying through the air.

I wonder how he knew how a flying dragon sounded.

In the evening Ed and I usually have a pint in a dark pub down on the canal and then we cook. Sometimes we stay to watch rugby there. Ed loves rugby. He is not the blithe boy I remember. His eyes have narrowed against failure and his hair is losing its vitality. As we are sitting down in the kitchen for Ed's signature dish – chilli crab with linguine (the crab comes from the covered market), my phone rings.

I hear only two words before the phone cuts out:

'Richie, please . . .'

'Noor, Noor, where are you?'

I shout, hoping my urgency will somehow reach across the dead space between us. My chest contracts violently. When I try to call her back, the number is apparently unknown. I try her Jerusalem mobile, unsuccessfully. I am beginning to panic. She sounded distraught. I try to call her father in Canada, but that number too is not in service.

'What's happened, Rich?' Ed asks. He is still eating; bits of linguine trail from his mouth as he talks. Perhaps he is trying to maintain a sense of normality.

'Something terrible but I don't know what.'

'Like what?'

'I don't know. Something bad. My girlfriend tried to call me. Her father's number no longer exists. Her phone is dead.'

Suddenly I remember Haneen and call her.

'Hello?'

'Oh, thank God. Haneen.'

'Who is this?'

'It's Richard. Richard Cathar, Haneen. Noor . . .'

'Don't call this number, whoever you are.'

She puts down the phone.

'What's up, Rich?'

I am stunned. Ed reaches across and briefly places his hand on my forearm.

'Tell me.'

'I have no idea. In Jerusalem I was going out with this Canadian girl, Noor, who is a journalist. I told you a bit about her. And that call was from her but it was cut off suddenly, and when I called back it was out of service. Her father's phone number no longer exists and her aunt in Jerusalem won't take my call.'

Ed says I am hyperventilating. He has had a course in first aid. He puts a Tesco plastic bag over my head and holds it closed around my neck.

'Breathe deeply. You are taking too much oxygen.'

My breathing calms down and he removes the bag moments before I suffocate.

'Here, have some pasta.'

I try to eat, but I feel sick. Something terrible has happened to Noor. I explain everything to Ed.

'The best thing to do would be to call the Canadian Embassy in the morning. Where was she calling from?'

'When I left Jerusalem she was in Cairo. We are engaged, Ed.'

8

Richard Arrives

TWO YEARS PASSED *before Richard set out for the Holy Land. Before he left, he reneged on his commitment to Alice, daughter of the King of France, and his fellow Crusader's sister, who he had been betrothed to for twenty years or more. As a very young girl, she had been taken to England as a sort of marriage hostage by Richard's father, Henry II, and there were rumours that he had seduced her. Some writers believe that was a reason for Richard to ignore her for all those years, despite pointed enquiries from her father. When in 1190 Richard finally took ship for the Holy Land, he stopped off in Sicily. The Norman King of Sicily, Tancred, had been holding Richard's widowed sister, Joan, and he had refused to hand over her dower from her late husband, William II of France. He also held some galleys and plate that should have gone to Richard's father and which Richard now demanded.*

Tancred was small and ugly: he was described as a monkey with a crown on its head. Richard would not stand for this presumption: Joan was released and, without any help from the reluctant French, he took Tancred's Messina 'in less time than it would have taken for a priest to say Matins'. Enthusiastic plundering followed. Philip was angry when he saw Richard's banners flying over Messina, because a banner above a city meant that its owner had sole rights to the plunder. Richard finally allowed his banners to be taken down, but Philip's resentment grew stronger.

Which in the French King did create
Envy that time will ne'er abate
And herewith was the warring born
Whereby was Normandy sore torn.

Finally Philip demanded that his sister's honour be restored, but Richard said that his father had had a child by her, and he could never marry her. To add insult to injury, Richard's mother arrived with Berengaria of Navarre. Eleanor, who was a great strategist, had lined her up to marry Richard to form an alliance with the kingdom of Navarre, and so to secure their southern borders. Berengaria was described, by the kinder scribes, as sensible rather than attractive. They were never to have children, and this too led to the rumour that Richard was gay. Walter of Guisborough, however, writes that, even while dying, Richard ordered women to be brought to his bed.

In the spring Richard set sail for the Holy Land after agreeing a settlement with Tancred. He took with him enormous riches to help in financing the Crusading.

Some of Richard's ships were wrecked on Cyprus and their crews and some Crusaders held. Richard sailed to their rescue; after a short battle, with Richard inevitably in the lead, Isaac, the ruler of Cyprus, Isaac the Despot, was deposed and Richard installed his own Angevin officials. On the 12th of May he married Berengaria. He saw very little of Berengaria for the rest of her life. She becomes a footnote of history, in that damning phrase.

Whether it was done by accident or design, the taking of Cyprus proved to be a very good move, because it meant that the Frankish Kingdom now had a strong base, just a day's sailing from the coast of Lebanon. After the disaster of Hattin and the capture of Jerusalem, the Crusaders' coastal castles were hanging on with difficulty as Saladin's troops bombarded and besieged them. The key city of Acre had been held by Saladin's armies for two years. In April, King Philip of France arrived with weapons of bombardment. He seems to have been rather listless. When Richard finally arrived in June, it was noted that Philip's six galleys were as nothing compared to Richard's twenty-five. Richard's own galley was red, with red sails bearing a white cross. The Muslims had heard a lot about the red-haired, six-foot-five warrior, who had absolutely no scruples about killing men, women and children and they were very afraid.

Baha al-Din ibn Shaddad wrote:

The King of England, Malik al-Inkitar, was courageous, energetic and daring in combat. Although of a lower rank than the King of France, he was more renowned as a warrior. On his way east he had seized Cyprus, and when he appeared before Acre with his twenty-five galleys loaded with men and equipment for war, the Franks let out cries of joy and lit great fires to celebrate his arrival. As for Muslims, their hearts were filled with fear and apprehension.

By July the Crusaders had retaken Acre. Duke Leopold of Austria, who had been on Crusade for some time, planted his banner by those of the Kings of France and England. It was torn down on Richard's orders, and Leopold immediately left for home. It was an insult he was never to forget. By removing his standard, Richard was proclaiming that Leopold was of little importance and not entitled to his share of the plunder. Philip sailed for home at the end of the month. He, too, had been humiliated by the dashing Richard, a soldier hardened by twenty years of campaigning and a man who loved combat. Philip had none of these attributes. Although it was agreed and sworn publicly that Philip would not attack his Angevin territories while he was on Crusade, Richard sent messengers to warn that Philip would undoubtedly try to seize the opportunity. As it turned out, the uncertainty of being on Crusade while his enemies plotted against him made it impossible for Richard to stay long enough to recapture Jerusalem. One of his enemies was his brother, Prince John Lackland.

Some months after the capture of Acre, Richard ordered a massacre of prisoners. The agreed date by which Saladin would pay ransom for the thousands of prisoners held in Acre and Tyre was 20th of August. Richard believed that Saladin was delaying in order to hold up the Crusader advance towards Jerusalem. In the afternoon of the 20th of August Saladin's envoys had not arrived as planned. Richard moved his army out of the city walls of Acre. Soon after, three thousand prisoners, including women and children, were led out and in sight of Saladin's soldiers they were massacred.

Baha al-Din ibn Shaddad describes the awful slaughter:

On the afternoon of 27 rajab/20 August he (Richard) and all the Frankish army marched to occupy the middle of the plain. Then they brought up the Muslim prisoners whose martyrdom God had ordained, more than three thousand men in chains. They fell upon them as one man and slaughtered them in cold blood, with sword and lance. Our scouts had informed Saladin of the enemy's manoeuvres and he sent reinforcements to the advance guard, but by then the slaughter had already occurred. As soon as the Muslims realised what had happened they attacked the enemy and battle raged, with casualties on both sides, until night fell. The next morning the Muslims wanted to see who had fallen, and found their martyred companions lying where they fell, and some they recognised.

This massacre is high on any Muslim list of Crusader atrocities, but Richard – as Baha al-Din ibn Shaddad suggests – may have done it as revenge for the slaughter of the Templars and Hospitallers in 1187. In any case, Richard could not afford to keep and feed three thousand prisoners and at the same time move on to Jaffa, Arsuf and Jerusalem.

After the massacre, Richard wrote to the Abbot of Clairvaux:

The time limit expired and, as the treaty to which Saladin had agreed was entirely made void, we quite properly had the Saracens that we had in custody – about two thousand six hundred of them – put to death. A few of the more noble ones were spared, and we hope to recover the cross and certain Christian captives in exchange for them.

Recovering the cross was very important to Richard. He instructed his armies to be ready to move out. They were reluctant to leave the comforts and fleshpots of the city they had just captured, after being camped outside the walls for two years.

Imad-ad-Din al Isfahani, Saladin's secretary, describes the camp followers:

Tinted and painted, desirable and appetising, bold and ardent, with nasal voices and fleshy thighs, they offered their wares for enjoyment, bringing their silver anklets up to touch their golden earrings . . . made themselves targets for men's lances, offered themselves to the lances' blows, made javelins rise towards shields. They interwove leg within leg, caught lizard after lizard in their holes, guided pens to inkwells, torrents to the valley bottom. Swords to scabbards, firewood to stoves . . . and they maintained that this was an act of piety without equal, especially to those who were far from home and wives.

9

Mr Macdonald

I AM SITTING in the library reading. I can only concentrate for a few minutes at a time before thinking of Noor. I look up across the rows of students. A girl runs her fingers through her hair in an achingly natural female gesture. I am flooded with anxiety. The uncertainty of the frightening phone call has kept me awake for two nights. What was Noor asking me to do? I am helpless. I sleep only in snatches. I look at the girl again, so young, so blithe, still combing her hair with her fingers. I have never quite known what these gestures mean. Are they unconsciously seductive, or are they secret signs known only to women? I find myself wanting to tell this girl about Noor; I want to enter fully the complicity and mystery of the female world.

I have a text. I walk down the steps and out into the quadrangle beneath the Tower of the Five Orders. It's very cold here. The Old Schools Quadrangle is enclosed on all sides, so that the winter sun only briefly reaches ground level. King James sits there high on the face of the tower, looking down. There is a smugness on his face, and why not? The statue was paid for by a sycophant, who understood the value of flattering the new king. Originally the figure had a double coating of gilt, an extravagance that suggests just how keen the university was to keep in with James.

The text reads: *Canadian High Commission wishes speak u soonest. Call Mr Macdonald.*

He leaves a number. I am trembling, from both the cold and the fear, so that I have difficulty punching in the right numbers. Twice I fail. King James above me appears to be watching, his latest book in hand. Vanity publishing. I am becoming flustered under his sightless gaze.

'Macdonald.'

'Hello, I am Richard Cathar. I left a message for you this morning, and apparently you phoned back. To my digs.'

'Yes. Thank you. I have news about your fiancée, Miss Nassashibi. It's not good, I am afraid. We think she is alive and being held in Cairo by one of the many groups that have appeared since the Arab Spring.'

'Have you heard from her?'

'No. But our people there are making every effort to find her and to see what can be done to secure her release. I know it is very difficult for you and the relatives, but we do have tried and tested procedures.'

'Has she been harmed?'

'We don't know. To be honest the situation in Cairo at the moment is confused. We do know she never returned to her hotel after a meeting nearly three weeks ago. But trust me, we have very good people on the ground.'

'Why would anyone have taken her?'

'Mr Cathar, there are many possible reasons. I can't speculate.'

'Have you spoken to her aunt in Jerusalem?'

'I couldn't give you that sort of information, even if I had it. But believe me, sir, we are doing everything possible. I will keep you informed. And if you hear anything from her, by any route, please call me immediately.'

He gives me a twenty-four-hour number to use. My hands are so cold I have difficulty entering it onto my phone.

I feel as though I am going to suffocate. I have been foolishly paddling about in history – history which I only understand in the

sense that I have charts of the time-lines and the factual details –
birth, death, marriage, wars, et cetera, but I am not close to
understanding the human qualities of historical figures. If I understand Richard III at all, it is through Shakespeare. As for Richard I,
rex ille bellicosus, I can't even make up my mind if he was a giant
red-haired mass-murderer, anti-Semite and sado-masochist or one
of the greatest and most romantic kings of all time, a brave warrior
and a dab hand at the courtly songs of the *langue d'oc*.

I cling to the idea that there is a truth in fiction that isn't available
to historians. But it is very hard to tell what is true and what is not in
this story. The fact is I don't have much of an idea of the here and
now either; it appears to have fragmented. It was only a few weeks
ago that I was lying in bed with Noor, profoundly blessed. Now I feel
cursed, as though I must unknowingly have made a Faustian pact,
which has come to its inevitable end. Haneen said, 'She is a human
rights activist.' Now that seems to have sinister connotations.

I haven't told Mr Macdonald this. He probably knows anyway. I
try to remember any scraps of conversation that might have some
meaning. Mr Macdonald said, 'She is one of ours.' And I took this
to mean a Canadian, a paid-up member of that frozen polite opti-
mistic nation. But maybe it means more. Maybe Mr Macdonald
and Haneen are in cahoots. Maybe they are trying to raise a ransom
to get her back from some cheap criminals or some out-of-work
Hosni Mubarak fans. If there is a real world, I am getting a dunking
in it. As I try to think clearly, what I remember most vividly is two
large drops of blood orange rolling reluctantly between Noor's
breasts as we lay under the open window, stilling our beating hearts.

Now my breathing is erratic. I feel that I might have a heart
attack at any moment.

I try to work to dull my fears. I am looking at a manuscript that
describes the Battle of Arsuf, which took place soon after the retaking of Acre. But I give up and look on the internet to see just what
the Canadian Security Intelligence Service can do. It is responsible

for conducting operations, covert and overt, within Canada and abroad. This is reassuring. On the downside, I read that they lost some classified documents after an agent left them in his car while attending a Toronto Maple Leaf hockey game in 1999.

Something catches my eye as I look distractedly at the manuscript: Richard the Lionheart was fifteen in 1173 when he took part in a rebellion against his own father in Normandy. By the time Richard reached the Holy Land he had been fighting non-stop for eighteen years. This man knew no other life. When his father died and he came to pay his respects to the body, blood began to trickle from the nose, which was seen as proof that Richard had killed his father. In a sense he had, because of his hostility to Henry II, encouraged by Eleanor, his mother.

In my misery and confusion, I begin to choke. For a moment I see the young girl looking at me, concerned. I am longing to speak to her, to assure her that I am all right. I exit from the library into the suddenly fallen, iron-hard night.

I make my way back to Ed's house. I may be having a breakdown. Ed takes me by the arm.

'Are you OK? You look shattered.'

'Sorry, Ed, I had a bad moment. I'm OK now.'

'Sit down. I'll make some tea. The good old English tranquilliser.'

When he comes back to the little sitting room he has a tray with a real teapot and some crumpets on a plate. I see something of the Ed I knew ten or twelve years ago. He's throwing himself into my crisis. I am his project. I tell him about my conversation. He produces a large notebook.

'OK, I think we should keep a diary. It's going to get more complicated, that's for sure.'

'A diary of what?'

'Of all the phone calls, conversations, things you remember. Why don't we start with Jerusalem? There could be some clues there.'

To him it's a mystery to be solved by deduction. To me the whole thing is wrapped in a Levantine fog that the good-hearted Canadians, in their sensible shoes and monochrome outfits, will never penetrate. But I fall in with Ed because it will keep us busy and allow us to believe in the possibility of a rational outcome. I keep wondering if Noor is dead.

'Macdonald is clearly a pseudonym, or perhaps a *nom de guerre*. The High Commission building is called Macdonald House. It would be a very strange coincidence. His name isn't Macdonald and he's a spook in the Canadian Security Intelligence Service. Their headquarters are in Ogilvy Road, Ottawa. It's all on Wikipedia.'

'Ed, this isn't a spy novel.'

'You would be surprised how like spy novels these things are.'

He seems to be enjoying this. Perhaps he finds the Ph.D. is a little dull.

I tell Ed about Haneen and what she said about Noor's human rights interests.

'What we need to find out now is what is actually going on. It's quite likely that the people who are holding your Noor have no idea who she is; to them she's probably just a North American journalist to be traded to more important people. The Canadians will be trying to make a deal quickly, knowing this. One of these groups could decide she was working for the CIA or Mossad.'

I remember what Haneen told me about Noor's father, that he was suspected of being a little too close to the Israelis. Ed adds this information to his notes. I can imagine Haneen calling in favours from Hamas or the Israelis or even the Grand Mufti. (In 1941 the Grand Mufti went to Berlin to see Adolf Hitler to tell him that they had the same enemy, the Jews.)

'Look, Richie, there's a woman I know in St Antony's College. She's supervising me with part of my Ph.D. She knows quite a lot about the secret services. She's suspiciously knowledgeable for a philosopher-economist.'

'Is it still the spy college?'

'I don't think so. Except in the sense that it has people interested in the covert services. I am not sure they go out and leave notes underneath stones in Moscow and that sort of thing. Anyway do you want me to call her? There's nothing to lose.'

'Sure. As you say, we have nothing to lose.'

Ed gets on the phone.

'Lettie, look, I have an important question to ask you. Can I come round with a friend? He has a problem, he needs your advice. OK, we'll be with you in twenty minutes.'

'Are you shagging her, Ed?'

'Yes, once in a while.'

'Oh Jesus, Ed; do we really want to drag your squeeze into this? It's not some fucking game of Cluedo.'

'Give it a chance. You'll like her. By the way, she's just a bit older than me.'

'And her name is Lettie. Is that short for Lettice?'

'No, short for Letitia.'

'Good name for a spook. OK, let's go.'

It's raining. We share an umbrella as we walk through the damp-darkened streets. The stone of the buildings is running gently with streaky rivulets, and a network of lead gutters, downpipes, unhappy gargoyles and spouts is gurgling as it channels water away to the rivers on which Oxford is built. I remember my disbelief the day I arrived in Oxford into this world of beautiful stone buildings. I loved Oxford particularly fervently in the winter, in the barely lit back streets where the stone of the buildings – as now – spoke to me. I believed what it was saying, that beauty and high endeavour are essential human qualities. These buildings – gurgling and chuckling in the rain – are the evidence of that principle. Aquinas believed that beauty and truth go together and also that we seek order and harmony in beauty. I am with Aquinas on this, but personally, I have no harmony or order; I am disintegrating.

But as we walk up St Giles past the Eagle and Child, where

Tolkien and C.S. Lewis and the rest of the Inklings used to meet, I begin to feel that Oxford is embracing me again, reassuring me. At the same time I know that it is the sort of irrational conviction produced by extreme stress.

Ed is carrying a bottle of wine. He is talking about what he calls 'possible scenarios' as we walk. Our walk seems to be timeless. It's like the walks I had in my dreams as a small boy: then I dreamed about the mother I had never seen, and in my sleep I was walking endlessly to find her, without ever arriving. Now I think of the clamour of the wedding party outside my window in Jerusalem; I think of holding a salmon by the gills, one hand on its tight, slippery skin; I think of the blare of the sackbuts at the Globe; I remember when I first saw Noor in the bar, and I smiled at her because she was so lovely, so joyously alive.

I am being presented with edited highlights of my recent life, and the effect is disturbing: my brain is racing aimlessly.

Suddenly I feel Ed taking my arm. I had forgotten I was with him; I was aware only of the pavement passing beneath me like an escalator.

'Here we are.'

'Where? Where are we?'

We seem to be in a village street.

'North Parade.'

'Oh yes.'

He knocks on the door of a small terraced house. There's a sort of shuffle inside. A bolt is slid back.

'Lettie, this is Richard Cathar – Richie – and this, obviously, is Letitia Melrose.'

I see that she is indeed a few years older than Ed. She shakes my hand warmly and smiles widely. She has an upbeat manner, and rather large, dark entrances to her nasal passages.

'Come in, come in. Oh you're soaked. What a foul night.'

'This is nice,' I say.

'Thank you. It's small but it suits me perfectly at the moment.'

There seems to be the suggestion of a sexual hinterland; on the short walk to the sitting room I get a glimpse into a bedroom. It is mostly taken up by a large bed with a bright Indian cover. I guess that this is the field of endeavour on which Ed has been recovering his self-esteem. Ed gives Lettie the bottle of wine.

'Oh that's so kind. Would you open it, Ed? You know where the corkscrew is.'

She is wearing plum-coloured jeans and a sort of pink wrap, perhaps cashmere. Round her neck are some chunky black, red and blue balls, possibly fashioned from some responsibly sourced wood. I have noticed that academic women are sensitive to ethnic fashions. The men are sensitive to no fashion, although they are happiest wearing an old jacket.

'Have you known Ed long?' she asks.

'Since Oxford, although we had lost touch.'

She is surprisingly well coiffed for an academic. Her hair is absolutely rigid. Ed glances at me as he comes in with the wine. I give him a quick thumbs-up. He looks pleased, although God knows why my approval should be important to him. I am seeing Ed in the pupal stage; after his banking years he is becoming a decent and responsible chap, with modest tastes. This is his plan for the immediate future, anyway.

Over the bottle of Cloudy Bay, Ed talks.

'Lettie, my old friend Richie is in big trouble. Noor, his wife-to-be' (he hurries a little over the phrase) 'has been taken hostage in Cairo. Noor, by the way, is Canadian, but – am I right, Richie? – with Palestinian connections. Nobody so far seems to know what has happened to her. The Canadians in the High Commission told Richie that they believe she may have been taken by one of the militias in Cairo. I know you have intelligence connections and I wondered . . .'

'You wondered if I could speak to someone. Right?'

'Yes, if you can,' I say. 'Anything you can do would be great.'

'If you give me her name and dates and all the information you can, I will make a call. One of our fellows here is a leading expert on the Egyptian uprising and the aftermath, and I will ask him. He's keeping his head down just now because there is an unfortunate accusation of having aided CIA rendition for Gaddafi at one point.'

I tell Letitia all I know and what Noor said to me at Kerak, that she had seen something dreadful in Homs. I tell her about Haneen, and the phone calls. She is very keen to know Haneen's family name. She takes notes. Very quickly Ed and I have become freshmen in her tutorial. It was to win the tutors' approval that I worked so hard.

By the time Ed suggests we go out for a curry, I feel less anxious. It's like the feeling of relief you have at a visit to a sympathetic doctor: the professionals are in charge. But I know that in the night I will again be seized by fear and dread.

In the restaurant, Lettie changes from rigorous tutor to Ed's girlfriend, and defers to him and his expertise in curry. She also becomes flirtatious. Her stiff hair is neatly parted, reminding me of the curtains in my aunt's living room.

Two days later Mr Macdonald calls me again. I now believe, with Ed, that he is not a Mr Macdonald at all.

'Mr Cathar.'

'Yes. Good morning.'

'It's Macdonald here, Canadian High Commission.'

I felt a deep tremor presaging the certainty of bad news.

'Are you there, Mr Cathar?'

'Yes, I am.'

'We have located your fiancée in Cairo, and have every hope of having her released in the next few weeks.'

He pauses.

'Thank God. Is she all right?'

'There is nothing definite to say that she has been harmed.'

'But?'

'There is no but about (*aboot*) it. Although in our experience, people who are kidnapped are almost always severely traumatised, and that is something we will deal with. We have specialists at the Embassy in Cairo who will assess and assist your fiancée in every way. She will be taken directly to Toronto.'

'Have you spoken to her aunt in Jerusalem?'

'I'm sorry, I can't give you details. This is ongoing.'

'Has a ransom been paid?'

'Same answer, I am afraid. Please don't think, Mr Cathar, that we are being insensitive, but as I said, we have to be very cautious. As soon as I can confirm that Ms Nassashibi is safely in our embassy, I will revert to you. And for the moment, don't contact anyone or speak to anyone. Particularly not the press. You understand, I am sure.'

'I do, Mr Macdonald. Will you tell her that we have spoken?'

'She will be informed, of course.'

When he has gone, I feel abandoned. I have been co-opted into this drama without having been given a script. I guess that my allotted role is that of the troubled, loyal husband-to-be. My destiny is in redeeming marriage. I must be married to make the narrative a happy one.

I have scanned the internet and there is nothing to confirm Mr Macdonald's story, and there is not a single mention of the kidnap.

Lettie texts me. She also has information for me. She tells me where I should meet her. I walk up from Bodley to the small hotel she suggests. It was once a parsonage. She is sitting with a cup of coffee in front of her by a fire. The wood scents the panelled room, reassuringly. The logs burn slowly, almost without smoke. I imagine that this is where the parson warmed himself after his short walk from the church next door. From the church comes the peal of bells, as if to endorse my thoughts. It is evensong. How sensible that word sounds. How comforting.

'Hi, Richie. Thanks for coming.'

'Well, actually I am grateful you texted me. It's been tough.'

'I can imagine. Just one thing. I don't think we should tell Ed about this meeting.'

'Oh, OK, but why not?'

'It's always a good idea to tell as few people as possible. Particularly friends.'

'I would feel a little dishonest.'

'Welcome to the world of espionage. I'm joking, honestly. Look, my contact has found out who is holding Noor. First, let me say there are no reports that she has been harmed.'

'Thank God.'

'It's a small group who are probably criminal rather that freedom fighters or jihadis. They are thought to be negotiating with the Canadians. Have you heard anything?'

'No, nothing. Although Mr Macdonald from the High Commission said he would call.'

'Will you tell me if he does?'

'Of course.'

'Ed's so pleased you are here. He's cheered up a lot.'

'I'm his project.'

'You are my project.'

I lean forward.

'Are you a spook?'

'No. Although the more I deny it, the more you will think I am. The not-so-glamorous truth is that I know quite a lot, but in an academic way. I couldn't kill you with a rolled-up newspaper, for instance.'

'In an academic way, do you think it's going to be all right?'

'My contact says it's pretty well standard. He doesn't rush into making wild statements. So I would say yes, it is going to be fine. But it may take some time.'

'How long?'

'A few days to a few weeks. It depends on all sorts of factors: rivalry, jealousy, ransom payments and the Egyptian Government and the Army's involvement. If they want to get involved it could be slow. What we don't want is for the Egyptian people to try to free Noor by force. But my contact thinks, as I said, that it's all pretty standard. Is her family rich?'

'I don't know.'

She wants to talk about Ed. She is keen to know more about his past, particularly about his ex-wife. But, I tell Lettie, I hardly knew her and lost touch with Ed himself some years ago, although occasionally I would meet up with him for lunch in the City at Sweetings. It was the sort of traditional restaurant he liked, with its hard-bitten, inexpertly and cheaply blonded waitresses. Their hair was as stiff as candyfloss, a budget version of Lettie's. All this was played against the bull-calf bellows of City boys that turned into a sort of male chorus as they grew steadily louder. Ed was in his banking pomp then.

I wonder why Lettie is so keen to know the details. She may be looking for areas of weakness she can exploit. She is disappointed that I can't give her the low-down. The skinny. We chat inconsequentially about Oxford. After a few minutes, she looks at her watch.

'OK, Rich, I have to go now. See you soon, and keep in touch if anything happens.'

'Thanks so much.'

When she has gone I sit by the fire. I wonder what her real reason for excluding Ed was. Could it be that she was following the rulebook?

The soft, unhurried country-smoke curls almost imperceptibly upwards. The scent is calming, narcotic. I am aware that Ed will be waiting for me, ready to go to the pub, but I order a beer to establish my right to sit here. I have never been completely at ease in restaurants or hotels.

Lettie didn't want me to tell Ed we had met, and I didn't tell her about Mr Macdonald's call. I don't want to be recruited into anyone else's version of what has happened. I am also wary of the role that is assigned to me: the dutiful fiancé whose destiny is marriage. It seems to me a trivialisation of our relationship. And I wonder if it was a coincidence that Mr Macdonald and Lettie should have given me the same information on the same day. I had feared Noor might be dead; now that I know that she is alive, I want, in my traitor's heart, to get out of this. Marriage is never the end of a story, as in many nineteenth-century novels.

When Noor asked if I would marry her, I saw it as a gesture of love. I was in the state Haneen called *sous le charme*, infatuated. But the more I think about it, the less I want to be the bride-groom in a Toronto wedding, the idyll no doubt reported in the papers and on television.

Also, who knows what Noor has suffered? Her flaming hair and her belief in every woman's entitlement may have been seen by her captors as a deliberate provocation. I know where this leads, and I don't want to follow. Those awful few moments when she called, choking, begging me to help, and the sudden breaking-off of the call have entered my dreams, so that four or five times a night I try to answer her desperation. Ed heard me when I was shouting, uttering last night; he brought me a cup of tea.

It is one thing to lie in bed with Noor in scented Jerusalem, the reed flutes and the hand drums floating erratically in on the night air. But it's another imagining married life with Noor. In the past few nights I have thought about what Haneen said and what Mr Macdonald said, and I have wondered what exactly Noor was doing in Cairo. I don't trust Mr Macdonald or Lettie. And now Haneen won't speak to me, and I have no idea of her reasons. But it all seems to suggest that I didn't know much about Noor.

I even wonder if our engagement was some kind of cover.

10

Richard and Saladin

AFTER HE HAD been in the Holy Land for eighteen months, Richard turned his thoughts to the Holy City and the Holy Cross. On his mind, too, was the knowledge that John, his brother, and Philip, King of France, were collaborating to take his lands in Normandy and Aquitaine. Messages sometimes took months to reach him; he was constantly anxious for news. So the Cross became for him a symbol, perhaps a synecdoche. If he could get it back from Saladin with a guarantee of free access to Jerusalem for Christian pilgrims, he would be able to claim that he had achieved the aims of his Crusade. And Richard longed to meet Saladin. He perhaps thought his famous ginger charm could work on him.

Months before, Richard had tried to set up a new Kingdom of Palestine, ruled by his sister Joan and al-Adil, Saladin's brother: she would marry al-Adil, Richard would give the coastal towns as a dowry and the new kingdom would remain part of Saladin's domains. Richard would have bought time; it was a stopgap plan so that he could return to the Holy Land after securing his Angevin empire. He would, he said, leave for home if this was agreed. For a few years at least Richard could then have claimed that his family were joint rulers of Palestine, and that Joan's husband was going to convert to Christianity. What would it matter if al-Adil signed a few documents and had a little chat with the Primate of Jerusalem, in the way that some of my friends have been to see the local vicar and listened to an endless homily, just to secure the beautiful old church in the village for their beloved's big day?

Baha ad-Dinibn Shaddad wrote that Saladin went along with it, but he said it was all a trick or a game by Richard. Joan, when she was eventually informed of her proposed new job, said that she would be damned if she would marry an infidel. Richard was running out of time. He urgently wanted a face-to-face meeting with Saladin, but Saladin refused: agreement must come first before kings could meet. Baha ad-Dinibn Shaddad records Saladin's meeting with Richard's envoy:

> The King says: your friendship and affection are dear to me. I told you that I would give these parts of Palestine to your brother, and I want you to be the judge between us in the division of land. But we must have a foothold in Jerusalem. I want you to make a division that will not bring down on you, brother, the wrath of the Muslims or on me the wrath of the Franks.

Richard marched towards Jerusalem to speed up negotiations. Saladin had turned down his request for a face-to-face meeting, yet Richard needed Saladin. When he was ill, it is recorded that he sent to Saladin for fruits and snow, which Saladin supplied generously. Each was intrigued by the other. But time was on Saladin's side: he knew that Richard had to go home and scorned his threat to stay another winter.

When negotiations broke down on the 6th of January, Richard advanced from Latrun towards Jerusalem, probably to concentrate Saladin's mind, because he had no real prospect of holding Jerusalem even if he could capture it. The advance stalled amidst disagreement and Richard decided to secure instead the strategic castle of Ascalon, which dominated the road to Cairo. He also wanted to make sure that the Kingdom of Jerusalem would be left in the hands of a strong military leader, and King Guy de Lusignan was not that man; he was still *dogged by his defeat at Hattin. Various barons and councils voted for Conrad of Montferrat; his coronation was quickly arranged, and Richard gave Guy de Lusignan Cyprus as compensation, but a few days later Conrad was killed by the Assassins, professional killers, on the orders of their leader, who was known as the Old Man of the Mountains. It was clearly a contract killing.*

Muslims thought it was done on Richard's orders because Conrad had been dealing separately with Saladin. But why would Richard have killed him after setting him up as King of Jerusalem? Nobody has suggested a plausible answer. Still, the French supporters of Conrad quickly spread the rumour that Richard had murdered Conrad, and this rumour found its way all around Europe. Henry of Champagne, Richard's nephew, then became King, and he married Conrad's twenty-one-year-old widow, Isabella. All this took just a few days.

But more bad news arrived for Richard: Philip of France was also spreading rumours about him, and at the same time planning to take his empire, with the help of Richard's brother John. With great misgiving, Richard agreed to stay on and to take Jerusalem. The Frankish armies, now united without Conrad, moved forwards. During a reconnaissance Richard caught sight of Jerusalem. It was as close as he was ever to get. It is said that he wept and held his shield over his eyes, begging God to forgive him for not being able to deliver the Holy City. The weather had turned, and it was clear to Richard that he was in no position to take Jerusalem, so for the second time he withdrew. Morale was somewhat restored by the appearance of a holy man who produced a piece of the True Cross which he had fortuitously hidden near by.

Richard moved to Ascalon, destroyed some months before by Saladin, to oversee the rebuilding of the castle and the city. But Richard's armies were disturbed and discontent and he restarted negotiations for an orderly exit after four months. It was agreed that Henry of Champagne would control the coast, and pilgrims would be allowed to visit Jerusalem. But there was a catch: Richard had to tear down Ascalon which he had spent so much time and money rebuilding. The negotiations broke down again. Saladin then ordered a surprise attack on Jaffa. The inhabitants agreed to a surrender and the Muslims rushed in to plunder the town. They raised their standards, but the citadel was still holding out.

Richard set off from Acre in a fleet of galleys. His red galley, flying a banner adorned with two lions couchant, was the first to make land the next morning. Richard took off his leg armour and jumped into the sea and, followed by all his men, charged the enemy.

Within a few hours Richard had relieved Jaffa. It was an astonishing victory and he was in jocular form: to Saladin's emissary, Richard said, 'This Sultan is mighty, and there is none mightier than him in the Land of Islam. Why then did he run away as soon as I appeared? By God, I was not even properly armed for a fight. Look, I am wearing my sea boots.'

But Richard was soon asking Saladin's emissary to speak to Saladin urgently:

Greet the Sultan from me and beseech him, in God's name, to grant me the peace I ask. This state of things must be stopped. My own country beyond the sea is being ruined. There is no advantage either to you or to me in allowing the present condition of things to continue.

He added that he would return to his own country immediately if a truce were agreed, without having to spend another winter here. Saladin called his bluff:

The King will have to stay the winter anyway, since if he goes everything he has conquered will fall into our hands . . . How much easier it is for me to stay here winter and summer in the heart of my own country, surrounded by my household and my children. The soldiers who serve in winter will be replaced by others who serve in summer. And, above all, I know that in acting thus I am doing God's will . . .

But Richard would not give up Ascalon. Again Saladin tried a surprise attack, this time on Richard's camp outside Jaffa. Richard had warning just in time; he placed his knights in battle array. For nine hours they fought. One chronicler claimed that Richard and six knights were more than equal to three thousand Saracens. Whatever the truth, Richard and his knights, Count Henry of Champagne, Robert, Earl of Leicester, Hugh de Neville, William de l'Étang, Raoul de Mauléon, Bartholomew de Mortemer, Gerard de Furnival, Roger de Saci and the knight who carried Richard's lion banner, Henry Le Tyois, secured their place in legend.

The chronicler, Ambroise, who travelled with Richard, wrote:

> The brave king of the English isle
> Went with the galleys by the sea.
> They were all armed so splendidly,
> No panoplies could be more fair.
> One saw the Earl of Leicester there,
> Likewise Andrew de Chauvigny,
> And also Roger de Saci
> And Jordan des Homez. This last
> Knight died before the year was passed.
> And also Ralph de Mauléon,
> Who has a lion broidered on
> His banner. Ancon du Fai.
> Many a Saracen smote he—
> As well as those of Preaux, who
> Were of the royal retinue,
> And many another known to fame
> Of whom I have not learned the name.

Richard de Templo wrote that Richard's right hand:

brandished his sword with rapid strokes, slicing through the charging enemy, cutting them in two as he met them, first on this side, then on that.

Ambroise added:

You never saw anyone like him. He will always be at the front. Always at the place of greatest need, like a tried and tested knight. They (the Saracens) call him Malik Richard.

For all the hyperbole, Richard was undeniably a supremely courageous, perhaps even reckless, knight and an inspirational king. Many reports confirm that the enemy often ran away when they heard he was coming: even King Philip of France had a tendency to depart quickly when Richard was expected. Despite his failure to take Jerusalem, the legend of Richard's heroism in the service of Christ grew and spread to all parts of Europe. His enemies feared his return.

Negotiation started again immediately. Abu Bekr, al-Adil's chamberlain, reported that Richard had said, 'How long am I to go on making advances to the Sultan that he will not accept? More than anything I used to be anxious to return to my own country, but now the winter is here and the rain has begun, I have decided to remain.'

Richard fell ill with a fever again and once more demanded from Saladin peaches and pears and snow. There is something of the petulant child seeking signs of affection from a parent.

He also told Abu Bekr that he should speak to al-Adil:

Beg my brother to think about how he can induce the Sultan to make peace. Ask him to let me keep Ascalon. Then I shall leave and then he with little effort will be able to recover the rest of Frankish territory. My only object is to retain the position I hold amongst the Franks. If he insists on his claim to Ascalon, then let Al-Adil find me some indemnity for the expense I have incurred in fortifying Ascalon.

Richard sent Bishop Hubert Walter, his right-hand man, to conclude the deal, as he was too ill to leave his bed. Saladin agreed to allow Christians to travel to Jerusalem to fulfil their vows. Walter, speaking for Richard, agreed to demolish the walls of Ascalon. But what was it that persuaded him to give up Ascalon without being indemnified for his expenses?

When the truce was signed, four parties of pilgrims set off for Jerusalem. Hubert Walter led the first. In Jerusalem he had long conversations with Saladin, and was shown the True Cross. Saladin offered him any gift he desired, and he chose to have two Latin priests installed in the Holy Sepulchre. It is highly significant that Hubert did not ask for the True Cross, which he would undoubtedly have done if it had not already been granted. It is likely that Saladin, who knew he was going to die soon, gave it as an act of kindness; war had exhausted and weakened him. He understood perfectly Richard's predicament. And he, too, wanted to keep the detail secret. There was to be no public disclosure.

Richard did not go to Jerusalem with the pilgrims. He had announced that he would be coming back, and it was known that he thought it demeaning to enter Jerusalem, except as conqueror.

11

Finding

FOR TWO WEEKS I have been going through uncatalogued and recently acquired or bequeathed material in the Bodleian. There were a few news references to the havoc the Muslims had wrought on Jerusalem in 1187, but nothing on the lost art. And then yesterday I spotted an entry in the print-out of recent donations: *Gift of Descendants of the Earl of Huntingdon.* I remembered that my father's friend was called Huntingdon. And I knew that an Earl of Huntingdon had gone on the Third Crusade, and probably sailed with Richard the Lionheart; I asked the Deputy Curator if I could look at them. She told me that the boxes had not yet been opened because of the programme of digitisation that was occupying the experts, but she had no objections to my looking at them.

'Some of these bequests contain Victorian versions of medieval documents, and some – very rarely – contain important documents that change our view of history, even in a small way. That's the exciting part. The Huntingdons were associated with Robin Hood, as I am sure you know. There is even one living member of the family whose name is Tarquin James Robin Hood Huntingdon. Something like that. It's all legend, I believe. A recent research paper suggests that Hereward the Wake is the original source of the Robin Hood legend. Anyway, if you see anything interesting for your paper, get it scanned and we can find an expert to translate.'

The boxes arrive. They are placed on a table and I pull on white cotton gloves.

The first box seems to contain household accounts in Anglo-Norman French. I go through the second box. It holds more household accounts and a few documents about local matters that I can more or less decipher. The dust in this box, a fine tilth of old manuscripts and leather, may have been in these covers for seven or eight hundred years untouched. The third box appears to hold charters and shrievalties granted to the family by King Henry II and by William Longchamp, in the name of Richard I. Now an assistant arrives with a dictionary I have requested.

'Anything interesting?' she asks in a whisper.

'Pretty routine. But there's a way to go. Thanks for this.'

She hurries off.

Late in the day, as I am sorting through the fourth box, King Richard's name leaps out at me from a sheet of vellum and immediately beside it, I see the Arabic title of Saladin, as used by Baha ad-Din ibn Shaddad. It is addressed: *From Richard, King of England, Duke of Normandy to Salāh al-Dīn Yūsuf ibn Ayyūb – Righteousnesss of the Faith.*

Lower down I see the words: *la Veraie Croiz.* My heart has become very volatile; is beating against my chest. This must be about the True Cross, which Richard was so keen to retrieve from Saladin, the cross that was lost at Hattin. The cross which Helena, the mother of Constantine, found in Jerusalem in AD 328.

Richart, rei des Anglois et duc des Normands vos salue, cher ami Salqh al-Din Yusuf ibn Ayyub

Mis frères, sumes ambedui travailliez. Avons devastet se pays, comme savez, avons tot despenduz nostre tresor. Mes propres sires menace mes terres d'ostremar, maugres en ait nostre trieve juratz; y retornar me fast.

Vos clamez ke mie otroierez ke nos gardiens Ascalon a

nostre depart en mer, et avez promis de nos en compenser; en plus, me faites saveir que vos tenez en main sa Veraie Croiz com carte maistresse. Mais jo vos fais sermenz en nom de Dieu ke non partirai mie senz sa Croiz, ke vos ne prisiez plus que seigne, et nos plus ke tote chose. Jo tiens en main non sa carte de s'espee des tarot, mas bien m'espee Excalibur; ne m'en refuse mie, mes freres. Por destorner cest malheur ki vos tombera desus, il faldra me rendre sa Veraie Croiz, sinon me verrez respandre se sang en tote sa Terre Sainte tresk'a sa prise de Jerusalem. D'issi tres jors, vos enverrai mon neveu Henri de Champagne avuec cinq de mes plus fizels cavaliers por prendre en main sa Croiz. Ese fera chemin soz ma garde a moi, e prendra emplace‑ment eternel dins sa cathedrale de Rouen.

De cez matieres ne deit nessun riens saveir.

I take the document for scanning. The assistant doesn't ask me any questions. It's just another old document after all. She even gives the scan to me on a USB, and makes me two prints.

I hide the original document in another box, and I spend the rest of the day and most of the night translating as best I can:

Richard, King of England, Duke of Normandy to Salāh al-Dīn Yūsuf ibn Ayyūb:

My brother, we are both tired. You know that we have laid waste to the country and expended our treasure. My lands across the sea are threatened by my overlord, despite our sworn truce, and I must leave. You say you will not permit us to keep Ascalon after I set sail for my lands, and you have promised to pay compensation. You have also sent word to me that the True Cross is a trump that you hold in your hand. I declare on God's honour that I will not set sail without the cross which to you is nothing more than a piece of wood, but to us is of infinite value. In my hand I hold not a card, but Excalibur. Do not, my brother, deny me. The only way you can avert the disaster that will fall on you is to return to me the True Cross or I will cause the Holy Land to run with blood until I have taken Jerusalem. Three days from now I will send my nephew, Henry of Champagne, and five of my most loyal knights to your camp to receive the cross. The cross will travel with me and be placed in the cathedral of Rouen for evermore.

    No other person must know.

Richard sails for Sicily on 9 October 1192. It is late in the sailing season; the winds are unpredictable and the Mediterranean is lined with his enemies, old and new.

I see his squadron leaving Acre, heading through squalls. The one hundred large ships and high-prowed galleys he sailed in from Messina eighteen months earlier are scattered. Richard's sister, Joan, and his neglected wife, Berengaria, have gone ahead with a dozen ships. Many other ships have returned to Messina, many have been lost. Richard's fleet now consists of twenty large ships and ten fighting galleys and the biggest, described by the chroniclers, the Buscia magna, is transporting the most famous and most feared king in the world.

    Somewhere, hidden below deck, is the Holy Cross, which is destined for Rouen Cathedral.

12

Mr Macdonald

MR MACDONALD CALLED me in the middle of the night. Sometimes when you are asleep you are taken without your consent into a world of uncertainty and anxiety; at other times you are serene and even blithe. You have no control of it. I was in one of the deep but disturbed sleeps when Mr Maconald called. I woke shakily, utterly confused.

'Macdonald here. Sorry to disturb you.'

'Oh yes. Mr Macdonald. What's the news?'

'It's good. Ms Nassashibi is in our embassy in Cairo, having medical examinations and some assessment.'

'Is she all right?'

'She is thin apparently, and traumatised, but I think that is to be expected after three weeks as a hostage.'

'What happens to her now?'

Ed has joined me, in flannel schoolboy pyjamas, and sits on the narrow bed. His face has a sympathetic strawberry flush to it, creeping up from inside the pyjamas.

'As soon as the doctors give the word, she will be flown to Ottawa.'

'Didn't you say Toronto?'

'Yes; well remembered. I did, but there's been a change of plan.'

'Can I speak to her at some time?'

'I don't think that will be possible. Only family members are allowed to speak to her.'

'We are going to be married.'

'The situation may change. She may request a call to you. But I believe that at the moment there is an embargo on all phone calls outside the immediate family.'

'What do you mean there's a fucking embargo on phone calls? I have waited more than three weeks to speak to her. She's my fiancée for Chrissake. I want to talk to her.'

'I am only the messenger, unfortunately. All I can do is tell you the situation as it is relayed to me.'

'Can you pass a message to her at least?'

'I am afraid not.'

'Why not?'

'I believe the family has placed this embargo on calls.'

'What time was she freed?'

'It was two days ago, I believe, at 9 p.m. That would be about 5 p.m., British time.'

'Why didn't you tell me?'

'As I said, I am only the messenger.'

'You are the organ grinder's fucking monkey – is that what you are saying?'

'Perhaps I am. I am so sorry to disturb you in the middle of the night, but I thought you would like to know that your fiancée is safe in the Embassy. I will do my best to keep you up to date. Goodnight. Once more my apologies, Mr Cathar.'

Ed has tried to piece together the conversation.

'You called him the organ grinder's monkey?'

'Yes. Fucking monkey. He's a slimy shit. He's a sort of Uriah Heep and Richard III in one.'

'Tell me what he said.'

'Basically he said that Noor is safe, rescued, recovered two days ago, and that she is traumatised and will be flown to Ottawa – not Toronto as he said last time – as soon as the doctors give the word. And I can't call her.'

'Why not?'

'Because the family have requested it, he says, she can't accept any calls.'

'It's probably just because journalists have been trying to get a story.'

'Do you think so? I don't. They are trying to freeze me out.'

'Well if Noor loves you . . .'

'Which she does . . .'

'Which she does, she will find a way of speaking to you.'

'Are you sure?'

'As you know, I didn't have a fantastic record of success in understanding my own wife, but yes, I think she will.'

'Nice pyjamas.'

'Annabel gave them to me a few years ago.'

'And you are still wearing them.'

'They're comfortable.'

'And you are still in love with her.'

'Yes. What can I say?'

'How did we get to this?'

'I don't know. It's . . . It seems to have happened very quickly.'

I think he is trying to talk about lost innocence.

'Let's have a cup of tea.'

'Good idea. I'll make it. Toast?'

'Yes please, with lashings of Oxford Thick Cut.'

'You must be happy, Rich. I mean, you know, that she's safe.'

'Yes, yes. Yes, I am. Underneath I am ecstatic, over the moon, mate, but a little fucked up.'

'I won't be long.'

As he stands up I see a gap open between the top and the bottom sections of his pyjamas. The revealed skin looks strangely patterned, like an orchid.

I try to remember Noor in the American Colony. Of course I can remember her – the outline of her – but I can no longer summon up those vivid, erotic, blessed hours; they have passed into another, desiccated, world, like Sandy's butterflies, in a glass display, beautiful but without vibrant life. It seems to me that she has acquired the insubstantiality of a dream.

Our revels now are ended.
These our actors,
As I foretold you, were all spirits, and
Are melted into air, into thin air . . .

When Ed comes back he is wearing a dressing gown. It's as though he has regressed to his first term at boarding school. He's carrying mugs of tea and a mound of toast.

'We should speak to Lettie, Rich. She will be able to ask questions.'

'Are you sure she's not a spy?'

'No, I'm not, but I don't think she's actually a spy, but I think she's on the lookout for talent. I think she puts names forward to be approached.'

'How do you figure that?'

'She asks about people I know.'

'What did she say about me?'

'She likes you, but she hasn't asked any, you know, pointed questions.'

'Ed, why did Annabel leave you?'

'She had an affair.'

'Who was he?'

'She was, is, a girl.'

'Oh Christ. Sorry. Was that a terrible shock?'

'To be honest, I knew something was wrong for a year or more. Before I was fired I used to get in to Snaufels and Montacute at 6 a.m. and come home at nine or ten at night, but after I was sacked I hung around the house all the time and finally she said she was leaving me and told me the reason.'

'You never guessed?'

'I did, I think, but I just pushed it to the back of my mind. We were in deep trouble, and I was under extreme stress. I knew the hedge fund was going tits up but of course you can't imagine what it's like to find that the fund you launched, with others, by the way, had lost nearly one billion pounds. I couldn't think of anything else. When Annabel told me she was going, I wasn't really listening. It seemed like a minor problem by comparison, easily dealt with.'

'How? Aversion therapy?'

He smiles wanly.

'I thought we could live with it. But I wasn't rational. I was in a blind panic. I would throw up two or three times a day thinking about the money we had lost. The bank wanted to pin it all on the three of us, the maverick rogue traders, as we had suddenly become. What really fucking well destroyed me was the ruthless way the inner circle, who of course loved the fund when it was making huge amounts of cash for their bonuses, buried us. I am OK now, but it's taken time. Look, Richie, I am sorry, I am burbling. Your Noor has been freed. That's the main thing. The important thing. I'm sorry.'

He sits on my bed; the strawberry rash is stronger, and making its way up his neck towards the fatty substance that has blurred the line of his jaw. The dressing gown has hearty, Jermyn Street, stripes of red and black. It's a rich garment, made for a prince of finance, but in this small bedroom, lined with a sort of knobbly paper, which is aggressively mildewed in one corner above the flimsy skirting board, it seems to be signalling a message about human frailty.

'Jesus, what a fuck-up,' Ed says, generously including me in his assessment.

Three days have gone by. I have tried to contact Haneen again, wanting to believe that the reason that she has not contacted me is because she is under pressure from various directions. But her phone numbers no longer exist. Then I had a thought: Father Prosper has seen nearly fifty years of Jerusalem, the turbulent Holy City. He would know something.

I called the École Biblique. He was summoned from the library. I could hear his shoes slapping on the stone floor as he approached the desk. I could even picture the phone booth off to one side, under a mosaic of St Catherine of Siena.

'Hello, Father.'

'Who is that? Is it Richard?'

'Yes it is.'

'I believed that you would call me one day.'

'Yes, I should have spoken to you earlier. You have heard the news, of course.'

'Yes, Richard, I have. Noor is safely in Ottawa, so I have heard.'

'And Haneen, where is she?'

'She is in Toronto. Her house is all closed.'

'She wouldn't speak to me.'

'She told me you called, but she could not speak.'

In the background I hear the bells of the church start up.

'What's going on, Father?'

'I don't know precisely. I think you should talk to Haneen in Toronto.'

'Have you got a number for her?'

'No. But she will call and I will let her know that you want to talk to her. I believe she has some private matters to discuss with you.'

'Do you have any idea what they are, Father? The private matters?'

'It's complicated. *Raconter tout serait impossible* – de Maupassant. It means it would be impossible to tell everything. This is Jerusalem. Nothing is ever complete, nothing is completely true.'

'I don't know what you mean.'

'Haneen will tell you. I know that, as a fact, she is very fond of you. I have to go now to vespers. Goodbye, my boy. God bless you.'

I envy Father Prosper, walking to the chapel through the cypress trees, the doves warbling their Gregorian chants decorously and timidly as the evening thickens, the bells sounding boldly as they have always done, wrapping him in the comfort of ritual. If he lacks for anything, it is human sensuality. The church has drained him; he lives amongst ossuaries and parchments in a dry world. On the other hand his life is calm, bounded by bells and based on simple rituals. It occurs to me that, safe in the École Biblique, he is like one of those fish I saw in Aqaba all those years ago through my cheap, fogged goggles, holed up in the coral, peering out at the flux of marine life. Also, it is clear to me that he and Haneen have conferred over Noor's kidnap.

Later that day Lettie texted me; she wanted to meet urgently. She suggested the coffee bar in Blackwell's. I left the Bod, as we regulars call it, and crossed the road. She was sitting in a corner, wearing a short skirt and black leggings. Her face glinted impatiently. I saw that she was a woman with a taste for the higher intrigue.

'Hello, Richie. How are you?'

'Bearing up.'

'That's the spirit.'

I think it was said without irony.

'And you?'

'Oh fine. I have a few things to tell you. I'll get the coffee. What would you like?'

Around us students chattered. Snatches of their conversations came to me, flirtatious and cheerful. There was always a mist of youthful sexuality hanging over the place, invisible but pressing. Already I felt the distance between me and them stretching away, unstoppably. I wondered if they had ever read what Plato wrote, that philosophy is the study of death. Religion and death also have an intimate association. Religion's unique selling proposition is that it can offer a way of avoiding death absolutely. I remembered A.J. Ayer:

> *Since the religious utterances of the theists are not genuine propositions at all, they cannot stand in any logical relation to the propositions of science.*

They may not, but for many people, the propositions of science are a dry and narrow way of looking at the world, not applicable to daily life.

Against a backdrop of espresso machines and muffins and rising steam, Lettie came back carrying two cups of coffee. She looked to me like a character in a romcom.

'Sorry it took so long.'

There were hearts on our coffee, corporate romanticism, which is an oxymoron.

'Tell me what you know, please.'

'Absolutely. Look, this is quite complicated. My contact says that a Canadian Christian Arab consortium raised half a million dollars to get Noor out. Actually the group that was holding her treated her badly. They accused her of being a Mossad spy, and it could have been much worse for her, but the Canadians applied a lot of pressure, mainly on the subject of future financial aid, and the President's office intervened. The money was delivered. Noor was released onto a street at midnight, and the group holding her were arrested; one or two were killed later, after a fire-fight. Amateurs, according to my contact.'

'What do you mean by "treated her badly"?'

'That is all I was told. But, Richie, I don't think you can rule out rape. I'm sorry.'

I sat silent, winded.

'Is Noor a spy?'

'Yes, I think she is. At least my contact believes she is. She works for the Canadians and they are in close touch with Mossad. Journalism is her cover, of course.'

'Lettie, tell me, why would she spy?'

'Spying isn't simple stuff. It is more about intelligence gathering than invisible ink. Governments naturally want to know what is really going on in the Middle East. And journalists hear things. If you ask me, she was probably recruited when she was at McGill and she probably believed it was a great cause. The Christian Arabs are having a hard time all over the Middle East.'

I asked the question that had been worrying me:

'Do you think I was cover?'

'It's possible, but I don't have that sort of knowledge.'

'She hasn't spoken to me or even sent me a message.'

'Have you tried to speak to her again?'

'For starters, I don't have a working phone number for her and also the Canadian High Commission is stonewalling.'

'That's their job in a case like this. It doesn't look as if Ottawa wants to go public.'

'Lettie, please, tell me what I can do.'

'I don't think you should do anything. Just sit tight. But remember, the facts may never come out.'

'I have to ask you this, Lettie: are you working for anyone?'

'I am not on any side, no. I'm an academic, a visiting fellow. I teach and I am writing a book about the role of the covert services in international economic relations. That's it. Nothing more sinister.'

'And you are helping Ed with his Ph.D.?'

'I am his supervisor, on part of it. I understand his subject.'

'He is very vulnerable.'

'You and he both.'

She stood up and kissed me on the cheek.

'I have to go to a departmental meeting now.'

'Thanks, Lettie.'

I walked across the road, towards the thirteen busts of Roman emperors, and I wondered what she meant by saying 'you and he both'.

Back at my desk I find it impossible to concentrate. Noor has been hurt and abused and I am unable even to speak to her. I feel a panic rising. I take my papers and leave the library and walk down towards the river, passing onto Christ Church Meadow through a gate, beyond which the vista opens dramatically. It's a cool afternoon, and the river in the distance is blue. The cows that graze on the meadow are being taken in. I have no idea where they are housed. Is that big wooden building over there a barn? There are joggers, more women than men, running in all directions with grim determination. Most of the women clutch a water bottle.

I believe in my heart that Noor has been raped. Her contemporary kind of beauty would probably be an affront to some.

I am on the Paddington train. Yesterday Haneen called and asked me to meet her in London, at a hotel in Knightsbridge. I don't know what she is doing there. She spoke unusually quietly.

I find that train journeys often produce contemplation; as we fly though the damp countryside I remember, quite arbitrarily, a photograph of my father. He is wearing a long military overcoat and a button that reads: *Help Stamp Out Reality*. What he understood by this, I think, was that life, as the establishment wished it, was dull; a new and exciting world was at hand. The old idea of reality was restrictive. The brain, with chemical help, could lead you to the true reality. I think that technology, all that idolatry of smartphones and iPads and so on, is just another version of the escape from the tedium of the real.

Now I can't understand how I came to be in this Kafkaesque situation. Kafka is one of my favourite writers, when confined within his books; I don't want the interactive experience myself.

But it seems I have no choice. I have tried to find in writers I admire a reflection of myself and I have sometimes tried to adopt their preoccupations. All too clearly I see now that my preoccupations are a lot more real to me than any I have borrowed over the years from writers: mine have real consequences. And they may not have a happy ending, or any sort of ending.

As the train hurtles heedlessly towards London, I feel again that Noor has left my world. A hatred for her kidnappers, even the two or three who were shot, consumes me. The presumption, the contempt, the callousness of seizing Noor and raping her and throwing her out on a dark street is not so different to what happened to Kafka's family when the Germans reached Prague. These people would probably have killed Noor without a thought if the money had not been delivered.

When I first read that Richard the Lionheart took captive women for his enjoyment – for a little ravishing – it seemed to me like a jolly medieval romp; *bit of slap and tickle, know what I mean, guv'nor*? Now it seems to me a hateful expression of contempt for women, an unspeakably awful and deliberate defiling.

Haneen comes down to the lobby. She is very elegantly dressed; there is no trace of the rich orientalism she favoured in Jerusalem. She is in a black dress, with a shiny red belt around the middle. Her eyebrows have been thinned and she has a shortish, professional woman's haircut. Her back, I see for the first time, is slightly hunched.

'Richard my boy. How worried you look.'

We embrace. To my heightened senses she smells of Jerusalem – of almond and zatar.

We sit in a corner of the gloomy bar, dark wood and lighted cabinets of expensive whisky, and Eastern European waitresses and glass bowls of limes and maraschino cherries and olives and fancy cocktail sticks and chromed cocktail shakers and black-and-white pictures by Bailey: all those 1960 poses of empty self-importance. Just like my father. I loathe this kind of place; it suggests that the world of plush furniture and cocktails and trite sycophancy is what we all really want. These places, in my, admittedly limited, experience, are always inhabited by businessmen, making banal but upbeat conversation, and by slightly foxed Holly Golightlys and personal assistants and PR people drinking champagne in the hope of impressing their clients with their sophistication. I am at the same time aware that my teenage years were spent beside a river in the Scottish rain.

'Dreadful hotel,' Haneen says, as if she can read me. 'Now I have some very important things to tell you. Would you like a drink first?'

'Is it that bad?'

'It's not so good.'

'I'll have a glass of red wine.'

We order from a tall, pale girl from the Baltic. Her skin has the texture of plain yoghurt, and her hair is almost white, so that she looks like the Snow Queen.

'Richard, you can never see Noor again.'

'I beg your pardon.'

'You can't see her.'

'Is she traumatised? What is the problem?'

'I am her mother, not her aunt. She was born out of marriage. I was engaged to a boy, a good boy but boring and traditional. I went to Toronto, and Noor was adopted by my brother and his wife. It's very complicated, but you must trust me it was all we could do at the time.'

'I am sure that's true.'

'Your father is her father too.'

'Oh, God.'

'Yes, your dear father was her father.'

She lingers on the word 'dear', perhaps offering me some

guidance to his true nature. I am gulping for air and my heart appears to be racing.

'Are you my mother?'

'No. Your mother died giving birth to you, because your father wanted to have some crazy natural birth in a cabin in the mountains miles from a doctor. There was a problem and she bled to death before help arrived. A few months before, your father wanted to see me on some urgent matter about world peace – he had a solution – and he came to Jerusalem. As I said, I was engaged to my first husband at the time, but Noor was your father's child. To tell you the truth, my fiancé and I did not have sex before marriage.'

'Is she all right?'

'No. She was badly treated and raped. We raised the money and the Canadians did the negotiation. I couldn't speak to you when you called me in Jerusalem. It broke my heart because I knew you were desperate, but we were in the middle of negotiation and certain that all our phones were being tapped. Then I left Jerusalem and went to Toronto to be with my brother. I also saw Noor in hospital in Ottawa, and she wanted to speak to you, but the Canadians vetoed it.'

'Did you tell her that she is my half-sister?'

'I had to. She was pregnant and wanted to keep the baby, because she was sure it was conceived before she went to Cairo. You can see why I had to tell her.'

I am breathing too fast. My blood is draining away somewhere.

'Excuse me, Haneen.'

I walk to the marbled men's room, and fill a basin with warm water and hold my face under as long as I can go. My panic subsides. I dry my face and hair in the fierce blast of a Dyson Airblade.

When I come back to the bar, Haneen suggests we go up to her suite, where she will order some food. It is apparently obvious I need food. As it happens I haven't eaten all day because of my anxiety.

'Why didn't you tell me earlier, Haneen?'

'I couldn't. It was a dilemma. I couldn't tell you or Noor that you had the same father and, *évidemment*, I had no idea that you had become engaged just before Noor went to Egypt.'

'How did she react when you told her you were her mother?'

'Actually, we told her when she was old enough to understand: I couldn't keep her in Jerusalem because my new husband would never have accepted her. But we were close, and after my divorce she came to see me every year, and I went to Toronto. But she didn't know who her father was.'

She waits for me to say something. I am stunned.

'My husband was a jealous man and he didn't want any talk of your father. By the way, when he married me he knew that your father was the love of my life. Also, even then, having a baby with your father would have been regarded as a scandal, particularly in our community. My husband was not a bad person, but he had the idea that a man's pride is very important, possibly even sacred. If I had kept Noor, the scandal would have been terrible. It was a bad time for us, from both sides.'

The regal, haughty woman I have come to know has suddenly begun to tremble. Her face, so patrician, looks older and in a state of flux.

'I am so sorry, Richard, I am so sorry.'

'I wish you were my mother.'

She smiles, as she wipes her tears with a napkin.

'Do you really mean that?'

'I do. My whole life I have wanted to know my mother and when I first met you I had a strange feeling that if I had a mother – sorry, I must be drunk – if I had a mother she would be someone like you. In Scotland I grew up with this sense of being cheated of my own life. It was only when I got to Oxford that I saw what was possible. Haneen, can I see Noor one day? We can't get married, but she is my sister.'

'She had a termination in Ottawa.'

'Oh Jesus, is there anything else?'

'No.'

There is a terrible pause; our breathing sounds unnaturally loud.

'Could it have been mine?'

'Noor was certain that it was yours. She went to Cairo knowing she was pregnant, she said. The gynaecologist said that the pregnancy was in the range of four to eight weeks. I had to tell her then that she was your sister, so either way a termination was the only option.'

'Was she upset when she was told she couldn't speak to me?'

'Yes, very upset. Also, you must understand, my brother doesn't know that you were sleeping with her and I decided that it would be better not to explain anything to him and his wife. Noor understands. Richard, I desperately wanted to speak to you earlier. I knew you must be suffering with the silence. But it was impossible.'

'I have to speak to her.'

'Give it some time. She's having counselling and medical assessments and then she has to decide what she is going to do. You can imagine how shocked she was when I told her. It was awful. She loves you and of course that is terrible – terrible – for both of you. Sometimes I think we are *une famille maudite*. Cursed. As I get older, I believe that there is malevolence everywhere in the world. We thought it would get better. Your father was full of ideas about the new world. But look, look at the so-called Arab Spring: it's turned vicious, it's anarchy. With these people nothing has changed since the Crusades. The Enlightenment, which I studied so eagerly at the Sorbonne, passed the Muslim world by. Now girls are threatened if they don't cover themselves, or killed if they want to go to school. You know why?' (I do have theories, but she doesn't stop.) 'Because these bearded fanatics are frightened of the modern world. They don't want their women to have ideas and they don't want anyone to suggest that there could be more than one way of understanding the world. It's absolutely absurd, but you can die for saying so. So now I am here to buy an apartment. It has come to this. I am buying a flat from some people called the Candy Brothers. As a family we have been in Jerusalem for more than a thousand years. We were already Christians long before your father's friend, Richard the Lionheart, arrived there.

'Amin Maalouf wrote: "The Arabs feel like exiles in the contemporary world, strangers everywhere. They feel defeated and humiliated. They are always thinking about how to reverse the direction of history and they always refer to past history to explain their problems." Amin Maalouf, by the way, is a Christian from Lebanon, and he left Beirut for ever many years ago.'

'You told me in Jerusalem that you had warned your brother that Noor was in danger. I tried to speak to him.'

'I know.'

'But you didn't tell him about me?'

'No. He asked me who you were after you called him. I told him you were a friend, that's all. He must never know the facts.'

Haneen and I talk into the night. She tells me about my mother, another seeker after enlightenment. Her name was Moonchild Gemstone and she was mostly whacked. She worked in a shop in the King's Road. I see my father wandering in one day, his long – already outdated – Indian scarf wrapped in loose folds around his neck, and seeing Moonchild Gemstone dancing to sitar music, which fills the shop, the *boutique*, as I am sure it was called. He starts to dance too, his scarf unravelling and floating behind him. Their eyes eventually manage to lock onto each other's, after an initial period of poor focus. Maybe they go a little later into the back room where they keep the good stuff and question each other about their star signs to see if it's an auspicious moment to have sex.

Eventually Haneen says she must go to sleep and she gets the spare duvet from a cupboard and makes up a bed for me on a sofa.

I have the unexpected but comforting feeling that I have come to rest. Maybe I am regressing, tucked up under this huge, pristine duvet, which has a remarkable lightness, as though the down in it has been harvested from delicate hummingbirds.

In the morning when I wake, Haneen has gone. She has left a sealed envelope for me. Inside it is a single sheet of paper.

Dear, dear, darling Richie,
Auntie Haneen has told you what happened. It was awful, but I am going to be alright in time. When Haneen told me about our father, I was shocked, but I still love you. We have done nothing wrong. If anything, I feel closer to you than before. I can't see you for a few months, but when we meet we will talk about everything. In the meanwhile try not to worry too much about me. I am stronger than they think. Dearest Richie – I need you. Your Noor for ever and a day xxxxx

I am sobbing. I haven't wept so often since I was eight years old. I can't bear the thought of her in agony. There is no address to reply to. Anyway, what would I say? That we should marry in secret? That we should be sterilised? That our father was a dangerously irresponsible and selfish person who took drugs? I have no hinterland: I am adrift in the world and now, implausibly, the woman I love turns out to be my half-sister. As Haneen said, we are a cursed family. Yet the sense of being at rest has not gone: Haneen is fond of me, Noor loves me. Things have changed: we are bound together by blood and secrecy. The complications and the intrigues are age-old.

13

Shipwreck

RICHARD WAS WITHIN *three days sailing of Marseilles, when he heard that Raymond of Toulouse was on the lookout for him. Richard had made many enemies, and he was the object of vilification by Philip and his allies. The wintry weather and the strong prevailing winds ruled out a passage through the Straits of Gilbraltar, which were anyway overlooked by Muslim powers. His plan was probably to travel to the lands of his brother-in-law, Henry the Lion, in Saxony. He turned back towards Corfu, where he abandoned his great ship and set off in two galleys with a few of his most trusted knights and their squires, among them William de l'Étang, Philip of Poitiers and Baldwin of Bethune. They were blown ashore in the Adriatic.*

There is no record of his great ship, which was transporting the True Cross. This ship came to be known to scholars as the Frankenef, but it has recently been shown by an alert German academic that this was a confusion: 'Frankenef', it turns out, was an early name for 'Frankfurt', close to where Richard was to be held for some months. A charter to be granted to the church at Chichester was signed by Richard and reads: Apud Frankenef, which was taken to mean 'on board the Frankenef', but in fact means 'at Frankfurt'. Richard would anyway not have been likely to have signed a charter on board ship in the middle of the Mediterranean. The only witness was Philip of Poitiers, one of Richard's companions in the Holy Land.

Richard and his knights could not have been shipwrecked in a more dangerous place; the ship was driven ashore in the territory of Duke Leopold, whose banner Richard had ordered torn down at Acre. Leopold was the nephew of Conrad of Montferrat, who was believed in these parts to have been murdered by Richard, and Leopold's over-lord was the Emperor, Henry VI, who was at odds with Richard over his support for his enemy, Tancred of Sicily. Richard and his knights dressed as pilgrims to avoid drawing attention to themselves, but after some harum-scarum adventures, Richard was recognised in a tavern and arrested on the 21st of December by Leopold's men and held in the Castle of Dürnstein on the Danube, in what is now Austria. Large sections of the ruined castle still stand. Leopold wrote to the emperor: 'We know that this news will bring you great happiness.' It was in Castle Dürnstein, legend relates, that Blondel, Richard's troubadour, found his master by singing familiar songs loudly outside various castles, until Richard heard him and joined in.

The news of Richard's capture travelled fast around Europe. Philip was thrilled: he reminded Leopold that Richard had set the Assassins on Conrad of Montferrat. But many people were outraged that a Crusader king should have been arrested on his way home after retaking Acre and the coastal castles and towns and routing Saladin.

I am keen to find out just what happened to this ghost ship, the former *Frankenef.* There is no name for it on record. Hubert Walter, the man in charge of the negotiations with Saladin, arrived in Sicily from the Holy Land. There he heard that Richard had been seized; the chronicles show that he set off for Rome to supplicate of the Pope, who excommunicated Leopold, and then he hurried to his master's side. They met, talked, no doubt, about the True Cross before Hubert Walter set off for England to raise the huge ransom that was now being demanded by Henry VI and Leopold – 100,000 marks, two hundred hostages and the delivery of twenty war galleys. As Emperor, Henry had the ultimate right to receive the ransom. Complicated negotiations finally resulted in Richard being transferred into the imperial custody at Trifels in the southwest of Germany. He was to stay in the area for eighteen months as bids and counter-bids were made for him.

The ever-faithful Hubert Walter set off for London. He took with him letters to Eleanor, Richard's mother, and his brother John. The letter to Eleanor about Hubert Walter is evidence that she had a very strong hand in the governance of England:

> To secure our release he has expended his efforts and his money in the Roman Curia and has made a long and dangerous journey to us in Germany. We know full well his loyalty and constant love for us, and he is now working on the Emperor and the nobles of the empire for our deliverance with affection and efficacy.

Walter was given special powers as Regent; his duties included subduing the rebellions stirred up by John in England and in Richard's Continental empire; he was to stiffen the resistance to Philip, who was threatening Normandy. Both Philip and John wanted, for obvious reasons, to keep Richard in jail as long as possible, ideally for ever.

Richard's trust in Walter was total. To survive in this charnel house, you needed trusted and loyal friends. He was not only Regent but soon to be Archbishop of Canterbury. He was Richard's Thomas à Becket, without the tragic ending.

A report suggests that the *Frankenef*, as we will still call it, set sail for Marseilles. Unknown to the knights on board accompanying the cross, Philip's armies had taken some of the border castles of Normandy and were closing in on Rouen. It would be dangerous for them to travel to the north with their precious cargo.

On 21 March 1193 Richard was tried in the emperor's court. Theoretically the outcome could have been death for the murder of Conrad and for betraying the Holy Land by dealing with Saladin, but in reality this was a show trial, as the terms of the ransom were already settled and Hubert Walter and Eleanor were busily raising taxes to pay it. The trial itself was a triumph for Richard. His eloquence and calm and his account of his achievements in the Holy Land were well received. Taking the cross was still a mystic and noble cause, and Richard had defeated Saladin and had led from the front. He proclaimed, 'I am born of a rank which recognises no superior but God', and many people would have accepted this judgement.

One chronicler, Philip's court poet, wrote:

When Richard replied he spoke in so lionhearted a manner that it was as though he had forgotten where he was and the undignified circumstances in which he had been captured and imagined himself to be seated on the throne of his ancestors at Lincoln and at Caen.

The Emperor, moved by his words and his demeanour, gave him the kiss of peace, although he was not to be released for another eleven months. In the meanwhile Richard occupied himself with matters of state, sending a stream of messengers to England. Most significantly, he ordered his council to proclaim Hubert Walter Archbishop of Canterbury: from Castle Trifels, in Speyer, Richard sent a message to his council in England, which gave it no choice:

The whole world knows to what pains and perils the venerable Hubert, Bishop of Salisbury, exposed himself and his men in the land overseas for the sake of God's name and the relief of the East, and how many services pleasing to God and Christendom and ourselves. And since we have ample experience of the Bishop's discretion, loyalty, and constancy and of the sincere love he bears us, we wish to promote him to the Church of Canterbury. Therefore we command you and firmly ordain that you hasten his appointment with all speed. For we are sure that it will be pleasing and acceptable to God and men. It is most necessary for speeding our release, defending our country and preserving peace, *and, with God's aid, it will be very profitable to you all. Myself as witness, at Speyer, 30 March.*

On 29 May 1193, Hubert Walter was installed as Archbishop of Canterbury. On the 8th of June, Richard smuggled another letter to his mother, apparently unaware that Walter was already Archbishop:

Whatever I have written or may write in the future about this business it is our fixed and unchangeable wish that the Bishop of Salisbury be promoted to the Church of Canterbury. We want this and nothing else. Myself as witness, at Worms, 8 June.

Richard shared with Hubert Walter a deep friendship, a friendship forged in battle in the Holy Land; he trusted him completely. And it was Hubert Walter who negotiated the destruction of Ascalon in return for the delivery of the True Cross after Richard had spent a fortune restoring Ascalon. But the True Cross was worth any amount of gold.

In captivity Richard wrote a song in Occitan which expressed his deep bitterness at his betrayal. The rhyme scheme and the repetition of phrases and words are in the tradition of Poitou. Richard is acknowledged as an accomplished troubadour in that tradition. His grandfather, Duke William of Aquitaine, was the first known troubadour. Richard was familiar with the codes of chivalry and courtly love of his mother's native land.

I

Ja nus hons pris ne dira sa raison
Adroitement, se dolantement non;
Mais par effort puet il faire chançon.
Mout ai amis, mais povre sont li don;
Honte i avront se por ma reançon
—Sui ça deus yvers pris.

131

II

Ce sevent bien mi home et mi baron–
Ynglois, Normant, Poitevin et Gascon–
Que je n'ai nul si povre compaignon
Que je lessaisse por avoir en prison;
Je nou di mie por nule retraçon,
—Mais encor sui [je] pris.

III

Or sai je bien de voir certeinnement
Que morz ne pris n'a ami ne parent,
Quant on me faut por or ne por argent.
Mout m'est de moi, mes plus m'est de ma gent,
Qu'après ma mort avront reprochement
—Se longuement sui pris.

I

No prisoner can speak truthfully
Unless he speaks as one who has suffered injustice;
To console himself he may compose a song.
I have many friends, but they have fowled me.
They will be shamed if I am confined for the ransom
—For another year.

II

They know full well, my barons and my men,
Of Normandy, England, Gascony, Poitou,
That I have never had a vassal
Whom I leave in prison for my own gain;
I say it not as a reproach to them,
—But a prisoner I am!

III

The ancient proverb now I know for sure;
Death and a prison know nor kin nor tie,
Since for mere lack of gold they let me lie.
I grieve greatly for myself; for them still more.

After my death they will be tainted for ever
—If I am a prisoner long.

It is the story of his betrayal in a fickle and shifting world. He was deeply affected by this disloyalty.

Walter travelled from England to Normandy and on to Poitiers. I have been making charts of all his and Richard's movements. They cover one whole wall of my cramped bedroom in Ed's house. As I colour the journeys and revise the information endlessly, my charts look like the contents of my aunt's knitting basket. Walter's well-documented journey south, as far as Limousin, suggests that his aim was to meet the knights escorting the cross. I have established that when Richard took to the galleys, Huntingdon, Roger de Saci, Hugh de Neville, Raoul de Mauléon, Gerard de Furnival, and Master Robert, the clerk, were ordered to stay on the *Frankenef* to deliver the cross.

I have decided to say nothing about the letter to Saladin for the moment. After all, nobody has taken any notice for nearly a hundred years. The description of the contents is sketchy, hand-written in about 1895 by one of the Huntingdon family, I would guess. The truth is I don't want anyone else to see the document. I know that I have no excuse for keeping secret a valuable document from this venerable library. I will announce its discovery when I am ready.

I have hidden the letter in a neglected box. Its label reads: *Domestic Accounts of the Bishop of Winchester 1186–1199*. It's easy to become secretive; while I am down here in the stacks. I am not aware of the outside world or what's going on there. I am like a mole burrowing blindly through old tunnels. The second Huntingdon box contains a copy of a letter, sent by Walter in November 1192, just about the time Huntingdon and Richard and the knights were embarking in Acre, clearly stating that

Master Robert is to use the money they have been entrusted with for the holy cause. *Causus sacris*. And the knights are exhorted: *Crux sancta sit vestra lux – Let the Holy Cross be your light*.

What would Master Robert have done with the equivalent of £100,000? It was probably intended for bribery and to buy horses for the knights; it may also have been to pay off the crew of the so-called *Frankenef* when the knights disembarked for their journey to Rouen, via Arles. I see Master Robert as a sensible fellow, an administrator, a bean counter, a little scared of the knights, and perhaps just a little humble too. Huntingdon appears to have been an exceptionally resolute knight. He was also immune to disease. This was attributed to his blameless life.

North of Arles there would be pockets of trouble with armed soldiers and mercenaries along the road, subjects of various warring noblemen, trying to extort money or goods.

By the summer of 1193 the whole of Europe knew that Richard was to be released. Philip sent a premature message to John, Richard's treacherous brother: *Look to yourself – the devil is loose*. While there was still time, Philip and John were securing as many towns and castles as they could in Normandy and fomenting rebellion further south. It would have been difficult, if not impossible, for the small group of knights bearing the Holy Cross to get to Rouen. There was a very real possibility that Philip would soon take the city.

It would have been difficult, if not impossible, for the group of knights bearing the Holy Cross to reach Rouen. Anyway, I have looked through the cathedral's records online for that time, and there is no mention of a treasure or a relic arriving at the soaring, beautiful cathedral of Rouen, now sanctified by the wonderful and ethereal paintings of Monet. It is difficult to imagine what the world was like when Gothic Cathedrals were young. Rouen was one of the earliest, modelled on St-Denis in Paris, and greatly admired by Richard.

Assuming that Hubert Walter headed that way for a purpose, I would guess that the Cross was left in Limousin, near Limoges. I picture a small group of knights crossing the River Dordogne or the Lot to find the devastation of war and the bewilderingly changed alliances which had happened while they were on Crusade with Richard. I see them deciding to hide the cross and to travel because it would be dangerous to go on beyond Limousin. I try to imagine the turmoil that was in their hearts. They believed absolutely that this was the Cross on which Christ was crucified. Their king had charged them with returning it to Christendom; before jumping into the galley, he reminded the knights – was Master Robert excluded? – of their sacred duty. I search online the records of Hubert Walter both in Salisbury and Canterbury for some further mention or letter, but I can find nothing that provides a clue to where the cross was hidden.

The more I learn about these times, the more I find myself wondering how people managed to live in an age of fear, with the dark clouds of violent death, the plague and lawlessness always ready to rain thunderbolts on them. I doubt if it is fully possible to inhabit their minds. It is hard enough to understand the minds of others in your own time and in the same room. In the absence of any other places to turn to, myth, the Church and relics like the Holy Cross provided necessary comfort. People who do not have – or do not accept – rational explanations have always turned to whatever they could find to serve the purpose. My father was one of these.

At the same time I am becoming increasingly confused. Already my notes have filled ten Ryman's wide-ruled pads.

Still I carry on: if I am right, Richard and Hubert Walter would have found time when Richard had exacted revenge on his enemies to dig up or seize the True Cross wherever it was hidden. Clearly they didn't find it, but it must still exist. In the meanwhile, in my increasingly volatile mind, I see some bedraggled knights burying the Holy Cross in a southern churchyard, attached to a simple Romanesque church, before separating and heading for home.

But I can no longer follow all my own notes or my charts and maps.

14

Crack-up

ED SAYS HE is worried about me. When I ask him why he's worried, he says that I have been behaving erratically. Also, we no longer meet in the pub and I seem to be too preoccupied to watch the rugby internationals.

'I know you have suffered and it must be terrible, but you must not work so hard. And you aren't eating.'

His words are well intentioned, but they irritate me.

'Ed, I am grateful to you. You've been a pal. But if you have had enough of me, and I wouldn't blame you if you had, I'll go.'

'I didn't mean that at all. It's just you have stuck all sorts of charts to the wall. A lot. And you are often up most of the night.'

'Dates, Ed, key dates, key places. But I see that you and Lettie need some space. Some personal space. To grow, to grow boldly.'

'Not at all. You've been wonderful for me.'

'All good things come to an end. You've been great and I will for ever be in your debt, *amigo*.'

'Why are you speaking like this?'

'Like what? I'm telling you the truth.'

'Lettie will be upset if you go.'

'She is one in a million, Ed. Follow your destiny.'

'Please, Rich. You are not well. Have something to eat. Have some cottage pie.'

'Don't mince your words, Ed. I'm fine, as good as gold. Right as rain. Like a pig in shit. Top of the world.'

And I know in one part of my mind that I am cracking up, but only on the rational level. Deep down I am fine. I am speaking important truths to Ed.

'Reality as we know it, Ed, is fundamentally mental, mentally constructed or otherwise immaterial. I copied that from Wikipedia, Ed. My Noor has been raped by five or six towel-heads, Ed; that's not immaterial. Or do you have another view? Do you come from another school of philosophy? Ed, my advice is, fuck this thesis about Adam Smith. Fuck Lettie, metaphorically speaking – I wouldn't want to intrude on your personal life, what goes on tour stays on tour – but she looks like trouble to me, if I am honest. Fuck your thesis. Ed, I'm worried about you, mate. You don't give a toss about Adam fucking Smith and his touchy-feely side – nobody does – but you were hurt by your rejection by the City, deeply hurt, so you are trying to rebuild your shattered self, because only by putting the self together again can you be happy. Solipsism, Ed, is what you need to study, that's the theory that the self is the only reality. Am I right? You have been schtupping Lettie the Lettuce, ace spy by the way, my contacts tell me, a woman seeing forty approaching like a fucking express train on the wrong track. The age that frightens women – prospects of childbirth low et cetera, and you're thinking she's a halfway house to my full recovery from humiliation, which will only be complete when I have a worthy thesis accepted by the owl-aspected examiners – that will show those hedgies and shorters and gamblers – a well-received, even acclaimed, Ph.d., or D.Phil. as we like to call it in old Oxford, Ed my old chumba-wumba. And your rehabilitation will be complete when some foxy publisher's editor with nice little tits, not too large and not too floppy and common, but nicely perky, and wearing just the right clothes from Joseph, sexy but not obvious, asks you to write a small book, for a modest advance, less than some of your lunch bills at Nobu, a book expanding on your thesis, and putting it into the kind of accessible language every dim-shit can understand and use to big himself up with his unspeakable friends – no women will buy it – and you will have a tumultuous sexual experience with this young woman, who falls for you totally, introduces you to the real Italian food in her tasteful flat in London Fields – not far from the Lido, once a green and frog-loud relic of outmoded thinking – *get the little thin-chested, consumptive Cockneys out in the fresh air* – now the Mecca of the not-quite-rich-enough middle classes – this woman with the nice tits invites you to the Groucho Club where you will meet interesting people who never talk about medium-term gilts – in fact they haven't a fucking clue what they are – but about life, its meaning, and what a lot of shits publishers are and mine's a Sauvignon Blanc, no, I said big glass. Bingo – pig in shit. I know these things, Eddie, because down the road in the old wank factory that is Bodley, which made me the unscrupulous opportunist I am – those are your words, Ed, one day to be spoken – yes, down in the bowels of the Bod, another loser is trying to come to terms with the fact – the material fact – that his fiancée – horrible chavvy word, "fiancée", you are thinking, am I right? – has been raped by gyppo beardies and that our baby was terminated by doctors in Toronto after a departmental conference, the bland leading the bland. They could have done a DNA test, but no, that would have involved the alleged father giving some samples, and that would have been messy, in both senses.'

'Stop, Rich, stop.'

So it seems I *am* actually speaking to him.

'Ed, this is the talking cure that you – and I – have been avoiding for so long. While we were watching rugby over a pint down at the old Red-Arsed Ferret, on the ninety-inch plasma screen, we were really thinking we're both fucked. Lettie the Lettuce confirmed it. We are both vulnerable. She said it. The Ace Spy said it. Maybe her contact told her. I would watch out for him, by the way, he's dodgy.'

'When did she say this?'

'Oh, off the cuff. Totally impromptu. Unpremeditated. But she smacked the monkey, didn't she, eh, Jimmy, know wha-ah mean, pal? Richard the Lionheart, three lions on his chest, that's the story. The genocidal ten-foot-high ginger-haired anti-Semitic poofter is my fast track to fame. Just like your bright idea of a thesis which isn't going to happen by the way, we both want to produce something, an actual, actual something in this world to tell them we are here. That we exist. *Somos màs*. But, Ed, you're ahead of me: you're already on Google, admittedly only because you and your pal lost nearly a billion, but I am not. I haven't registered a flicker on the public consciousness, not even a mouse's fart. I must go to bed, Ed.'

Wheh – wheh-wheh-wheh – w-hooop-w-hooop.

When I wake some time – some days later – it takes me time to understand what has happened. I am, I decide, after a long, detached inspection of the pale blue curtains and the tubes attached to my arm, in a hospital. To judge by the strange hyena cries, it's probably a mental hospital. I have read about the powerful drugs they use in these places and I wonder how long I have been sedated. Some hours later, the cries die with the dawn light and a doctor comes in to see me. She tells me I am in the Warneford Hospital, Headington. She is a tall and blonde woman of about my age. Despite the chronically tired, greyish skin that hospital doctors acquire, her eyes have come through unscathed. They are friendly, ceramic blue, like Delftware, like new-born babies' eyes.

'Ah, you are awake, Mr Cathar. I'm Dr Wettinger – Ella – and I am in charge of your case.'

'My case.'

'You, yes. It looks as though you have had what we call a psychotic break. We like a label; it's just a convenient term. A psychotic break is most usually brought on by extreme stress. Now that you are with us, I want to take your history. Particularly I want to ask you about stress. Have you had bereavement or other catastrophic disruptions to your recent life? And have you had this kind of episode before?'

'Yes, to the catastrophe, and no, I have never had this kind of episode before.'

'Can you tell me about it? I will probably need to talk to you again tomorrow, and by then you should be out of bed and walking around the grounds.'

'I feel very strange now. Am I heavily sedated?'

'No, not heavily. Your motor was racing too fast when you were brought in, so we gave you some beta blockers and benzodiazepines. You needed a period of calm and sleep. And boy, did you sleep.'

'How long?'

'Two whole days.'

'Am I going to be all right?'

'In what sense?'

'I mean, I'm not officially bonkers now, am I?'

'No, no. A psychotic break is usually a temporary condition as I said, and often a one-off event. Do you want to tell me now what happened in your life?'

'Can you tell me who brought me in?'

'An ambulance, and your friend Edward Laing brought you in. He was very worried about you. Apparently you were ranting for an hour.'

I am touched. Big, lonely, chubby Ed. I am the lodger from hell. He was looking for friendship. He was looking for empathy.

'Last thing I remember, I was shouting loudly, screaming in fact, at Ed and telling him he was a loser.'

'Don't worry, he didn't take it to heart.'

She smiles. She has a nice smile. A nice smile is not a meaningless cliché. Hers is warm and interested and she has lovely regular teeth. I am grateful for it. For a moment, which I am sure seems like ages to her, I stare at her smile. I desperately want her help and approval.

141

'As we doctors say, are you ready to answer some questions?'

'I'm certainly ready to ask some.'

'It doesn't really work like that.'

'Oh, sorry.'

I feel that I can trust her. It's a relief to hand over to her my self, some of it, anyway. I see that she's not going to subject me to that sub-Freudian nonsense which I had inflicted on Ed.

'One last thing, can I ask you if my friend was really not angry with me?'

'No, not at all. He was just very concerned about you. In fact he came in yesterday and sat by your bed for an hour.'

'Thank you. He is one of the good people.'

'Surprisingly, there are lots of them around, I find. OK, let's carry on.'

I decide right away that I must answer almost all of her questions. My medical notes are open in front of her and she has a notebook.

'Do you take drugs?'

'No, I never have. Probably because of my father. He did.'

'Before this incident, were you more or less stable in your life?'

'I think so. I've been working on a project in the Bodleian Library and in London. I went to Israel to do some research and I met a Canadian journalist, and we fell in love. We were planning to get married. But she was taken captive by an armed group in Cairo. That was very stressful. She's been released, but there are all sorts of things I don't understand and haven't been told. She was raped and that has really upset me. I don't mean on my own account, but on hers. I can't imagine what hell she went through. Actually I can. That's the problem.'

Slow down. Slow down. I am gabbling.

'Where is she now?'

'She's back in Canada.'

'Have you seen her?'

'No, they won't let me. But I have spoken to her aunt.'

Does this sound paranoid? Psychiatrists explain the world in very different terms.

'Who are the people who won't let you speak to her?'

Over the next two hours I tell her the whole story, minus only the incest. She listens calmly and takes notes. I am aware as I talk that this is not so much my psychiatric history, as a kind of narrative that I am stringing together, partly for my own understanding. She may even think I am a fantasist.

'If you ask me,' Ella says, 'I think it is a classic case of extreme stress leading to a psychotic break. To be honest, I think you have coped with it pretty well. It's often uncertainty that triggers these incidents. We are designed to look for answers and conclusions. Ambiguity and uncertainty, as in your case, are destructive.'

'Are you married?'

'I am. To another doctor. He's a GP.'

'Are you happy?'

She smiles. Her smile is now more wintry.

'It's my job to ask the questions. So why did you ask me?'

'Because I have a feeling that after the way I was brought up I don't understand family life. I'm interested in it, in other people's lives. I don't understand quite a lot of mundane things. My father was a sort of hippy, as I said, with grand but delusional ideas, and we never spoke for years. I have a very weak idea of what normal domestic life is. At this moment, talking to you, I want to reconnect, but the problem is I don't know what that entails. With Noor I could see where I was going and now that's been taken away.'

'OK. Let's talk some more tomorrow; you look very tired. You should sleep, but I will come in tomorrow and tell you all about my delightful and happy marriage.'

'Do you believe in the talking cure?'

'Not in the Freudian sense of unlocking deep mysteries, no, but I do in the sense that conversations, like the one we have just had, are helpful. I mean that, at the most basic level, I will find out what may have triggered this episode, and I am able to give it a name and tell you that this condition will pass quite quickly.'

When she's gone I lie in bed very conscious that I am a psychiatric patient. I wonder if this means that I am in some way weakened, with fissures opening. Cracked.

Some time later – I have been dozing – Ed comes in with biscuits. He seems a little nervous, as though he's expecting the nutter to jump out of the bed and start screaming again.

'Ed, I am so sorry about the other night. I flipped.'

'No problem. We all know what you have been through.'

'Ella, the doctor, said you had been great. I can't remember much after I started shouting. You have been so kind to me and I abused your friendship and hospitality.'

'What have they put you on? You don't do remorse as far as I know?'

'I mean it, Ed. I am ashamed.'

'Some of the things you said were true, sadly.'

'What sort of things?'

'Like why I am doing a Ph.d. And also about Lettie.'

'Oh shit, sorry.'

'I am going to give up my Ph.d. It was killing me.'

'Don't do it because of what I said. Although I can't really remember clearly what I said.'

'I'm not. I realised some time ago that this academic stuff was not for me. What you said was true. It is all the higher bollocks at this level. How are you feeling?'

'I have had a psychotic episode, which was apparently caused by stress, and it is temporary. Anyway, they sedated me for two days.'

'I know.'

'Thank you; you sat by my bedside. Ed, I feel disembodied as though I am talking about somebody else. It is a weird feeling. It must be the drugs. By the way, could you bring in my laptop so I can see if Noor or her aunt has been in touch? I feel a bit out of it.'

I can't remember if I told him that Noor is my half-sister. It seems to me to be a holy secret, a kind of sacrament. I also wonder if I was wrong not to tell Ella. I thought it could open up an Aladdin's cave of psychiatric bollocks, to use Ed's word. The higher inanities are everywhere.

'They kept you here for a couple of days just to calm down. Has it helped?'

'I think so. As I said, I feel strange. I feel as though I have a clear picture of my situation, almost a vision. And thanks, Ed, for being such a pal. I can honestly say I don't deserve it.'

I wonder whether the drugs my father took and those I have been given don't have similar effects, a nudge off the true that produces some kind of spiritual understanding. I feel a current of affection flowing between Ed and me. It seems important to tap into this enhanced sensibility, but at the same time I know that all the absurdity and waste of my father's life – his auras and revelations and cosmic love – were triggered by drugs. In his mind he had discovered the many mansions in God's house. Perhaps I am suffering from the same delusion.

Ed possesses a sweet decency. We talk for an hour until a nurse comes in and declares that I need rest.

'I'll be back to you with the laptop. Would you like me to come and get you tomorrow or whenever they let you out?'

'I would be very grateful.'

I am moved. Tears are pressing for release. It's strange that nobody really knows why tears are set off by strong emotions. More and more, showing your emotions – *having a good cry* – is recommended, as it releases the tensions that are building within you. The analogy is with a volcano.

I slept and woke up again, two hours later, knowing that I had a long night ahead, a night troubled by drugs and inchoate fears. I dreamt of Richard imprisoned. I saw him held in Dürnstein. I heard the strains of Blondel's songs, in the original Occitan, rising up to Richard's chambers, which were sumptuous: he may be a prisoner, but he is still a king. Richard went to the Gothic window. Instead of singing along with Blondel, he sang *C'mon, baby, light my fire*. I saw medieval tapestries of hunting scenes, chunky furniture, a long table, a hawk sitting on a perch with an Arab hood over its eyes. On its legs were those leather tethers, *jesses*, I think they are called, with bells attached. I saw that my dream has a theme: the Lionheart imprisoned, Noor kidnapped, and me, held (am I held?) in a mental hospital.

It's a lonely place to be at night. Nurses flit by from time to time, carrying medication. I fear the male nurses; I think they are the muscle. If I call for a taxi to take me home, I don't believe they would be helpful; I think they would reach for the syringe. Someone is howling in a cubicle not far away. Her torment is pitiable.

When Ella comes to see me in the morning I am dressed and waiting in a grimly functional day room.

'Ella, am I being held here?'

'No, you are a voluntary admission.'

'But I didn't have a choice. Nobody asked me.'

'You were in urgent need of treatment. You weren't making much sense. But trust me, we are not going to section you or forbid you from leaving if you wish.'

'But you could stop me leaving.'

'In theory, if I thought you were a danger either to yourself or to the public, I could. But all I want to do today is to make sure that you are all right and to make sure that we support you properly in the unlikely event you need help. I just need to complete my notes. I am recommending that you are discharged tomorrow morning. Your friend Ed is coming to get you. He insisted.'

Ella takes me back over some aspects of my family history. What happened to my mother, for example. I answer her questions truthfully until she comes to the subject of Noor. Again I can't tell her that I was sleeping with my half-sister; however enlightened Ella may be, she would be bound to refer to Freud, who believed everyone has the inclination to incest. Or maybe she would be familiar with Westermarck's theory that young children, brought up in close proximity, related or not, develop a natural taboo against incest. As Noor and I did not meet in childhood, there was no taboo. Or did we recognise, subconsciously, shared characteristics we were naturally attuned to, which is another theory about incest? How could any psychiatrist pass up the fun of exploring the dark secrets of our relationship?

But Ella is nothing if not reasonable. She seems chronically tired, but she is always patient and cheerful. She tells me again that it is highly unlikely I will have another episode, and that if I do I must go immediately for help, preferably here in the Warneford. She accompanies me on my obligatory walk. After just a few days of sedation I feel a bit shaky, and she takes my arm.

'You said you would tell me about your wonderful marriage.'

'Yes, I did. It is not so wonderful,' she says.

'Do you have children?'

'No.'

We have swapped roles. She tells me that her husband has fallen in love with someone else. He believes that falling in love is not just an excuse; it's an irresistible mystical event. Behind a yew hedge, I kiss her.

'This is not very professional,' she says anxiously.

'No, but then I am not a professional.'

I hold her close for a moment. Obviously I haven't quite moved to a higher plane.

'Thank you, Ella, you have saved my life. Can we see each other, non-professionally?'

'No. At least not in Oxford.'

'Can I have another accompanied walk tomorrow?'

'No. You are recovering well, I think.'

'Yes, we non-professionals find the kissing cure works every time.'

Glancing around to make sure there are no gaps in the hedge, she squeezes my hand and slips her card into it.

'Text me. My number is on the card.'

Her skin has surrendered some of that mortuary tone to the blush of sexual intrigue.

'Ella, I honestly can't imagine how any man could have left you.'

'Thank you.'

'It's true. I mean it.'

And I do. Patients often fall in love with their doctors.

When Ed comes for me – it comforts the administrators to know that you have at least one sane friend – his mind is on Lettie.

'I spoke to Lettie last night, about our future or lack of it, but she asked me if my doubts were because she is seven years older than me, and of course I said no, no, no. Then she asked me what the problem was, and I said, which is partly true, that I needed to get back on my feet. And she said so I was just a little bit of light relief, fluff. Of course not, I said, no, not light relief; nobody could call you fluff, it's not like that at all, but it wouldn't be fair of me not to tell you the truth. It seems she didn't want the truth.'

'I kissed my psychiatrist.'

'Where?'

'Only on her mouth.'

'I mean where in the hospital?'

'Oh, we were behind a hedge in the garden.'

'Are you crazy?'

'Did you mean to use that word? The answer is "no longer". I was certified sane, by Ella.'

'After you kissed her?'

'Yes.'

'Jesus, as if your life wasn't complicated enough.'

'I'm fine.'

But then, as we get into Ed's car, I begin to choke.

'Don't take me back, Ed. I am OK, really. It's good to cry.'

'I won't take you back, Richie.'

Ed has a three-year-old Porsche, which the bank allowed him to keep. We roar away, although it's difficult to roar in Headington. It is a stately sort of place.

15

Lords

MY FATHER'S ADMIRATION for Richard seems to have been born out of legend rather than history. What was he proposing to do with the document that he left in the urinal in Paris? His shambolic notes – mine are heading in the same direction – claim that there was incontrovertible evidence that Robin Hood and Richard met. I wonder if my father's pal, Huntingdon, is still alive. Google reveals that he is, and that he often pops into the House of Lords if there is any talk of the European Union, which he detests. I write to him explaining who I am, and to my surprise he answers my letter promptly and invites me to lunch at the House of Lords. He remembers my father with affection.

Ed is certain that I need a suit for the occasion. He comes with me to Ede & Ravenscroft, in the High Street, astonished to hear that I have never had a suit, in the sense that the top half matches the bottom half exactly, and he feels he should guide me. He thinks a blue shirt will go well with the suit. I consider myself in the mirror, and I do have a lordly look. Ed insists on paying the bill. I take him aside, while the lugubrious man who has congratulated me on fitting perfectly into one of his suits, no alteration required, waits, tape measure around his neck: *It doesn't happen as often as you might imagine, sir.* He admires it so much he offers a free college tie to complete the ensemble. He likes my college tie, because it is simple. *Not too many griffins and escutcheons and so on, just a few subtle light blue stripes, sir.*

'Ed, I can't pay you back, as you know. I had no idea a suit could cost so much.'

'Pay me back when Richard the Lionheart comes in for you. Remember what you said, the genocidal, red-haired poofter was your meal ticket? Consider this an investment by me. By the way, the cuffs on the shirt are great, aren't they?'

I haven't noticed that they have some fancy detail on the inside which can be displayed by turning them back, to achieve the serious but informal look, that little touch of the dramatic. The atmosphere in the shop is equivocal: on the one hand the young gentleman must be accommodated, on the other, there is a suspicion that I may not be the sort of young gentleman they would like to serve, if they had a choice. The gentlemen they want, with their casually patronising self-assurance, have not been seen in numbers since my father's day, but the myth of the English gentleman lives on. I feel they are looking right through my £800 suit and seeing the wee ghillie, his hands raw and his clothes smelling strongly of ash-smoked salmon. The scent clung to me for months.

The suit is placed within its own tent and handed to me carefully like a baby passed to the vicar at a christening. There is, it is true, something ritualistic about this suit buying and fitting.

'He's going to the House of Lords in this,' says Ed, perhaps hoping to impress.

'Good luck, sir.'

He says it as though he doubts that I will be well received.

Outside the peers' entrance is the immense, rampant statue of Richard I. It is truly enormous, not just in the remembered impression of a boy. I imagine that every time Lord Huntingdon enters on important business, he basks in the knowledge that his unhistorical ancestor, Robin Hood, was a close chum of the Lionheart.

The entrance to the House of Lords is heavily protected, so that I am photographed and given a tag and passed through a metal detector, before being asked to sit and wait for his lordship, who is expecting me. Peers pass by, many of them former Members of Parliament, enclosed in an ineffable mist of self-regard. I think that, if you wanted to understand politics, you would need only to see the sort of people who are passing through here, eager to be important, eager to be recognised, eager to attach themselves to power and influence. The doors and screens and wallpaper and carpets are adorned with Augustus Pugin's endless patterns of medieval Gothic motifs.

An usher calls me: Lord Huntingdon is here. He seems surprised to see me, as though he were expecting somebody more serious-looking, or generally older. Perhaps my suit is too new. His certainly isn't: it is shiny with age, although this may be a desirable patina. The double-breasted jacket hangs very low; the vent at the back is under pressure from his comfortable backside, and gapes.

'Ah Richard,' he says, 'how do you do and what jolly good fun to meet you. I am so glad you wrote.'

We shake hands. One of his eyes is a little glassy. It occurs to me that it might actually be glass. His face looks as though it has been lightly scorched on one side.

'I was very fond of your father, you know. Shall we go through to the dining room? I can't stand it: they have tried to become trendy and with-it, but they have mercifully left a few things on the menu that the old buffers can eat. Now it's full of salad with goat's cheese and raw tuna, and stuff like that. But I suppose we must move with the times.'

As we are shown to our table there is much *Yes, milord* and *This way, milord* and *Is the table suitable, milord?*

We order; he opts for the salmon fishcakes and I, who have taken an oath never to eat salmon again, order pickled razor clam risotto. Huntingdon looks concerned.

'Are you sure?'

'Yes, I think I will give the razor clams a go.'

'They may give you a go.'

We laugh at his witticism.

'I had a minor stroke last year, which accounts for my harlequin appearance. It's not much fun getting old. I'm seventy-six. Lovely man, your father. Delightful. We were great muckers. Great muckers. You look like him, as a matter of fact. Now, what can I do to help? You said you are writing a thesis at Oxford.'

'Well, thesis may be overstating it, but I am writing a paper on Crusader art. As of course you know, your ancestor was at Acre and other places during the Third Crusade. I just wondered if you had any historical records or recollections of your ancestor from that time.'

'Look, the truth is we are not directly related to that Earl of Huntingdon in any way. The title was revived three times, but we do have some archives that go back a long way. It was mostly collected by my grandfather. Your father borrowed a document from the archive. When I gave it to him to show to experts, he managed to lose it. It wasn't really his fault; I think we had had too much of the old magic mushroom the night before. I can't say I blame him entirely. But there's lots more that hasn't been cata-logued. My grandfather was very keen to establish that we were related to the first Earl, who was the grandson or son of the King of Scots, and he also bought all sorts of stuff about Robin Hood – there's a whole network of Robin Hood loonies. He was sure he could discover a connection. A year ago we sent a few boxes to Oxford, and we have given some other things to a local museum. But there's a lot more, and you could take a look at that. I would be grateful, as a matter of fact. It's perfectly possible that my namesake helped himself to Crusader art, although the only things I believe we have from that time are the remains of some banners from Acre . . . oh, and some ghastly icons. I can't stand icons. Do you like them? The women all look as though they have moustaches and the paintings are frightfully gloomy. Fat babies and depressed women, all in sepia, probably from the incense wafting about. Dreadful.'

The food arrives with a carafe of red wine.

'House plonk,' my host says, 'but after the first few glasses it is just about drinkable. Right, where was I? Oh yes, the so-called archive. Come up to our place next weekend. Do you shoot?'

'Yes, I do.'

I am relieved to be able to tell the truth; I recognise a test question from a long way off.

'Jolly good. Got a gun?'

'Not here. Mine's in Scotland.'

Technically this gun is not mine. It was given to me on permanent loan by my aunt. It may even be the gun that my aunt's husband, Sandy, used to blow his brains out. I always felt it was too delicate a question to ask her. I learned to shoot on the job, with clays and then with the grouse on the beaters' days and on informal shoots.

'Not a problem,' Huntingdon says. 'We have quite a lot. Too many. I'll get my secretary to send you directions. And I will ask her to give you directions to the museum in Ashby too, just in case you want to drop in. My father's coronation robes are on display there, by the way. My wife donated them. She didn't ask me, as it happens. Come up for the weekend. Friday evening. How are the razor clams? My fishcakes are jolly good.'

I find myself succumbing to his charm. He has a kind of holy innocence, no doubt the product of years of privilege, but innocence all the same. A lifetime of secretaries and farm agents and nannies and – I see on Wikipedia – three wives has made him a sort of human cork, bobbing, unsinkable, on life's waves. He tells me he is a 'working hereditary', meaning that he was kept on when the House of Lords was reformed. He is one of ninety hereditary peers who were elected because of their expertise or diligence. His expertise is in the working of the European Union: he loathes it. He sees a Britain happily free of the rest of Europe, giving full rein to its own glorious history, unique talents and generally special qualities. I wonder if this history encompasses Richard the Lionheart, who cared so little for England. In Huntingdon's opinion, the European Union is an enervating force trying to stamp out individuality in favour of uniformity.

We start on another carafe of wine. It does get better after a few glasses. I am already drunk and amusing myself by thinking of implausible outrages committed by the Europeans, from banning mince pies, because they contain no minced meat, to refusing curved bananas, and on to demand that Latin names be displayed for the fish sold in fish and chip shops. All these are Euromyths, dreamed up by the tabloids.

Getting drunk with an elderly peer is working wonders for my state of mind.

I can see the time on one of the little monitors dotted around to keep the lords in touch with what is going on in the chamber. It's four o'clock. When we leave the restaurant, a little unsteadily, Huntingdon tells me he must be in the chamber soon. He has to alert the world to some dastardly plan by the French to increase subsidies to their peasant farmers at our expense.

'Goodbye, dear boy. It was wonderful to meet you. And we look forward to seeing you at the weekend.'

He shakes my hand warmly, and I watch him marching purposefully into battle, just like the first Earl of Huntingdon at Acre.

On the way out, I pass beneath the baleful presence of the triumphant Richard on his horse, his massive sword raised in triumph. My father thought it was a magnificent statue and brought me here to look at it when I was thirteen and about to be incarcerated at Pangbourne College, to have my small, sensitive testicles coated with shoe polish.

I must find my way to Oxford in a haze of bonhomie, which I know will wear off soon and become a headache. On the train I realise we have not spoken much about my father, although he has made approving noises, a bit like a seal barking. And for the first time in weeks, I haven't thought of Noor for hours on end. Now, rapidly becoming remorseful, I struggle to bring my fuddled brain to bear on Noor, as though she needs my full attention and love. She hasn't written to me. Surely she has access to email? I have emailed her, but the emails have failed. I try to imagine why she is not able to contact me. And I try rather forlornly to remember and re-create the happiness of our weeks together. I remember her body recoiling in the shadow of Kerak; she didn't say it, but I think she was afraid of going on assignment.

Ed is excited by my invitation to a shoot. In the City, shooting was big. It betokened a devil-may-care attitude to money – *after all, you can't take it with you* – and a manly attachment to what is elemental and deep-seated, and also a lack of squeamishness. This squeamishness, best demonstrated by the anti-hunting brigade, is the touchy-feely way of looking at the world, an attitude which is dragging the country down. How often I heard this kind of thing up on the moors as the grouse whistled towards the butts, by their deaths lending backbone to a decadent people who couldn't punch the skin off a jar of custard or stamp on a cockroach.

For some reason I don't fully understand, Ed wants me to look the part; he offers to lend me his Porsche. I protest unconvincingly. On my way north – all shooting is north – I head for Ashby de la Zouch, where a destroyed castle of the Hastings family, Lord Huntingdon's family, lies. Here the third Earl of Huntingdon was jailer to Mary Queen of Scots.

I park the Porsche outside St Helen's Church in Ashby and head for the Hastings Chapel. Here some scraps of Crusader flags are on display, but it is not clear which Crusade they belong to. Still, I find it moving that these flags were carried, a thousand years ago, to the Holy Land and brought back home; they may have survived Hattin or been flown at Acre. The particular Earl of Huntingdon who built this church was beheaded by Richard III. I recall Mark Rylance: *I will shortly send thy soul to heaven.*

The castle, ruined by Cromwell's men, is a Huntingdon possession acquired much later; it had nothing to do with our Henry, Earl of Huntingdon. The museum is in a modest house. I speak to the curator; yes, she has some documents and parchments from the time of the Third Crusade. She takes me to a locked cupboard and brings them out. They are written in a florid, antique prose, which means that they are probably Victorian. A third letter, in Anglo-Norman French, appears to be from Henry of Huntingdon to his wife. He says that he has landed that day at Marseilles – '*Marselha*' in the *langue d'oc*. It is dated 15 January 1193: Huntingdon assures his wife that he will now be home before the Feast of St John, Midsummer. He adds '*je n'en mantirai*' – 'trust me' – a very contemporary promise.

The librarian makes scans of the letter, so that I can study it with my dictionary to hand. I offer a donation of £10, which she says is very generous. My bona fide is assured by the fact that I am staying with the family over the weekend.

Late in the afternoon I pause at the gates of Huntingdon's house. Some way down the drive I can see the house. It's pretty grand, a classical building, in the style of Palladio, as I have discovered on Wikipedia. It looks a bit like a bank, only more domestic. The drive is long and straight, bordered by oaks. Just before the house I cross a clear stream by a beautiful stone bridge. My professional opinion is that the stream almost certainly holds brown trout. Lord Huntingdon appears at the top level and sets off down the lichen-mottled steps. He walks stiffly, placing his feet carefully like a man in a dinghy. He is wearing a tweed jacket over a mustard-yellow, V-necked jumper.

'Welcome. Did you have a good journey? I'll take your luggage. Park your car round the side, under the magnolia. Tea is waiting. And I have put you in the best draws for tomorrow.'

I have no idea what a magnolia looks like, but there, beside a wing of the house, is a huge, glossy tree of broad leaves like dark green spatulas, which must be the magnolia. Huntingdon has made it up to the first level with my bag, and I pick it up and follow him up one more level of steps and into the house. The most recent Countess comes forward rather grudgingly.

'This is my young friend Richard Cathar, darling. He is the son of my friend from Oxford, Alaric. I told you about him. And Richard, this is my wife Venetia.'

She must be thirty years younger than the earl. She is blonde and wiry with an unnatural tan. She is wearing a cashmere poncho and tight white jeans and short brown boots. It is the Argentine polo look, favoured by the young royals.

'Sorry,' she says, 'I haven't had time to change; just been for a ride. Tea is ready. And I believe that David is going to show you the archive. Did you say you had looked at the stuff we sent to Oxford?'

'Yes, I have had a quick look through it.'

'His father was a great chum of mine. Great chum.'

'Yes, so you have said.'

She goes ahead to summon tea.

'Venetia hates the shooting,' says Huntingdon. 'We've cut the season to only eight full days, plus a friends and family day. That's tomorrow's entertainment. Would you like a whisky? I tend to need one about this time of day.'

'Not for me, thank you, sir.'

'Call me David.'

He pours himself a double from a decanter.

Through the huge windows, I see that it is becoming darker, one of those late-winter days when the weak sun is doused by the mist and the exhalations of the damp countryside.

'No, Venetia hates the shooting. She prefers polo and horses. She goes off to Argentina. We have an estancia there, not huge, where she breeds polo ponies.'

Of course, I picture her cavorting with those dashing Argentine polo players. Highly sexed, horse-disfigured hidalgos. It's widely known that sitting on horses enhances the libido.

I wonder if my mind has completely recovered from its episode; it seems a little erratic in its opinions.

Venetia appears again and immediately behind her, pushing a trolley, comes the woman from the village, in a floral housecoat. Thanks to my days as a ghillie, I know that these women are selected from among the locals for their degree of devotion and desperation. They also have a belief in the ancient wisdom that *everyone knows their place*.

'This is Mrs Wilbraham. This is Mr Cathar, the son of a friend of his lordship.'

'Pleased to meet you, sir,' she squeaks.

Perhaps she is disappointed that I don't have a title. She retreats, sidling backwards for a few steps, like someone receiving an MBE at Buckingham Palace, before turning slowly to see if she is possibly needed on some noble whim.

'What sort of tea would you like?'

'Oh, just builders'. I have simple tastes.'

'What a pity,' says the Countess.

'What was that, dear?'

'Young Richard likes builders' tea.'

'Jolly good. Now we have some absolutely terrific lemon sponge bought at the church sale. The only problem, being the laird, as you would say up in Scotland, is that you have to buy a lot of sponge cake. And huge onions. So eat up. Or if you prefer, there are sandwiches. By the way, jolly smart car you have.'

'Sadly, it's not mine. It's way above my pay grade. Actually I don't have a pay grade at all.'

'Too bad. But you look like a bright fellow to me, like your father.'

'Unfulfilled promise, I think is the phrase. I would love some lemon sponge, it looks delicious.'

'The proof of the pudding is in the eating,' Huntingdon warns.

It is strange how easily I fall into this familiar and superficial conversation, which often involves dogs and horses, the management of shoots and the bloody useless government. It is a defensive way to converse, one that establishes shared values, while avoiding any form of intellectual pretension.

After tea – excellent sponge cake – Huntingdon leads me to the archive, which is housed underneath the first floor in a semi-basement that was once, he tells me, a storeroom for food and supplies because it is always cool and dry. He shows me five huge dark wooden cabinets, each with four drawers.

'This is what we call the archive. It's never been properly catalogued, but I have looked through most of it at one time or another. You're interested in the Crusader period, aren't you? My alleged ancestor was on the Third Crusade, you said. There are some papers or parchments, which are probably Victorian, collected by my grandfather. To be honest, I think it was one of these your father lost, nothing too valuable. And here's a picture of your father and me. I got it out for you. Look at the size of those spliffs. You look quite like your father.'

In the photograph are two slender young men, with long hair and patterned trousers, standing in a punt, smoking weed. They are smiling, sharing a beautiful cosmic joke. My father never lost that look of satisfaction with his induction into the inner workings of the universe.

'Different times, different zeitgeist. But good times. Good times. I would start on cabinet two if I were you. Cabinet one is mainly estate bills from the nineteenth century. Let me know what you find, and I will arrange with the secretary to print it out for you.

You should perhaps stay until Sunday night to do justice to the material? Can you do that? Good show. Dinner will be at seven forty-five. No need to dress.'

I have brought my new suit, just in case.

In the picture my father, I have to accept, does look like me. I recognise the eyes, quite widely spaced, and the thin nose. His smile, although a little skewed, is also like mine. When this picture was taken, he and Huntingdon were younger than I am now. I see that they are both wearing Afghan – possibly Pakistani – embroidered waistcoats. Wisdom and deeper understanding were believed to spring from the East. The West, according to Herbert Marcuse, was clapped out, on its last legs; the one-dimensional society could not last. Liberation from the affluent society, from false needs, would free the West, particularly in the matter of repression. Marcuse was big on repression; he spotted it lurking everywhere, but particularly in sexual politics.

I have two dictionaries with me, Anglo-Norman French and Latin, and I start eagerly – feverishly – on the archives. My plan is to have a quick look through and to put aside anything that may be of interest. I know that Henry, Earl of Huntingdon was already in Acre when Richard arrived. I also know that, although he set sail from Acre in Richard's ghost ship, the *Frankenef*, he did not go with him when the King and a few knights turned back and set off from Corfu up the Adriatic in two galleys. We also know that the *Frankenef* was later seen in Brindisi, but it is unlikely that Henry of Huntingdon and his companions would have struck out for home from there. Marseilles is the obvious jumping-off point, and the letter in the museum seems to confirm that Huntingdon was in Marseilles in January, which could mean that he was planning to make his way via Normandy to deliver the Holy Cross to Rouen before returning home, as he promised his wife. *Je n'en mantirai.*

But I need confirmation. Also, I have no idea how big the cross was. Presumably it was the bigger portion of Helena's cross, which was carried into battle twenty times. The Crusaders triumphed in every one of these battles until the catastrophic defeat at Hattin. In Ridley Scott's movie, *Kingdom of Heaven*, the cross is a huge, silver-encrusted and bejewelled object that glints in the sunlight. This film reliquary seems to be a grand version of the one in Barletto, Italy.

After two hours I have retrieved three documents that could be interesting. One mentions a Templar *commanderie* on an island beyond the port of Marseilles. It may be that Richard of Hastings, who was Master of the Templars in England between 1160 and 1185 and a relative of Henry Huntingdon, helped them on their way.

It's time for dinner. I have put aside the three documents, two on parchment, and one that is clearly a later copy on paper. I go to my bedroom, which overlooks the darkened park, studded with huge trees, and dress hurriedly. I am breathing too fast. I adopt Ed's remedy and put the plastic bag which contained my new shirt over my head, and breathe in slowly until my hyperventilating stops.

We take a sherry before dinner in a bigger drawing room, hung with plenty of family furniture and ancestral portraits. The ancestors in grand houses always look smug, as though they have delightful private memories. Their skin is pinkish and their eyes are small. This look may just be the rictus of sitting for a portrait.

'Did you find anything interesting?' Venetia asks.

'Yes, some very interesting letters, or at least copies of letters. They are not in themselves amazing, but the dates and places mentioned may help me build up a picture of what happened when Richard the Lionheart sailed for home.'

'Did he have important Crusader treasures with him?'

'That's what I am trying to find out.'

'We have had this stuff under our noses for hundreds of years, but we've rather taken it for granted. As one does,' says Huntingdon.

We go in for dinner. Candles are burning on a long table. A

young woman waits on us. She is studying catering and hospitality at a local college; she comes in to help when the family has visitors. She has that soft covering that is increasingly the norm; her face is creaseless. The first course is a plate of smoked salmon, which I try to hide under a lettuce leaf.

I ask Venetia about her polo ponies.

'Are polo ponies really ponies?'

'No, they are not ponies, as in Shetlands or anything like that, but they are usually quite compact, so they were called ponies. In Argentina they are often the gauchos' workhorses, and the best ones are used for polo.'

'Venetia has about thirty at any one time, don't you, darling?'

For a moment I think he's talking about gauchos.

'Yes, I do. I sell them to English players if I can.'

'Loses money of course. When we were married the idea was that it should wash its face. Hasn't happened so far.'

'Do you have a significant other?' Venetia asks.

'I do. She's a Canadian journalist.'

'Where is she now?'

'She's in Toronto.'

'Do you visit her there?'

'No, not at the moment. I met her in Jerusalem, but four weeks later she was taken hostage in Cairo. That was a couple of months ago and she's still recovering.'

'How awful,' says Huntingdon. 'How absolutely beastly. Was she harmed?'

'She wasn't treated well.'

'Poor you,' says Venetia. 'And poor, poor girl. What's her name?'

'Noor. She's half Palestinian.'

'I'm desperately sorry.'

She puts her hand on my forearm for a moment.

Huntingdon pours us all another glass of his favourite Sangiovese. He knows the grower, a wonderful fellow called Aldo:

'Down-to-earth chap, who knows how to live. *Vivre pour vivre*, as the French say.'

I ask how he squares this *vivre pour vivre* business with his dislike of the European Union.

'The problem with the EU is that they want to impose a sort of straitjacket on all of us. The French, the Italians, even the wretched Greeks. The Greeks would be far happier pottering about in their little boats trying to catch the odd octopus for supper or renting their spare room to tourists, than trying to keep up with Stuttgart and Frankfurt. They'll never do it, so what's the point? Different temperaments. Different culture. One size does not fit all.'

'Boring,' says Venetia in a loud singsong.

Huntingdon doesn't take offence. Actually I think he makes some sense: in my experience in Jerusalem, for instance, Arabs and Jews, despite hundreds of years living side by side, seem to live only to proclaim their differences. The Scots see their prime virtue as not being English and the Canadians take comfort from not being Americans.

'Sorry,' Venetia says, 'I am afraid my husband is something of an obsessive.'

'We are having a beef stew now. Or roasted vegetables,' says Huntingdon.

'Two of our many children are vegetarians, so we are always prepared for the young,' Venetia explains, as if to apologise for the vegetable dish.

'Stew for me,' I say, not wanting to look like a self-obsessed food faddist.

'That's the ticket. Your father was great fun, you know. Great fun. Rather wild. The girls liked him. He was what you young call a "babe magnet". There weren't many girls in Oxford in those days; there were only enough to go round if they went round fast enough. Your father was very good-looking and, as far as I can remember, he was never without some young girl. He regularly climbed over the walls of the women's colleges late at night.'

'I never really knew what happened when he was sent down.'

'It was really a grave injustice. Your father didn't supply drugs to Sam Gordon-Mowbray. There was no commercial transaction. They both smoked a bit of weed, and dropped acid occasionally, but because Sam was the son of the Foreign Secretary, they had to find a scapegoat. I am afraid your father took the rap because he had spent the evening with Sam before he died.'

'Was he as good-looking as Richie?' Venetia asks.

'Very nearly.'

The suggestion that I am good-looking always makes me anxious. It's unearned.

I quickly ask Huntingdon, 'Do you think the incident ruined my father's life?'

'Yes, I do, to some extent. I think that is true. He was bitterly disappointed to be sent down. Humiliated. And – I have often thought about this – possibly it drove him to his – forgive me for saying this – sillier ideas. But I still kept up with him. All our meetings were joyous. The difference was that when I got married for the first time I settled down. When he got married a few years later, to your mother, he kept right on with the alternative life. It had become a mission. I think possibly that it was, as you suggested, a reaction to Oxford. He often said there was more to life than Oxford. He felt that the people in charge were repressing us, and of course he had clearly suffered a miscarriage of justice. Being in court was humiliating for him.'

He pauses. He seems to be considering carefully. A small speck of spume has gathered in the corner of his mouth. Venetia reaches across to wipe his mouth with a napkin.

'It was a great shame. I loved your father. But it was a life lost. Absolutely.'

After a few glasses of port in front of the fire, which is still crackling quietly and persistently, Huntingdon is dozing, his mouth open. Venetia asks me to sit next to her on the sofa and she whispers in my ear: Huntingdon is impotent and she wants to have sex with me when he's gone to bed. She breathes a warm, alcoholic dew on me. I am not sober either.

'I'm engaged.'

'I'm married. Don't be a wuss. I'll come up to your room when he's gone to his bedroom.'

Almost as if he has heard his cue, Huntingdon wakes up.

'Sorry, I dropped off. I'm off up the wooden stairs to Bedfordshire.'

'I'm off too,' says Venetia. 'Goodnight, Richard.'

With a few small groans Huntingdon stands up. On one side, the fire side, his face is brick red.

I feel affection for him and gratitude for his generous assessment of my father, who is becoming more visible and substantial to me, as if I hadn't been able to see him properly.

On Sunday, as I was leaving for Oxford in the Porsche, Venetia came down to see me off, near the magnolia tree. I apologised for my behaviour the other night. I told her from inside the car that she was fantastically attractive, but that my personal life has been so traumatic that I could not have lived with myself if we had gone to bed. I was very uneasy.

'That's all right. I was tipsy and wanted to sleep with you. You can't imagine what it's like here in winter. I was a model, with lots of boyfriends, and then I married David and came up here. At first I loved it, but I missed London. I missed all sorts of things, actually. I go to our place in London once a month, but it's often full of mad Eurosceptics. My escape now is my three months in Argentina.'

'Do you have sex with gauchos?'

'What sort of question is that? Not gauchos, usually with the professional polo players or the estancieros. Richard, it's worse to have once been young and beautiful.'

'You are still beautiful,' I say, but without the conviction required for effective flattery.

'I know enough about men, too much, to know that if they really find you attractive the scruples aren't an issue.'

'I'm so sorry. Please, believe me, it's more complicated than that; I didn't want to offend you. I certainly didn't mean to.'

'I was hurt. But that is life. Off you go, dear Richard.'

The Porsche's boot is in the front and it holds my bag, three precious folders of copied documents and a brace of pheasant. Huntingdon and his friends were impressed by my shooting, particularly by a couple of left-and-rights. After shooting speeding grouse, pheasants appear to be on a suicide mission.

Before I set off, Huntingdon told me again that the Robin Hood document, which my father lost, was probably a forgery, commissioned by his grandfather, who wanted to believe that he was descended from Robin Hood. I saw that Huntingdon was trying to boost his friend in my esteem. I was touched.

Still, Sherwood Forest is not far from the family estate, and Richard the Lionheart did ride out there one day in 1194.

16

Noor

My darling Richie,

I am recovering slowly. I have had five operations, but they are now almost over. As I lay in hospital I remembered our time in Jerusalem together. Through all the pain, I clung to that; it was a lifeline because I was very low.

I have never been so happy as I was in Jerusalem. I felt blessed to have met you, and I still do. The shock of the discovery that we have the same father threw me into deep despair; I had so wanted to be married to you. I loved you so much that I even had to ask you to marry me. Were you surprised, and do you regret saying yes? It must have been obvious to you that I was totally in love with you. Your room in the American Colony became in my mind our small heaven. We seemed to be perfect together.

Sometimes, very briefly, I wish you had never smiled at me in the Cellar Bar, because of the pain it has caused both of us. Whatever our future holds, I will never, never regret what happened. I heard from Haneen that you had a short stay in hospital after a break-down. I pray (in a secular way, I know you believe in rationality) that you are better. I wasn't going to write to you so soon, but I was just so worried. Are you alright now? When I heard the news, I knew that I had to write to you, even though I have been advised – I have had counselling and some psychiatric treatment too – that it is too early and might impact my recovery. But I couldn't wait.

The thought that you had suffered because of me and my work was hard for me to bear. I am so, so sorry. I wanted to call you, but I decided that I would not have been able to speak to you without cracking up, and also because any calls I make would be monitored, I am sure. When they captured me, I was able to make that call before they took my phone, and it broke my heart when I heard your voice for a moment. Even now, as I write these words, I am crying again.

I must tell you the whole story because I didn't tell you everything. The truth is that I worked for the Canadian Government, for the Security Intelligence Service, which has contacts with Mossad. My job as a journalist was to interview people in the Middle East, because of my Arabic, but I was also filing intelligence assessments to my contacts in Ottawa. I had a mixture of motives; the main one was to try to help human rights activists in various countries, by publicising them. Some of these activities were through committees that the SIS subsidised. The other motive was more personal, to try to help bring the plight of the Christian Arabs to the world. They are being treated very badly.

In Egypt, just before I was captured, I interviewed the new Coptic Pope. Do you know that the Coptic Pope is chosen by a blindfolded boy drawing a name from a bowl? Isn't that wonderful? Bishop Tawadros II is the one hundred and eighteenth Coptic Pope of Egypt. The Copts are very worried, my people in Jerusalem and Lebanon are worried, and as it goes on, possibly to destruction. I so wanted to talk to you about my assignment, but I couldn't. In Cairo I was captured by a small group who were tipped off by some pro-Mubarak elements in the police that I had visited the Pope in St Martin's Cathedral. (Which is magnificent.) They didn't like that, but also they thought they could sell me on to some extreme Islamist group. But mostly they just hated me for being a woman, for not being married, for living in Canada, for not covering myself at all times and, of course, for being a Christian. I was abused

– raped – and beaten for three days. Two of my front teeth were shattered. I thought I was going to die and I tried to remain strong by thinking of you constantly. I have been having orthodontic work, and also some internal reconstruction surgery. My teeth will not be right for another two months. What upset me most was that I had to have a termination, which Auntie Haneen told you. I was sure I was pregnant when I left for Egypt, and very happy about it. She has come twice to Toronto to see me.

You remember we were at Kerak and I had a panic attack? I couldn't tell you at the time, but what I saw in Homs was the bodies of a whole family just after they were executed. It all came back to me in Kerak. Three small children shot in the head lying on the floor of the house next to the bodies of their mother and father. At night I still see the flies feeding on their wounds. It has haunted me ever since.

I have lived a life of so many deceptions over the last few years, that I no longer know right from wrong except at this level: nobody at any time or under any circumstances should kill other, defence-less, human beings. Our government has good intentions but I had already decided I couldn't be involved any longer; Egypt was going to be my last assignment. I now believe that the democratic countries should simply help where they can – education, health and so on – and should by their own example offer a better life, but that they should not try to influence other countries by covert operations or force anything on puppet governments. The prejudices, the beliefs, the thousands of years of custom can't be changed by the secret service. Anyway, I am now a retired agent – I have been awarded a medal to prove it.

None of what I have written to you is authorised. I am still being debriefed, and I am supposed to stick closely to the rules of the service for life, but, Richie, how could I let this deception and uncertainty drag on? I have been given the best treatment available, first in Ottawa, and now in Toronto, but my nights have been terrible, thinking about you and our situation, and it was all much worse when I heard from Auntie Haneen that you had been in hospital. Are you better now, my dearest, dearest lover and brother?

It sounds crazy, doesn't it? How did such a thing happen? But of course there is a connection: all roads lead to our father, through Jerusalem and Haneen. In her heart I think Haneen wanted to bring us together, although not in the way it happened. She played a big part in my release, too, and sold property in Jerusalem that had been in the family's possession for eight hundred years to pay for the ransom. Haneen has been wonderful. She also said to me that your (our) father had great difficulty bonding with you because he was so guilty about being the cause of your mother's death. He thought he was cursed. He told Haneen all this when he came to Jerusalem. Even though she was engaged, Haneen was still in love with him and they became lovers again. I am sure Haneen never told him that they had a daughter. And now, to pile deception on deception, I can't tell my uncle and his wife, my adoptive parents, anything at all. They see what happened to me as confirmation that they were right to get out of the Middle East thirty years ago. And also they think – they don't say it, fortunately – that I should never have got involved in, as they understand it, human rights organisations. Deep down, despite the Canadian citizenship, they still have some old-fashioned ideas.

How is your Crusader art dissertation going? As we say in the secret services, it's just cover for something else, isn't it? And that something is Richard the Lionheart. I think you should write a personal memoir of your (our) father and Richard. It's definitely a threesome. With your talent for expression – by the why you never told me you were awarded the top first class degree at Oxford – you could also write a wonderful novel. Just leave out your lover/sister. Nobody would believe that anyway.

Richie, please write me. I will accept whatever you decide (old-fashioned values). I have no ground to stand on at all, particularly as I didn't level with you about Egypt or Haneen. Another thing: I have read that most men can never come to terms with rape. But that's too dark a thought – I don't want to go there, it makes me feel utterly abandoned. What I really want from you is to hear that you still love me, even if it is as a younger sister.

Yours, for ever,

Noor xxx

PS. I have set up a post box where you can write me privately. I can't use email or the phone safely. It is what we in the trade call a dead drop. This is from that post box, smuggled out.

Fed Ex to Poste Restante, Box 3114, Moose Creek (yes, really) Callington, Canada. Postal Code L1C 3A6.

17

Richie

My dearest Noor,

I can't really tell you adequately just how happy I am to get your letter. I am overwhelmed by joy.

It is true that I spent a few days – four – in the Warneford Hospital in Oxford. As my psych said to me, my motor was running too fast and I needed to slow down. I don't think this is strictly a medical diagnosis. Its technical term is a psychotic break. It was relatively minor, though scary, and I am over it. The worst thing was abusing my friend Ed, who has been such a good friend to me. But he has forgiven me. People in general treat me leniently. I wonder why.

I think you are very perceptive when you say that all roads lead to our father. (By the way, I am delighted to share him with you.) There is a sort of phantom controlling influence at work somewhere. And your suggestion that Haneen wanted us to meet, if only to compare us, may be true. She asked Father Prosper – you met him once, the sweet old Dominican in the huge black shoes, you said they were like small boats. Anyway Haneen asked him to introduce me to her. Nothing in Jerusalem ever passes Haneen by. I think now that she probably knew some time earlier that we had met in the Cellar Bar. She also feared for you going to Cairo. It may be that someone from there tipped off people in Egypt.

Noor, I am very, very happy to have you as my sister. And as I said to Haneen in London, if I had a mother, I would have wanted one just like her.

The question you raise about your treatment in Cairo and – by implication, what you fear my reaction to it might be – is something you should put out of your mind. The only thing on my mind is that you should come out of this terrible experience and be happy. You didn't deserve what happened to you and you have not in any way been demeaned in my eyes. What you are thinking, I am sure, is that I may find it difficult, as if rape had somehow defiled you. I am sorry to speak so plainly, but I really want you to understand that I love you, and in some ways even more intensely now that I know you are my sister, and I want you to know that our weeks in Jerusalem were, for me too, the most wonderful of my life. As I lay next to you in the American Colony and watched two drops trickle down between . . . well, you know what I am referring to . . . and outside our window there was that magical music adrift on the spiced night air, and the two of us in our room, free and enchanted, in some way floating above the world, buoyed up by the night music and the scent of jasmine, avid explorers of each other, I realised for the first time that when you are truly in love you lose yourself in the other person; you want both to possess that person and to share your essences. The cruel, but astonishing – almost unbelievable – fact is that we do share our essences, our DNA. I apologise if I sound both sentimental and banal, but your letter has released such a torrent of emotion in me that I feel I have to tell you, in my turn, everything.

My work on Crusader art has been made easier, because there is essentially just one person who knows all about it, and I have plundered his work ruthlessly and added some bits and pieces from the Rockefeller Museum and little-known stuff that Father Prosper put me onto, in his big shoes. But in the meanwhile I have discovered a letter totally by chance, which suggests that Saladin gave Richard the True Cross, also known as the Holy

Cross, as part of the deal for Richard to go home to save his lands. I think I am quite close to discovering where the True Cross ended up, which will be very big news if I can find out. I have become obsessive and fraught, partly because I was so strung out worrying about you that I couldn't bear to go to bed where the demons would attack me. Why is it that at four o'clock in the morning everyone is a pessimist? I am sure you wouldn't, but please don't breathe a word of this to anyone. One day, one year, I think I will be able to stand this up. You probably wonder why I should care about the True Cross at all, given that it is almost certainly nothing to do with the piece of wood Christ was crucified on. But the important fact is that to Richard the Lionheart, and to many Christians, it was accepted as just that, miraculously discovered by Helena, the mother of Constantine the Great, in AD 328 in a well under Golgotha. When the cross was lost in 1187, the Cistercian monk, Henri of Albano, described it as a second crucifixion of Christ. Reality doesn't come into it: belief is everything. The more deeply I get into this story, the more I see that symbols of something, anything, that suggested hope, were of profound importance in life as it was lived. It seems to me this is still true for many people, maybe for the majority.

Our father – sounds like the beginning of the Lord's Prayer – our father, who art in heaven, was one of these people, always looking for the miraculous. His take on the world – I hope I am not upsetting you by speaking ill of your father – was that mind-expanding drugs would create a new reality and a better world. When you write that you think our role is to offer an example or an option to others, I am with you. When Obama talks about the American Dream, as though it is something real and wonderful, rather than what it is, just a figure of speech, I can't help thinking that this contains within it the assumption that the dreams of other nations, say Palestine or Britain even, are not in the same league. Only America is in the major league of dreams. As far as we can tell,

Afghans have no interest in the American Dream. They have their own aspirations and longings and sense of what is right.

From my point of view, much more can be understood from the literature and culture of a country than from the phrases of politicians.

Forgive me for this bombast – I have fallen back on my own thoughts too much in the last weeks. I may even be becoming a crank.

As for your remark that you will agree to anything I decide, I'm afraid that I can't accept the burden of that. We have – let's be honest – a terrible dilemma to resolve, and the question is, can we make a life together now? I love you in every possible way, but even I can see that it won't be easy. My suggestion is that we wait patiently until you are better, and, when you are ready, we escape somewhere, say Greece, for a month or two and make any decisions then. Whatever we decide, you will always be my sister. Ask Haneen for her advice. I will try to speak to her in London. She's the only one who knows everything. I feel as though we need her onside.

Noor, I am like the blindfolded boy you described, dipping his hand into a bowl. Our lives have taken the strangest possible turn, but I believe something good and wonderful can emerge out of this.

All my love,
Richie xxx

18

Oxford

I AM WALKING up the Banbury Road to the FedEx depot in Summertown. For my last year as a student I lived up here in North Oxford. I know every road; I know the house where T.E. Lawrence lived, No. 2, Polstead Road. Strange to think that he sprang from these Victorian Gothic houses in this solid suburbia. How would you adapt to desert and camels after this?

There is something satisfying for me about sending this parcel. It is on its way to Moose Creek; this simple act seems to be an affirmation that I live in the world; at times I have felt myself drifting away. Although I still have a few questions, Noor's letter has calmed me. Things seem simpler. Perhaps I was depressed. Richard the Lionheart became depressed and ill when he was torn two ways, to take Jerusalem or to return home to secure his lands. He lay in his tent outside Jaffa for days, unable to move. Even the peaches and pears and melted snow that he requested from Saladin failed to revive him.

If I am honest, I can't see how Noor and I can live together, and I can imagine the whispers that would follow us. And I can't bear the notion that she might feel she has been shamed in some way. There are plenty of instances of women being blamed for their own rapes. I wonder if this kind of attitude doesn't linger in her family in Toronto, as she seemed to suggest.

I want to ask Lettie just how she came to find out what was going on in Cairo. I think that she must have been passing information from me back to her contact. Ed must have mentioned what had happened to Noor, and she would have suggested a meeting. I wouldn't be surprised if she had a direct line to Mr Macdonald.

Back home, I am trying to translate Henry of Huntingdon's letters from the museum in Ashby; one contains the word *'tesaur'*, which is 'treasure' in Occitan. There are some lines addressed to Hubert Walter, but these appear to be an extract from a poem, or a *chanson de geste*. I transcribe this letter (if it is a letter) onto a large sheet of unlined white paper and stare at it:

> *mes qui le porte, et chier le tient*
> *de s'amie li resovient,*
> *et si devient plus durs que fers;*
> *cil vos iert escuz et haubers*
> *et voir einz mes a chevalier*
> *ne le vos prester ne baillier,*
> *mes por amors le vos doing gié.*
> *Or a mes sire Yvain congié:*

Word by word I translate with the help of my dictionary:

> *But he who carries it, and cherishes it*
> *Remembers his friend,*
> *And thus he becomes stronger than iron;*
> *This will be your shield and hauberk*
> *And truly never before have I wanted*
> *To lend it or give it to a knight,*
> *But because of my feelings of love I give it to you.*
> *Now Lord Yvain gives you permission to leave.*

When I have finished my translation, I am sure that these must be lines from a *chanson de geste*. *'Qui le porte'* could mean 'whoever wears it' or it could mean 'whoever carries it'. Perhaps Huntingdon is quoting a poem that is familiar both to him and to Hubert Walter. Suddenly the penny drops: this is a form of code. They are about to carry the Holy Cross to its destination. But who is the Lord Yvain who has given his permission?

I email my text to Father Prosper, along with my translation, asking him to identify the piece if he can. Within ten minutes he replies:

> *Mon cher Richard, what you have translated, quite good, is from Chrétien de Troyes's 'Yvain, le Chevalier au Lion'.*
>
> *It is a narrative poem. In this* geste, *Yvain is the knight with the lion. Does this help with your question? Email me some more if you have questions. Lionheart, the 'knight with the lion.' Is this a coincidence?*
>
> *I hear from our mutual friend that the one in Canada is recovering slowly.*
>
> *Have patience, my son. Father P*

This is the way Hubert Walter and Henry of Huntingdon agreed to communicate. 'Yvain', as Father Prosper suggests, can only be Richard; they are saying that they have set out with the treasure, the cross. The second copied letter appears to have been sent from a Templar *commanderie*. I have discovered that there was a *commanderie* on an island near the port of Marseilles, and another outside Arles, which still stands. Here Huntingdon's letter is just one sentence: *Sire, ne sait que face*, which means, 'My lord, I don't know what to do.'

The third note seems to refer to this plea: *Pensez de tost venis arrière a tôt le moins jusqu huit joz après le Saint Jean.* This translates, more or less as, 'Be sure that you come back in time eight days after the Feast of St John.' On June the 23rd. I compare this note with Chrétien de Troyes's text. It has been subtly changed to answer Huntingdon's cryptic message. I think it suggests that Huntingdon and his party should wait until midsummer, after Richard's release. We know from the chroniclers that Hubert Walter was headed for Angevin to stiffen the resolve of Richard's vassals by assuring them that Richard would be released and he would immediately go on the attack. He, Archbishop Hubert Walter, was the King's man, the Regent.

My theory is made more likely by the communication between Huntingdon and Hubert Walter about a treasure, and it is hard to imagine what that treasure could be if it were not the True Cross.

After 1193, there are no letters and documents in the Huntingdon cache because Henry of Huntingdon died that year, soon after he reached home, his reputation for never becoming ill on account of his blameless life intact. His horse slipped and fell on top of him.

But there is a letter in that year from Hubert Walter to the Master of the Templars in Arles. It is mentioned by a chronicler in his biography of the great man: it asked the Master to aid the friends heading for Rouen and home. Hubert Walter says – quite possibly an adornment by the chronicler – that it is the duty of all Christians to help these knights who served the Lord in the Holy Land so steadfastly. Huntingdon, spelled 'Huntington', is mentioned as their leader and as a relative of the Master of the Templars in England.

After a troubled night I call my former tutor, Stephen Feuchtwanger, and I ask him if I can come to see him. I tell him I am running out of money and that I am confused. He is delighted to help. Come for the weekend. He gives me directions: he can no longer drive, but I should take a taxi from the station. He adds that his partner, Larry, is there, and he is a marvellous cook.

'The weather is bracing. Cold, with high winds off the sea, but dry. I can just about manage a short walk these days. You can tell me all about what is worrying you. And I will see if I can get you some more money from the college.'

He is related to the novelist Lion Feuchtwanger, author of *Jud Süss*, one of Weimar's finest, which the Nazis appropriated for anti-Semitic propaganda. His family emigrated, some to America, some to England. There is still just a trace of German in his voice after all these years. He said to me once, 'I am one of the last of the *Kindertransport* children who revived the English intellectual and artistic worlds.' He loved to be numbered with Karel Reisz, Frank Auerbach and Vera Gissing. He is an emeritus fellow of the college and much loved. He told me that when he came to Oxford and stood in the Broad outside our college, he thought he had woken up in heaven.

The taxi veers down a narrow, enclosed lane and at the bottom of it the sea is crawling dark green and grey. Off to the left a hill rises, almost conical, like a small, extinct volcano, and seagulls are swooping and crying out. We pull up at a small Victorian cottage. Stephen Feuchtwanger, author of *Hovering. Towards an understanding of the Poetics of Gerard Manley Hopkins,* appears at the door as I pay the driver, who has entertained me all the way from the station with his impressions of London, where he has just been for the first – and last – time. It's a shithole, is his considered opinion.

Stephen's hands shake a little. He is a still wonderfully good-looking eighty-one-year-old, with clear intelligent features and imposing grey hair, as if he were a judge of the Supreme Court or the president of a Swiss bank. His partner, Larry, stands behind him, looking over Stephen's shoulder at me. He was once Stephen's graduate student.

'Larry has made a cake in your honour. I have told him that you were one of my most talented students ever.'

Inside the cottage is all lightness, with light blue-painted floorboards and colourful curtains. I guess this is Larry's work. One whole wall is taken up with blond bookshelves and neatly stacked books.

We sit down in the small living room which looks out over a low stone wall towards the sea beyond. Larry is tall and thin. He wears mustard-yellow jeans with a preppy belt and loafers. I would say that he is a youthful forty-year-old. He came to Oxford from Michigan, he tells me, and he has never once been back to Battle Creek, the home of Kellogg's. It's the sort of statement that we provincials utter, expecting, but never receiving, applause. He produces a glossy chocolate brownie cake and pours the tea. Stephen watches me solicitously as I take a slice of the cake: 'Brilliant. The best chocolate cake I have ever eaten.'

We settle down comfortably to talk. I have a longing for a warm and kindly home life. I imagine Noor sitting next to me in a room like this. After half an hour, Stephen stands up.

'Now, young Richard and I are going for a walk. A short one along the sand dunes and back via the beach.'

Stephen pulls on a huge green anorak, he takes my arm and off we go down the lane. He points out the church where Betjeman is buried: *minor poet, major self-publicist.* The conical hill is called Brae Hill and crops up in some of Betjeman's poetry.

'Now, Richard, tell me your problems. And before you start, I have some good news, the college will pay to give you more time, another four months.'

I hear that familiar, faint, Germanic note: 'Mo-ar time.'

'Thank you. I honestly don't think I deserve it.'

'You are highly talented. The college is honoured to help you. Don't forget that. You seem to be a little down. Here I am, with Parkinson's, eighty-nine years old, and still eager. For what exactly, I don't know, but eager nonetheless.'

I tell him everything as we walk along a path in the sand dunes between the beach and the sea before we skirt Brae Hill on another path directly above the sea, which is lapping the base of the hill. I tell him about Noor – without the incest – my breakdown and my problems with the quest – even as I use the word I feel uneasy – my quest to discover the True Cross. I tell him why I think Richard was given the cross by Saladin and that I believe it reached Marseilles while Richard was in captivity in Germany. I tell him my problems of translation, and I tell him that I can't go any further.

After a few minutes he says, 'I think I have the answer for you.'

He doesn't say what it is. We walk back along the beach. At the cottage Larry is cooking. He is wearing an immense apron, embroidered with three red chillies.

'Do you like fish? I have some beautiful sea bass from Padstow, straight off the boats.'

'I love fish. I used to be a ghillie.'

This is not one hundred per cent true: I hate salmon after having gutted and cleaned them and looked into their glassy, vacant eyes.

'Larry is a wonderful cook,' says Stephen. 'He spoils me.'

We sit down with a glass of wine: for the first time in weeks I am completely relaxed. Stephen tells me he only goes up to the college about four or five times a year nowadays, for meetings or various dinners. Outside it is very dark, the deep rural dark. In the cottage I feel as though Peggotty is caring for me.

Stephen's eyebrows are vigorous, probably nourished by the rich intellectual matter within. He seems wonderfully pleased to see me and, eager as I am for human warmth, I am grateful. He is a very old man, but he is still relaying something sacred, which I first heard from him, the belief in the transformative power of literature. I see that Larry has made him happy. Larry reads to him and cooks for him. In return, Larry receives the help and advice in his own writing from a great man, who is generous and unselfish.

Later, Larry shows me to my bedroom under the roof. A small fire burns in the grate. The bed is covered with a patchwork quilt, and a blue bottle of Cornish Natural Spring Water stands by the bed.

'He often talks about you.'

'I don't deserve it, but I need his approval just at the moment.'

'He told me he wanted you to sit for the prize fellowship.'

'Yes, but I didn't think I was up to it. How is he, by the way?'

'It comes and goes. At the moment he seems very happy and well.'

'I can see you are good for him.'

'I hope I am. Anything you need? No? Well, sleep tight.'

I have a bath and jump gratefully into bed. In my bedroom at Ed's house, now on the market, everything is damp and soiled. Here, all is crisp and clean. I have six pillows with embroidered pillowslips and there is a bowl of tulips by the mineral water. I sleep untroubled for the first time in weeks. My aunt would have said it was the fresh air, or the ozone.

After a late breakfast, Stephen suggests we go for another walk. We head up a lane, and emerge on the golf course, and cross a fairway, heading towards the stumpy, isolated church.

'Stephen, I didn't tell you the whole story.'

'Do you want to?'

'I have to tell you that Noor, who was kidnapped, is my half-sister.'

'How exciting.'

'Well, when I met her I didn't know and she didn't know either. But after she was taken, her mother, who lives in Jerusalem, told me. My father and her mother had a relationship a year or so after I was born. Haneen – her mother – felt she had to tell me when she realised we were proposing to get married.'

'Quite common amongst the Hapsburgs and Hohenzollerns, of course. What are you going to do?'

'We're not going to get married, obviously. She's in Toronto having counselling and psychiatric treatment, as well as internal operations.'

'Dear boy, what an extraordinary and awful thing.'

'I really wasn't meaning to involve you, but I thought it was dishonest not to tell you.'

A man in plum-coloured trousers and red fleece comes down the hill, led by his Labrador, which is pulling hard on the leash.

'Hello. Stephen, hello.'

'I see the dog is taking you on a walk, Mark.'

'I would have died years ago without him. It's a consensual arrangement.'

'A retired High Court judge,' says Sephen when he has gone by. 'Richard, can I ask you, as your old tutor and great admirer, to listen to what I have to say?'

'Of course.'

'Your quest, as you quaintly called it last night, is troubling you, because it has no obvious outcome. Is that more or less what you were saying?'

'That is exactly what I was thinking.'

'Perhaps it is a diversion. You should write about your experiences in Jerusalem and your quest to find the Holy Cross in any way you like. Use your imagination. From what you have told me, it's about belief. The power of fiction at its best is to make the reader believe, to enter into, what you, the writer, are writing. That's all it is. By reading, and giving his consent to be beguiled, the reader becomes complicit with the writer, to some extent creating his own fiction. You have a wonderful opportunity. Even if it turns out not to be the True Cross, and even if there is no neat outcome, you can write about that. You must free yourself. Dear Richard, nothing could give me greater pleasure and satisfaction than to be able, before I die, to read the book I know you are capable of.'

We are standing near the ninth tee of Trebetherick Golf Club, the wind blowing in from the estuary; Betjeman is at rest two hundred yards away. I feel treacherous tears welling again. Even now I wonder if my treatment in hospital has altered me for ever at the cellular level, somewhere the emotions arise. Stephen's hand on my arm is shaking. His thick grey hair is flying wildly. His cheekbones and the surrounds of his mouth are raw from the wind so that he has a cadaverous look, as if prefiguring his death.

'Thank you, Stephen. Thank you.'

'Shall we go home?'

I take his arm under the elbow, in the way we were taught at Boy Scouts to escort a blind person across a busy street. I did not have the opportunity to put it into practice as I never saw a blind person and, anyway, the streets were rarely busy.

19

January 1193, Marseilles

MARSEILLES WAS A busy port. From Pisa and Genoa, Venice, Milan, Corfu, Rhodes, Acre, Alexandria, Constantinople and Brindisi, ships from the modest to the magnificent docked. The Crusades had led to an increase of commerce and traffic and there was a constant bustle around the quays, and the markets on the quaysides; the huge warehouses, which looked like rural barns, were full of goods for onward transit. A new world of trade and commerce was emerging in the counting houses, factors' offices and merchants' storerooms. All the languages of the Mediterranean were spoken here, including Arabic. The merchants and factors were highly organised. In order to cope with the many nationalities and the complex agreements, Latin had become the language of trade.

The sailing season was officially closed for the winter; the sea could be violent and the winds could rip sails; galleys powered by slaves could be swamped. But this did not deter the few brave, or desperate, captains who set sail for home when they saw a break in the weather. Ox- and horse-drawn carts departed at all hours on the first stage of the long journey inland, as far as Paris and Antwerp and Rouen and La Rochelle, Dieppe and Amsterdam. Glassware, silks, spices, Flanders cloth, skins, wheat, wine carried in tuns, and much more, were loaded and unloaded.

On the 15th of January, a large sailing ship docked. It was rumoured that it carried knights who had come from Acre and Corfu. This mysterious ship had a high prow, which made it capable of crossing the Channel to England, but at this time of year there was no question of leaving the Mediterranean through the Straits of Gibraltar into the Bay of Biscay: the prevailing winds made that impossible.

An armed guard from the Templar commanderie waited for the five knights who were escorting the precious cargo to disembark. These men were among Richard the Lionheart's most loyal knights. They had taken the cross and they had all fought at Richard's side in Messina, in Cyprus, in Jaffa, in Acre, in Arsuf and in Ascalon. They had about them a sort of dignified sanctity: a third of their fellows had died of disease, drowning or wounds over the past two years, and they had seen death and blood and massacre. All of them bore scars. But they had received Almighty God's grace by entering the Holy Sepulchre in Jerusalem, so fulfilling their vows.

Word had got out that the Templars were receiving these important knights, who were on the business of a king. Rumours were circulating furiously around the quays. Henry of Huntingdon understood that rumours were dangerous. In truth, only the Master of the Templars knew their business. But here in Marseilles, not even the brotherhood of the one hundred leaders of the crafts and businesses of Marseilles, which had its own courts and regulations, would dare to offend the Templars by asking questions. The Templars were very powerful and in Marseilles, which was in practice an autonomous state, they were particularly potent.

As they disembarked, the knights were wearing their light mail without cuirass. The mail was covered by a plain white surcoat on which was stitched a simple cloth crotz; none of them wore the arms of their captive King because there were many enemies of their overlord here in Provence.

Messengers from Hubert Walter had prepared the Templars for the arrival of their guests. Henry of Huntingdon, William de l'Étang, Gerard de Furnival, Raoul de Mauléon, Bartholomew de Mortemer, Roger de Saci and Master Robert walked beside a wooden box, draped with a brown Flanders cloth. Huntingdon was the only one of the knights heading for England. The others were going to Anjou and Normandy. An outer ring of Templars led them solemnly from the great ship towards a waiting galley. The merchants and factors stopped their work briefly to watch; they had seen many strange sights. It may have looked to them like a religious ceremony, as, in a way, it was. To reach the Templar commanderie, an island fortress, the knights, their escort and the treasure had to travel by boat. The galley moved swiftly, leaving behind the bustle and rumours and spies of the port. The Master himself came out of the castle to greet the travellers, and led the procession through the main gate. As soon as they had shed their mail the knights were seated at a long refectory table, where the Master gave thanks for their safe arrival from the Holy Land, through danger-ous waters, and blessed them for their successes against the infidel. Huge fires at either end of the refectory warmed them. Flagons of Provençal wines were brought in by the squires, followed by platters of mutton, and lampreys and beef from the marshlands of the Camargue, known in Occitan as Camarga.

Weary and sick though they were, Huntingdon and his brothers in arms made their way to the chapel of St Bernard de Clairvaux, the patron saint of the Knights Templars. The chapel was devoted to the cult of the Virgin Mary, and Richard's knights gave thanks on their knees for their safe passage and prayed that the Virgin would continue to protect them on their sacred mission. For two weeks they waited for a message as they rested in the Knights Templars' care.

Henry of Huntingdon was particularly anxious to set out for home. He hadn't seen his wife for three years. But, unlike Marseilles, Arles and Toulon were under the suzerainty of the Counts of Provence and the journey to Arles and onward would be dangerous. If it were known that Huntingdon was leading a small group of knights who were escorting precious treasure for Richard, there would be a free-for-all, and the knights would be seen as candidates for ransom, like their sire.

The whole world knew that Richard was held in captivity. There was a cloud over England and the Angevin empire.

When the message came and the terms were agreed, and the silver was handed over, the Master of the Templars prepared to provide an escort of twenty knights to ride as far as Arles; Huntingdon's men were given Templar cloaks and robes and armour for the journey. Their shields, on a black-and-white background, were inscribed with the words: In hoc signo vinces – In this sign you will conquer, the motto of Constantine the Great, the first Christian Emperor, who saw a vision of the cross, the chi-rho, in the sky before the decisive Battle of the Milvian Bridge. The new world that was emerging still had roots in the classical world. The bridge, where Constantine received his revelation, still spans the Tiber, almost one thousand seven hundred years after Constantine's apocalyptic vision.

For Henry of Huntingdon himself, no challenge was too difficult, no danger too great, but he was apprehensive: to lose the Holy Cross now was unthinkable. The contingent, apparently of Templars, set off well before dawn in a galley; the horses were restless, tied head to tail in a flat barge, before they were led onto the quay and the knights mounted, to ride out beyond Marseilles, away from the marshes and islands and the teeming port. The treasure was in a covered wagon pulled by four horses. Two more draft horses were tethered to the back of the wagon in case they were needed. Only the master of the commanderie knew what was being carried in the large wooden box, secured with metal bands and wrapped in Flanders cloth. Initially the knights followed the route of the Roman Road, skirting the mouth of the Rhône. Roger de Saci rode with his favourite falcon from the Holy Land on the pommel of his saddle. It was in jesses and bells and an Arab hood covered its head.

'That bird won't last long in this weather,' said Huntingdon.

The bird was crouched, its feathers plumped up.

'She is strong. If she dies, that will be a very bad omen for all of us.'

From within its hood, the falcon squeaked.

'You are a mysterious man, Roger.'

'I trust fate. I love the bird. I want her here, close to me. If she dies it is God's will.'

Henry had seen many men who clutched at straws after the horrors they had witnessed.

The knights were headed in the direction of Aix, because it was a safer journey; ten miles north of Marseilles they took the road across the Camarga, in the direction of Arles. Wind and rain swept in over the marshlands. There was a low sky of tarnished silver plate above them, and little movement on the road ahead. The horses' heads hung low and the riders pulled their cloaks tight. Nobody spoke. Henry of Huntingdon gave thanks silently that the day was so foul. Perhaps the Virgin was looking after them. All day they struggled towards Arles. Sheets of rain like a silver curtain drove in from the south. Master Robert sat slumped on his horse, his back bent, his hood pulled across his face, his hands resting on the pommel. He may have been asleep. Now the cart had to be pulled out of a deep rut, and the two extra packhorses were harnessed for the task. It was a frightful, demoralising day. Wet through, cold and exhausted, they finally arrived at the commanderie of Arles. The gates opened onto a courtyard and the horses were taken away to be fed, while the treasure was moved under escort to the chapel by Knights Templars, as if they were conducting a vigil for a hero.

Although Templar rules forbade falconry, Roger de Saci's bedraggled bird was housed in a chicken coop and fed two dead mice, which it ate quickly and without joy or gratitude, watched closely by Roger de Saci. Henry was surprised it had survived the journey.

'Did you pray for the bird?' he asked.

'I did. As we rode, I was praying to the Virgin for my family and my falcon.'

'But perhaps not in that order.'

In the Latin Kingdom, de Saci had been an avid falconer. His sire,

Richard, also enjoyed the sport. De Saci's devotion to this bird, with its ruthless eyes, was a mystery to Henry.

The Master, Guillaume Soliers, greeted them as they assembled. He spoke on behalf of all Templars when he beseeched the Lord to aid them in their mission and he thanked them for their noble work in the Holy Land. He reminded the assembled that these men had fulfilled their vows and were bound for heaven and eternal life. During the meal a choir sang the Templars' own Gregorian chants. After they had eaten, Soliers and the knights retired to discuss the way ahead. The Templars were strong enough to provide an escort, but not far beyond Arles, Soliers said, nothing could be guaranteed. He recommended that they travel as ordinary pilgrims, returning from the Holy Land.

Despite their vows of poverty and service, the Templars had acquired a very high opinion of themselves. You could never be certain where they saw advantage. But it helped Henry's cause that his relative had been the Grand Master of the Templars in England. Hubert Walter had prepared the way, and Soliers had been receiving intelligence of what lay ahead on their way to Rouen. It was in Arles that they received the news that Hubert Walter was their king's choice as Archbishop of Canterbury. It pleased them that a brave companion and a justiciar of the realm should receive this honour. They drank to Hubert, and de Saci gave his falcon a lump of meat, impaled on the end of a dagger.

Soliers passed to Huntingdon a message from Hubert Walter, which instructed them to wait before moving north. The message to move out would be 'stronger than iron'.

> He who carries it, and cherishes it
> Remembers his friend,
> And thus he becomes stronger than iron;
> This will be your shield and hauberk.

For ten days they waited. The news from the north was that John and Philip were desperately trying to make gains before Richard was released and many nobles of Richard's kingdom were trying to decide where their advantage lay. Some were for John and Philip. Master Robert, the clerk, sought information wherever he could; he discovered that the Count of Angoulême was turning towards Philip of France. He noted which castles John had bought or captured. He was watchful and meticulous.

Huntingdon said that he would gladly kill John in combat, if John were man enough to accept the challenge.

'You know perfectly well that he is a coward. Is that why you will issue the challenge?' said de l'Étang.

'He is a coward, and what he is most frightened of is our sire.'

They drank to their incomparable king. They praised his bravery and good nature and his singing voice. They were full of bitterness for the traitors who had taken him prisoner, men who themselves had sworn to aid all who had taken the cross. They had lost their souls for gold. The knights swore that there would be a price to pay. Bartholomew de Mortemer recited some lines of Richard's 'Ja Nus Hons Pris':

> They knew full well, barons and my men,
> Of Normandy, England, Gascony, Poitou,
> That I have never had a vassal
> Whom I leave in prison for my own gain;
> I say it not as a reproach to them,
> —But a prisoner I am!

Mortemer wished them eternal damnation:

After my death they will be called to account.

In the dark of night, Henry of Huntingdon prayed, as he did every night, to the Virgin that she might guide them to deliver the Holy

Cross to Rouen, the very cross on which her son was crucified, and then he prayed that she should permit him to go home, his vows fulfilled, his sacred task complete. He was longing to see his wife and children and his lands again. But the message to move out did not come for two months. And the King himself was not to be released until the following year:

I grieve greatly for myself; for them still more.

20

Port Meadow

STEPHEN HAS SET me free. I am happily writing my account of Richard and the Holy Cross.

Emily emails me. She has a new boyfriend, actually more of a partner. She felt she owed it to me to tell me. They are living together. He knows about me. They have no secrets. Would I like to meet him?

No, I fucking well wouldn't. And in this respect, at least, she doesn't owe me a thing. She wants to buy me out of the unsold flat in Hackney. Her boyfriend has a legacy and he is offering to put up half the asking price; taking into account the outstanding mortgage, he is prepared to pay me £10,000. And – great news – he has a very good eye, and believes he can smarten up the place relatively cheaply.

I email my congratulations, and accept the offer. I write: *I am very happy for you*, which is both ungrammatical and untrue. I have detected, I think, an attempt to make me jealous; she wants some sign from me. She doesn't want to think that our many months together have left no traces on me.

It is a long email. Her partner is in music. He specialises in finding promising young acts, like Speed Wheels, who I have never heard of. Her writing is going well. She has submitted a short story to a competition. She has also sent it to an agent.

This picture of an interesting and creative lifestyle could be translated by the cynical – me – as meaning that her boyfriend has some money left to him by his granny, which he is squandering, and that she is heading inevitably for literary rejection, so that she will have to take the teaching diploma and embark on a career, an important component of which will be eating biscuits in the staff room as refuge from the delinquent pupils. And her partner will eventually become a minicab driver or go into garden design, laying turf for lawyers. But I am happy about the money.

I end on an upbeat note: *He's a very lucky man, and I think your offer is fair and generous*. I append my address and my bank details to speed up the transaction.

I have been in an ecstatic phase, jumping out of bed to get back to my narrative, my novel, my historical biography, my picaresque, my reverie – call it what you want.

Ella and I went for a walk on Port Meadow yesterday. It was the first time we had met since I was discharged from hospital.

A large part of the meadow was under water. Swans and ducks and geese were making merry, where earlier cows and ponies – some of them Shetlands – had grazed calmly. At any moment Noah might appear in his DIY ark. It seemed happily disorderly to me – ducks swimming about everywhere – but then, how would these birds, with their tiny brains, distinguish between flooded grassland and legitimate, bona fide lake or river? Or Mount Ararat. A whole new world had opened up to them.

Ella was heavily disguised in dark glasses and a hooded jacket. The fact that we had done nothing wrong, apart from the solitary kiss, which took place at a time when my mind was disturbed, suggested that she felt some sexual tension between us. Of course, she was recently my shrink and I was just an irresponsible lay person, helpless against the forces of derangement. Also, she had shown me the path out of the dark forest. But now her nervousness began to inhibit me. The water was just below the bridge as we crossed the river – it was running alarmingly strongly, and contributed to the sense of Old Testament disorder. We walked through the wet afternoon to the Perch. She went ahead of me into the pub, presumably as a precaution against running into somebody who would report her to the BMA for consorting with a lunatic. I followed a few minutes later, as though I had arrived separately. This was her neurotic plan. The pub was empty, apart from a barmaid polishing glasses, and two young men looking at their phones. Somewhere off stage was the sound of plates being stacked. The atmosphere was torpid. We ordered red wine.

'Ella, this is crazy. You must be able to talk to your patients.'

'I know. But it's more than that. You shouldn't have kissed me.'

'Nobody saw us. Anyway I was drugged – by you.'

'I know, but it made me think about Clive, and how I can't really stand the idea that he is *seeing* (she makes quotation marks in the air) someone else. Fucking someone else. When you kissed me – by the way I am not making any demands on you, not at all – when you kissed me, it brought up a lot of issues I was suppressing.'

'That sounds quite Freudian.'

'Whatever. Actually, Freud was a total fraud. It started me thinking about what I was going to do.'

'Ella, when I told you that I couldn't imagine anybody leaving you, I meant it.'

She looked at me, appraising.

'You have an elusive quality.'

I wondered what this elusive quality could be.

'Why don't you just tell him to fuck off. Or is that not the professional way?'

'It's not that easy. He's moved into her flat. She's called Chelsea, can you credit it? I told him I was going to call myself Holland Park. It's so fucking banal and predictable and actually sick-making when he says, as if he is prey to forces he can't control, that against his will he has fallen hopelessly in love. I am supposed to understand.'

'And obviously, you don't.'

'No I don't.' She stared at the fireplace. 'Thanks for listening to me. I'm sorry to vomit on your shoes.'

'Come, let's go to my place.'

'Are you sure?'

'Yes.'

She looks at me and I kiss her, emboldened by wine. The two men in a corner barely notice us.

Now that she has something to be properly guilty about, she puts on dark glasses and pulls her hood down and avoids eye contact with walkers. She behaves so furtively that she is conspicuous. I laugh.

I know that Ed is away. We go straight to my little bedroom. In my mind it is not a betrayal of Noor, but a form of therapy, possibly for both of us.

Later, we lie in the tangled sheets, oddly content. Just the act of sex has calmed her completely. Outside my small, and smeared, window, the light is fading. At another time the crepuscular tones might have been the signal for melancholy, but I feel strangely happy.

'Richie, that was wonderful. I just can't explain what it is like to be ditched by someone in this way. It was shattering. It was a stab to the heart. But somehow sleeping with you has trivialised my worries. Was it OK for you?'

'Lovely, wonderful. But look, I'm very sorry, but I can't see you again, because if we had a relationship, I would be doing something terrible to Noor that might finish her. It's very complicated, but I couldn't do that. I hope you understand.'

'I do, of course I do, but it is difficult. This is the first time I have felt happy for months.'

'Me too.'

She had a high colour. Her lips were bruised. She held on to me tightly for a moment. It is a strange, spiritual, thing – two bodies trying to become one in this way. Two near-strangers doing something so elemental, so intimate and so irrational.

'Where's your friend Ed?' she asked, some immeasurable time later.

'Oh, he's in London having an interview for a job in Australia. He's hoping to be the investment manager for the University of Western Australia in Perth. Ella, what did you mean when you said I was elusive?'

'You are hard to pin down. It's very attractive, by the way.'

I could tell her that I am not elusive, merely half-formed.

21

To the Auvergne

THE MASTER OF the commanderie was becoming restless. Although his position in Arles was princely, there were rumours in the town, no doubt reaching the Count of Provence, that some of the Lionheart's knights had taken refuge with the Templars. Of course, the Templars were duty bound to help pilgrims who had been to the Holy Land, but these were not ordinary pilgrims; the rumours had it that they were important men, carrying something of importance with them. The region was in even more turmoil than usual, and Soliers had to avoid offending the powerful. Particularly he had to avoid the impression that the Templars were becoming a law unto themselves.

He called Henry of Huntingdon to his chambers. Soliers was wearing the white surplice that Knights Templars were obliged to wear at all times.

'Henry, you have become a good and true friend.'

'Thank you. You, Master, have in turn been a generous host and an honest friend. You wanted to speak to me?'

'Yes, it is a delicate matter. Nobody here has broken silence, but nonetheless there are rumours in the town about the knights lodging with us. They say that you are guarding something of great value. There are rumours that you are conveying treasures from the Temple of the Hebrews, or that Richard the Lionheart has placed the bones of Our Lord in your care, or that you have brought from the Holy Land the Grail. As you know, we have been accused of possessing the Grail ourselves. And, of course, the Ark of the Covenant. The Grand Master has heard these rumours. He has decreed that you should move on as soon as possible. We have for some time been the object of suspicion. We are even rumoured to practise witchcraft behind our walls.'

Huntingdon knew that the Templars were envied and increasingly feared. Despite their vows of poverty, chastity and obedience, they had become very wealthy because of their role as bankers to thousands of pilgrims. But they were also feared because they had ridden willingly to their death in many battles, most famously in the Holy Land. To die in battle was a great honour for a Knight Templar.

'I understand,' said Huntingdon.

'The Grand Master wishes you to know that for the honour of your uncle, he will do all he can to see that you are protected on your journey.'

'We are grateful.'

'I will pray for you. You are doing the Lord's work.'

'I know that this journey will be difficult while your king is in captivity and I have prayed for his early release too. But there is turmoil everywhere. The Marche is especially turbulent. You should head for the Auvergne. The Grand Master has decreed that I send an escort of ten knights and their squires, twelve spare horses, and ten sergeants with you. And you should wear at all times our surcoat and the cross until you arrive in the Auvergne, when you should dress as pilgrims. These are the Grand Master's directions. We will arrange two guides who will accompany you through the mountains to Lo Puèi de Velai and we will alert Count Robert of Auvergne, who is a former vassal of your king, and we will also alert the archbishop that you are to be given safe passage as pilgrims, returning from the Holy Land. My knights may go no further with you.'

'I thank, you, Master.'

'I am very sorry, my friend.'

'I understand.'

Henry of Huntingdon spoke to his companions. They did not trust the Master. They did not trust the Templars, and they would have preferred to wait for the signal from Hubert Walter, the king's voice, but they had no choice other than to prepare to leave. Each Knight Templar selected for the journey north was to be accompanied by his squire and the squires had to be summoned from their homes and families. Henry of Huntingdon sent a message to Hubert Walter in Poitou. He did not hold out much hope that Walter would get it before they arrived in the Auvergne. The message read: Et si devient plus durs que fers: He becomes harder than iron – the confirmation that they were riding out.

In fact it was two weeks before the convoy could set out, one morning before dawn. The weather had changed, and there was the scent of almond blossom in the air as they rode towards the shuttered town. The horses clattered through the silent streets. There is something stirring and also menacing about the sound of many horses moving through a town before dawn. The iron rims on the wheels of the wagons scoured the cobbles loudly. The journey to the relative safety of the Auvergne would take them five days. The knights, in their white surcoats emblazoned with the Templars' red cross, were silent. Inside its hood, even Roger de Saci's falcon was quiet. Nobody came out to watch this cavalcade passing through like wraiths of past battles, and past deaths. The Templars' reputation for witchcraft ensured that the citizens of Arles knew better than to be seen to be inquisitive. In the wagon there was almost certainly a corpse, and who knew what uses the Templars had in mind for it?

Huntingdon was glad to be moving. He had found the delays hard to bear. His family was always on his mind. But he believed, as Guibert de Nogent famously expressed it, that 'God has instituted in our times holy wars, so that the order of knights and the crowd running in its wake . . . might find a new way of gaining salvation.'

It is time to go home. He has found his salvation. He trusts in God to guide him.

22

Oxford and London

I AM AFRAID that when Noor and I meet again I will see someone broken. People who have suffered severe trauma are often changed physically and mentally. My aunt, with her disappointments, her acute sense of the humiliation she had brought on herself by a lack of judgement when she left her husband, Andrew, the stockbroker from Fulham, for Sandy, the gamekeeper, is one. She and Sandy married, romantically, at Gretna Green as soon as the divorce came through. There is a photograph of them together. Sandy is every inch the outdoorsman, rugged and vigorous in his deerstalker and camouflage kit, with a large gun cover on his back. My aunt, if not beautiful, is slim and lively. She is wearing green wellington boots, and a dark blue skirt with polka dots. Her hair seems to have been modelled on Princess Diana's. Her nostrils are flared eagerly, like an excited pony's; something is in the air.

A few months after this picture was taken, my aunt's ex-husband, who had moved his personal assistant, Arabella, twenty-six, into the family home, was cheerfully spreading stories that her marriage to Sandy was already on the rocks. Sandy was out on the moors most of the time, and in desperation my aunt was going into Banchory in search of a cappuccino or a reasonably recent copy of *Tatler*. Sandy believed she had a lover there. When he was at home, he barely spoke, and drank too much. If she questioned him, he became violent. She was ashamed to visit the doctor to have treatment for a fractured eye socket. Then Sandy blew his brains out and the colonisation of her face, her biblical punishment, started its march. She had a breakdown, but there was no one to turn to. From deepest Fulham, only waves of *Schadenfreude* reached her. My father visited once, but he didn't like the vibe; suicide upset him. He left, after suggesting to her that she should drop out in Ibiza.

By the time I came to live with her, she was showing reclusive tendencies and, looking back, I could have helped her more. Her movements were prematurely slow and painful, as if she were willing old age upon her, but for all her misery, she went on reading. She understood the world through Dickens and Jane Austen and Elizabeth Gaskell and Thackeray. She surprised me by recommending two authors I came to love, Saul Bellow and John Updike. I read solidly for four years and we discussed the books. We never talked about Sandy. My theory was that she had seen something elemental in Sandy that her husband, the stockbroker, lacked. That something, sadly, turned out to be a kind of Celtic resentment.

How will Noor be after her awful experience? Her upper jaw has required work, including implants. This kind of thing takes place too close to the brain. If I speak honestly – I appear to be borrowing from the Lionheart's song – I don't know how I am going to deal with the question of rape. I have had visions of Noor with a born-again look, like a reformed alcoholic, with a stoicism brought on by suffering. In my sleep I sometimes see her smiling vacantly, her gaze a little odd, her glorious red hair cut short, in a penitential gesture: *I am shriven.* Worse, Noor might decide that her kidnap has made her a better person, with a deeper understanding. She might start a foundation, because nothing can be explained in this world simply as evil or inexplicable.

But what I fear most is that the innocent days, the blood-orange-trickling-between-her-breasts days, are over. We could become locked into something dutiful, her terrible abuse tying us together.

I want to talk to Ella about these worries; I want to know if they are normal; I want psychiatric absolution. But if I do talk to her, I think we will end up in bed together. And what are words really, but a palliative, a groping for comfort and reassurance? Hamlet, tersely to Polonius: *Words, words, words.*

I call Haneen and to my surprise she takes the call.

'Haneen, how are you?'

'Fine. I have just arrived in London – ten minutes ago – and was going to call you myself later. Can we meet?'

'When is good for you?'

'Tomorrow. Come to my apartment. Eleven a.m.'

She gives me the address.

'We have lots to talk about.'

'How is Noor?'

'She is brave. A very brave girl. She's improving, but it breaks my heart to see her like this. We will speak tomorrow.'

I am already cheered by hearing her effortlessly imperious and unequivocal voice. It brings back Jerusalem as keenly as the sound of bells. She will share with me some of her Levantine wisdom. I am anyway due in London for a visit to an exhibition of Crusader art at the British Museum, and I have to sign an agreement at a solicitors' office in Hackney, which is required for my pay out. I am infused with dynamism.

Haneen lets me into her Candy Brothers apartment. It has a balcony with a view of the Albert Hall, and just beyond that, of some huge trees, semaphoring proximity to Hyde Park, one of the holy places. She embraces me, and starts on a tour. The furniture is low to the ground, and impersonal, as in an airport departure lounge. She says it was a show flat and they included the furniture and fittings. She says that they were surprised at her skill haggling.

'You know what Woody Allen said, the only crime in our family was buying retail. I could have bought a large piece of Jerusalem for what I paid, but I am not going to have regrets. The time has come. *Sans doute*. Definitely. How are you, my boy?'

'I'm fine. How's Noor?'

'Well, hopefully, she has had all the operations. Six of them. She's very upset because the doctor told her that there is little chance of her having a child without intervention. And of course, she is unsure of her future. Also she is frightened. She wonders how you can have a future together.'

Perversely, I feel a surge of relief, that she doesn't have blind faith in the love-conquers-everything mantra.

'What I was going to say to you is that we think – Noor and I – that it is best for you two not to meet again. She has to make a new life. She knows in her heart that she can't be involved with her half-brother romantically. She can't be in love with you. It's not possible. Her mental state is very fragile. Richard, I love you as my son, and I have tried to think of some way out that is good for both of you, and really, to tell the truth, I have failed. The first thing is to get Noor well, but I don't think she is ever going to recover if she thinks that in some way you will be able to live together. She knows this is logical, but she doesn't want to believe it.'

'My idea was that, when she was better, in her own judgement, we would go to a Greek island and have a long holiday together.'

'Richard, I think you have to give Noor the chance to forget. You know what psychiatrists say and what they all believe? They say that there is no such thing as true forgetting. All experiences leave a trail. If you go to this Greek island, what's going to happen? I can tell you. You will, both of you, feel obliged to find a solution and then – or perhaps a few months later – you will feel trapped in your past and your obligations to each other. I believe, and Noor accepts it, that you must have a complete separation. You knew her for five or six weeks only and a terrible thing happened to her that will live with her for ever. Richard, you aren't the answer to her problems:

she can't marry you, she can't have a physical relationship with you, she can't have your baby – she's lost one already – and she can't forget what you might have had, and she will for ever feel cheated. So how can you be part of her life? In my opinion you can't and believe me I have lain awake for nights without end worrying about it. She must move on, as they say. Am I right?'

'Probably. But can I think about it?'

'Of course. But remember, it's even more complicated because my brother and his wife don't know all the facts. Can you imagine the hell she would go through if my brother – who is her adoptive father – knew that you were her brother? This secret must remain our secret. Nobody – except maybe me – has done anything wrong, but I don't think my brother could deal with that news. Already he is hinting to me that Noor overreached herself. It makes be mad, but I can't react. He thinks we Christian Arabs should keep our heads down. Just what many German Jews thought. And the French Jews. He believes I encouraged Noor in her folly. To him human rights are deliberate mischief-making. All that sort of nonsense. By the way, you can use my spare room whenever you want. I won't be in London again until the end of summer and it will be good to have someone here from time to time. I have a key for you and I will give the doorman your name.'

'This is perhaps a little grand for me.'

'It's never a surprise to me how quickly people adjust to luxury. I've made up the bed for you if you would like to stay tonight. I want you to feel you can come here any time. I loved your father and now as I grow old I see you as part of my family. Is that acceptable?'

She speaks with a kind of resonance – waves booming in a sea cave, and her accent is of a higher order, not belonging to any one country or time. I think the aristocratic Russians probably spoke French in this way. There is just a hint of her provenance in the word 'acceptable' which she pronounced harshly, as 'accept-tibill'.

'That's very generous. Thanks. I do have business at the British Museum – they have an exhibition of works from the Scriptorium of the Holy Sepulchre and a reproduction of an icon from Bethlehem, which demonstrates that Latin and Byzantine art had integrated in the twelfth century. There are also many more Western influences in the rebuilding of the Holy Sepulchre, and some drawings to illustrate this. But you probably know more about it than I do.'

'How is your project coming on?'

'I put it aside for a while, but now I am trying to get it back on track.'

'Noor tells me you are doing something on Richard the Lionheart.'

'Yes, I am. It's a sort of novel.'

'Your father wrote a history of Richard.'

'Yes, I've read it. It was more of a dream sequence than a novel.'

She smiles. We are affectionately complicit.

I understand why writers are reluctant to discuss work in progress. As Beckett replied when asked what his writing was about: *It's about the writing.*

In the night I think about what Haneen has told me. She seems to be saying that Noor is terribly damaged and that pinning her hopes on me would be disastrous. I can't believe it. We will meet on a Greek island, for better or for worse. Haneen said there can be no true forgetting. Psychiatrists are bound to say that, because there would be a lot fewer of them in employment if the inexhaustible archive of doubtful memories was declared off-limits. And how would you prove that there is no such thing as true forgetting? Something that has been truly forgotten would be just that?

23

Richie

DEAREST NOOR,

I spent last night in Haneen's new flat in London. I am sure she told you about it. It's pretty flash. Is that a term you know? Anyway, she said it was time. I think she feels she has been disloyal to Jerusalem. I read only a few days ago that some cities exist as much in the mind as in the material world, and the writer mentioned Jerusalem. I find myself thinking about Jerusalem, and Room 6, far too often. I have the feeling that I – and maybe you – will never be so happy again as we were in the pasha's harem. I can see why Haneen would feel torn.

One thing she said disturbed me. She said that it is a fundamental belief of psychoanalysts that there is no such thing as 'true forgetting'. She feels it would be disastrous for your recovery if we met again. What is untrue forgetting? A kind of willed amnesia? And would that be a bad thing? Anyway, enough pop psychology already. The simple question is, *will you see me again?* If you are sure that it is best for you to forget me, and everything that reminds you of me (true forgetting?), then I will accept that. Only a few weeks ago you told me that you would accept anything I decided; we seem to have exchanged roles. Will you tell me exactly – don't spare me – how you feel about our future?

As for my plans, I have decided on an island for us in the Dodecanese. I went there once with my father – our father – on our one and only family holiday and I thought it was magical. I dreamed of it for years. It's called Symi, and has an ancient stairway of three hundred and sixty-five stone steps between the port and the upper town. It is called Kallistrata – beautiful, or good, road. Donkeys carry the heavy stuff. There are almost no cars on the island because there is hardly anywhere to go that can't be reached by boat. But in my memory there is also a small island just off-shore, with a chapel on it. I want to visit it again with you. (Does this sound like the plot of *Mamma Mia!*?) I was only about twelve at the time and I was probably passively inhaling my father's dope, so I am anyway an unreliable witness.

We stopped off in Rhodes to see the Castle of the Knights Hospitallers, who set up shop there after the fall of the Kingdom of Jerusalem in 1291. My father loved a castle. He thought he could read the stones. When you saw Kerak, as you reminded me in your letter, you saw corpses. Our father saw glory and mysticism. Oh, and in Symi he fell out with the patriarch of a huge monastery at the far end of the island. He believed that swimming naked was a human right, and he did it in full view of the monastery. I hid in a dark café as the recriminations started. The credulous had a habit of throwing bottles with prayers in them into the sea; our father wrote: *Let it all hang out for world peace* on the back of a menu, rolled it, and placed it in an ouzo bottle. I didn't know what that meant. I was instructed to hurl the bottle off the boat as we cleared the bay. Outside the bay, he said, there were currents that might take the bottle anywhere.

The strange thing is that I have met a number of people recently who tell me what a wonderful person he was.

And finally, I would accept, if you told me yourself, that you believe we should not meet. For myself, I believe that we will meet on the Island of Symi one not-too-distant day. Write to me and tell me your thoughts.

All my love,
Richie xxxx

PS. I enjoy writing: *Moose Creek* on the package. In my mind's eye I see a herd of moose knee-deep in snow eating bark. Close?

24

Emily

TO MY SURPRISE, Emily is at the lawyers', in a small office next to a launderette, a few streets back from Hackney Town Hall. She says that the documents for the flat transfer have to be witnessed at the same time. She says this as a matter of universally known fact. Do I mind? Of course not. Can we have a coffee afterwards? OK. We sign the legal paper. Briefly I wonder if there is a warehouse or a limbo where this unloved stuff ends up. The lawyer, Derek Cocks, is wearing a brown suit with a blue shirt and a tie of the same blue so that the tie vanishes into the shirt. He has a cold and holds a handkerchief over his face; mostly all we see of him is his eyes. His voice is slightly muffled when he speaks.

'Right, that was short and sweet. All done and dusted. Bye for now.'

A little later, I find myself in a kind of barn in a narrow lane where, Emily says, good coffee of origin is served. It is served by a cheery man with a ring in his nose and three more in each ear. I have nothing against the visual aspect of his cartilaginous bits, but I wonder about the delusion that they represent. There is a lounging area where two women are feeding their babies. They radiate a fecund sanctity. Not much money has been spent on creating this resource; I imagine the coffee guy and his friend going out in a clapped-out van to collect the assorted lumber from skips.

Emily and I sit on a battered leather sofa; for a table we have a large fruit box, labelled: *Weald of Kent Apples*. I see that, behind the counter, which rests on two barrels, they sell health-giving organic fruit and vegetables and they are all set up with a yellowed Magimix to make smoothies. Instead of thinking, *How wonderful*, I think of the conspiratorial beliefs that have led to this dump.

'Great café,' says Emily. 'It's really become popular with the locals since you left.'

The locals are invoked to lend some moral weight to the place. There also seems to be an implication that my departure encouraged them to take care of their health by downing pomegranate and celery smoothies.

Emily's face has become thinner, even more Virginia Woolf-ish, her nose apparently longer and her eyes more distant from the action, so that she looks strangely like an icon. She has the aspect of a writer – serious, a little worried about where it's going, but also – I am reading way too much into this – the comfort of belonging to a superior caste, the writing caste, people who write about funny domestic misunderstandings, people who make up history, people who write about detectives who drink too much while still able to solve crimes, people who see pathos in autism, people who write about how to overcome sex addiction, people who write the autobiographies of sportsmen and sportswomen, people who wrote their own *Bildungsroman*, retired politicians who rewrite their careers, people who write about tasty ten-minute recipes, people who write about the failings of men, people who write celebrity novels, people who write comic novels, people who write spy novels, people who write epistolatory novels. And so on. Writing is still highly esteemed, even more so than reading.

Emily seems to be in a very good mood, made all the better by having the opportunity to demonstrate to me what I am missing.

'Where's the wedding, Emily?'

'Islington Town Hall in two weeks' time. I discussed it with

Freddie, but he felt it would be uncomfortable if you came. Sorry. Freddie is quite traditional; he's Anglo-Indian, by the way.'

'Good. No need to apologise. Mixed marriage is the future. How's the writing going?'

'Oh, it's going quite well. I've written nearly fifteen thousand words of my first draft.'

'Emily, on your climb up the greasy literary pole, are you finding that the precepts of your old chum from Sheffield, Edgar Gaylard, are helping?'

'God, you are such a bastard.'

'It wasn't me who went off and shagged a beardy literary man. You said you needed your personal space, remember?'

'Richie, I feel sorry for you. Are you OK?'

'As a matter of fact, I do have one or two things on my mind, yes, but our comic interlude in this organic toilet has cheered me up enormously.'

Emily grabs my arm. She speaks quietly but urgently.

'I brought you here because I wanted to tell you that two men appeared at the flat, saying they wanted to speak to you. They produced identity, which said they were from the Metropolitan Police, Special Operations. I told them that you hadn't lived here for some time. They wouldn't say what they wanted, but they said I should tell you if I saw you that you should contact them.'

'Did they say what it was about?'

I am alarmed.

'Just what I told you. Nothing more, but they seemed quite reasonable.'

'Did you give them my details?'

'I don't know any details.'

'My phone?'

'No, of course not.'

'I have to go, Em. I really do wish you all the best for your wedding. And I apologise.'

'What for?'

'For everything. Anything you can think of.'

'They gave me a card, a number for you to call.'

She retrieves it from her bag. It has a name: *Detective Sergeant Alandale, SO15*. My first thought is that I need to speak to Lettie.

'Bye, Em. Have a good one.'

'Good luck, Rich.'

I wonder if this luck to which she is referring is specifically in relation to the fact that two Special Branch officers are apparently looking for me, or if it contains a general assessment of my future. I turn as I go out: she is sitting there, against a sombre still life of leathery, pocked apples.

The exhibition in the British Museum is demonstrating the degree of integration that took place in the art of Outremer, in architecture, painting, and craft. Among a display of elaborate reliquaries is a True Cross reliquary on loan from the Church of the Holy Sepulchre, Barletta, Puglia. This cross fragment – there are thousands – is contained within an ornate box, finished in gold and silver, highly sophisticated work. It suggests to me that the Holy Cross carried by the four knights may have been housed in something similar, perhaps even more grand, made by the local Frankish craftsmen, who had been working in the Holy Land for over a hundred years.

Fulcher of Chartres, the chronicler of the First Crusade, wrote in 1124:

> *For we who were Occidentals have now become Orientals. He who was a Roman or a Frank has in this land been made into a Galilean or a Palestinian. We have already forgotten the places of our birth; already these are unknown to many of us and not remembered to many more.*

The most important article from the Scriptorium of the Holy Sepulchre is on display. It is the psalter of Queen Melisende of Jerusalem, probably made in 1138. Seven craftsmen are believed to have worked on it and the intricately carved ivory covers and the silk spine of the book are thought to be distinctly Western. It is a beauiful object.

When Jerusalem was captured after the catastrophic defeat on the Horns of Hattin in 1187 – and the Holy Cross was lost – Imad ad-Dinad-Isfahani wrote: *Jerusalem was purified of the hellish Franks*. Saladin had the Haram purified with rose water before he would enter. It was the end of a long period of Crusader dominance and the end of the golden age of Crusader art.

I see, if I need to be reminded, that art and its creation are a kind of affirmation – *Look, we exist*. There, in the blazing summer heat and the winter chill, amongst the alien rocks and parched hills, the former citizens of Reims and Chartres were proclaiming that they too were engaged in the work of humanity, to rise above the material world.

Strange, mad, noble and persistent.

I wish I could say that my mind is fully focused on these lofty thoughts, and their application to my, as yet, fledgling dissertation; instead I am wondering what the people from SO15 want to talk to me about. Am I obliged to get in touch with them? If they are the Met's counter-terrorist arm, what do they want with me? I am worried; I know from my reading that injustices happen daily: *Someone must have slandered Josef K, for, one morning, without having done anything truly wrong, he was arrested.*

I call Lettie from the train and ask her if she can speak to me urgently. She suggests the coffee shop at Blackwell's, and I tell her I will be there in just over an hour. I have read that spies often choose very crowded places to meet. Lettie has bagged a table near the windows overlooking Broad Street. I can just see two of the Roman emperors across the road.

'Hello, Richard.' We kiss rather unconvincingly. 'What a surprise. It's your turn to get the coffee by the way; mine's a double macchiato.'

'Anything to eat?'

'No, nothing, thanks.'

I order for myself a latte and a large round biscuit that looks as if it were fashioned in playschool. I need the comfort of a sugar rush.

'What's up?' Lettie asks.

'The usual. I have been researching my dissertation at the BM. It is interesting that in Palestine in the eleventh century, Byzantine and Western art were coming together, don't you think?'

'Gosh, I never knew that. Fascinating.'

'Lettie, I have something to ask you.'

'Shoot.'

'I don't know if this is the sort of question I should be asking you, but I was told that two men from SO15 are looking for me . . .'

I fumble in my pocket and hand her the card. She looks at it for a moment.

'SO15 is a branch of the Metropolitan Police. They make the arrests for the secret services.'

'Arrests?'

'That's their most public activity. They rush into houses before dawn, fully tooled up, and drag Muslims out of bed. It has to be said, they often get the wrong people and the wrong street.'

'What would they want with me?'

'It must be something to do with Noor's kidnap. Don't worry, they are also sent out on the street as information gatherers, to do routine police work.'

I see that she enjoys the higher intrigue.

'Do you think I should call them?'

'Yes, but give it a day and I will see what my contacts think might be going on in the investigation into the kidnappers and their links. Your name may have cropped up and you might have been put on the watch list as a result. You haven't joined the Oxford branch of Al-Qaeda without telling me, I hope?'

'Sorry, yes. It was that or Scientology, and I opted for the rational choice.'

'Very droll.'

'You told me once that Noor was a spy. Could that be it?'

'It may be that there are some details about just who she was working for that need to be confirmed. Or they may think that you, without even being aware of it, have information, what they call 'pocket litter'. By the way, you don't want these people to come into Ed's house. One will look for pocket litter while the other keeps you busy. To you, what's in your pocket or beside the bed is nothing, but to them a credit card transaction, a train ticket, these are dates which help them. Or it may be they want to talk to you about who paid the ransom, and why. Do you know?'

'No.'

'OK, let me ask a few questions before you call.'

I wonder what questions she is going to ask.

'Have you heard from Ed?' I ask.

'He sent me a postcard of a kookaburra sitting in the old gum tree and I had a text today. He is hoping to get the job after a good interview. By the way, he told me you have had a bad episode. I am sorry.'

'It wasn't great, but it only lasted a few days. Officially I had a syndrome brought on by stress. There was a lot going on and I couldn't cope; suddenly I flipped. Ed was an angel. I really owe him big time. Are you an item again? I hope so.'

'Yes, we are, although no thanks to you. He told me what you said by the way.'

'Oh shit. I am sorry. I really was ranting.'

'You probably did him a favour by discouraging him from continuing with his doctorate. It was making him miserable.'

I feel a sudden warmth for Lettie and I am glad that my unkind – although chemically induced – words didn't drive Ed and her apart. She is edging towards the first stages of middle age. Her neck is just a little wobbly, and there is a skein of tiny lines around her eyes, visible when she turns towards the light. There seems to be a moment when young women lose the bloom of youth. Men are given more latitude. This may be a scandalous inequality. I see Lettie, high-powered spook-academic, clever, successful, and with a taste for the higher mysteries. At the same time I see Lettie, the woman who is wondering if she will be fertile for much longer, desperate to be married to my old chum, Ed, so that she can bask in the warm currents of domesticity, even if she knows in advance that it will be unfulfilling.

When we step into Broad Street I embrace her. Across the road the Roman emperors are grimacing.

'Lettie, will you forgive me? And will you find out what you can?'

'You're forgiven. And yes, I will do what I can. I'll text you when I have anything and we should meet. Rich, don't worry about it; this is just about what they call *humint*, human intelligence, in covert operations. It's getting information from real people.'

I cross the quad and go to the Upper Reading Room. I try to imagine what might have happened to the small party of Richard's men when they left Arles for the Auvergne. I remind myself what Stephen Feuchtwanger said, that there can be profound truth in fiction. At the same time, real life seems to have found me, in the form of SO15. Already I am beginning to fear that I will be badly treated. They may cite my psychiatric episode and threaten to have me locked up. Or they may question me about Noor's background or our trip to Jordan.

25

Noor

Dearest, dearest Richie,

Thank you so much for your letter. About Moose Creek – no moose there any more, sadly. For your information, their favourite meal is aquatic plants.

I love to hear about our father. Maybe you and he didn't get on so well because of your mother. Do you think maybe you blamed him, without knowing the facts?

Rich, I am not saying that we should *never* meet again. But I don't think we can do it soon. I can't put a time on it, and that breaks my heart. I think the tragedy is that I won't ever get over you, which is what the counsellors and psychiatrists say I must do. My biggest worry is that you won't love me in my fragile state and that you won't be able to forget – talking of the impossibility of true forgetting – what happened to me. And this is before we try to come to terms with the fact that Room 6 is a thing of another time. We were shown heaven and then banished. I can't even begin to imagine how I could explain this to my adoptive father. It's all so, so unfair. The message from my shrink is that I have to start again and I have to find someone else. I don't want to find someone else: all I want is you. But then she goes on: if I tried to have a chaste (her words) relationship with you, it just wouldn't work and we would destroy what is so beautiful and innocent and we would deny ourselves children. By the way, only this one shrink knows the whole story.

Do I make sense? I am crying again. Look, just under the word 'again' is a large teardrop.

I am having physiotherapy every day and I am becoming stronger, physically. In my mind I am preparing to swim with you to that little island you mentioned, both of us singing 'Mamma Mia'. There is comfort in the cheesy.

Richie, please have patience, and please write to me about our father, as I have a lot of catching-up to do.

All my love, my darling,

Noor xxx

26

SO15

LETTIE IS MEETING me in the café in St Mary's Church. I once climbed the many steps winding up the inside of the steeple to a balcony from where you can see the whole of Oxford spread out before you. Way below, entering All Souls that day, I saw a procession to install a new vice-chancellor. Academic gowns flew in the breeze, exposing bright undersides, like the wings of tropical birds. I felt like Jude the Obscure then, gazing at the steeples and towers and ancient colleges, each one of which hid within its walls secret gardens, and I looked at the wooded hills beyond, and I was thinking that I would never fully belong.

The café is busy, in a measured kind of way. I know already just how the cappuccino will be: thin, weak, bubbly foam, sprinkled liberally with cocoa and watery coffee, which will taste as though it has already had a turn in the espresso machine. Of course the coffee will be sourced responsibly in some far-off land. The Church of England has abandoned souls for gesture politics.

I sit nervously for five minutes before Lettie arrives. Under her arm she carries a fat document folder. Is this about me?

'Hello, Richard.'

We kiss. She places the folder on the table ominously; the word 'brief' comes to mind.

'What would you like?'

She comes back with our coffee in rude mugs.

'Right. The boys in blue do want to talk to you. They just want you to tell them – by the way you don't have to tell them anything – what you know about Noor's background, and if she had any contacts with the UK, also if she had been targeted for kidnap or whether it was an entirely opportunistic job. When you do see them, don't do it at Ed's place or wherever, as they are inclined to have a little look around later.'

'You told me that. What do they want from me?'

'There is obviously something missing. Maybe they think you can fill in some details for them.'

'Like what?'

'Well for instance, what do you know about her covert work?'

'Nothing. I don't know anything.'

'Whatever you do, don't tell them any lies.'

I am beginning to wonder whose side she is on. Supposing they know that Haneen is her mother. That Noor is my sister? They would find that really interesting. And how plausible would it be that I had met my own, unknown, sister by chance in the famous Cellar Bar, nest of spies?

'So you think I should call Detective Sergeant whatsit to fix a time for a cosy chat?'

'Yes, I do.'

'And if he doesn't believe me?'

'Get a lawyer.'

I think of the lugubrious lawyer, Derek Cocks, who wore the brown suit with the cleverly camouflaged tie, and who presided over my signing of the sub-agreement. I don't think he will do.

'Lettie, the whole thing is absolutely crazy. I don't want to talk to SO15, whoever they are. I don't want to be part of this investigation. I don't want my life fucked over by these people. In fact I don't want to be dragged into it at all. I am not involved.'

'From what I have heard, I don't think they believe you are involved.'

'Lettie, tell me, how do you know details like that?'

'You asked me to find out, and I did. If you want my advice – which, can I remind you, you requested – talk to them, try not to become angry and tell them what you know.'

'What did Ed tell you about Noor and me?'

'Why?'

'Because I don't trust you any longer. You may already have given your contact all sorts of bits of information. You tell me how I am supposed to answer if they ask me how I met Noor. You know it was in the Cellar Bar in Jerusalem, you know that it is famous for clandestine meetings, spook central, and you know they aren't going to believe the truth, that I was staying there while researching for my fucking project on Crusader art, and that I met Noor by chance, and you know that I went to Jordan with Noor, and you know the reason they want to speak to me is that they want to discover if I am some sort of jihadi myself, or Noor's controller, and one with delusions to boot. Have you told them I was in the Warneford? Did you tell them that your lover took me there? That he has been talking to me, and passing it on to you, at least until he left for the land of the kookaburra? Did you warn me off meeting the plods at Ed's place for a reason, that it could have been embarrassing for you? You know what I think? I think you are a spook, not the pocket-litter type of spook of course, but the high-altitude, well-connected, *gosh isn't this exciting* type of spook. Am I right?'

'No, you are totally wrong and you are incredibly ungrateful, not only for what I have done, but especially for what Ed has done. Goodbye.'

She walks out of the café, composed, but rigid with anger. I sit frozen. If anybody has been watching this scene, they will think we have been having one of those lovers' arguments where the more injured party stands up and walks majestically away, leaving the other looking guilty and embarrassed, even if he or she is in the right and as blameless as a newborn lamb.

I am overwhelmed. The spooks want me and, for all the *Mamma Mia!* shtick, Noor has all but rejected me, and my five brave knights, who are supposed to make my name as the writer of an upmarket *The Da Vinci Code*, are stranded somewhere, both in my mind and in the region of the Puy-en-Velay in the Auvergne, now best known for its lentils. And Richard the Lionheart is still a prisoner, and becoming bitter:

> *Honte i avant por ma reancon*
> *Sui ça dues yvers pris.*
>
> *My friends will be shamed if for my ransom*
> *I am imprisoned for two winters.*

In Germany the negotiations drag on. Winter approaches.

I decide that I must speak to Detective Sergeant Alandale:
'Detective-Sergeant Alandale.'

'Hello. Yes, it's Richard Cathar here. I believe you wanted to speak to me.'

'Oh, yes, I've got it. We do want to speak to you. Thank you for calling. We would like a little help with an investigation. I am sure you understand. Can you meet us soon?'

'I'm in Oxford at the moment, doing research, but I could get to London tomorrow.'

'Thank you. Can we meet at your place? In Hackney?'

'It's not my place any more. What about in the British Museum, in the covered courtyard? I could be there at eleven. I'll wait for you at the bottom of the staircase.'

'OK. That sounds fine. I've got your mobile number now, so I'll call when I am at the museum.'

'Are you coming on your own?'

'Yes.'

'OK. I look forward to meeting you, but I have to warn you I don't know anything much about what happened in Cairo.'

'I am sure you can help us.'

The sun is shining through the grid of the clear roof, so that it creates a geometric pattern on the stone floor below. I am early. I am wearing my suit. I want to be sure that there isn't back-up hanging about. I imagine the back-up will look different from the tourists and I will be able to spot them. I half believe that they will arrest me on some grounds, perhaps as an encouragement to get me to talk. I feel as though it may be obvious that I have guilty secrets, and sex with my half-sister is the one I least want to talk about to Detective Sergeant Alandale.

When he arrives, I pick him out immediately. He's wearing casual clothes, a windcheater and jeans, but it's obvious he is a little uneasy: he is off his turf. My phone rings.

'Morning, I'm standing just at the bottom of the steps.'

'I see you.'

He is about fifty, with a congealed face, like ice floes backing up; his cheeks are encroaching on his eyes from beneath, and his fore-head is encroaching from above, so that eventually he will be snow-blind.

'Morning, Mr Cathar. Thank you very much for helping us, sir.'

I attribute the 'sir' to the suit.

'Morning, I'll do my best.'

'Can't say fairer than that.'

'No.'

There is nothing in the formalities to worry me yet. But I have the feeling that I have strayed into genre fiction. I am never sure how to pronounce 'genre'. Is it French, all eliding together, which sounds pretentious, or is it 'john-re', which is clumsy? As we walk to the café with its long communal tables, I ponder the idea that you could divide all your experiences into literary genres. This would be a thriller. I have never liked thrillers, because the authors withhold information improbably.

Alandale takes his coffee long and white. Not too strong. He takes out a notebook and a pen.

'Right, this is very informal. These notes are only to remind me of what we have discussed. But first, I have to tell you formally that I am Detective Sergeant Wayne Alandale of the Metropolitan Police's special operations department, SO15.'

'Can I ask you what you do?'

'We do police work around possible terrorist acts. At the moment we are trying to help our colleagues in Canada, who want to know about your relationship to the woman who was kidnapped in Cairo, Ms Noor Nassashibi, a Canadian citizen.'

'Well, I was in Jerusalem researching – I am writing a dissertation funded by my Oxford college – and I met Noor in a hotel, the American Colony. We met a few more times after that and a relationship developed.'

'Are you engaged to her, as our colleagues in Ottawa believe?'

I wonder if Mr Macdonald, or Lettie, has been behind this interview.

'Yes. Informally, a week or so before she left for Cairo. She hadn't told her parents, as far as I know, and I don't have a family to tell. Obviously, we will have to consider everything when her treatment is complete. As you know, she was badly treated by her kidnappers.'

'I didn't know. I am sorry. Did you have any other contacts in Israel?'

'No, apart from a Father Prosper Dupuis at the French Bible School. He helped me – he's still helping me – with my research.'

'Can I just check the spelling of Dupuis?'

I tell him.

'And do you know' – he reads uncertainly from his notes – 'a Mrs Haneen Husayni?'

'Yes. She knew my father many years ago, and I was introduced to her by Father Dupuis.'

'Were you aware when you met Ms Nassashibi that she was an agent?'

'No. I thought she was a journalist. I don't know anything about any other activities, even now.'

'Did she ask you to do any errands for her, or deliver letters, or send email for her?'

'No.'

'And can you tell me why you and Ms Nassashibi went to Jordan?'

'I was looking at castles and we took a break.'

'Castles. Are there castles in Jordan?'

'Yes, there are. Crusader castles.'

'I see, and why were you looking at Crusader castles?'

'This may be a bit boring, but it was because in the eleventh, twelfth and thirteenth centuries these castles were built by the Crusaders, mostly by the Franks, that is, French-speaking. At the time, by the way, that included the English. They brought their own art and religious books and ideas of architecture with them and in effect the whole of what is now Jordan, Lebanon, Palestine, Israel and Syria became the Kingdom of Jerusalem. It is also known as the Latin Kingdom. Anyway, my particular interest is in how these cultures – the Muslim, the Byzantine and the Christian – drew one from the other. I warned you it would be boring.'

'Very interesting, actually. But why would you look at castles for that?'

'Because castles are durable and they contain architecture and art. The churches have different styles over the years – Byzantine, Romanesque, Gothic – and there are even some frescos still visible. After the fall of Jerusalem in 1187, Richard the Lionheart . . .'

'Three lions on his chest.'

'That's him, Richard the Lionheart arrived on Crusade and defeated Saladin, but he could never capture Jerusalem.'

'Wasn't he gay, by the way?'

'Who?'

'Richard the Lionheart.'

'Probably not.'

'All right, so you and Ms Nassashibi went sightseeing in Jordan. Did she speak to anybody or meet anybody during that time?'

'No.'

'Not a Mr Hasad al-Sayid?'

'I think he was the owner of a shop, selling antiquities. He tried to sell us something.'

'What was the exact relationship between Ms Nassashibi' – he glances at his notes – 'and Mrs Haneen Husayni? Am I pronouncing that correctly?'

'Yes, I think you are. Mrs Husayni was always referred to as the aunt of Noor Nassashibi. Her father in Toronto is Mrs Husayni's brother.'

'You said your father knew her?'

'Yes, he met her in the seventies. I think I said that my father knew Father Prosper Dupuis.'

'You did. Did you know that Mrs Husayni has bought an apartment in London?'

'Yes, I did. But I am not sure why this is your business if you don't mind my saying so.'

'I am just here to gather background information. Do you know why she bought a flat in Knightsbridge?'

'It's in Kensington, I think. I imagine – I really don't know – that she felt the time had come to have an alternative home.'

'I see. Why had the time come?'

'I think it was mainly a religious thing. She and her family are Christians, a very old sect, going back to a time before the Crusades, but I think she feels that Christians are increasingly under pressure in the Middle East.'

'Have you had political discussions with Mrs Husayni?'

'We have talked about all sorts of things.'

'And she never mentioned Mossad to you?'

'No, I don't think so. Not specifically, anyway.'

'Did she ever suggest to you that Islamist groups were targeting her or her niece?'

'No. Look, I am sorry but I don't want to speculate about things that I don't really know anything about. Mrs Husayni was very kind to me when I was working in Jerusalem. We talked a lot – she helped me with the art particularly. She's very knowledgeable. But also, as I am sure you know from your line of work, you can never fully know the mind of another.'

'No, I think that would be true. Did she ever tell you about threats to her life?'

'No. Still no.'

I remember Lettie's warning about not becoming angry.

'And has Ms Nassashibi been in touch since she was flown back to Canada?'

'No. As I understand it from her aunt, she is not well enough and her doctors have suggested that it would be very upsetting for her to see me or write to me. Possibly because she wouldn't want me to see her in this condition.'

'Have you ever considered the possibility that she was using you as cover?'

'Do you know something I don't?'

'No, I am just collecting detail for a fuller picture.'

'No, I don't believe I was used as cover.'

We seem to have been talking for a very long time, when Alandale finally closes his notebook.

'Thank you, Mr Cathar. Your cooperation is greatly appreciated. Do you know that I have never been in this beautiful building before. Correction, I have been to the museum on a school trip from South London to look at the mummies, but that was long before this was built. It was all black and sooty then.'

'Will you want to speak to me again?'

'I would never say never, but it's not likely. If you have any information that you think might help us, or you wake up one morning and you remember something you didn't tell me, please give me a call.'

He gets up a little stiffly and shakes my hand. I have the feeling that he has left a threat on the air. And I am conscious that I have told him a few lies. Perhaps that is what they want.

27

Richie

DEAREST NOOR,

I have had an intimation of what life must have been like for you; I was contacted by the Special Branch (they have a new name) to 'help them with some background'. The man who interviewed me asked about you and Haneen and about our trip to Jordan. The picture he was building up is of some sort of complicity, involving me and Haneen and even the man in the antiquities shop in Kerak City. I told him about my friendship with Father Prosper, and then I wondered if that was a good idea. Who knows what his involvement has been? I don't trust anybody now, and I wish I hadn't spoken to this man, but I was advised by someone (I don't trust her either) that I should speak to him. I have nothing to hide, yet I found myself becoming evasive and telling lies, or at least not giving him the whole truth, and I feel somehow guilty.

I don't know how you could have lived this life of deception and ambiguity. What I wanted to ask you, and please answer me truthfully, is whether you were using me for some reason. That is what the man I spoke to, first name Wayne, was suggesting. As I remember our first meeting, I saw you and I couldn't help myself. I smiled at you because you were so lovely that I was unable to do anything else. If you arranged that, please explain how you did it.

All my love,
Rich xxxx

28

Auvergne, April 1193

THE BISHOPS OF *Le Puy-en-Velay have a history of crusading: Bishop Adhemar de Monteil carried the Holy Lance into battle in the First Crusade. He died of typhus in the Holy Land, revered for his evident spirituality and bravery. The present Bishop, Aimard, was a shrewd and ambitious man. He was aware that while Richard was in captivity the whole region was in the balance. If he were known to have helped Richard's knights, who could say what might happen if Richard were never released, and his brother John and Philip of France or the Viscount of Limoges claimed the territory? Or if the Count of Toulouse or the Count of Angoulême became the sovereign lord? All of them would be likely to make a claim to the Auvergne. But the Bishop could not refuse the request of the Grand Master of the Templars to receive these men returning from the Holy Land, so his solution to a difficult political problem was to hide Richard's knights from view in a remote abbey belonging to the bishopric until they could be moved on.*

Henry of Huntingdon and his men were housed on the edge of a deep valley, near the headwaters of the Loire. The long days were unnaturally quiet; at night wolves howled. Only Roger de Saci was happy. He took his falcon out every day and she adapted very quickly to this wooded land, with its great stretches of open fields and deep forests, a landscape utterly different from the arid hills of the Holy Land. Huntingdon had conversations with the Bishop, never failing to remind him that his uncle had been the Master of the Templars in England. It seemed that the Bishop was waiting for confirmation of the release of King Richard, which was rumoured to have been agreed. His explanation was that it would be too dangerous for the knights to move towards Limoges, where the Viscount was favouring the uneasy alliance of Philip and John. Huntingdon understood: they were hostages until the Bishop had seen the writing on the wall. The Bishop made it clear that he wanted his hospitality and care to be noted, if Richard were to be released, and he wanted it rewarded. He also made it clear that they could not leave without his approval.

Huntingdon felt the weight of delay pressing on his shoulders. He had no secure means of passing a message to Hubert Walter, who was said to be in Angevin, travelling tirelessly to encourage Richard's vassals to remain loyal, assuring them that Richard would be released soon. He had the Pope's and the Emperor's personal promise.

Now Huntingdon could wait no longer. He found it intolerable that he, who had fought the infidel and escaped death many times, should be held up by this minor bishop in a godforsaken corner of the world, a man made greedy for enrichment and fearful of reprisals. They would leave with or without the Bishop's blessing, and without his escort. The Bishop had a small contingent of spies among the monks, and the knights only spoke of their plans when they were out in the woods hunting or exercising their horses.

Huntingdon invited the Bishop to speak to him: he said that he wished, as an act of gratitude, to show the Bishop the treasure they were carrying. Huntingdon wore his surplice and his soft boots of deer-skin to welcome the Bishop. He took the key from a pouch that hung from his neck and unlocked the sliding bolt of the chapel and pushed open the door. Fully armed, William de l'Étang, Raoul de Mauléon, Bartholomew de Mortemer, Roger de Saci and Master Robert waited for the Bishop in the locked vestry off the chapel where the cross was kept in its gold-and-silver-banded cruciform reliquary.

'In here, my lord Bishop, is the sacred relic. Pray go ahead.'

Roger de Saci emerged from the deep shadows and seized the Bishop's arms from behind, as Raoul de Mauléon closed and locked the door. The Bishop was forced into a large oak chair. When he was securely tied to the chair, William de l'Étang lifted his episcopal robes and Roger de Saci produced his dagger – the same one he used for feeding his falcon – and expertly made a small incision in the Bishop's scrotum. The Bishop screamed, as a thin stream of blood fell onto the chair and the floor.

'My lord Bishop,' said Huntingdon, 'be silent. To hear you squealing like a pig is of no consequence to us. We have seen thousands of men mortally wounded who behaved with more courage than you at the moment of their death. You are a snivelling poltroon, a traitor, a worm, looking for advantage while our sovereign lord, the noble King Richard, who took the cross and defeated the infidel, is in captivity, in defiance of all the covenants safeguarding those who take the cross. His captors have been excommunicated by the Holy Father and yet you, a cleric of no standing, ignoring your pope, have reached well above yourself in asking for payment and by attempting to hold us here, we who are on the King's and God's sacred business. If you wish to retain the ownership of your testicles, swear now before God that you will aid our departure in the direction of Limousin and swear that you will repent of trying to obstruct God's work. This is your only hope of salvation. You should be ashamed of yourself: instead of behaving like a Christian, you have been plotting against our sire, Richard, whose prowess against the infidel exceeded, as the jongleurs testify, that of Roland at Roncevaux. Do you swear, before we make a eunuch of you?'

'I swear, by almighty God,' the Bishop said. He was sweating and trembling, and his words emerged as a thin falsetto.

Huntingdon produced a piece of parchment. The Bishop signed. Huntingdon saw that his damp face was as white as a woman's breast. Perhaps he was losing too much blood. Fortunately Master Robert was standing by with a pot of vinegar; now he doused the wound *liberally. The Bishop screamed again. He was taken to a sparse guest room and locked in. In the very early morning, well before first light, Huntingdon and his comrades, led by a guide they had enlisted at a remote farmstead, rode out in the direction of Limousin with five spare horses tethered to the cart.*

The fact that Huntingdon's men set out for Limousin is supported by a note in the rolls of the cathedral of St-Pierre in Poitiers: Master Robert, the rolls record, has arrived from the direction of Limoges, having come home from the Holy Land. He has returned the Crusader cross he has worn for four years to the Bishop of Poitiers, as a token that he has fulfilled his vows to God. The Bishop blessed him.

No more is known of the rest of the party, except for the sad story of Henry of Huntingdon, who was killed on his own lands two months after the Feast of St John, when his horse fell and crushed him.

29

Ella

ED HAS EMAILED me from Australia. He has been offered the job, and he has taken it. He says that Lettie was very upset because I had told her I didn't trust her. He suggests that I should apologise; if I don't it will be difficult to have me living in his house. He is, he says, going to rent it out anyway now that he is living in Perth: *keeping a base in the old UK in case the job goes tits-up.*

I picture good-natured Ed in Australia. I see him hot and russet on the beach wearing his flowery Vilebrequin cozzie. He is worrying about the Great Whites, but also worried that he has offended me. He is very sensitive about upsetting anyone and perhaps that is why his career in hedge funds came to a premature end. In Perth – a town, I once read, that is full of white cockatiels flying down the main street – he will want to settle this rift immediately; I email him right away.

> *Ed, all I can tell you is that Lettie seems to know an awful lot about Noor and her kidnap. For better or for worse, she was advising me on what I should do. The whole business has made me oversensitive, a little paranoid, and I am worried about having another episode. You can't imagine – or perhaps you can – how awful it is to lose control of your self. In your rational mind you know what to do, but you simply can't do it. I am terrified it will happen again. But I will apologise to Lettie.*

I have been seeing Ella, informally, and she is a great help. Forgive me, Ed, and congratulations on your job. Perhaps I can come and visit you in Perth and we can wear one of those hats with the corks when we are downing a few tinnies. You need to learn the lingo fast, mate. Talking of sharks, I read about a graffito near a beach in South Africa: Great Sharks Eat Whites.

I have been having sex with Ella, despite my good intentions. She is still troubled – even paranoid – about the consequences of being seen with me. Our relationship is unstable because of her anxiety. She has an urgent need for sex; her husband's infidelity has left her with the fear that nobody desires her, and having sex with me is helping her over this fear, and helping her to catch up on her due quota. While Ed has been away I have been meeting her at his house most evenings. We have a drink, we kiss, and then she takes her clothes off and places them neatly on a chair. Her eyes turn inwards, so that she looks like a blind seer, and she moans. I think of Noor. I don't make comparisons.

Ella comes to me with a faint scent of the hospital, which reminds me that I am not in Jerusalem. This clinging hospital aroma is the smell of death. All the more reason to think of Noor in the scented, golden, historical, ancient light of Jerusalem. In my mind, *in medias res*, I am fucking Noor, struggling to hold on to her.

When Ella comes, she cries, a brief Freudian squall, bringing relief to the parched sexual prairie, and she clings to me, sometimes almost strangling me, for a moment or two and I feel trapped both in a headlock and in a terrible lie. In the past I have spoken to close friends about imagining sex with someone other than the person you are having sex with. It was surprising how many said they did it often. The strange thing is that I am very fond of Ella and I think she is almost beautiful, but at a certain level – the atomic level, perhaps – I don't find her sexually attractive. I can't explain it, but some small tics, some aspects of her body, some of the things she says, small turns of phrase, cause me to resent her, as if she is trying to take Noor's place, and I can only regain my equilibrium (and the necessary ardour) by thinking of Noor, moist and golden. If I never see Noor again, this will be the image that will for ever remain in my mind.

I long to capture the ecstasy of Room 6 and I am always disappointed. Ella talks calmly and sensibly afterwards, before rushing to her empty house to turn on the lights, making sure that she is seen there. By whom, she never tells me, but I assume it is by medical and psychiatric people: health professionals.

So Ella and I are on different tacks; she is recovering her self-esteem, which requires me to be sexually ardent, and I require the comfort of human intimacy.

I am taking refuge in the Bodleian, although I am moving back to London to stay in Haneen's apartment as she is in Jerusalem for the next few months. I feel that I must write, and Haneen's flat is so bland, so detached from life, that I imagine it will be perfect. Yesterday I explained to Ella that I had to go back to London, and she cried.

'Why do you have to go now?'

'I have to deliver my dissertation and I need the British Library.'

'It looks as if you are trying to get away from me.'

'No, I am not, believe me. You've helped me in so many ways.'

I have the familiar feeling that I have disappointed Ella, only the latest in a line. It weighs on my spirits.

'I've helped you, but now you want to go?'

'I do want to go. Ed's going to rent this place and it won't be available. Anyway, you don't want me to come to yours, which I understand. But because you are terrified of being seen in public with me, I am finding it difficult. I need a period of peace to write and to sort things out.'

'So I am dispensable.'

'Ella, please, don't do this. You're wonderful, but there is a cloud hanging over both of us: you still love your husband, and I love Noor. You know as well as I do, probably better, that this has been a kind of interlude.'

'I could love you, I'm sure.'

We were lying in my bed almost naked; the light of Jericho outside the windows was feeble, enervated, dismal.

'Ella, this isn't the real thing. You know that.'

'Do I?'

'I think you do.'

'Maybe I do. Maybe I should have realised sooner that it is one way only with you, that you are a taker.'

She turned away from me and hid her face in a pillow. I felt for her and at the same time I was resentful; I saw myself as innocent, but still it was obvious that I was contributing to her unhappiness.

'I wish you had never kissed me,' she said, muffled by linen.

'I was mad then.'

'And I am mad now.'

When she was gone I felt terrible unease. I don't want to be the agent of anyone's unhappiness, but it seemed to me unfair that after having sex with her in a therapeutic spirit I should have been declared the guilty party by a tribunal of one. In our encounters I had never felt ecstasy. I made love to her diligently; I ran through the whole repertoire, the whole rigmarole, and all the time I was fully conscious, detached. She wanted me to say I loved her, but I couldn't. It would have been better if I could have lied convincingly; many people like the company of implausible flatterers. But also there was something I could not have told Ella, that having sex with her made me think of what I had tried to avoid – Noor being gang-raped – and that squeezed my heart so painfully that I feared it would stop.

Noor was right, it would never be forgotten; it would rise to the surface like the leisurely and odorous exhalations from the depths of a stagnant pond.

I lie in the bed, the sheets definitely in need of a visit to the laundry in Walton Street, while the miserable unrelenting rain taps on the dirty window with soft persistence.

Maybe I should go to sunny Perth and take my chances with the Great Whites. Maybe I should give up this task of writing an account of Richard the Lionheart and the True Cross, and get on with my dissertation. I want to get to the essence of Richard I, but I only understand medieval monarchs via Shakespeare, just as everything I know about Russia comes from Russian novels. My father saw historical figures as his confidants, who were talking to him about many important subjects, such as the spirit of a nation.

I was thinking about these things earlier, as Ella straddled me, holding my hands and rocking feverishly back and forth, like a child on a playground horse. As it happens, I don't know much about children either.

30

Noor

DEAREST RICHIE,

First, I just want to assure you that you were not used in any way by me. In fact it was against the rules for me to have a relationship with you at all. As you said in your letter, you smiled at me, and I thought like what a lovely smile and how good-looking you were. And the rest is history. It really was a *coup de foudre*, as we say in Montreal.

I don't really know why your guys would be questioning you. As you said, you have nothing to hide.

I am feeling a little down today, because I am having another operation tomorrow. By the time you get this, I will have had it, hopefully the last. Something didn't quite work out as the doctors believed it would. There is nothing I can do except try to be patient. I will be in hospital for about four or five days.

If you trust me – which I know you do – you will believe that I didn't use you as cover or in any other way.

Look after yourself, my dearest brother and lover, and I know we will be together in the not too distant future. I am clinging to that hope.

All my love, and then some more,

Noor xxxx

31

The Devil is Loose

LOOK TO YOURSELF – *the devil is loose.*
     King Philip Augustus of France, to Prince John, brother of King Richard.

John is becoming desperate as Richard's release date approaches. He fears being hanged for treason. In many people's opinion, he deserves it. He makes agreements that cede most of Normandy, his brother's duchy, to Philip. He recognises Angoulême's claim to be independent of Aquitaine, his brother's other duchy, and he surrenders key castles all over the place. He is so desperate to oust his brother that he is trying to bribe Richard's vassals, at the expense of all that his father and his brother have achieved. Nobody trusts him. Philip despises him, but he needs to work with him.

When the Emperor announces that Richard will be released on the 24th of January, Philip and John jointly offer him £1,000 a month for as long as he keeps Richard in captivity. They have an alternative offer too: 80,000 marks to hold him for the rest of the year, when the campaigning season will have closed – and they will have consolidated their gains – or 150,000 marks to surrender Richard to them. The Emperor postpones the release, possibly to consider these offers. He orders a conclave in Mainz for the 2nd of February. Eleanor, Richard's doughty mother, arrives to bring her considerable political nous to bear on this meeting. She loves Richard: a German chronicler describes

Richard as the son Eleanor loved most particularly. Two of his closest advisers, Archbishop Walter of Rouen and former Chancellor, William de Longchamp, have hastened to be at his side. A number of Rhineland princes also support Richard: he has spent his time in captivity assiduously making alliances. The Emperor sets a final demand: that the Kingdom of England should be made over to him, although it will be ruled by Richard as a fief. After a tense meeting, Eleanor persuades Richard to accept this demand. She understands that nobody in England will take much notice of a formality, but it will allow Henry VI, whose empire is relatively meagre for an emperor, to puff himself up.

As is the custom, Richard leaves behind hostages: the Archbishop of Rouen, a son of King Sancho of Navarre – brother of his neglected wife, Berengaria – and one of his most trusted knights, Baldwin of Béthune. In the event they aren't held long.

All this has come about because Richard was blown, fortuitously, onto the Emperor's shores. Finally, on 4 February 1194, he releases Richard and the devil is indeed loose. The lord of St Michael's Mount, won over to John, dies of fright when he hears the news.

Richard has been working on alliances, preparing for this day, and now he sets off for the Lowlands to enlist more support on the way home. A huge fleet is waiting at Antwerp to take him to England. He arrives finally at Sandwich on the 25th of February. Jubilation seizes the country as he embarks on a royal progress, crown on head, wearing his white Crusader cloak with its red cross. His first stop is the shrine at Canterbury and after that he moves on to Bury St Edmunds. His manner is typically gracious.

As the Cistercian Abbot, Ralph de Coggeshall, writes:

No tribulation could cloud the countenance of this most serene prince. His words remained cheerful and jocund, his actions fierce or most courageous as time, peace, reason or person demanded.

John, for all his brother's cheery countenance, is terrified, and stays on the other side of the Channel, well away from his brother, although he desperately wants reassurance about his future. Richard believes in the notion of honour – pretz – which requires forgiveness for high-ranking enemies, if not for the lower-ranking. John has his hopes pinned on his brother's chivalric nature.

Some months before, Richard's right-hand man, Hubert Walter, set in motion the recapture of the few castles in England still holding out for John. Nottingham Castle is now the only one still defiant. It takes a visit to the scene from the Lionheart himself to finish the job. He arrives, wearing a light coat of mail. He is announced with a fanfare of trumpets and horns. The defenders believe it is a ruse. They scoff, tapping their noses knowingly: bottled up in the castle, they have clearly been a little out of touch with current affairs. Richard, characteristically, takes part in the siege, surrounded by men with large shields. The defenders are driven into the keep as night falls. In the morning, just in case they misunderstand his intentions, Richard orders gallows erected and has some prisoners hanged in full view. He is a great believer in the persuasive effect of public execution; it concentrates the mind. He also orders that some Greek Fire should be ostentatiously prepared, and he has a captive brought to him.

'Well, what can you see? Is it me?' he asks the terrified man, who is sent back into the keep.

When it is reported to the defenders by the captive that King Richard is indeed here, right outside in fact, they immediately agree to surrender. It's all over in less than two days.

With time on his hands – it's like a cricket match that ends unexpectedly – Richard makes his one and only excursion to Sherwood Forest, which he is curious to see. None of the chroniclers who note Richard's movements in detail over the next few days reports a meeting with Robin Hood, or Robin Hod, or the Green Man, but somewhere in the depths of the race memory this brief trip is lodged, to be pulled up like a bucket in a well to be commingled with the legend of Robin Hood.

Although Richard never met Robin Hood, and although the Sheriff of Nottingham never fought a duel with Robin Hood, these encounters are half real in many minds. No king of England, excepting perhaps the legendary Arthur, has entered the national mythology so deeply. Richard's return after his exploits in the Holy Land and his unjust captivity have made him a figure of veneration in England. A public procession in Winchester, the King in full regalia, with two swords carried before him and a collection of earls, knights and barons behind, becomes a near mystical occasion, watched by thousands.

The huge nineteenth-century equestrian statue of Richard, by Carlo Marochetti, outside the Houses of Parliament, depicts him as the embodiment of national pride. Two bas-reliefs show the capture of Ascalon and Richard pardoning Bertran de Born, once a rebel and an acclaimed troubadour. The message to Victorians is clear: to be English is to embrace bravery and compassion.

As soon as he could, Richard moved to the new port at Portsmouth to be ready to sail for Normandy to begin the difficult task of regaining his lost territories. He is reported to have been impatient to get on with it. His chancellor, the more than capable Hubert Walter, was left in charge. Walter knew that the knights had hidden their tesaur; he may not have known exactly where that was. But Henry of Huntingdon was dead and the other knights were dispersed.

The fleet was delayed by bad weather; characteristically, Richard decided to set sail in his great ship. At the end of the day he was forced to turn back. His fleet finally left harbour a week later. He was a man of the warm south of Provençal song and sunburnt mirth. London was on the cold periphery of his orbit. He was to spend most of his remaining time in Normandy and Anjou.

When he landed at Barfleur he was welcomed riotously; there was dancing in the street and drinking and calls for the death of the French King. For all that, Richard had a nearly impossible task ahead of him if he wanted to restore his lands in full. It may be that he regretted taking the cross to leave his territories exposed.

The major thrust by Philip came from the north-east of Normandy, where the crucial Castle of Gisors had been handed over to Philip by a nervous castellan. It was only thirty-two miles from Rouen, and massively fortified.

Further south in Aquitaine, the Count of Anjou and many others were in revolt against Richard. These were the people he reproached in his song, 'Ja Nus Hons Pris: mi home et mi baron – Ynglois, Normant, Poitevin et Gascon'. He was obsessed with bringing them all back into line, and was determined to teach them that retribution would be swift and terrible and was inevitable after their treachery, a treachery made worse by the fact that they had broken God's law in attacking the lands of someone who had taken the cross.

During Richard's weather delay, Philip had attacked the Castle of Verneuil, his last great opportunity before Richard reached Normandy. But John, his brother, had decided to change sides. He rushed to Lisieux where Richard was staying overnight soon after landing, and threw himself at his brother's feet and begged forgiveness. Richard gave it to him – generously, those present recalled. He said to his brother, 'Don't be afraid, John, you are a child. You have got into bad company and it is those who have led you astray who will be punished.' John was twenty-seven.

John of Alençon, Richard's host, told John forthrightly that he had been treated far better by his brother than he would have treated Richard in similar circumstances. He added that John was sans desert – not worthy.

Already, propelled by the sheer terror Richard aroused, the tide was turning. Philip was beginning to vacillate. He retreated from Verneuil, Richard took it, and in the process captured all Philip's artillery. In turn he kissed every man of the garrison, which had held out. Philip continued sporadic attacks, even threatening Rouen, but Richard quickly captured three important castles. He was doing what he did best, undermining and taking castles; he was an expert after more than twenty years in the field. But perhaps just as important was the knowledge of his ruthlessness and bravery; the rebels were considering their positions carefully.

At his swashbuckling best, Richard took the castle of Loches by storm in just one day. Touraine was his again. Now Richard set out for Vendôme, the key to Aquitaine. Philip rushed to stop him, but when he heard that Richard lay immediately ahead, thirsting for a decisive battle, he turned and fled. Richard, with the help of his chief of staff, Mercadier – in effect a mercenary – who provided him with fresh horses, galloped after Philip. Richard had offered Philip single combat to the death, but Philip knew his limitations. Richard caught up with the army, but somehow Philip managed to escape. Richard was reported to be disappointed, déçu. Nothing would have pleased him more than to make Philip pay for his duplicity and treachery with his death. But he had the consolation of capturing the immense French wagon train that supplied Philip's travelling court. Richard had a childish delight in taking other people's supplies and other people's money. He viewed what he had captured: hundreds of war and draft horses, siege engines, the royal archives, which contained many names of people prepared to give their loyalty to Philip. He also took possession of huge amounts of Philip's treasure.

Mercadier was another who had sailed with Richard to the Holy Land, but when news reached him that Philip, breaking his public oath to Richard, had started to invade his lands, Richard sent Mercadier back to defend his empire. When he returned from captivity, Mercadier was always at his side. Richard had the highest possible regard for him, and rewarded him with the lands of some of his rebellious vassals, which included an estate of the Viscount of Limoges.

32

Kensington

HANEEN IS RIGHT; it's not difficult to become used to luxury.
I am quickly at home under the flattering urbanity of the Rothko
prints and soothed by the view of the park and kept perfectly warm
by the air which seems to come from vents in the floor in response
to my unspoken needs. Sometimes I see the Household Cavalry
passing through the park on their huge black horses. I think of the
Templars and Richard's knights riding through Arles. You don't get
pageantry in Hackney, but then in Hackney you might be in
another country. This seems to be a characteristic of world cities,
and probably always has been, that not far from wealth there is
often grinding poverty.

Here, everything is controlled and groomed: lawns, trees,
window boxes (now showing daffodils and early tulips) and in the
corner of my vision there is an artful drift of crocus, pale lavender
or purple; these colours come first, before the yellows and whites.
Here, the window frames are all painted and so many layers of
white paint have been applied to the stucco over the years that in a
certain light the rows of grand houses look as if they have been
iced. Dogs walk the streets towards the park on leads. There are no
Rottweilers or psycho bull terriers. Here they go in for amiable
breeds like Labradors or small, neurotic dogs, like dachshunds. In
the cold weather these little creatures trot along wearing a coat just
in case they should become distressed, or even slightly put out.

Some of them refuse to walk at all when faced by a puddle and then they are picked up and carried comfortably under the arm, as if they are baguettes. They sail complacently along above the ground. I am thinking happily about these things when my phone rings.

'Good morning, is that Richard Cathar?'

'Yes.'

'Are you able to take a call from Lord Huntingdon?'

'Absolutely.'

'All right, I am putting you through.'

'Richard, hello. How are you?'

'I'm fine, thank you. Are you well?'

'Probably as well as can be expected at my age. Look, I have two things I want to tell you. One is that I have found another box of papers collected by my grandfather, and there is one manuscript, which seems to be in ancient French. It was in the old tack room. I thought you might want to look at it. Would you be interested?'

'I would love to see it.'

'I can't make head or tail of it, but there is something about "*croiz*", spelled c-r-o-i-z, which must mean "cross". There is also the word "*yglise*", that would be "*église*" in French, I would imagine.'

I try to hide my excitement.

'Do you have a copy of it?'

'Ah, I am ahead of you. I do. Can you come round to my London house to have a look at it? I don't want to take the risk of sending it to you.'

'Understood.'

'Right, come round for supper. I have a pie from the Ginger Pig and some good claret, which goes well with it. Seven thirty. I also have something else to ask you, but we will save that for later. My secretary will email you the address. Venetia is in Argentina, so it will be just the two of us.'

There is something wonderfully cheering about Huntingdon; he has an unstoppable good humour, as though his life has been a long succession of treats. Which it probably has. My dictionary tells me that a tack room is 'a store for bridles, saddles and harness, usually in the stable block'.

Richard's movements after his release are covered in some detail. From 1194 to 1196 he waged war almost without pause. Although he had humiliated Philip and taken a number of his castles, there was still a threat from the north-east: the heavily fortified castles on the Seine, in the area known as the Vexin, were still in Philip's hands. Crucially, these castles commanded the routes to Dieppe and Rouen. Philip's tactic now was to encourage and finance rebellion in the south to divert Richard from the Vexin. But by 1196, although it was clear that Richard had secured almost all his territories, the Vexin was the key to successs, and it was still in Philip's hands, so that he was in effect winning the war for the north-east of Normandy.

Richard decided that he would secure his position for ever by building an enormous castle on the Seine; he appropriated the Manor of Andely from his ally, the Bishop of Rouen, who was furious; he had been a hostage held by the Emperor to guarantee payment of Richard's ransom. But nothing would stop Richard: with the labour of thousands of men, he built Château Gaillard, the best fortified castle in Europe, in just two years. The Castle of the Rock – *Castrum de Roka* – was protected by the river and was set on a ninety metre-high promontory, with a stockade across the river. He spent an unheard-of sum of money, greater than the expenditure on all the castles of England at that time. It was an astonishing feat, driven by Richard's determination to make his Normandy safe. He supervised all the work and he brought his knowledge of siege machines to bear, so eliminating 'dead angles', sections of the walls vulnerable to attack because they were out of sight from the battlements; the castle was encircled by a curvilinear wall. He also commissioned fast, shallow-draft boats which could bring supplies up quickly and safely. Richard had learned in the field that supplies and reserves win battles.

The great English chronicler, William of Newburgh (Newbury), reports:

At that place, while this great undertaking was in progress, a wonderful event is related to have happened. For, as some not ignoble persons – who assert that they were present themselves aver – in the month of May, a little before the solemnities of the Lord's Ascension, as the King drew near, and urged on the work (for he came frequently to point out and hurry its completion, and took great pleasure in beholding its advancement), suddenly a shower of rain mixed with blood fell, to the astonishment of all the bystanders who were present with the King, as they observed drops of real blood upon their garments, and feared that so unusual an occurrence might portend evil: but the King was not dismayed at this, nor did he relax in promoting the work in which he took so great delight, that (unless I am mistaken), if even an angel from heaven had persuaded him to desist, he would have pronounced anathema against him.

William of Newburgh was always alert to supernatural intervention; his account brings us closer to Richard the obsessive, the compulsively active, the insatiably belligerent. It is significant that Richard seemed able to dismiss this portent lightly, in a time when omens were taken very seriously.

Richard was happy at Gaillard. He said, 'Behold how fair is this daughter of mine.' He built himself a palace on the Isle of Andely beneath the castle. Gaillard had the great advantage of keeping Philip at bay. His Castle of Gisors was only seven miles away, and Philip was keenly aware that Richard had blocked his attempts to reach Rouen. From his throne room within the castle, Richard carried on vigorously with the administration of his kingdom;

many charters and writs were issued, made law with his seal of two lions. (The third lion was adopted three years later.) So it was that Château Gaillard on the Seine became the King of England's favourite residence. Château Gaillard was intended to be the expression of all that he had achieved and an advertisement of his dominance. It was designed to last for ever. To this day its ruined walls and towers with their machicolations – protruding battlements from which rocks could be launched directly downwards – are overwhelming in their scale.

Huntingdon's London house is in a small terrace just off the river not far from the Tate Gallery. He comes to the door himself. He seems, even for such an equable man, to be in an exceptionally cheerful mood. Perhaps the Countess's absence is the reason. He gives me a martini and then we sit down to the promised game pie and sprouts, and a bottle of red wine.

'Do you like game pie?'

'I love it.'

I say this hoping in some way to inflate my credentials: *Look, here's a chap who eats grouse and venison and woodcock. He's not just some vegetarian wonk.*

'We have bread-and-butter pudding for afters. Venetia likes with-it food,' he says rather wistfully. 'When she's away, I relapse, I am afraid. Mind you, we do both like a good curry.'

After dinner he takes me into the small study and produces a thick, padded manila envelope.

'This is the manuscript that I thought might interest you. I have had a copy made for you to take away. It looks to me like a map, but you will know, or find out, I am sure.'

Very carefully he slips out the manuscript.

'Look,' he says, 'this is my grandfather's, the Robin Hood fanatic's, handwriting. It tells you where he bought the manuscript in 1908. And this is a copy for you.'

It is just one sheet with about five lines on it, some unreadable.

'What do you make of it?' Huntingdon asks.

'If it's a forgery, it's a very good one. I think it is right for the period, and I think it uses carbon ink, which fades, and is used in everyday correspondence, rather than for illuminated addresses, like the addresses to Saladin in the Bodleian that I was shown. It needs X-raying and some other tests, but I will come back to you when I have what's readable translated. Is that all right with you?'

I try to feign academic detachment. It seems to be the outlines of a simple map.

'Absolutely fine. You can take the copy away with you, of course, but please, don't show it to dealers or experts. In my time I have popped quite a few family heirlooms, and my experience is that the dealers are all posh crooks, either trying to buy your heritage cheaply or trying to inflate the value for their commission. And the experts always think that whatever you show them would be better off inside a museum, looked after by them. They don't really believe in individuals holding on to important objects or rare manuscripts or master pictures.

'Now, Richard, I said I had a proposition to make to you. Would you like to do a trial stint as a researcher for me? I have a number of speeches to deliver on Europe over the summer, which I would like you to research, and possibly you could make policy suggestions. You would have access to the Lords and to the parliamentary archives and so on. You strike me as a chap with a very good mind, well above my level, I can assure you. How do you feel about Europe?'

'Ambivalent.'

'That will do. We draw the line at Europhiles with mad eyes staring out towards a future European super-state. Can you consider it?'

'I'm looking forward to it already.'

'Good boy. It's not frightfully well paid, but for someone like you it should be interesting. I will pay you £30,000 a year and your initial contract will be for six months, to see how you get on. Something tells me you are going to be a great find. Now, how about some bread-and-butter pudding? I even have custard.'

'I would love to give it a try. The job I mean. And the bread-and-butter pudding. But I have to tell you, I have never had a proper job.'

'Sometimes I think working in organisations deadens the mind. Everyone begins to sound the same. First thinking is what we need. I'll get my parliamentary secretary to sort it all out. She's a wonderful woman; couldn't live without her. Her name is Elaine, by the way. Can I give her your number?'

'Of course.'

When I get home to Kensington, nodded in by the doorman, I spend the next hour or so writing out, word by word, the faded and indistinct words from the photocopy. I come across a few words I recognise, *'yglise'*, for 'church' as Huntingdon said, is one of them, and *'tesaur'* is another. Parts of the original manuscript were obviously scuffed and the ink has faded. There are many words I am unfamiliar with. It might never have been sent to the intended recipient – perhaps Hubert Walter – or it could have been a copy that remained in the baggage of Henry of Huntingdon.

One word puzzles me particularly: it looks as though it might be a person's name: 'Chasluç'. I have the strong intuition that I am getting closer to the hiding place of the True Cross. Now I need to discover who 'Chasluç' was.

33

Richie

DEAREST NOOR,

I am very sorry it has taken me so long to reply. I should have written sooner, but I have been – as usual – deep in research and writing and also I have been offered a proper job working in the House of Lords as a researcher. I start in a few weeks. It's all slightly eccentric.

I can't bear to think of you suffering so much. Please tell me how the operation went. At the moment I am staying in Haneen's new apartment which I think I mentioned to you. Has she told you about it? I am sure she has. From the balcony I can see Hyde Park, a bit of it anyway, and in the distance I can often see the Household Cavalry taking their horses out for exercise. Sometimes they go out in their full ceremonial outfits to escort dignitaries. It's magnificent, but I can't help wondering what the point is of riding around London dressed up for a cavalry charge.

Yesterday I was handed a piece of parchment, with some words in Old French. It looks like it is a map, and I have a feeling this will provide the link I have been looking for to where Richard's knights, who were escorting the True Cross from the Holy Land, left it. Trust me, before you denounce me as a fantasist, the evidence is mounting up.

Darling Noor, I am living in the belief that we will meet again soon. It keeps me going. At the same time I feel helpless, but every day I try to send you my love in some way, and I hope it arrives safely in the land of the moose. It's the secular version of prayer.

Get better, my dearest sister, and think of Jerusalem when you are feeling low. I do.

Richie xxx

34

Philip is Humiliated

1198. RICHARD THE Lionheart, King of England, Duke of Normandy, is winning the battle with Philip Augustus, King of France. He routs Philip's forces outside his own Castle of Gisors. Richard is so eager to get at Philip that a chronicler writes: He looked like a starving lion who had caught sight of his prey. In the scramble to retire into the castle, Philip falls, humiliatingly, into the river. Richard loves to tell the story of how Philip had a dunking before being hauled out of the water half drowned. By the autumn of the year, Philip seeks a truce; he is prepared to make concessions. In truth he has no option. In November a short truce is agreed.

Richard takes his fast boats up the Seine to meet Philip. For some unexplained reason – perhaps because Philip is nervous in the presence of the ferocious, red-haired Richard – he remains seated on his horse. They agree to separate meetings with the papal legate, Peter of Capua, as mediator. He is renowned for his sonorous and emollient speeches, dressed up in the kind of sanctimonious humility that Richard detests.

At the first meeting with Peter of Capua, at Château Gaillard, Richard refuses to compromise: all his lands must be restored. Peter argues that while war continues the Kingdom of Jerusalem will remain in danger; his master, Pope Innocent, is particularly keen to launch another Crusade. Richard is angry. He stands up and advances on the legate.

'Let me remind you, if it had not been for Philip's malice, which forced me to return, I would have been able to recover the whole of Outremer. And later, when I was falsely imprisoned, he conspired to keep me there so that he could steal my lands. It is wrong to make peace or a long truce while my enemy still holds lands and castles taken unjustly and illegally.'

Peter of Capua, his hands clasped piously, makes an ill-advised comment.

'Ah, sire, how true it is that no one can have everything he wants. The Holy Land demands that we all make sacrifices.'

Richard, barely containing his anger, sits down. He says he will accept a five-year truce.

'I will allow Philip to retain the castles he holds, but not a foot more.'

'Sire, I will take your proposals to Philip Augustus. I have, sire, another matter on which His Holiness has asked me to speak to you.'

Richard turns to his counsellors. After a few moments he turns back to Peter.

'What is it he wants?'

'His Holiness asks that you release the Bishop of Beauvais, the cousin of Philip Augustus. He is both anointed and consecrated, and it is wrong to keep such a man under lock and key.'

William the Marshal, a famous knight and close friend of Richard, later writes that the Bishop of Beauvais was the man Richard hated most in the whole world.

'By my head,' Richard shouts, 'by God's legs, he is de-consecrated for he is a false Christian. He has accused me of killing Conrad de Montferrat, who I had appointed King of Jerusalem; he has maligned me all over Europe. He has been his perfidious cousin's lapdog. It was not as a bishop that he was captured, but as a knight, fighting and fully armed, a laced helmet on his head. Sir hypocrite, what a fool you are. If you were not an envoy I would send you back with something to show the Pope, which he would not forget. Nor did the Pope lift a finger to help me when I was imprisoned and needed his assistance to be freed. And now he asks me to set free a robber and an incendiary who has never done me anything but harm. Get out of here, Sir traitor, liar, trickster, corrupt dealer in churches, and never let me see you again.'

Peter of Capua flees to Gisors, rightly afraid that, if he stays a moment longer, Richard will have him castrated. Richard goes to his chamber and has all the shutters closed and flings himself on the bed in a paroxysm of rage and resentment, brought on by his reminder of the many injustices done to him while he was imprisoned.

> N'est pas mervoille se j'ai le cuer dolant,
> Quant mes sires met ma terre en torment.

> It is no revelation that my heart is sad and pained
> When my own sires despoil my lands.

The bitterness of 'Ja Nus Hons Pris' has seeped into his bones, like rainwater into porous stonework.

William the Marshal is sent in to speak to Richard. He tells his king that Philip will never hold the castles he has taken illegally; without lands the castellans will not be able to sustain themselves. Richard simply has to blockade these castles to take them.

'They will fall into your hands, sire, like ripe plums.'

Richard is duly soothed. Some suggest that his rage is a tactic. Others believe his rage is not only real but easily understood. William the Marshal takes the credit for being able to talk the King round. They have known each other since they were jousting in Poitiers as adolescents.

Soon Richard is back on the warpath, planning to bring to heel the perennially troublesome half-brothers, Aimar, the Viscount of Limoges, and Ademar, the Count of Angoulême, who are Richard's vassals. He sends Mercadier south to lay waste to their lands. Without lands, there is no hope of survival. Fear, devastation, and starvation are to be visited on them. Mercadier knows only one way to fight a battle, and that is with utter ruthlessness and unsparing cruelty. But Richard is not content to leave the work to Mercadier. He has a score to settle with Viscount Aimar, but more importantly he is on the trail of the True Cross, which will vindicate him. His revenge on Aimar will be all the sweeter when he has retrieved the Holy Cross, *sancta croitz*, and he can parade Christendom's most sacred relic throughout the streets of Rouen. It is the cause of great bitterness to him that he has not been given his due for having defeated Saladin and for securing the coastal towns of the Latin Kingdom. He knows that the True Cross will be a potent symbol of his success. As he wrote to Saladin: *The cross, which for you is simply a piece of wood with no value, is for us of enormous importance.*

In great splendour, Richard progresses towards Chinon where he spends two nights. His mother is at Roncevaux, near by, and he visits her there. Then he goes on to Loches, one of the most important castles he has recovered. He basks in the restoration of his empire and the welcome from his grateful subjects. They don't see themselves as English in any way, but as Angevins, and Richard is their lord. There is a growing realisation that Richard has won the war and they are eager to demonstrate their undying allegiance as ostentatiously as possible.

Richard can have no other reason for heading towards the negligible castle of Châlus-Chabrol in Limousin when Mercadier and his routiers – as the chroniclers report – have already wasted Limoges's lands.

35

Father Prosper

My dear Richard,

I thank you for your email, with scan of a document which you suggest may be a map or diagram written by Henry of Huntingdon in 1194. Even from the copy I can agree that the original was written on *vélin*, which is 'vellum' in English.

As you said, it is necessary to look at the original document under the conditions of science, using X-ray and ultraviolet to be certain; but by appearance, I am confident that it could be a manuscript from the time of the Third Crusade. The words that you are trying to translate are a mixture of Anglo-Norman French and Occitan. A man like the Earl of Huntingdon would most probably have written in Anglo-Norman French.

Here are some of the words you wanted me to confirm: *'amagat'*, means 'hidden', sometimes written as *'amagada'*. *'Tesaur'* is *'trésor'*, 'treasure', as you know; *'relicar'* is 'reliquary', *'soterror'* and *'aterror'* are variants of *'enterrer'*, 'to bury', and all your other translations except one are correct. Maybe the one important thing I can tell you is that 'Chasluç' is the Occitan name for 'Châlus'. Châlus-Chabrol is where your Richard was killed. I have not had the pleasure of reading Dan Brown, but this seems to be his territory, from what I understand. It is definitely not my 'bag' as your father used to say. These mystical treasures are always found in a *grotte profonde,* as your manuscript suggests.

I cannot tell you much more. But considering what you have sent to me I think you must show the original to an expert at the British Museum and I attach the email address of my colleague, Dr Keith Philpott. He has the most advanced equipment in Europe. Let me know if you wish that I should send him a note to introduce you.

Our friend in Toronto has been released from hospital. Will you see her?

Amitiés,

Prosper

36

The Death of Richard the Lionheart

Now 'Chasluç' makes sense. It is 'Châlus-Chabrol', and that is where Huntingdon and his companions must have hidden the True Cross. They could not go on to turbulent Normandy with the cross because Philip was closing in on Rouen. But by 1199 things are different and Mercadier and his *routiers* have pacified and laid waste to large swathes of the south, and Richard is ready to reclaim his treasure.

The story of Richard's siege of Châlus-Chabrol was told by Richard's almoner, Abbot Milo, who was present, to Abbot Ralph de Coggeshall, who in turn wrote:

> *During Lent Richard took advantage of the opportunity of peace with King Philip to lead an army of his own against the Viscount of Limoges. Moreover, there are some people who say that a treasure of incalculable value was found on the Viscount's land. The King ordered him to hand it over; and when the Viscount refused, the King's anger was further aroused. Then he devastated the Viscount's land with fire and sword as though he did not know that arms should be laid aside during Lent. At last he came to Châlus-Chabrol.*

Yes, at last he came to Châlus-Chabrol – to reclaim his treasure. The castle was occupied by only thirty-eight men and women.

While his sappers undermined the castle walls, Richard's bowmen fired at anyone who appeared above the parapet. It wasn't a big castle and surrender before the walls collapsed was increasingly likely. Surrendering early might lead to clemency, but holding out to the end would certainly lead to disaster. The acrimony between Philip and Richard had seen an increasing number of atrocities against prisoners, and these included castration and blinding.

As darkness was falling on 26 March 1199, Richard left his red tent, wearing no armour except for a helmet. A rectangular shield held in front of him by four men in armour was all he had for protection. Richard carried a crossbow, a weapon he loved, hoping for a little target practice. But there was only one possible target, also equipped with a crossbow, high on the parapet. His name was Pierre Basile. He was taking the occasional potshot at the besiegers below, and using a frying pan as a shield. The lone defender was providing light entertainment; the besiegers particularly appreciated the frying pan as a comic prop in this comedy of a siege.

Pierre Basile aimed at Richard the Lionheart. Richard applauded and then – just too late – ducked behind the shield. The bolt struck him in the left shoulder. The reports say that he made light of it and walked back to his tent calmly so as not to cause alarm, although it is hard to see how, with an arrow protruding from his shoulder, he could not have caused consternation. The bolts on these crossbows were shaped like an arrow, or like a ragged artichoke. Pierre Basile may have had the bigger, defensive crossbow, which was much heavier. But it seems unlikely that one of these struck Richard. If it had, he would not have been able to walk away; it would have shattered his whole shoulder.

Back in his tent Richard tried to pull the bolt out by the wooden shaft; the shaft came away, leaving the iron (or lead) bolt deeply embedded. Mercadier summoned his own doctor to the King. By torchlight – it was now late into the night – the surgeon removed the bolt with great difficulty. One report says that Richard had become very fat; whether his obesity or inept surgery was to blame, the result was great trauma to the tissues. Almost inevitably septicaemia or gangrene set in. Richard knew that he would die. He sent a message to his beloved mother, asking her to come to his bedside. He wrote immediately to William the Marshal and to Hubert Walter. He ordered William to take command of the castle and the treasury of Rouen. Rouen and much of Normandy would again be vulnerable once Philip heard of his death. There is a story that he ordered up some local women to pleasure him, perhaps on the widely held principle that sex was a defence against death. William the Breton describes him as indulging in 'the joys of Venus'.

Eleanor arrived from Roncevaux, near Chinon, where she had been staying for some time; there is no record of what was said, but they would undoubtedly have discussed saving the Angevin empire and what to do with Richard's heir, his treacherous brother John, who was clearly not up to the job of conserving Richard's territories. He probably left instructions for Hubert Walter to work with him. And Eleanor was to play an important role.

Richard allowed only four of his most trusted companions to enter his tent; he knew that news of his imminent death would embolden his enemies and that all he had achieved since his release would be undone. His reputation had always been his most potent weapon. It is not difficult to imagine his distress in those last days.

He asked for Pierre Basile to be brought before him.

'What have I done to you that you should kill me?' Richard asked.

'You killed my father and two brothers and you intended to kill me. Take what vengeance you will. So long as you die, I shall willingly suffer any torments you may devise.'

Richard, perhaps out of respect for his mother and her civil and gracious principles, pardoned Basile and ordered him released, although all thirty-eight defenders of the castle were hanged. As night fell on the 6th of April, Richard confessed his sins to his almoner, Milo, and died. Milo closed his eyes.

Mercadier did not release Basile as ordered, but had him flayed alive as soon as Richard was dead.

Richard's body was divided: his brain and entrails were buried at Charroux, on the border of his beloved Poitou, and his heart was buried in the cathedral of Rouen not far from his brother. The remaining parts were buried at his father's feet in Fontevraud Abbey, along with the regalia and crown he had worn at Winchester. All this was according to his instructions. There is a later effigy of Richard lying next to his mother in Fontevraud. Eleanor is holding, and looking intently at, an open book. This could be a reminder of her lively intellect, or an indication of piety. Richard's neglected wife who, like my aunt, had faded from the official narrative, was buried some years later in a Cistercian abbey near Le Mans, forgotten and erased, having served her purpose as part of a strategic deal. The feet of her effigy are resting on a very small lion. On her head is a queen's crown, although she never set foot in England.

Richard's death was a joy to some and an unbearable sorrow to others. He was dead after twenty-five years of relentless warfare. It was said of him that he sought victory rather than conquest. He was addicted to war and danger. There are soldiers and foreign correspondents who become adrenalin junkies. Maybe Richard was one of these people who are easily depressed and bored when they are thrown back into domestic life. But Richard was widely admired for his contempt for danger and his generosity of spirit. These two qualities came to be seen as English virtues, despite the fact that Richard spent so little of his life in England itself, where, he said, it was cold and it rained all the time.

Rumours immediately sprang up to explain his death, and what he was doing in Châlus besieging this insignificant castle. There was talk of a Gallo-Roman treasure. Around Europe the news of his death changed at a stroke the balance of power. John was soon to lose almost

everything Richard had held. The contrast with his brother caused
some to wonder why God had cut short his life:

> *Oh death, if heaven allow it,*
> *I chide even God.*
> *God why did you fail?*
> *If you recall he defended your Jaffa*
> *Against many thousands;*
> *Acre too he restored to you . . .*

Legends sprang up. One German legend – 'Richard Lowenherz' –
has him locked in a room with a lion while in captivity. Richard kills
the lion by sticking his hand down its throat and ripping out its heart.
It was believed that a lion would not kill a true king. This legend had
wide currency, and nearly two hundred years later, Shakespeare knew
it well enough to use it in King John:

Lady Falconbridge to her son, Philip Falconbridge:

King Richard Coeur-de-Lion was thy father
By long and vehement suit was I seduced
To make room for him in my husband's bed.
Heaven lay not my transgression to my charge!
Thou art the issue of my dear offence,
Which was so strongly urg'd, past my defence.

Philip Falconbridge:

Now, by this light, were I to get again,
Madam, I would not wish a better father.

I think of the Globe and *Richard III* and Emily with her earnest
nose, and her sexual fervour. I try to think clearly of Noor too, but

she is becoming faint in my mind, as if she only existed as a preliminary sketch, like the master drawings Emily and I once went so earnestly to see at the Royal Academy.

When I try to understand Richard the Lionheart, a man who died relatively young, I am struck by the fact that I am myself more than a third of the way towards the end of my own life, and that I am alive only by chance at this moment in all the millennia that have passed and will pass. I am not warming up these feelings for literary purposes: I have learned with frightening clarity how insubstantial and arbitrary a life is. Noor described Kerak Castle as a necropolis. Who would disagree? We are, after all, resting on the bones of the dead.

From the balcony I see the Household Cavalry trotting pointlessly along. Some of the horses are steaming.

37

The Map

ACADEMICS MAY BE out of touch with the world, poorly
barbered and prone to wearing sandals with socks, but their job is
to represent the idea – at the very least – that there is rationality in
the world, and that it must be explored. And that puts me in a difficult position, as my quest is not entirely rational. As I walk around
one of those airy squares in Bloomsbury looking for Dr Philpott's
office, I wonder what he will make of it. There is a huge bronze bell
knob. He comes to the door.

'Keith Philpott, how do you do?'

'Fine, thanks, and very grateful that you have given me the time.'

He is dressed in a denim shirt and shiny blue trousers. His hair is
curly and tousled and he has that perennially boyish manner which
male academics often retain, as though their hair is fixed for ever in
a certain time. I would guess he is about forty-five.

'No, it is my pleasure. It sounds interesting. And we have just the
kit you need to look at your document closely. Cup of coffee before
we begin? I do a rather fancy coffee. I took a course.'

I think his accent is from Somerset, a sort of reminder of the
rustic world that has passed.

'Coffee, that would be great.'

He has a huge old coffee machine. It rests on a table under a vast
photograph of Jerusalem, the classic view across the Old City
towards Al-Aqsa and its golden dome.

'I did some weeks at the École Biblique.'

'Yes, so Prosper told me. Lovely man. He says he knew your father.'

'Yes. Back in the '60s.'

'Latte?'

The coffee machine is obscured by clouds of steam. The place looks like the station café in *Brief Encounter*. Philpott takes some time to pour the milk into two glasses, producing, by some magic, the design of a Prussian eagle on each of them.

'That's amazing.'

'I find it strangely enjoyable. Yes, Prosper is a remarkable man. I have been out there often, looking at manuscripts, parchment and vellum, even papyrus, trying to date them and so on. I don't really read them, so much as analyse them and conduct DNA tests. Prosper gave you a very warm recommendation. So let us march boldly on. Can you show me on the manuscript all the words you have identified first? Shall I get it out of the box and set it up?'

There seems to be something about me that attracts charity. I persuaded Lord Huntingdon to let me have the document X-rayed. He was reluctant, but I told him that his vellum might have a clue to where King Richard's treasure was buried. He was animated by the mention of Richard; anything that brought him closer to Richard was a bonus. Every day for the past month I have passed under the gaze of the Lionheart, his sword aloft and a rapt look on his face, which recalls his one and only sight of Jerusalem.

My job is to write speeches for Huntingdon and research arcane facts about the European Union. At the moment we are looking closely at the residences of the important people in the EU's foreign office. Huntingdon calls the functionaries who are allotted them *les grands fromages*. His next speech should make clever play, he says, on the scandalous protection these people are accorded against auditing of their expenses; and he will make a connection with the way that France's two hundred and forty-six cheeses receive special status. (His ire is directed primarily at the French.) *Les grands fromages* should fear for the onslaught that he, armed with my choice phrases, is about to unleash on them. I am enjoying it, crazy though it is.

Dr Philpott extracts the manuscript carefully.

'From what I can make of the ink and the few visible words, it is twelfth century. Let's get it on the rostrum and have a good look. I am sure you know that these sheets of vellum were often used a few times. We may find words that have been written over, or we may find details which will allow us to identify both the place and a date. Presumably that would be important for you?'

'It would be wonderful.'

He turns off the lights and fires up the machine. He tells me it is a Synchrotron, which throws an intense beam at the object. On the screen a ghostly, almost submarine, image is appearing.

'Yes, I think you are right, it is a simple map, just what you would expect from someone in the field,' Dr Philpott says. 'There, under the remains of the note, look. Do you see just under that line? Just there is a church, and over there is the outline of what is a town. Are you interested in the church? OK, let's go in closer.'

Philpott says that this kind of medieval map or diagram uses a number of familiar symbols for river, castle, church, abbey, city wall, and forest. He points to what he says is a pictogram of a cross beside the church and also to the words *'grotte profonde'*; as he zooms in he says he can read *'sanc . . . croitz'*.

'Are you looking for a cross?' he asks.

'Yes. We are looking for the True Cross, lost to Saladin. I don't want to offend you, but will you keep this entirely secret?'

'Of course I will. Father Prosper told me that you were on to something very important.'

'Look, I think that this may be the cross that Richard brought back from Jerusalem. We think it was hidden on the way to Rouen. When I looked at the chart again I could see *'Chasluç'* which is

Occitan for '*Châlus*', and that was where Richard was killed. We think Richard was there to look for his treasure, which many of the chroniclers mention. It was a piddling little place, and there can have been no other reason for the most important king in Europe to have been there, in person, to subdue thirty-eight people.'

'OK, sounds reasonable. Now you need to know if what you have is enough to identify the place? Am I right? The church may still exist, and that would be a great help; if you think the treasure was hidden in the crypt or somewhere in the church.'

' "*Grotte profonde*" seems to suggest that it was left in a crypt or cave, I would say. "*Amagada*" means "hidden".'

'Yes, and the church, which we can just see outlined, seems to be to the south of a town, beside a castle. This little shape of a tower here, this could be your "Chasluç". Now I have a fancy trick to show you. I can overlay this on a Google map of the area and we can see what we get. We will start with the presumption that this is Châlus. Is it Châlus-Chabrol? Right, this will take a little time. What we want is to find the few clues that your man left behind and then we can see if we can pinpoint the spot. Let me just use the computer to mark up the places of interest on the screen because they won't read when we overlay. OK, done. This is exciting – a quest. Another coffee while the computer sorts itself out?'

I am light-headed, but I say yes. Keith Philpott is rushing about, perhaps crazed by caffeine himself, now making his exquisite latte, now checking the progress of the map overlays. I knock back my latte, this one decorated with a fern.

'Why did you take a barista course, Keith?'

'My wife left me, and I wanted something to do that wasn't work. So that's when I took the course. Being a boffin, I have naturally looked into all the mumbo-jumbo and the science of coffee and how to make it. Now I blog. I am known on the web as Prof Mike Macchiato.'

'Do you mind me asking, why did your wife leave you?'

He looks at me briefly before answering.

'She really hated me. That was it. She hated me for not being someone else.'

'Who?'

'Anybody. It's a very unpleasant feeling, to be hated. Particularly if, in your own mind, you believe you have been quite reasonable. My wife said I had Asperger's, very common amongst academics, she claimed. The strange thing is that now that she has gone I have never been happier. I feel guilty for being happy, but the upside is that, if I feel guilt, I can't have Asperger's. OK, let's see where we have got to. Right, this is a river, the Tardoire, and, look, it corresponds, roughly anyway, to the river running beside Châlus. I do this all the time, by the way, for projects on British medieval villages and early Norse settlements. Your church would be about here, if it still stands. I'll go in. And lo and behold, here is the outline of a church. Your "*yglise*". Up to the north-east is a town and here we see, in exactly the right place, the city of Limoges.'

'The castle belonged to the Viscount of Limoges. He had been a thorn in Richard's side for many years.'

The day passes happily. It is amazing what Keith Philpott can find and interpret. He overlays medieval maps on our map. He looks at deeper levels of the vellum; he produces ink analysis.

There is a ring on the doorbell, and the door opens; a young woman with a pale, ethereal, seamless face appears. She has a little snow on her woolly hat. Keith introduces her. Her name is Ann. She is his colleague from Gothenburg on a project about early Norse villages in the pre-Christian era. She shakes my hand and I feel a little insistent pressure like the grip of a chameleon. Of course I am wondering if this pale woman has contributed to his new happiness.

'Right,' he says, 'our time has flown. Ann and I have to do a little work. I will draw up a usable map for you, containing all the information I can get from your manuscript, overlaid with existing rivers and ancient buildings. Can I ask you, what are you expecting to find? A complete cross, a piece of wood, or something more elaborate?'

'I think the cross will be in a reliquary, probably of gold and silver bands around a wooden casket. Although it may not have travelled in that alone.'

'You have done a fantastic piece of detective work. Wonderful. I hope you can come round tomorrow and I will take you through the detail. And don't worry, the chart will be locked away for the night. Goodbye, Richard. This has been one of my best days.'

'Me too. Thank you.'

He hugs me, unexpectedly. Although it's March, it is snowing lightly outside on the square, and the snow and the arrival of the ice princess seem to be connected.

38

Richie

DEAREST NOOR,

Tomorrow I am going down to Limoges to look at the castle where Richard was killed to see what I can find. It was a very minor siege, and Richard was there to find hidden treasure, definitely not just to demolish the castle of his enemy, the Viscount of Limoges. My research suggests that it could have been the Holy Cross, as Richard would have known it.

I have been working in the House of Lords, doing research for Lord Huntingdon on the European Union and its follies – as my boss sees them – and writing speeches for him. You will be as excited as I am to hear that we are about to deliver a knock-out blow to the bureaucrats who are wasting our money in Brussels. This is the raison d'être of my employer, who is charming but deluded. I don't have to believe anything much – my job is simply to bring up the bodies.

Rumour has reached me via Father Prosper that you have left hospital. I am so happy to hear this, but I wondered why you hadn't told me yourself. Are you on the way to recovery? I hope so, because I have made enquiries in Symi and I have provisionally rented a house for three weeks overlooking the main harbour, starting on the 1st of May. Are you going to be able to come to stay? We will have a small boat moored outside and we will chug around the island to my favourite beach, the one I mentioned which faces a small island with an even smaller chapel just out to sea.

Write to me as soon as you can. I haven't seen Haneen for a while, but I think she is in Jerusalem. She once told me – when we came back from Kerak, I think – that you don't find treasures or lost manuscripts or paintings by looking for them in the obvious places; they are almost always neglected and unrecognised in collections or museums or private houses. Anyway, my dissertation on Crusader art should soon be sent off for judgement.

I have to tell you that I dread the idea that we are drifting apart, not because we want to, but because it seems too difficult (and perhaps too painful?) to meet up. Please give the idea of going to Symi a chance. We will work something out.

Noor, I think of you every day, sometimes five or ten times. Strangely, it is only thinking of our time in Jerusalem that keeps me sane.

Love from your brother and lover,
Richie xxxx

39

Heading South

ON THE TRAIN down from Montparnasse, heading south towards Eleanor's and Richard's dominions, I was reading a book, published about eighty years ago, which described Eleanor's Courts of Love. Outside on this winter's day the French countryside rushed past the window of the *train à grande vitesse*. The countryside seemed to be deserted. For miles the only movement I could see was flocks of scavenging crows.

It was in this book on that journey that I learned that Eleanor had been on the Second Crusade and had fallen in love with the art and architecture of Byzantium and the freedom of the Latin Kingdom. She saw that Byzantium was a far more sophisticated and elegant place than Paris, where she had lived for many years. She was astounded by the art, the luxury, the clothes, the jewellery and the manners of the people. I have incorporated all this in my dissertation. Finding without seeking. It happens quite often, in my experience.

When she set up her court in Poitiers after she had left Henry of England, Eleanor was determined to improve the huge hall the Plantagenets had built next to the castle. She also intended to improve the manners of the locals. Soon she had licked them into shape:

Here there was no disordered bivouac littered with the straw bedding of a feudal soldiery; no depot for the forage of routiers; no draughty harbourage with unglazed mullions and flapping hangings lighted with the slant beams of flares and traversed by wind-blown smoke; no armoury for shield and helmet, trophies of the chase, the litter of hounds and falcons. Here was a proper setting for majesty, a woman's place in the sun, a fit stage for the arts, a foil for beauty, a comfortable house . . .

At her court, Eleanor and her eldest daughter, Marie of Champagne, fostered the idea of *l'amour courtois*, loosely based on Ovid's *Ars amatoria*. Here, topics were argued semi-formally, such as the possibility of love after marriage. (Decision: not possible.) Eleanor's ideas spread to many of the courts of Europe.

According to my book:

It had the effect of freeing woman from the millstone which the Church of the first millennium hung about her neck as the author of man's fall and the facile instrument of the devil.

Where men in Poitiers, including the Bishop, had previously been content to dress in sheepskin and fox pelts, they now took up the new fashions. One disapproving chronicler wrote:

Today the humblest would blush to be seen in such poor things. Now they have clothes fashioned of rich and precious stuffs in colours to suit their humour.

Eleanor insisted that her court should have an artistic sensibility; men were required 'to be purged of the odour of the kennel and the road, and to be free of spurs and falcons' when they entered Eleanor's halls. They were also encouraged to see themselves as belonging in the realm of romance, and to think of themselves as the property of women. They were to see themselves as supplicants to women, through poetic addresses.

Eleanor brought up Richard in this extraordinary place, from where he was paraded as her favourite son around her lands so that her people could see their future lord. I find it impossible to get a clear or consistent picture of Richard from the chronicles; only episodes of his life are vivid to me. But it is clear that he acquired some of his mother's sensibility. At the same time, he was also an utterly implacable and ruthless enemy, and it is difficult to reconcile this ruthlessness with the ideas of her court. His treatment of Alice, who lived for years at the court in Eleanor's custody, certainly owed little to the precepts of the courts of love. But how do we know that Richard's reluctance to marry Alice did not spring from having seen her running around the court as a young girl, more little sister than bride, for years? It may be that Westermarck's theory, that young children brought up in close proximity, related or not, develop a natural taboo against incest, applied to Richard.

As for Richard's belligerence, it can be traced to Poitiers' famous season of tournaments, which were patronised by:

> the rabble of soldiers, fighting cocks, jousters, springers, riding masters, troubadours, Poitevin nobles and young châtelaines, adolescent princes and infant princesses in the great hall of Poitiers.

The tournaments became so violent and involved so much money as ransom, that they were eventually curtailed. Still, these tournaments, virtually small wars, produced a crop of renowned and brutal knights every year. One of the most famous products of this training was William the Marshal, Richard's friend and companion, described as the greatest knight who ever lived. There is an effigy of him in the Temple Church, London. He had skinny shins, I noted.

As we raced through the countryside it appeared to me that France was sleeping. Looking across the fields and copses and stunned villages, with the occasional church steeple breaking the horizon.

I was struggling to fix Noor in my mind; she had become a memory, a phantom . . . I didn't in truth know what she had become, but it was not substantial. She was now part of a story, a story that involves someone who was, as in a fairy tale, my sister.

I checked in to my cheap hotel, quite close to the station of Limoges. The station has an impressive spire, which, from the train, I had mistaken for the tower of the cathedral. It was eight fifteen when I presented myself in the lobby. Nobody could be more suspicious of a stranger than a receptionist in a small French hotel: she told me with joy in her heart that dinner was not served after eight. She said that I was *en retard*, but she might as well have said I was a retard for negligently missing my dinner. Just to rub it in, she reminded me that dinner was part of the *formule* I had paid for. I told her the train was late. She shrugged: 'It is not our responsibility.' Before I could ask the question, she told me that there would be no refund.

Outside on the empty boulevards, a few people in taupe or pink anoraks were visible, looking in shop windows cautiously. Pink seems to have become the sub-prime of colours. A chicken rotisserie van was standing in a small square near the cathedral and I ordered half a chicken. The rows of chickens rotated steadily and aromatically; the effect was almost balletic. I sat down on a bench beneath some brutally pruned plane trees and ate the chicken with plastic cutlery from a styrofoam box. Juices ran down my chin. I could see elderly, bowed couples, and a few African women, entering the cathedral for an evening service; I guessed they would be huddled in the vast interior like the small bands of Native Americans painted on the endless prairie by George Catlin. I walked down towards the river and across St-Martial Bridge, built on the supports of the original Roman bridge. Richard the Lionheart's father, Henry, had destroyed it in 1182 to punish his disobedient vassals.

St Martial, I had read, was an important saint in these parts, and the first Bishop of Limoges.

For all the neglected grandeur, I thought that there was a sense of sadness in provincial cities like Limoges – the cafés serving the immemorial *croque*, the *baguette* with *saucisson* or cheese or ham, the poor coffee, the trees butchered in homage to some forgotten notion of rationality, the rows of dilapidated Mansard-style houses, the dreary shops. There was *no joie de vivre* here. A group of Algerian boys – I assumed they were Algerians – came towards me with their razor-cut hair and giant trainers, and I felt nervous. Strange that they appeared to be dressed just like the Palestinians I had seen in Jerusalem. All my better feelings told me they were just boys, out and about, but my instinct warned me to be wary. I have often had this feeling in Hackney. In Kensington – where, courtesy of Haneen, I am now living – we are all harmless strangers, although sometimes in the elegant garden squares I can hear the full, orotund English spoken, loudly and especially cheerfully on a Friday when these people are loading the Range Rover for the trip to the country house, enthusiastically supported by their congenitally cheerful Labradors.

As I walked along the River Vienne, I was wondering what I thought I might find at Châlus-Chabrol. Richard's life had been appropriated by many of the local guide books, his heart, innards and skull – if you believed them – were scattered in local churches and crypts and even in a field. This appropriation of the glamour of Richard had reached a scientist, dubbed by the French press *the Indiana Jones of pathology*. He was granted a small section of Richard's heart – a few cells, a thin slice? – to determine just what had killed him. He might, apparently, have been poisoned.

In Jerusalem Father Prosper had told me of a DNA test on the thirteen headlice found in Qumran. Headlice live only a few hours without blood, and the plan was to discover the DNA of the last people the headlice were feeding on when the Romans sacked the place in AD 70, which would have provided, rather neatly, useful information about the inhabitants of Qumran. Unfortunately none of the blood in the headlice yielded DNA.

In bed in my small room I felt very alone, and plagued with doubts. What was I doing here? Was it to make a name for myself, or was I competing with my father, in some way that had not been revealed to me? I slept fitfully, waking up in this rabbit hutch every few hours, feeling miserably uncertain. Just before dawn I woke finally and I remembered one of Stephen's favourite sayings: 'Literature interprets the chaos of life and gives it meaning.' I thought that I now understood what Stephen had tried to tell me in Cornwall; he was telling me to free my imagination to explore the chaos of life.

On my laptop I found two emails, the first from Noor.

Richie, I am a free agent. (Jeu de mots – get it?) Let's go to Symi in May.
Noor xx
PS. More detail to follow. I love you.

My heart lurched, as though the ballast inside me had shifted in a storm.

The second email was from Keith Philpott; I had asked him if he had the time to look at any research done on the churches and abbeys of the region and their crypts or tombs. He said he would look through the data. He said that he could probably extract more information from the document and the map. He also said he had found the words '*Saint Martial*', only visible under a minutely focused beam, near the pictogram of the *yglise*. He had taken the liberty of doing some research on St Martial, and discovered that he was the patron saint of Limoges. The church on the map was certainly named after him, and it would have been an obvious hiding place, some miles from troubled Limoges, particularly as there was a dispute between the Viscount of Limoges and the Abbot of St-Martial; the Abbot would probably have been willing to help an enemy of the Viscount.

Keith also sent me a link to something called *Les Ostensions*. This, I learned, is a yearly ceremony to which the faithful are invited to view the relics housed by the Confrérie de St-Martin. They are paraded around the town and the priests in attendance implore God to intercede with the saints. It is an ancient custom, revived some years ago after St Martial's crypt was discovered. As Keith put it, 'This could be interesting, no?'

I emailed Noor and told her we would talk about Symi later when I got back to London. I told her how happy I was to hear that we would, after all these months, be together again. I emailed Keith to thank him for his work. I found myself plumped up with optimism. I thought how odd it is that often, just when you are at your lowest, the gloom can clear unexpectedly, even arbitrarily.

I took a taxi to a village near Châlus. The driver told me that Richard the Lionheart was killed in Châlus and that the English do tours of the castles of this region. '*Mais Richard Coeur de Lion ne parlait pas même un seul mot d'anglais*.' I had an appointment with a woman called Cathérine Sieff, whose brother I had met in England. He told me that his sister owned a bookshop called Parola, Occitan for 'words', in a small village near Châlus, and she had become the local historian. She was very well known in the region and her bookshop was, as he put it, a 'destination'; she had a café in the old mill that housed her bookshop where she made wonderful coffee, served with *madeleines* or *friandises*. She also loved exotic teas; Emily would have been right at home. Cathérine Sieff had been married for eight years to an Englishman who had died less than a year ago. Jean Sieff said she would be delighted to see me.

The taxi pulled up in a small square, priested by plane trees, with a fountain in the middle. I walked through an old, rounded doorway that might once have been the main entrance to the mill. The bookshop was just as a bookshop should be: roof to floor it was stacked with books in those evocative and serious paperback French covers. There were photographs and paintings of local interest, there was a small art gallery upstairs and there were giant pots of bougainvillea on the terrace at the back, which looked over the stream that had once powered the mill. A half-sized piano rested in a corner of a room on a lower level.

She appeared from the café.

'You are Richard, I am sure. I am Cathérine. It is wonderful to meet you. Come, my brother says you like good coffee, *à l'Italien*.'

'I do. And he says you make great *madeleines*.'

'I hope. I have just made some.'

She was wearing a simple light dress in blue cotton, and her hair was long and darkish blonde, falling down to her shoulders, artfully natural. She was in her early thirties, I guessed, very young to be widowed. She was slim in that French way. I was reminded of a picture of a 1960s singer, Françoise Hardy, with my father. She is holding his arm lightly in the picture. He hinted that he had had an affair with her in St-Tropez. It's not impossible: after all it was the 1960s and he was one of the new species of laughing freemen, complete with Jim Morrison hair, poised silkily on his head. His hair had a life all of its own.

Cathérine made me a latte and decorated it with two hearts. She watched my reaction. Wonderful, I said. The bookshop had been financed by her husband and they had a house in the countryside near by, where she now lived full-time. He was a banker – *not a crook, not at all* – and she was devastated when he died suddenly of pancreatic cancer, aged thirty-six. He died within three weeks of diagnosis. I had another coffee. I was beginning to feel the effects of the caffeine: I was overrun by the possibilities a life could offer and, despite my plans for Symi, one of these was to have sex with Cathérine. We talked in general terms about my mission here. I told her that I was writing a dissertation on the art of the Latin Kingdom and its influence on Eleanor, and that some treasures of Jerusalem were sent to Normandy, but documents I had read suggested that they had been held up near Limoges. I needed her help to locate a church, only identified as St Martial, just south of Châlus-Chabrol. Now that, thanks to Keith, I knew something of *Les Ostensions*, I asked her if she could help me get to see the relics in storage.

I had two *madeleines*. They were the shape of a scallop-shell, quite large and destined to rest in the memory for ever.

Cathérine knew about the church of St Martial. She told me that there was nothing much to see, because it had been destroyed during the Hundred Years War, but I would be able to walk the outlines of the building and look at some collapsed parts of the crypt. I thought this crypt might be the *grotte profonde* on Huntingdon's chart. She told me about *Les Ostensions*, which she described as kitsch: the relics and bones of various saints, some of them local, were processed around town. A reliquary holding St Thomas's finger bone was one of the main attractions, as well as various other reliquaries, one containing a piece of the lance that pierced Christ's side.

'It makes me a little mad to see them parading this stuff around the city. Anyway, what exactly are you hoping to find?'

'I am looking for reliquaries of Latin Kingdom or Byzantine origin, which are being recognised as important artworks. They demonstrate that, over a hundred and fifty years, artistic fusion was going in Outremer. It may be that one or more of these ended up here. I am sure you know that when Richard besieged Châlus-Chabrol, just before he was killed, he was looking for hidden treasure, which the Viscount of Limoges would not surrender to him?'

'Yes, I do know the story, but in those days hordes of treasure were often mentioned in a miraculous way to explain things. You know, like the pot of gold at the end of the rainbow, or by a mythic holy quest. The story of the treasure that the Viscount would not surrender is fiction. It was supposed to be a fabulous horde of Gallo-Roman gold. But it is strange that it was never found, no? The treasure of Rennes-le-Château is another example. This crooked nineteenth-century priest, Bérenger Saunière, made a huge amount of money from selling thousands of indulgences, but the source of his money was said to be from some treasure he had found in his church.'

In the afternoon, she drove me to Châlus-Chabrol. The remaining tower was quite small and unimpressive. She told me where Richard was supposed to have been killed; nobody really knows for sure, because a new castle was built on the site.

'Most of the original castle, except for the keep, has been demolished, and this later castle, these ruins over there, was also destroyed,' she said. 'OK, I must go now.'

She smiled, and shrugged apologetically. I thought I could detect sadness, a certain wariness about the eyes. As I stepped out of the car she said, 'Do you have a hotel reservation?'

'Yes, in Limoges.'

'Would you like to stay at my house? I can come with you to the church tomorrow. I am free in the morning.'

'That would be great. My room is a dog-kennel. But, by the way, I have no clothes. Obviously.'

'You can have a clean shirt from my husband's cupboard. There are many. I haven't been able to throw anything of Harry's clothes away.'

'Thank you.'

'Now I will try to persuade the *Confrérie* to let you see the relics. They have no idea what they have and they don't really care as long as the – how do you say? – the credulous, come out to look.'

I was leaning on the windowsill of her car, looking across at her, and for a long moment, as she leant towards me, I saw her breasts; small but not negligible. It was impossible to look away, because that would have suggested guilt. Instead I tried to look serious.

'Thank you for that. I will see you later.'

'OK, Richard, that is great. I will come and get you here just after six when the shop will be closed.'

I walked round the castle tower and entered the keep, where Pierre Basile, the man with the frying pan, could have been positioned with his crossbow. It was not possible to climb up to the top of the remaining battlements. But it was clear that the scale of the siege was unworthy of the attention of the most famous king in Europe, unless he had something else on his mind.

Later that night when we were lying in bed, Cathérine told me that her brother had said she would like me.

'And was he right?'

'Absolutely, although maybe he was not expecting us to jump into bed.'

'No, probably not. Men are protective of their sisters.'

'Do you have sisters?'

'Just one half-sister.'

'Are you close to her?'

'She lives in Toronto. I didn't even know about her until a few months ago.'

'Do you have *une petite amie*?' Cathérine asked.

'No, not at the moment. Do you miss your husband very much?'

'I miss Harry, and every day I think of him, and every day when I wake up I have to remember that he has gone. It is terrible.'

I couldn't tell her about Noor while lying under the old Limousin oak beams on her big, lavender-scented bed, a foaming cataract of embroidered sheets and pillows. I couldn't tell her that I had fallen in love unwittingly with my half-sister and that in Egypt she had been gang-raped. My relationship with Cathérine, so far, was more like a bitter-sweet French romance of a young widow and an English stranger meeting fortuitously and consoling each other, although down the road there was undoubtedly going to be a phase of existential angst and introspection. My true story was far too implausible, with dark undertones that would not survive the examined life.

'Why did you come to live in this place?'

'*La France profonde.* Just because it is deepest France, that is why I come. We had a small apartment in Paris, just by St-Sulpice, but I have for a long time an idea of a bookshop in *la France profonde*, and we bought this place. Harry was working in Paris and I spent more and more time here. I became fascinated by Occitan – we have our own Limousin dialect even now – and I was looking more and more deep in the history of our language, which is endangered. Anyway, I become over the last eight years known and now our bookshop – and our tea and coffee – are well known.'

Her body has a fine, aromatic sheen. A new lover has intriguing little aromas and textures. I feel blessed to be lying next to her.

'Are you happy? You don't think it is a mistake?' she asks, looking genuinely concerned.

'I am ecstatic. I have been through some bad times.'

We kiss. Her lips have calmed down now and are gently solicitous, tenderly exploratory. This kissing business surprises me even now, because it is so intimate. I remember my first proper kiss in Aqaba, with Judy McAllister, and the shock of her wet and falafel-flavoured tongue exploring the inside of my mouth.

'Cathérine, did you intend to seduce me?'

'No, no. In French we say it was *un coup de foudre*. Do you know what that means?'

'Yes. I do.'

'I had not planned anything at all. In fact you are the first man I have fucked with since my husband died.'

I am taken aback for a moment by the word 'fuck', but I guess that she thinks it is nothing more than argot, like '*merde*'.

'I am honoured.'

'We only meet this morning. Is that a matter of concern for you? Do you think I am a *salope*?'

'A cause of concern? No, it is beautiful. A miracle. I haven't been so happy for many, many months.'

'In our local Occitan we say "*gorrina*" for "*salope*".'

'You are the most wonderful *gorrina* I have ever met.'

'Have you met many?'

'Quite a few.'

In the morning she is not quite so serene. We have slept a little uneasily.

'Are you all right?' I ask, as she brings in some tea.

'I am fine, but I found it strange. This was our bed, and two or three times I woke up and thought that it was Harry next to me. I had dreamed about that so often.'

I put my forearm under her thigh, and pull it gently onto my stomach, and we press against each other, taking counter measures against doubt. I feel a little anxious, aware that I am in the unseam'd bed. I could even things up by telling her all about Noor, but it is not possible at the moment – or ever. In truth Cathérine is lovely in the morning, hardly rumpled, and radiating a gentle warmth. We go out to a café for breakfast and I am pleased because I think that this means she is happy to be seen with me. She has given me one of her husband's shirts to wear: perhaps unconsciously, she has chosen nothing particularly distinctive. It fits me well; Harry appears to have been about the same size as me.

There is something wonderfully conspiratorial about breakfast after a first night of passion, of intense longing, of secret appraisal.

At the *yglise* – '*egleisa*' in Occitan, she tells me – Cathérine leads me around the outlines of the building. It was a Romanesque church, she says. It once had a crypt, now full of rubble and what looks like bistort and yarrow, although I can't be sure; heathers are more my bag. St Martial himself was buried in the Cemetery of Martyrs in Limoges. There was once a chapel above his tomb, which became a pilgrim shrine. The abbey in Limoges, which bore his name, was founded in AD 848 by Benedictines, and destroyed during the French Revolution. When the abbey was torn down, St Martial's tomb was lost, but it was found and excavated in 1960.

'What are you looking for here?' Cathérine asks.

'As I said, my research suggests that an important reliquary of fine Byzantine and Crusader work, which was supposed to go to Rouen, was buried here in St Martial's Church in 1193 to wait until Richard was free again.'

'OK. Well I don't think it will be here. Most likely it was removed when the church was destroyed and taken to Limoges and placed in St Martial's tomb in the *abbaye*, the one that was discovered in 1960. But that was excavated. So there is a possibility that whatever was found was taken to storage. Now the relics, not the archaeological objects, are controlled by the people who organise the *Ostensions*. I will explain that you are an academic from Oxford – we all love Oxford – and that you wish to look for reliquaries that may have come from Outremer. What are you going to do with these objects if you find them?'

'I just want to photograph them and decribe them for my dissertation. I have a picture of a reliquary in the Church of the Holy Sepulchre in Barletta, Puglia. It may be that it would be similar.'

I also tell her about Queen Melisende of Jerusalem's psalter and I say that until recently few people had realised the extent of the influence of Outremer on art back home. The Latin Kingdom was not just some flyblown outpost. As I say it, I wonder how much of this my father understood. His expectations of Richard were of the spiritually significant variety.

Cathérine has to go to a dinner party with friends. She feels she can't bring me along because everyone would be wondering if we were lovers and her husband only died eleven months ago. I understand. She drops me off at the hotel. The receptionist looks at us with disapproval; I have obviously been up to no good, a dirty stop-out, and missed more meals so generously included in the *formule*.

The world of priests and canons and abbots and bishops and monks and cardinals seems to be remote from life as the rest of us know it. For a start these people believe in the incredible. We meet Father Fabien Pelous at the cathedral of St Étienne in Limoges. I can't make up my mind if Father Pelous, a strongly built, peasanty man, believes that parading the relics and asking for God's intercession with the saints – it seems a rather roundabout procedure for attracting God's attention – works in some way, or whether it is merely a cultural custom of long standing that has the benefit of attracting people into churches. Fortunately he appears to have absolutely no aesthetic or historical interest in the art of the Latin Kingdom, but he does see my arrival as a good opportunity for a story in the local press, under his byline. Cathérine is doing a terrific job of overstating my academic credentials.

'This English gentleman, Monsieur Cathar, is an expert from Oxford University on the art and artefacts of the Latin Kingdom. He wishes to see if he can identify any of these as coming from the Holy Land in the twelfth century.'

Catherine translates his answer, although I already have the gist of it.

'Yes, we may have some things which are of interest to Monsieur Cathar. *Allons-y.*'

The relics are in another building. We cross a courtyard and enter a Romanesque chapter house, on the south side of the cathedral. The floor is of huge flags. Our feet echo across it as we walk; the sound is moving ahead of us in rivulets. As Father Pelous grapples with some huge keys on a leather belt, Cathérine squeezes my bottom conspiratorially. I try not to laugh.

Father Pelous opens an iron grille, which grinds and squeals. He leads us down a long, vaulted corridor. At the end of the passage is another door, rounded in the Romanesque style. We are entering a crypt, he tells Cathérine, who tells me. Father Pelous unlocks the door. As he pulls it open it starts up its own ancient protest of creaking and arthritic oak.

The interior is a surprise; it looks a bit like a mortuary, with neon lighting falling evenly on stacks of drawers in pale grey; the effect is of bluish moonlight. In each drawer is a relic, Father Pelous says. He consults the labels and opens about twenty drawers for me. I am pleased to see he has very little clue of what's inside each drawer. I take photographs indiscriminately, so as not to draw particular attention to any of the reliquaries. I even photograph Thomas's finger bone. I have taken close-up pictures of about half the reliquaries, but I am very interested in *Tiroir Numero 37*, which contains something I have glimpsed, a cruciform box, labelled indistinctly: *Provenance inconnue*. Cathérine goes out to make some calls. For half an hour I carry on looking in the drawers. Father Pelous says he will be gone for a while: I may photograph for my records, but I must not touch anything.

I return to *Tiroir 37*. The interior of the drawer is dark and the contents are visible only by the flash of my camera, which confirms that it is a wooden, cross-shaped box, about four feet long. The gold and silver bands that would have bound the box have been removed. Gently I prise open the box, hoping that Father Pelous is not going to reappear suddenly. The wood is dry and crumbling. Lying in the box, I see a board, deeply incised with words that once read, in Hebrew, Greek and Latin: *Jesus of Nazareth, King of the Jews*. The original white pigment, that would have been in the incisions, is still just visible. It is the remaining portion of the *titulus* of the True Cross, attached to a single crossbeam of wood, about two feet long. I photograph it from all angles and in many sizes, particularly close on the script, which I know will match exactly the other section of the *titulus*.

My legs are shaking and my heart is out of rhythm as if I had run up two hundred steps: the *titulus* was sawn in two on Helena's orders, and the other half is in Rome, in the Church of Santa Croce in Gerusalemme; it was taken there by Helena, Constantine's mother, in AD 328. This is the cross Saladin took from the Templars in 1187 on the Horns of Hattin, and this is the cross for which Richard the Lionheart was prepared to give up so much. And it is the cross that Richard's knights brought across the Mediterranean and on to Chasluç and which they hid, probably in the lost church of St Martial.

I can't tell Cathérine the full story when she comes back inside. It's too soon.

40

Letter from my Aunt Phoebe

DEAR RICHARD,

I am sorry to have to tell you that I am dying. I have no one else close enough to me to convey the news to you. I am in Aberdeen Royal Infirmary, and I have been told that I will not live for more than three weeks. To be honest, I am not afraid of dying, in fact I welcome it. As Dr Johnson said, 'It matters not how a man dies, but how he lives.' Dying, I think he said, is a short interlude in comparison with a life.

If you can come and see me in the next few days I would be very happy. The years you lived with me were a great blessing for me. I hope that I didn't drag you down with my problems and my sense of inadequacy. You were always a bright and delightful boy and – as you proved – a very intelligent boy. I may not be able to email you again unless I can get one of the nurses to do it, as I am going to be all wired up, but I live in the hope of seeing you before I go.

I have also sent to your London address a letter, which your father wished me to give to you when he died. He said he had given it to me because he was not able to bring himself to see you again. He told me that he had behaved very badly towards you, and that he wanted to explain himself. But I didn't want to send the letter on to you immediately, because I was worried that, whatever the letter said, it might disturb you. It was selfish of me but your father was always erratic, for all his charm, and anything could have happened. Anyway, the letter has never been opened and now I will be spared having to read his vain and mawkish ramblings.

God bless you, if there is a God,

From

Your aunt, Phoebe, who loved you.

I had a picture of her in the infirmary, alone and helpless, and I rushed to King's Cross to get a train to Aberdeen. On the journey up I was keenly aware that I had neglected her and I was also aware of how much she had done for me in her dour way. As we crossed into Scotland, I called the hospital to tell them that I was on my way, but they said that she had died in the morning. They wanted instructions about where the body was to go; at the moment it was in the mortuary. The hospital had a list of local undertakers. My aunt had given me as her next of kin, but she had refused to give them contact details. I could only guess her reasons.

I called Ed in Australia – it was mid-morning in Perth – and congratulated him on his engagement to Lettie, which I had seen in the *Telegraph*. I told him about my aunt. I had to speak to someone. As always, he was warm and generous and keen to know how I had got on. I told him that I had found the True Cross that Saladin captured in 1187.

'Struth, that's bloody brilliant, mate.'

'You're taking the piss, Ed, but I forgive you. I miss you. Is Lettie with you?'

'She's on her way. She's got a job in the embassy in Canberra.'

'Spook-type job?'

'Who knows?'

'I'm going to the Greek islands with Noor.'

'How is Noor?'

'I don't know, to be honest. I'm nervous.'

'Have you got a Plan B yet?'

'No. But I've got to go now. A big male nurse is heading my way, with intent. It was great to speak to you.'

'No worries, mate.'

'Ed, serious question: have you had too much sun?'

'Got to blend in with my cobbers, Richie. By the way, Lettie wanted you to know that you are no longer on a watch list, whatever that means.'

'It means she's a spook. Bye bye, Ed.'

'Bye, Rich, I am very sorry about your aunt.'

'Thanks. She was a good person.'

I have no Plan B; I have fallen deeply in love with Cathérine. As a matter of fact, I don't even have a Plan A.

41

Letter from my Father

My dear Richard,

I have asked my sister Phoebe to pass this letter on to you when I die. It's not the usual load of clichés and meaningless sentiment and it contains no advice. But I feel that I should try to explain myself.

You asked me in the early days about your mother. I just couldn't speak about her to you. She was a lovely girl. I met her in Chelsea and it was love at first sight. She was already a heroin addict, although she hid the full extent of her habit. She believed that the occasional pipe was good for you. I never took H myself, but I was doing quite a lot of the other stuff, mainly acid. When your mother became pregnant we thought that we wanted to have a natural birth in the Rockies. I had persuaded her to get off the heroin, and that was one of the reasons we moved to the Rockies, so that I could be sure she wasn't taking heroin while pregnant. She suffered very badly for weeks, but stayed clean. When she died giving birth to you, somehow in my paranoid-delusional state I blamed you. I could not look at you without thinking of her. It took me years to realise that I had been living in a state of denial, because actually I was to blame for insisting on having the birth on the side of a mountain, miles from the nearest doctor. When we had that alter-cation and you left for Scotland, that was the catalyst for starting on my long journey back to sanity. I was stoned when we had that awful moment. It took me years of therapy and treatment to live a more or less stable life. My friend David Huntingdon helped me, both with money and with accommodation. Many other friends were kind, too, despite the dreadful things I had done to them, and their wives.

The worst of these, my boy, was to send you away to boarding school. It was a time when you needed a proper father, and I was no use at all, still believing I had some magical future.

When you were awarded your degree, I was so proud of you and I wanted desperately to come and see you and to beg forgiveness. You had achieved something wonderful, in contrast to my miserable Oxford fiasco. I waited outside the Sheldonian and tried to hear the acclamation. Afterwards you walked right by me, almost in touching distance, and I turned away. I was so proud of you, but I didn't want to spoil your moment.

I have asked my sister to give you this letter only after I have died, which event won't be long now. Not an event in life, as Wittgenstein remarked. You may choose to reject my letter completely and imagine that these are the ravings of a sad, deluded old man, and you may be angry, thinking that I am trying to excuse the inexcusable. Most of all I think that you will have contempt for the way I have lived my life. But please, dear Richard, know that I loved you and, far too late, understood what a mess I had made of my life and how tragic it was that we were never close. I have desperately wanted to see you again. Goodbye, my boy, goodbye.
Dad.

42

Symi

HANEEN IS AGAINST the holiday in Symi. She tells me that Noor is not ready for it just yet. But Noor emails me to say she is keen to leave Toronto, where it is still cold, to head for the Mediterranean. It will speed her recuperation. I suspect that Haneen, shrewd and very human, sees difficulties ahead. I see difficulties ahead. I speak to Haneen in Jerusalem, trying to reassure her that we will just swim and take it easy and spend time together, as brother and sister.

'Richard, be very careful with her. She is not right in any way. She needs peace and quiet and reassurance. Are you sure you can provide those?'

'I will try, I promise.'

She isn't convinced, but she gives her reluctant blessing. She has natural authority; you are obliged to seek her blessing, even if you find it irksome. I promise to call her immediately if anything goes wrong.

Lord Huntingdon is very pleased with the speech I have written for him about abuse of the financial allowances by *les grands fromages*. While I am away on holiday he wants me to work on another speech, about fishing rights and quotas. Only the British obey the laws, he says. He is particularly exercised by the diminished stocks of mackerel. He sees the mackerel as a peculiarly British fish, a plucky, unpretentious little creature that has become the object of a piscine holocaust. I advise him against using the word 'holocaust' in this context. Perhaps we could say 'dangerous over-fishing'. He sends me pages of fishing statistics. He proposes to call this speech 'Fishy goings-on in the EU'. I suggest 'The Need for an Urgent Enquiry into EU Fishing Policy'. If I can think of a more catchy title, he would welcome it.

I have been thinking about my aunt's dismal funeral and my father's letter, as if they are linked, which in a way they are. Only five people attended the funeral. It was the sort of wet, cold day that figures in novels when a funeral is involved. The Church of Scotland minister gave a plausible account of my aunt's virtues – patience and stoicism; as he said, not particularly contemporary values. I had the feeling that the minister was something of a philosopher: he had travelled the world in Deeside.

Two of the estate workers I knew were there, as well as a man I had never seen before who had the chafed cheeks of someone who spent a lot of time in the great outdoors. The minister told me that he was a gamekeeper who had worked with Sandy and had been very fond of him, but had moved to another estate when Sandy married. By implication, he had not been very fond of my aunt. The owner of the estate, Gunther von Schwerin, sent flowers for the brief ceremony and these flowers took a free ride on a coffin into the dank pit. Von Schwerin had also paid for a gravestone, and asked me to come up with an inscription.

In the end I wrote:

Phoebe McAllan, née Carter, born in Wimbledon, England, who has found peace at last, aged seventy-three, in this beautiful place.

I could not think of another thing to say about her or another person to invoke as a witness of her life. Her first husband sent me a note of condolence on expensive embossed paper. His vindictive days, after my aunt left him for the monarch of the glen, were apparently behind him. He hoped to meet me one day; he had read in a newspaper that I had made a discovery which shed new light on Richard the Lionheart and his relationship with Saladin: 'Sounds jolly interesting.' Sadly, he and his second wife had separated. Amicably.

I had struggled for some time to include Sandy in the inscription, but it was impossible:

Devoted wife of Sandy McAllan, who died so tragically. Wife and devoted helpmeet of Sandy McAllan, who died prematurely and tragically.

There were more drafts, all equally hollow, all travesties of a life. Everyone in the district knew that Sandy had become suspicious of my aunt – this silent man talked about it in the pub – and that he had convinced himself that she was having an affair, and also they all knew that he had shot himself in the game room, producing a truly appalling still life of human and stag carnage, intermingled.

I could have written: *Phoebe McAllan, devoted aunt and teacher of Richard Cathar MA (Hons) Oxford.* That would have been true. The funeral was Pinteresque, in the sense that a whole lot was left unspoken.

Noor arrives at Terminal Five. I have been standing outside anxiously for some time. She comes through the doors fearfully, like a forest creature breaking cover. Her hair is short and even at a distance I can see that her face is slightly distorted, in a way that unsettles me; her features seem to have moved without purpose in unexpected directions. She catches sight of me and scuttles towards the barrier. I seize her and hug her. She is crying.

'I am sorry, I have missed you so much,' she says, wiping her eyes. Her voice is strained as though it is playing at the wrong speed. I climb over the barrier.

'Noor, it's wonderful to see you.'

I kiss her, but she turns her face away. Now her body is racked by waves of sobs that roll through her like breakers. I feel desperately inadequate.

'Come, let's get a taxi.'

In the cab she holds my hand; her grip is cold and insistent. Like a baby's. I think she feels the need to be attached to receive some warming charge from me.

'Are we going to be all right?' she asks.

Her apprehension is poignantly evident.

'Of course we are. Of course we are. Your hair is lovely short, by the way.'

'Do you think so, really? It was cut in hospital before my last operation. I felt that I was being punished for something.'

'No, it's great. You've had a bad time. But we'll put it all behind you in Symi. I checked the weather; it's almost thirty degrees and the sea is warming fast.'

A little desperate, I show her on my phone pictures of the house I have rented, with a small boat moored out front. I tell her that it is in a perfect position – the agent assured me it was – with a view over the bay; all day the boats come by. I tell her, again, about the Kallistrata, the ancient stairway that leads to the upper town. She looks at me – her mouth is puckered as though she is struggling for breath – and then turns to stare out of the window as we slow in the traffic on the M4.

I have put flowers in Haneen's flat. Noor says she loves the place.

'Do you want to bath and rest?'

'I have been resting for months, but yes, I do want a bath.'

I remember how we shared our huge marble bath at the American Colony and argued about who would have the tap end. Through the door I hear her crying quietly now. It's a world away. I feel sick with distress. When she comes out she is wearing a white towelling dressing gown; she sits on the sofa, legs crossed.

'Haneen tells me that you have made the great discovery of the cross you were looking for.'

'Yuh well, maybe she was exaggerating a little. But yes, in Limoges I found the True Cross, not the actual cross on which Christ was crucified of course, but the cross that Richard the Lionheart wanted from Saladin. As I told you, I think, I was lucky to find a letter in the Bodleian Library that seemed to confirm that Richard had struck a deal with Saladin, and I went on from there. The historians and palaeographers are not overly impressed – not yet – because they think that the piece of the cross in Santa Croce in Rome is a medieval fake, and already some experts have said that the letter from Richard to Saladin is also a fake, a palimpsest, done in the nineteenth century. But what I found in Limoges – I had lots of help – is clearly part of the cross Richard wanted so desperately, and the fact that it matches exactly the piece in Rome makes it more or less conclusive. Dendrochronology and other tests are being done, both in Rome and in Paris. I've started to write a book about the whole experience.'

I tell her about our father's letter to me, and how I have regretted the fact that I turned my back on him. I tell her about my mother, Moonchild Gemstone – it's impossible not to smile – and our father's drug problem and – most moving of all – how he stood outside the Sheldonian Theatre when my degree was awarded, proud that I had done so well, and hoping, after eight years, to speak to me. I paraded right by without seeing him. I tell Noor that this has troubled me in case he thought it was deliberate.

I talk non-stop because I don't want Noor to feel that she is obliged to talk about her experiences. Also, I have been dreading hearing the detail of what happened to her.

We walk to the park to see the Household Cavalry practising for a parade. Noor thinks the Mounties are just as impressive. There is talk of the Household Cavalry being moved to the suburbs. Huntingdon is against it. He believes that Britain has a unique talent for pageantry, absolutely unrivalled anywhere in the world.

315

In the evening, sitting together on the sofa, I ask Noor if she wants to tell me her whole story and to explain, if she can, why I was interviewed by SO15.

'Rich, do you think this apartment is bugged?'

'I doubt it, but I don't know. I don't see why it would be.'

'Let's talk on the balcony.'

We sit outside. I can hear music from the Royal Albert Hall; it sounds like the Mass in B Minor.

'Richie, this is difficult. My job was to get inside information, the sort of thing journalists hear on assignment. But it seems that in Egypt someone knew about my other life. We now know who tipped them off – I can't tell you the name – but you were put on a watch list in the beginning, just in case. You have a friend in Oxford – I didn't know her name – and she kept her contacts at MI5 briefed about you. To be fair to her, she did send a dispatch saying that, in her judgement, you had no involvement. But it was her contacts who put you on a watch list. I am sure it all sounds very underhand to you, but actually what she did is kinda according to the manual. There was a report that the kidnap was all set up for the money. I didn't know any of this until months later, when I was being debriefed in hospital.'

Her voice is oddly thin and strained.

'Who is Mr Macdonald?'

'Oh, that is just any delegated intelligence officer at any embassy. Mr Macdonald is named for our first prime minister. On another year it will be another prime minister.'

'Noor, tell me if you can, what happened to you in Cairo. I think we should discuss it, even though neither of us wants to, I am sure.'

She is silent for a moment, her mouth is very mobile, searching for words, sucking them. 'You know what I was thinking over the last months? I was thinking about you and me in Jerusalem before all this terrible stuff and my heart was breaking. I don't want to remember what happened after. To see you and to know that we will never have children, and to have to accept that we can never marry, that's too much for me to bear. Terrible things happened to me, Richie – sick, awful things, which seemed to be aimed at women in general. I can't speak about it. Just hold me, Richie, please.'

Her tortured face is frightened and defensive as if she has seen the worst that the human race is capable of. And maybe she has. I have an awful image of those survivors of Belsen and Auschwitz, with the vacant, stunned look. Noor appears in the same way to have had some of her human essences leached out. I know now that she will never forget. She will never recover.

She sees me looking at her, concerned.

'Is it obvious?'

'What?'

'That I am broken, crushed.'

'Noor, don't say that, please. I was just thinking as I looked at you how beautiful you are and how much we are going to enjoy Symi. Day by day. Take it day by day.'

'I have never known what that means. You have no choice, unless . . . Quite a lot of doctors said that.'

'You just look subdued, which is totally understandable. I have faith in Symi.'

'Please hold me, Rich. I want to feel I can breathe again.'

In Rhodes we avoided the Crusader castles, those necropoleis. My father had shown me what he said was the Street of the Knights. I wish we could have gone to see them, because I imagined the Templar castle would have looked much like the Templar *commanderie* in Marseilles from where Huntingdon's knights set out with the cross.

We are in the comical hydrofoil from Rhodes, *Aegli*. Aegli was one of the three nymphs of the evening. This one looks as though it was made for an early James Bond movie, from discarded galvanised-iron water tanks.

I can see the castle as *Aegli* starts out of harbour slowly and clumsily, low in the sea, but soon the engines roar and she is speeding improbably, rising to the surface of the water to achieve a state of grace, while passing with élan alarmingly close to rocky islets. I remember it from my trip with my father, our only holiday together.

Now the man who took our tickets is slumped plumply over what looks like a kitchen table, reading a newspaper, *Proodos*. He has an intimate relationship with the paper; he is hunched, almost incubating it. Noor stares out over the sea. I do not know what she is thinking.

In the night at Haneen's flat we slept in separate rooms, but later she crept into my bed and begged me to hold her. She was alarmingly thin, with sharply protruding bones. I had a glimpse of small, drained breasts. I felt immeasurable sadness on her account, and perhaps also on mine. It was all I could do not to weep.

I knew it was true: she has been crushed.

As we approach Symi, *Aegli* sinks lower into the water again as it finds its way into the harbour; it's not flying now; it's more a case of butting its way through the water. Above us rise the strange classical houses of the town, built in a time of wealth from the export of sponges. The port is crowded with boats, but *Aegli* has her own mooring, and we head confidently there. From a distance, half submerged, I imagine she would look like a nuclear submarine.

A man with a handcart meets us and loads up. He speaks some English. He is lame and it seems a little demeaning for him to be pushing this cart, but he refuses my help. He moves pretty fast, almost skipping along the quayside road. Outside a whitewashed wall, he hands us the keys and points to a blue door. He follows us in with the luggage. Our house is a joy, with a balcony overlooking the harbour, just a narrow track between us and the water and a little courtyard at the back, shaded by an old, knotted grape vine, a blue table and two blue chairs in the deep shade. Small birds are busy in the vine. They rustle and whistle. Down below, tied to the sea wall, is our boat. I feel good about having a boat, as though it will enable us to explore freely and to be happy.

There are two bedrooms, one overlooking the sea and the other further back. The house is already stocked and a huge bowl of bursting figs rests on a table. The owner, who lives near by, comes to see us and asks if everything is OK. She speaks her small allocation of English confidently. She has strong, wiry hair. She looks at Noor, and says, 'You must eat. Greek food makes strong.'

Noor smiles. I think it is the first time I have seen her smile in two days.

It's evening. The port is busy as we walk towards the shops. In a long, straggling line, a flotilla of small dinghies, bearing children, is hurrying anxiously home, as small craft have done for millennia. Above us, high above, the bells of the church of the Virgin, Panaghia, ring around the bay. The sea is now golden and the hills beyond Emporios are being coated in a light wash of caramel so that their outlines melt.

We buy more food – *loukanica* and wine, and a warm loaf of country bread, *psomi*. In another shop, close to the start of Kallistrata, I buy a canteloupe. The shopkeeper sniffs the melon to make sure it is ready; she tells us it's good. When we get back to our house the riding lights on the working boats and the yachts and the grand palaces of the very rich and the very criminal are bright. The harbourmaster can just be seen gesticulating and blowing his whistle sharply and irritably, to indicate where the boats should wait their turn or where they should moor when their turn eventually comes. From the town, music drifts towards us. I think of Jerusalem. As the boats come in, we can hear singing and conversation. It's true that voices carry across water.

'This is a lovely place, thank you for bringing me here,' says Noor as we sit, interested spectators, on the balcony.

I look at her. She doesn't seem unhappy, but I am on edge.

'Tomorrow, Agia Marina for the day.'

I am speaking hopefully of tomorrow, but already I am dreading the night to come, when Noor will again be seized by her memories, which will cause her to convulse and moan, before waking up and clinging to me desperately, while I try to calm her. For now, we watch the last, late boats docking. Across the water there are strings of naked light bulbs on the quays and draped on the trees in front of the bars, and the music and laughter of carefree people reaches us. I hope that a few glasses of red wine will calm Noor – and me for that matter. She sips cautiously. Her legs are stretched out imploringly towards the sea. She turns to me.

'Please don't watch me all the time. You are making me nervous.'

'Sorry, I want you to be happy, that's all.'

I watch instead a small gecko hovering around the outside light. It moves quickly to catch the moths that are drawn to the light. Its eyes roll happily as it swallows. Noor turns to me again, the side of her face caught in the light from inside the house. She looks ethereal. I think of African spirit children, who are believed to be at risk of being recalled at the whim of the spirits; they barely have a foothold in this world.

'Richie, are you OK with being my brother?'

I don't know what she means. She may be asking if I am able to live as her brother rather than her lover, or she may be asking if I want – now that everything has changed – to move on. I can't answer her question. We sit in silence.

When I called Cathérine from London to tell her that my half-sister had been in hospital and I was taking her away for recuperation in the sunshine, she was a little surprised. She said she would go to a book fair in Paris for a week in that case; no problem.

* * *

Noor is staring fixedly at the sea now. She prises her gaze from the sea and turns to me.

'Richie, I haven't come to try to relive what we had. I know that's not possible.'

Her face, the map of her torments, is fully exposed to the weak, yellowish light. She wants me to say something but I cannot speak: I feel shame and despair. Here she is, helpless, crippled by her memories, and I . . . I have been cavorting cheerfully in bed with Cathérine. (Who looks like my father's lover.)

'I have come to say goodbye, Richie.'

'No, Noor, please. The whole point of this holiday is to make it work. To see how we can keep close for ever. I won't desert you.'

But I know I am not convincing her, even if that were possible.

'I am here to say goodbye, Richie. Haneen was right all along: it would have been better not to have had hopes.'

'Why? Why?'

I am deeply hurt, despite my treachery.

'Because even just seeing you, and knowing what we could have had, gives me too much pain. More than I can bear.'

'Come with me to Agia Marina tomorrow. We will take our little boat. And then tell me afterwards what you want to do. Please give me that time. I love you, Noor.'

'It may be true that you love the idea of me, but I am not the same person you loved. You know that, Rich, you know it.'

'You are down; it will change. Tell me how you feel tomorrow. And practise your *Mamma Mia!* songs. Will you give it a chance?'

'OK. But I would like to go to bed now, by myself. It's not fair on you to have to sleep in a room with me. I'll have the back room, it's quieter, and I will take a sleeping pill. Goodnight, Richie.'

I help her move her things out of the big bedroom, and I tuck her up, kiss her, and go out to sit on the balcony in the cooler air. I finish the wine and the salami. Noor is quiet, and I am pleased she is getting some rest.

43

Aftermath

IN THE MORNING she was dead. She had brought many sleeping pills and tranquillisers with her. It turned out that she had come to say goodbye, just as she had said. She had removed her turquoise ring from Sinai, and put it beside the bed for me.

As I picked up my phone, I had the feeling that it was going to be the most difficult telephone call I had ever made.

'Haneen, it's Richie.'

'Oh, Richard, morning. How is she? She called me last night very late, and left a message, whispering, saying goodbye. I was very worried. I tried to call her but her phone was off and so was yours.'

'Oh God, Haneen, this is awful, dreadful: all I can do is tell you that she is dead. I don't know how to tell you any other way. When I went in to see her in the morning – she went to bed early – she was absolutely still. Our landlady called the ambulance, and they declared her dead. She left a note reading: *Goodbye, Richie, my lover and my brother for ever.* I'm so, so sorry, Haneen.'

She is crying, and gasping.

'It's terrible. Terrible. But I don't blame you, Richard; I should have told you I was worried that she would try to take her life. She tried twice in Toronto, but I didn't want to tell you. Do you want me to come?'

'Please come, I can't do this alone. Thank you, Haneen. Thank you.'

I give her some details of how to get to Symi and she says she will ring back when she has a flight from Tel Aviv Ben Gurion.

The rest of the day is harrowing. The police ask a lot of questions, with the help of an Englishwoman who runs a local estate agency. I explain that Noor has been ill in Toronto, and that we had made a plan to go on a holiday together when she recovered; she was my half-sister, raised separately in Canada. I have to fill out ten pages of statements. Many of the questions seem to me to be misguided, ignoring entirely the human nature of what has gone on, as if suicide were a wilful nuisance that mostly requires assurances about payments as a redress. The questions are offensively practical. Was she a citizen of the EU? If not there is no repatriation allowance. And so it goes on.

The doctors confirm late in the day that she had swallowed a mixture of anti-depressants and sleeping pills; as she translates the doctors' report, the Englishwoman smiles and nods, as if to say she has been on my side all along. Later she tells me that the Greeks in these parts abhor suicide; they are superstitious about it. I don't know if this is true.

Haneen arrived from Tel Aviv, via Rhodes, on *Aegli*, the following day. I met her at the mooring. She came off first, with the fat man carrying her luggage: *noblesse oblige*. She hugged me. We stood for a while against the background of the harbour, rocking gently but insistently like ships at anchor. She took my arm so that we could stand out of the sun next to the butane gas depot to talk.

'Richard, the first thing to understand is that it is absolutely not your fault. I should have told you that she was suicidal, and had tried to kill herself before. But she said how much she was looking forward to this holiday and she said she was sure she would recover. I only half believed it, but I had to give her the chance. And I didn't want to be the one who told you how depressed she was. I am to blame, if any of us is. But of course those who are most to blame are those monsters in Cairo. By the way I have spoken to my brother and his wife. They are hysterical. It's terrible. Can we go to see her now?'

'Yes, it is all arranged. It's not far but a car is waiting.'

I can't go into the clinic again with Haneen. I stand outside and I call Cathérine. She is in Paris, at the book fair. I tell her that my half-sister has died, suicide, that this wasn't her first attempt and that I want to come to France to see her.

'Of course. I'm so sorry for you. Life is very cruel, I know. When will you be arriving?'

'I could meet you in Paris, day after tomorrow, and maybe we could travel to your house together?'

'Perfect. Forgive me, Richard, I was a little bit worried that you were really going away with a girlfriend. So in one way I am relieved. That sounds terrible; it came out wrong in English: I feel very, very concerned for you. It must have been awful. But I love you – I think you know this already. Is that a good thing?'

'It's everything to me. Everything.'

It takes me a few moments to compose myself.

I want to tell her that I love her too, but a few yards away Noor is lying dead, in a thin mortuary gown that reveals, mercilessly, her fragile body, and at the same time her humiliation and despair. Her bridge, replacing the teeth she has lost, is lying with her clothes in a wire basket. I just can't utter the word 'love'.

When Haneen emerges, she is silent. I hold her around the waist. She is rocking slowly.

'Haneen, are you all right?'

Her haughty eyes, her paprika eyelids, her arched eyebrows, her flared nostrils, her shrewd mouth, her long neck – they are all struggling for meaning in the chaos of life.

'She looked happy for the first time in months,' she says. 'That at least is a blessing.'

The cicadas on the hill are screaming. Haneen and I are bound together; only we know the full story.

44

Six Months Later

Before I left Symi, I took the little boat moored in front of the house, and set off to the monastery of Panormitis. After leaving the harbour I kept close to the coast. Thoughts of buying land – I was looking at a small bay with one or two deserted stone houses – seized me. Perhaps I could live here, with a boat for transport, and write what I know. I think it is true to say that I have enough material. Parched hills and small islands went by to my left; the landscape was absolutely free of life, although out to sea, in the direction of Kos, a low blue-grey form on the near horizon to the east, I could see small fishing boats. The entrance to the bay of Panormitis is narrow. After travelling for nearly two hours I wondered if I had missed it. But suddenly, as if looking through a narrow doorway to a painting beyond, I saw the bell tower of Panormitis, rising like a rocket at Cape Canaveral above the much lower, white buildings of the monastery. I had forgotten how wide and how nearly perfectly circular the bay was.

I moored the boat at the quayside and went straight to the bakery, through an archway. I remembered some pastries my father had bought for us. Particularly, I recalled the scent of a lemon cake. It's of course a truism that childhood scents can be evocative. I was dehydrated after my long boat trip, and bought two large bottles of water to go with the cake. I had brought some writing paper and a pen. I wrote a message just as my father had done, and I threw it overboard in one of the bottles as I passed through the entrance to the bay on the voyage homewards, followed by the diminishing tones of bells. I kept on going beyond the harbour of Chorio and anchored near the chapel of Agia Marina on its small island. It was dusk, the tangible, gilded, classical dusk. I stripped off and swam right round the island. I sang *Mamma Mia!* tunes untunefully, and mostly under water, to fulfil at least part of my promise to Noor.

The note in the bottle read: *It is not about something. It is the thing itself.*

I am home now with Cathérine as I write. She is pregnant. For the past few months I have been helping her in *Parola*, her bookshop, and my French is pretty good.

In my mind, she and Noor have merged. I haven't been able to tell Cathérine that Noor was my lover. It seems my life, which has been marked by deception, is continuing along that path. Cathérine does not know that we had planned to be married. She knows only that Noor was kidnapped and abused in Cairo and committed suicide. Unknowingly, Cathérine colludes in this deception because she is well up on the subject of rape, and embraces sympathetically evidence of its awfulness. She sees it as a rebuff to the rational mind. Like Haneen, she studied at the Sorbonne and those beautiful courtyards – where young students sit with their lovers, kissing carnivorously, and where the spirits of Diderot and Voltaire and Rousseau keep watch – have formed her. I could say something similar about Oxford's effect on me; it's the sense that there exists something ultimately worthwhile, something that will overcome obstacles and outlive all the madness and depravity.

Cathérine is very happy to be pregnant. Harry didn't feel they were ready for parenthood. It was possibly their only major disagreement. I see that Harry and I are becoming fused in Cathérine's eyes. She sometimes calls me Harry by mistake, but I don't mind, although I feel a little guilty that I am living his life and spending his money. And also because I love his Cathérine so profoundly. She has suggested that, if our baby is a girl, she should be called Noor, and if it is a boy, he should be called Harry. I think it is a wonderful idea.

My discovery of the missing portion of the True Cross has led to many invitations to speak all over the world. In a small way I have become known. Some people want to believe that this is the cross on which Jesus was actually crucified. It suggests to me that the longing to escape death and to make sense of a life will always be with us.

I enjoy being in the bookshop and I make a good cup of coffee or a pot of Dammann Frères tea for the customers. I have learned how to do latte art, and my favourite motif is of a lion couchant, although sometimes I do an open book. An increasing number of the customers emerging from the old houses they have bought in the nearby towns and deserted villages in the hills are British. Some of them know of me and my find. They don't say it, but I get the impression that coming for a chat and a latte, or an exotic tea, is the most exciting thing that happens to them on any given day.

Every second week I take the train to London for meetings with Lord Huntingdon. He has twice had Cathérine and me to stay in the country. The first time, Venetia looked appraisingly at Cathérine for a long moment, but they got on well. Despite his Europhobia, Huntingdon says he finds her very charming. I think he means sexy. It is true that she has a very natural and evident sensuality.

From home I provide content for Huntingdon's website and I write speeches for him. (We have brought much needed attention to the plight of the plucky little mackerel.) I see that our meetings are important to Huntingdon; he is increasingly fond of me. I told him recently of my father's letter and what he had said.

'I believe he meant it, Richard. He struggled with his problems for those last ten years, but he told me often that he had wasted his life. He was a dear man. He never really got over the drugs business in college. He was a lovely man, very human. You are very like him in some ways.'

I wonder what it is about me that so many people have seen qualities in me I am not sure I possess. Although I am well on the way to finishing my book, it will be too late for Stephen Feuchtwanger. He died a few months ago, and was buried in Wolvercote, not far from his friend Isaiah Berlin. A thousand people came for the funeral. I was one of them.

For myself I have two ambitions: one is to be a good father and the second is to live by writing. Both are forms of immortality. Perhaps the only two that are available.

ACKNOWLEDGEMENTS

John Gillingham is the master biographer of Richard I, and his books and papers have been my guide. Any mistakes in my book are certainly not his. The Bodleian Library has been more than helpful, and I particularly want to thank Christopher Fletcher, Keeper of Western Manuscripts. I would also like to thank Professor Robert Taylor of the University of Toronto who helped me cheerfully with some translations from and to Occitan. Selina Hastings was generous with her knowledge.

At Bloomsbury I have been helped and warmly encouraged by my editor, Michael Fishwick. Anna Simpson has been gently but firmly effective in putting this book together and Mary Tomlinson has read and corrected my manuscript with great diligence, as she has done for at least four of my novels. I am now something of a Bloomsbury veteran, and I am ever grateful to Katie Bond, Nigel Newton, Alexandra Pringle, David Ward, Kathleen Farrar and Trâm-Anh Doan, as well as to more recent arrivals, especially Laura Brooke, publicist.

My agent, James Gill, is way more than an agent: he has a frighteningly complete knowledge of European languages and is a fierce ally. I owe him a great deal.

A NOTE ON THE AUTHOR

Justin Cartwright's novels include the Booker-shortlisted *In Every Face I Meet*, the Whitbread Novel Award-winner *Leading the Cheers*, the acclaimed *White Lightning*, shortlisted for the 2002 Whitbread Novel Award, *The Promise of Happiness*, selected for the Richard & Judy Book Club and winner of the 2005 Hawthornden Prize, *The Song Before It Is Sung*, *To Heaven By Water* and, most recently, *Other People's Money*, winner of the Spears novel of the year. Justin Cartwright was born in South Africa and lives in London.

@justincartwrig1

A NOTE ON THE TYPE

The text of this book is set Adobe Garamond. It is one of several versions of Garamond based on the designs of Claude Garamond. It is thought that Garamond based his font on Bembo, cut in 1495 by Francesco Griffo in collaboration with the Italian printer Aldus Manutius. Garamond types were first used in books printed in Paris around 1532. Many of the present-day versions of this type are based on the *Typi Academiae* of Jean Jannon cut in Sedan in 1615.

Claude Garamond was born in Paris in 1480. He learned how to cut type from his father and by the age of fifteen he was able to fashion steel punches the size of a pica with great precision. At the age of sixty he was commissioned by King Francis I to design a Greek alphabet, for this he was given the honourable title of royal type founder. He died in 1561.